DEADFALL

EDGE OF EXTINCTION
BOOK 4

KENNY SOWARD
MIKE KRAUS

DEADFALL
Edge of Extinction Series
Book 4

By
Kenny Soward
Mike Kraus

© 2023 Muonic Press Inc
www.muonic.com

---

www.kennysoward.com
kenny@kennysoward.com

---

www.MikeKrausBooks.com
hello@mikeKrausBooks.com
www.facebook.com/MikeKrausBooks

No part of this book may be reproduced in any form, or by any electronic, mechanical or other means, without the permission in writing from the author.

WANT MORE AWESOME BOOKS?

Find more fantastic tales right here, at books.to/readmorepa.

If you're new to reading Mike Kraus, consider visiting his website and signing up for his free newsletter. You'll receive several free books and a sample of his audiobooks, too, just for signing up, you can unsubscribe at any time and you will receive absolutely *no* spam.

You can also stay updated on Kenny Soward's books by visiting his website at kennysoward.com.

SPECIAL THANKS

Special thanks to my awesome beta team, without whom this book wouldn't be nearly as great.

Thank you!

READ THE NEXT BOOK IN THE SERIES

**Edge of Extinction Book 5
Available Here
books.to/aVDQO**

LAST TIME IN EDGE OF EXTINCTION...

Zach and his friends returned to Fairbanks with Red Hawk's Marines after a partially successful rift mission, bringing back vital information about the Russian betrayal and two valuable scientists abandoned by Commander Orlov. As raging firestorms descended upon the city and dogfights tore through skies, Colonel Red Hawk established communication with Washington. Craig updated the President on the results of the Rift mission and heard from Stephanie that she'd been able to contact Zach's family in Stamford. The soldiers she'd sent to check on them found a message scrawled in Dutch on the wall, informing Zach that Wendy and the kids were okay and probably with his father, Morten. Unable to fly through the raging firestorms, Zach set out with Craig, Grizzly, Liza, and Nikolay in a well-supplied Humvee with orders to escort the scientists to the nearest US Air Force base and see that they got home to Washington.

They drove through the next few Alaskan towns, outrunning fiery weather and lines of traffic filled with panicked civilians fleeing the storms. People fought in the road, stole from each other, and caused accidents. Near Sacha, Alaska, they reached a congested bridge over the Tanana River, and a mysterious white van attempted to cut them off. Zach soon realized it was Scotty and Sandy, and they had more henchmen with them and were armed to the teeth. Not wanting a conflict, Zach ordered Grizzly to get off the road and take the next exit where they hid in an abandoned warehouse. After scoping the Tanana River for a place to cross, they returned to the warehouse where Scotty and his gang hit them. The intruders shot Nikolay and disarmed Zach and his team, but to his surprise, Gina Morosov was with them. Gina's loyalty quickly shifted to Zach, and she turned her weapon on Scotty, forcing him and his gang to leave. After speaking a few words over Nikolay's body, the team jumped in the Humvee and crossed the Tanana River where a log got stuck in the axle parts. They jacked the vehicle up and winched it to a tree so it wouldn't slide, allowing Grizzly to knock the piece of wood out and get them moving again.

Days later, Zach and his team approached the town of Whitehorse with radio chatter filled with Canadian and Russian voices. Once in town, they met a unit of Canadian Armed Forces, who tried to take their Humvee and supplies, despite Zach providing Red Hawk's written orders. During the stop, Russians attacked from the woods, killing several CAF soldiers and blowing up two Canadian Humvees. Picking his rifle off the pavement, Zach ran to their Humvee and positioned himself at the grill. He stood firm and held off the initial Russian charge, shooting at them until the CAF forces could reinforce him with support gunfire. When Zach was about to be flanked, Gina appeared with a semi-automatic shotgun to repel them with a vicious counterattack. Canadian troops finally arrived with enough force to send the enemy fleeing into the forest. During the battle, Zach was slightly wounded in his calf and on his right side, hit with shrapnel. CAF soldiers drove them to Whitehorse, where they met Colonel Leopold who thanked Zach and his team for their defense of the Canadian position. He offered to return their equipment and the shot-up Humvee after they got some food and rest. A few hours later, Zach and his people were about to hit the road when Russian paratroopers and heavy armor began dropping from planes that flew low across the blistering skies.

In Stamford, Connecticut, Wendy and the kids traveled with

Morten and Zach's extended family through New York and Pennsylvania, battling fierce rainstorms and flooding because of the domino effect from the Alaskan Rift. Walking patrols around their three wagons, and taking grief from Samuel and Lavinia, Wendy struggled to keep the kids positive and safe with danger lurking everywhere. They fought off some attackers, and Zach's kinder brother, Uri, was wounded. As Lavinia stabilized him, the harsh weather forced them to seek shelter in an abandoned garage, where they dried off and enjoyed some food and rest. Samuel and Lavinia were against Wendy and her kids even being there, but Morten settled their quarrels and was a steady source of strength for the entire family as they traveled. On the road, David and Wendy worked with Samuel to remove debris from the path and dig them out of a mudslide that threatened to destroy the wagons. They fought through crowds of refugees going south, warding off attackers at every turn and battling destructive winds that pummeled them the entire way.

Finally arriving at the Amish community in Pearisburg, Amish guards held them at the gate and summoned the elders. Morten argued for Wendy and the kids to stay, but the elders didn't want outsiders in their community. As the discussion dragged out beneath the stormy skies, a farm on the other side of Amish territory was attacked. The men rode to confront it, leaving Wendy, the kids, and the Amish women at the entrance. When a second assault came from the road, they defended the gate successfully and drove the intruders away, brave actions that earned Wendy a chance to speak at an elder meeting on her behalf. In Smithson's home, she stated her case to stay within the general community but was denied. Instead, they'd be forced to live on the outskirts on a lane of abandoned cottages that were in disrepair. Cracks ran along the walls, and the air reeked of mold and dust. After they settled in, Charlie was scared by men walking around the property, and when Wendy confronted them, they revealed themselves to be Smithson's guards.

The following day, an Amish family moved in next door, barely speaking to Wendy when she introduced herself and adding to her mistrust of the Amish. With Charlie frightened, and living under a disintegrating roof, they tried to leave but were met by Morten, who'd assumed they might flee and brought them supplies. He'd heard the elders talking about converting David and Charlie into the community without Wendy's permission, which sealed her decision to leave. With their backpacks, a small amount of food, and some weapons, Wendy and the kids set out west to find a true home.

Later that morning, they met a skinny, desperate family with two children who begged for help. The father demanded Wendy let his family travel with them or at least give them food. When Wendy didn't agree, the man tried to take her gun, forcing Charlie to shoot and wound him. Wendy guided the kids past them, but Charlie gave the family some supplies and left them on the road. Exhausted and weary, with the storm bearing down on them in relentless sheets of rain, Wendy took a chance on a driveway that ran up a hill and found a dry house with no occupants. It had food, a working faucet, and a beautiful stable filled with horses. Noting the moldy bread in the pantry and the dust on the kitchen table, Wendy figured no one had been there in a long time and that they'd claim it for the moment.

In Washington, Stephanie Lancaster continued her work, updating the refugee camp leaders across the US about the changing weather patterns and using the information to help supply line convoys reach their destinations. Thousands of citizens gathered outside the Pentagon, pulling down the barriers and fences, challenging the Marines and soldiers surrounding the place. The troops opened fire, driving them back but only angering the crowds more. A short time later, the President was led away to a secure location, leaving the remaining scientists and planners to serve the country. With the situation worsening outside, Senator Lauren Tracey fled the building after making a deal with some soldiers, adding to the shrinking staff. When an armored truck rammed through the military line and reached the Pentagon's front doors, Stephanie began to see how things would end. While she was on the phone with her kids, Colonel Davies entered and explained he was ordering all civilians to evacuate the grounds immediately. He placed her with the same group of soldiers she'd initially sent to check on Wendy and the kids. Along with a staffer named Laney, they prepared to abandon the Pentagon.

Across the world, the weather worsened. In Moscow, clear blue skies and a shifting upper atmosphere allowed UV radiation to surpass safe levels, melting snow and burning grass and trees. When citizens gathered at a park to take in the warm sun, their skin turned red and swelled with blisters that burst on their foreheads and arms. The ensuing panic caused endless traffic jams with people stuck in vehicles, baking in the sun's rays. Others attempted to climb out and flee, only to die on the streets diving for dark alleys or shadowy places to hide.

In Iquique, Chili, flash storms sent floods sweeping through the town, washing away buildings and people, drowning them, crushing them between piles of heavy debris and cars, and dumping them into the sea. At a small luxurious restaurant in the middle of the city, panicked customers stood on a second-floor balcony and watched citizens flail in the rubble that shot-up walls in geysers of bloody spray. The highways on the hills were washed out and crumbling away with the traffic, and the town of Alto Hospicio rode a thick gush of mud down the slope to crush the south side of the city, pushing debris through the narrow streets and suffocating everything in a layer of sludge, cutting off the cries of thousands as they perished.

And now, Edge of Extinction, book 4...

CHAPTER ONE

Zach Christensen, Yukon, Canada

Brisk winds swept through the slopes of the Yukon Valley, where snow and ice melted off in torrents of fast-flowing streams. Waterways wound down from the heights, splashing, foaming and carrying rocks, trees, and pieces of homesteads that had once stood on the hillsides. A flock of Northern Pintails coursed due south, weaving beneath the torrential sky, quacking as they dodged hydrocarbon fumes and streaks of lightning. Zach caught the eye of a horned mountain goat trapped on a massive boulder that split the floodwaters, the goat's expression as weary and annoyed as Zach's.

He sighed and shook his head, turning back to the task at hand. He stood outside the Humvee on Highway 2 as a flood rushed across the road and ran off the left-hand shoulder in a waterfall that fell a hundred feet to the valley floor. They'd been on their way to Carcross when the melting and rainfall had become a real problem.

"How deep do you think it is?" Craig asked.

Grizzly watched the flow and shrugged. "I guess three and a half feet... give or take."

"Give or take?" Craig shook his head.

"That'll ride over the hood of the Humvee," Zach said, shifting his rifle on his shoulder.

Liza stuffed her hands in her pockets and hugged her coat tighter around her, her accent thick as she spoke. "Can make such a crossing?"

"Looks pretty risky to me." Gina leaned against the idling Humvee. "We miscalculate this by a foot and we'll roll right off that hill and over those rocks. It would be a messy way to die."

"We're not going to die," Zach said flatly. "Either Grizzly can drive us across, or he can't, and we find another way."

All eyes turned to the burly Russian as calculations rolled around in his head. He studied the Humvee, measuring the tires and vehicle's height against the rushing flood. With a faint nodding that grew in enthusiasm, he reached a conclusion. "I see angle to take. Grizzly will get across."

"Are you sure?" Zach asked. "I can walk the cable across first and hitch it to a tree over there."

"It would sweep you right off road. You stay inside truck. More weight."

"That's what I wanted to hear," Zach replied. "Besides, the chances of us finding another way across would be slim, not to mention having to leave the Humvee behind."

"I am not a survivalist," Liza said in her Russian lilt. "But that would greatly reduce our chances of survival,"

"Not to mention it would be a hell of a walk to Carcross," Gina added.

Zach clapped. "Okay, everyone back inside. Grizzly's driving across."

Craig was standing on the left-hand shoulder where the water crashed over the debris-ridden slope and carried the forest refuse into the gorge.

Zach joined him. "What are you thinking?"

"It's not the steepest drop," Craig said, swallowing hard.

"No, but those sharp rocks and broken deadfall would cut us to pieces," he replied.

"That's an encouraging thought."

Zach grinned wryly. "Sorry. Didn't mean to put those thoughts in your head."

Craig shrugged. "Are you kidding? Those thoughts are in my head constantly, anyway. I'm starting to dream about floods and fire."

"I know the feeling, man." Zach rested a hand on his shoulder. "Come on. Let's go."

Everyone got back in and buckled up, gripping the armrests and whatever handholds they could while a faint mist sprayed across the windshield. Grizzly hit the wipers to clear it, and Zach gave the mountain goat a brief salute and nodded that he was ready to go.

"Okay, everyone," Grizzly said. "I will make sweeping maneuver starting on right side and keep grill pointed into flow. Flood will sweep us little bit... hang on."

"For dear life," Gina huffed.

Zach gripped the armrest and dashboard as Grizzly backed the Humvee up, put it in drive, and raced toward the torrid flood at thirty-five, slamming into it hard, rocking everyone in their seats as water sprayed up the side and over the hood in a wash of foam. They were knocked sideways instantly, drifting five feet to the left as the spinning tires sought purchase. The diesel growled and coughed as Grizzly went with the flow, allowing the truck to play before bringing it back hard right again. A shudder ran through the vehicle, vibrating the frame, shaking the floor and Zach's feet. Liza cried softly, and Gina groaned while Craig kept his face averted from the looming drop just outside his window.

Jaw locked tight, hands flexing on the steering wheel, the burly Russian wrestled for control of the three-ton truck, crashing it into the waves, backing off, then slamming his foot on the gas as they swept closer to the precarious edge. Water barreled over the front end and shoved it, eliciting an aggravated growl from Grizzly, but he fought the wheel and got them pointed straight again. The last three seconds of the ride were locked in slow-motion time, Zach clenching his jaw and preparing for the inevitable roll off the side of the hill. But then they were through, bursting from the swollen floodwaters in a jolt as the tires gained purchase on the pavement. Grizzly had been overcompensating to the right, and the sudden pitch in that direction sent them spinning, their tail end sweeping around, wheels spitting, until they came to a lurching stop in the middle of the road. The Humvee idled and dripped, with an occasional grumble and hiss from beneath the engine block. The vents kicked out a steady flow of air as the crew blinked and caught their breaths.

"Great driving, Grizzly." Zach patted the Russian on the shoulder.

Craig wiped beads of sweat off his brow and reached up to do the same. "Yeah, man. *Really* great driving."

Gina chuckled off the remaining tension. "For a minute there, I thought we were goners... no offense, Grizzly."

"I never had a doubt." Craig's voice shook.

"Oh, you had plenty of doubts." Liza rubbed her hand against her leg. "You were holding my hand so tight, I thought you would break it."

"Did I? Sorry about that. I only had doubts about the situation, *not* Grizzly."

"It is okay," Grizzly chuckled. "Many people doubt me my whole life, but I keep driving. Keep... moving."

Zach settled back in his seat. "Let's get moving, then. We've got a long way to go to Carcross, and I don't want to run into those Russians we saw dropping from the sky."

"Not just soldiers." Grizzly put the truck into gear and started down the highway. "They also drop heavy machines."

"APCs and all that fun stuff," Zach agreed. "That's why I want to get to Carcross before them. We could resupply there and get some news from the Canadian Army."

"They will attempt to cut off roads... stop supplies," Grizzly said.

"That makes sense," Craig replied flatly. "They'll try to choke them and keep people and troops from moving freely."

"Agreed." Zach rubbed his forehead.

"Our military is very persistent," Liza said. "When they decide to do something, they will keep at it until they make progress. And with Orlov leading these strikes, he will be ruthless in carrying out the plans of our generals... to what end, I cannot say."

"Would they actually try to extend this far into the Yukon?" Gina asked.

"I'm not a military expert," Zach replied, "but I'd assume the farther they drive inland the more they could solidify dominance in the oil fields and refineries. Just creating problems and distractions as they go would be enough."

The truck cab fell quiet as the road slipped by beneath them. The vast Yukon Territory stretched ahead in breathtaking views of vibrant green forests, patchy and brown from the storms but more alive than anything up north. Flocks of birds flew in masses, fleeing the hydrocarbons poisoning the skies, frantic wings flapping to escape, formations broken by turbulent firestorms, knocking some birds from the sky to plummet to their deaths.

Zach spread his legs and grabbed a water bottle from the floorboard, tilting it back to wet his parched throat as he hoped for a much smoother journey home.

CHAPTER TWO

Wendy Christensen, Pearisburg, Virginia

Wendy lay on her left side on the roof of the house, ankles twisted to keep her grip, cheek pressed against the rough shingles as wind and rain threatened to rip her off. She held the edge of a blue tarp in her right hand and a cinder block with a rope tied to it in the other. David was ten feet away, facing her, holding his part of the tarp and his own tethered brick, wincing at the constant gusts and sweeping winds, shivering as cold water seeped beneath their ponchos to chill their skins.

The latest storm had ripped across the hillside and targeted the east end of the house, tearing shingles off, causing the home to groan and shake. Soon after noticing some dripping on the kitchen floor, they concocted a plan to stop the leaky roof until the weather dried up and they could make a more permanent repair.

"Ready, David? Go!"

They rose together, lifting their cinder blocks, scrambling up the sloping roof, slipping as they hauled the tarp to the top. The high winds forced them to stoop, and their ponchos blew around their legs as they were buffeted from every direction. Below them, down by the gutters, Charlie stood on a deck ladder and leaned on the tarp, helping to keep it pinned to the roof with her weight, her blonde hair whipping from her hood. Wendy slipped and fell, dropping the cinder block with a heavy thud, her knees hitting the shingles and grinding on the rough asphalt material, eliciting a groan that was devoured by the wind.

David had almost reached the ridge. "Come on, Mom! You can do it!"

Wendy nodded and set her jaw. She only had five more feet to go. Gathering her strength, she lurched from her kneeling position, got to her feet, and surged toward the ridge, scrambling, swinging herself over, and dragging the tarp along with her. David did the same, and they stretched it tight between them. Then they put the cinder blocks down with heavy thuds. The ropes they were tied to ran over the ridge and down to companion blocks on the other side, causing both ropes to go taut and pin the tarp to the roof. Gasping for breath, knees and palms rubbed raw from the rough surface, Wendy got up and swayed, observing their handiwork, waiting for it all to blow away. The edges flapped noisily, but the largest section of the tarp stayed affixed no matter how hard the wind blew. She gave David a thumbs up and a questioning look, and he returned the gesture with a nod.

Wendy crossed to meet him. "That should hold, short of an actual tornado blowing through."

"It'll hold great!"

"Now, let's get the hell down from here!"

They moved to the west side of the roof, climbed over the ridge, and skidded on their backsides to where an extension ladder rested on the gutter. Charlie stood in the yard, holding the ladder against the gusting winds. Wendy grabbed the side rails, started to flip around and climb down, but the sudden movement, combined with a whipping gale, sent a wave of dizziness through her head, forcing her to sit quickly before she lost her balance.

"Are you okay?" David asked.

"I'm fine. Just a little dizzy." She waved. "I know it's only fifteen feet, but it might as well be a thousand to me. You know how I am with heights."

David gripped her arm. "It's okay. I'll help you. Just grab the side rails, stand and turn, and go straight back, if you know what I mean?"

Wendy nodded and did as he told her, turning sharply and walking backward until she found the top rung with her foot. She descended the rest of the way with wind and rain punching at her from all sides and getting into her clothing. She didn't care. As soon as her feet landed in the soggy grass, she grinned and hugged Charlie. Together, they held the ladder for David and then retracted it and laid it against the house.

"Should we put it back in the barn?" David asked.

"We'll keep it out here for now in case we have any more leaks. There are more tarps out in the stables if we need them. Later, we'll hammer on some of those spare shingles we found in the barn."

David grinned and nudged her. "Just remember not to put an even bigger hole in the roof trying to fix it."

Wendy laughed. "My dad was a construction boss. I've been on a lot of job sites. Believe me, I know how to hammer shingles, son."

Wendy adjusted the pistol on her hip and looked around. It wasn't an expansive backyard, thinner on the east side where the gravel tract led to the barn and where they had a few unexplored sheds. It opened wider to the west with a path of stones leading through overgrown gardens of wild honeysuckle and vine-covered trellises, promising something larger on the other side. The hill continued up from the backyard another three hundred feet, the angled slopes covered with trees and brush. The driveway ran up past the garage and curved to the stables, and the front yard was cut off at the nose where it dove to the road. It was a ranch-style home with a laundry room just off the garage, a kitchen–living room combo, and bedrooms and bathrooms on the west side.

"There are a lot of places for someone to sneak up on us," Wendy frowned. "I wish we hadn't slept through our first watch."

"We were exhausted." Charlie locked arms with her. "After what happened with that family, we all needed some time to unwind."

"You're not wrong, but it wasn't very smart. At least we're well rested and took care of that leak."

"Just in time, too." David looked up. "The rain is picking up again."

"I hope it stops soon." Charlie sulked. "It's downright depressing."

Wendy nodded. "Are you guys ready to feed the horses now?"

"I'm always ready to feed the horses." Charlie jogged off. "Come on. We'll introduce you to them."

Wendy hadn't been out to the stables yet because she was so busy investigating the homestead's first floor, and sleeping, though the kids had been out there several times already. They squelched across the wet yard until they reached the gravel driveway which drained only slightly better than the yard with streams of water cutting rivulets into the dirt and washing rocks away.

"You'll love it out here," Charlie said. "Whoever owned the place before was pretty organized. We fed and watered the horses fine. I can't wait for you to meet them. Let's see, there's Sassy, Darwin, and Ginger."

A single ridge ran the length of the stables, and the wooden sides were faded, warped, and cracked. At the far end, the structure opened into a larger barn area with a loft and storage section. Beside its plain, blanched color, the exterior had no additional markings. One gravel tract continued straight while another turned toward the barn entrance. Charlie led them to a door that stood open about a foot and swung it a little wider, and they all stepped inside and stood there dripping and looking around.

"How do you know the horses' names?" Wendy asked, arms crossed as she watched Charlie turn on some electric lanterns hooked to the wooden beams, illuminating an open area with saddles and bridles hanging on the walls and a desk with neatly stacked papers and tools.

"Come on, and I'll show you." Charlie practically skipped along the corridor where the horses watched them with their ears perked up. She stopped at the left-hand stall and pointed to a placard beneath a large, beige horse with a sparkling white mane. "Sassafras, see?"

"I see now," Wendy said, coming up to another chestnut horse on the right with a long white spot on his nose. "Darwin has his own placard, too."

"That's right," David replied. "Be careful around him. He's kind of clumsy. Almost squished me into the stall wall earlier."

The third horse stood in the last stall, her stunning blood-red coat shining in the lantern light.

"Ginger." Wendy patted the tiny white splash on her forehead. "I'm guessing this one is a mare."

"We assumed the same thing," David replied, "and based on being around them a little, the other two are geldings."

"So we won't have any baby horses to feed."

"I don't think so," Charlie laughed.

David and Charlie took buckets from hooks and marched toward the barn side of the building. A large riding mower with some field attachments was parked against the north wall, and a few tons of bagged feed and three hay rolls were stacked in the middle. Wendy strode over to the feed bags, noting the different brands with mixes of oats, grains, and concentrates.

"How do you guys know what to feed them? I don't know anything about horses, and you know even less."

"There's a list right here." David walked over to the wall and pointed to a chalkboard with the horses' names and their daily feeding schedule.

Wendy crossed her arms. "Okay, you're following directions. It'll make it easy to take care of them, at least until the feed runs out."

"But think about it." Charlie scooped feed into her bucket. "If we learn how to ride them, we could get around the area without using the roads. That has to be an advantage, right?"

"When you put it that way," Wendy nodded impressively. "Honestly, the thought hadn't crossed my mind."

"And don't worry." Charlie held the bucket handle with both hands. "We did the math on how long this food will last us. If we only use the feed, that's at least a few months, probably taking us into late summer or fall, which would give us plenty of time to find more."

"But it's not even that necessary," David said, "because we can take the horses out into the yard and let them graze. As long as all this rain doesn't kill the grass or something, they can eat as much as they want."

"And we still don't know what's on the other side of the property," Charlie said. "We were thinking about going out there either today or tomorrow, if it's okay with you."

"Sounds like you guys have this figured out pretty well. I admit, I wasn't enthusiastic about having horses around, but you're changing my mind. I can imagine riding them across the fields and into the hills where cars can't go. But keep in mind there's more to maintaining horses than just feeding and watering them. You have to take care of their hooves, too. Like with horseshoes and stuff. And the big kicker... we don't even know how to saddle or ride them."

Charlie grinned like she had it all figured out. "By then, Dad will be back and can help with that."

David had loaded his bucket and was standing next to her. "Or we can strike up a deal with the Amish. Horses are a part of their lives, so they'd have some experts over there."

"After leaving them like that?" Wendy asked. "I doubt they'd be willing to help us at all."

"Charlie and I talked it over, and while we can't trust them completely, we'd be coming at it from a better position this time. Maybe we can *trade* them some things for their services."

"Yeah, we'd be coming from a position of power," Charlie said.

"You mean, we'd have leverage?"

"Exactly. I checked the shed out back, and there's a seed box, so we could potentially plant some things as soon as the weather gets back to normal." She glanced up. "If it ever does."

"Wow. You guys have been busy." Wendy gestured. "Okay, show me what you do."

Charlie and David entered the horse stalls and dumped the feed in their troughs before scooping the dirty water into a bucket labeled "old water." They walked outside to collect rainwater from a downspout that fed an overflowing barrel. Wendy watched the horses while they worked, more than a little nervous about the horses' sheer size, forced to push aside images of her children getting trampled or bit. When Ginger only nipped at Charlie's hair and Darwin nudged David playfully, her concern was immediately put at ease.

"They really are beautiful." Wendy patted Darwin's neck as his wide rump bumped the side of his stall. He sniffed at her fingers and snorted loudly, and Wendy jerked her hand back and laughed. "What a character!"

"They have such cool personalities." Charlie finished with Ginger's water and stepped out to shut the stall door behind her. "We're just figuring them out. I can't wait to ride one someday."

"And you promise not to try it without some proper training, okay? No trying to ride bareback."

"We won't."

"They look like general stock horses to me, not thoroughbreds or anything. I wonder what the original owner did with them?"

Charlie shrugged. "No clue, but they took good care of them, it seems."

Wendy nodded slowly and smiled. "And I can trust you to keep that up?"

"Yeah, Mom." Charlie's expression brightened. "David and I already figured we could feed them and brush them in between our patrols. I don't think they'll be a burden at all."

"Well, we have to protect them, too, so we'll have to come out here when we patrol. Something tells me you two won't have a problem with that."

"No, ma'am," David said.

"Nope," Charlie agreed.

Wendy glanced toward the house. "I saw cameras mounted in the eaves. Are there any out here?"

"I didn't look," David said, coming out of Darwin's stall. "But we'll walk around and check before we leave."

"Speaking of which, why don't we head back now? We've still got a bit of the house to explore."

"Yeah, I want to see what's in the basement," Charlie said.

They bid the horses farewell and left through the east doors, walking the outskirts, David pointing at a camera on each of the two south corners.

"Now, if we can find the control panel for those and get them powered up," Wendy said, "maybe we can monitor things without standing in the rain so much."

They started back, kicking through puddles, hands stuffed in their pockets as the chill worked beneath their ponchos. They were about halfway there when a distant engine approached from the highway, stopping at the foot of the driveway in a squeal of tires, followed by a spray of gravel and a high-pitched roar as whatever it was tore up the hill.

"Someone's coming up the highway," Wendy said, stomach sinking. She unslung her rifle, raised it to her shoulder, and crouch-walked through the misty rain toward the garage. "David, spread out to the right. Charlie, take the left."

The kids nodded and followed Wendy the last ten yards before a white pickup burst into sight, weaving, wiping out bushes and brush on the way up, engine growling in fits. Tires sprayed gravel as the woman driver jerked the wheel back and forth, barely in control while the passenger sat limp with her head lolling around. The windows and fenders were riddled with bullet holes and blood smeared on the inside. Wendy stepped toward the garage doors and pushed David ahead, aiming at the windshield and shouting, "Stop! Stop right there!"

She leaped out of the way as the truck sped by, its tail end sliding by and spraying her with water and rocks as the driver showed no signs of slowing down. Charlie danced aside but kept her gun on the truck as the vehicle fishtailed past them and shot off the right edge of the driveway, slamming into a gnarled oak tree with a massive crash. Metal crunched, fenders buckled, and pieces of trim and plastic flew off as the grill hugged the tree trunk in a violent embrace. Wendy pointed to David and then at the passenger door, and he nodded and moved to cover it. She stepped in front of Charlie and pushed her back with her backside, holding her gun on the driver's door, ready for someone to come out firing. The tires continued spinning, spitting mud up the sides, the engine sounding like a chainsaw in the woods. Wendy slipped closer to the door.

"Right behind you," Charlie said from a little to the left.

"There's a lot of bullet holes in the truck, kids," she warned. "And blood on the windows. Do you see it?"

"Yeah," David replied. "The passenger window has two holes in it... I think the lady inside got hit."

"Okay, I'm moving in." She raised her voice to the driver, who lay forward over the wheel with her arms thrown on the dashboard. "Whoever's in the truck, come out! We're armed, so don't try to hurt us!"

When the driver didn't move, Wendy reached and popped the door, keeping her rifle trained on her as she backed up. The woman was short and thin, wearing jean shorts and a T-shirt. Blood smeared her pale skin. Her wild, red hair was held in a ponytail, the tangled mess hanging over her left shoulder.

"Can you hear me, lady?" Wendy asked, creeping closer to catch her soft moans above the throaty engine then backing off again. "She's alive but looks hurt bad. What about your side, David?"

He was about to reach for the handle when another truck tore up the lane, growling and throwing gravel.

"We've got company!" Wendy spun away and cross-stepped into the driveway. "Stay behind the truck, Charlie!"

A black pickup roared into sight and rounded the top of the hill with two big men taking up the front seat. When the driver saw them, he slammed the brakes and skidded to a halt twenty-five yards away, looking back and forth between the white pickup. They raised their guns, seeming uncertain of what to do.

Wendy didn't give them a chance to shoot first. She started pumping bullets straight into the grill and windshield, a steady *chink-chink-chink* punctuated by muzzle flashes. The AR rounds clinked and clacked with every strike, and when David joined in it sounded like heavy raindrops smacking a tin roof. The driver kicked his door open and rested his weapon on the frame, firing at Wendy one-handed. She was already cross-stepping to her left, making herself a harder target while continuing to shoot, rounds punching through his door and sending him ducking. David was backing up, taking cover as the passenger stood outside the truck and fired his pistol sideways like a gangster. Wendy switched to the passenger, leaning into her shots and puncturing his side of the windshield. Glass shattered and spilled everywhere, and the man yelped and dove behind the dashboard, giving Wendy and David a chance to close on them.

"Come on, David!" she hollered, ejecting her spent magazine and slamming another home, charging the weapon with a solid *clack*!

The two men got back inside their truck, firing wildly, raising long enough to shoot and then ducking again. Bullets zipped past Wendy's head, but she pressed forward and kept shooting steadily, jerking the rifle barrel at whichever man stuck his head up next. The truck suddenly lurched into reverse and spun out in the yard, doing a quick multi-point turn before racing away in a spray of gravel and grass. Wendy sent three more rounds their way, hitting the tailgate as they disappeared over the hill.

She lowered her weapon. "Are you okay, David?"

"Yeah, I'm fine." David exchanging his spent magazine for a new one.

"How about you, Charlie?"

"I'm good." Charlie circled from behind the pickup to join them. "What was that all about?"

"Seems like they were intent on getting to the people in this truck," Wendy replied, moving past Charlie and heading straight to the passenger door. It was still hanging open, and the woman inside lay slumped to the side, held in by her seatbelt. She looked like the driver but wore a white floral summer dress stained red with blood. Wendy lifted her hair to see a bullet hole in her right cheek and another in her chest, and she let the hair fall through her fingers with a sigh of disgust.

"I think she's dead." Wendy felt for a pulse. "Yep, she's dead for sure."

"Poor lady," Charlie said.

"I heard the driver groaning, so she might be alive."

They moved to the other side, Wendy handing her rifle to Charlie and pushing the woman back, her head flopping loosely against the seat. Checking her pulse, Wendy nodded. "She's alive but took a bullet to the arm and leg. Come on. Let's get her inside, David."

Together, they unbuckled her and pulled her from behind the wheel, David taking her shoulders while Wendy lifted her legs. As soon as the woman's foot left the gas pedal, the high-revving engine plunged to an idle, sputtered, and died.

"Keep her off the ground." Wendy grunted through clenched teeth as she waddled and tried to hold the woman's weight. "Charlie, get the garage door, would you? Let's put her in the spare bedroom and try to stop this bleeding."

"Okay." Charlie raced out ahead of them.

With her swinging between them, Wendy stared into her slack face, noting the blood smears on her cheeks and the bruise beneath her left eye. "Geez, lady. You sure know how to pick a fight."

CHAPTER THREE

Stephanie Lancaster, Gainesville, Virginia

Rain poured over them, hitting the Humvee's roof with heavy patters. Water dripped down the sides in wide rivulets, lit up by bursts of lightning and rolling thunder that rippled through the sky in waves.

They were outside Gainesville, Virginia, on Highway 29 with Specialist Jamison behind the wheel driving them steadily through the wreckage. Stalled and broken-down vehicles littered the road, many with their blinkers on and hapless people sitting inside. It was the most cars Stephanie had seen since slipping from the Pentagon's tunnels and shooting past the angry mobs trying to block the exits. The Virginia roads were dark and dismal, the highway filled with cracks from water damage and gradient slippage.

"I don't like the looks of this." Private Adelson was sitting between Laney and Stephanie with a worried look on his face.

"You said that in the last town we passed." Sergeant Gress poured over maps in the front seat.

"Yeah, but I *really* feel it this time."

"Just be ready to climb into that turret if we need you. Until then, let's not panic everyone, okay?"

"Okay, sir."

Outside Stephanie's window, businesses and department stores came into view with signs barely hanging from poles, glass spread like confetti across parking lots. Hurricane Jane's damage reached far and wide across the town. Wind-sheared roofs, overturned cars, and drifting garbage marked her passing, turning subdivisions into debris fields.

"It looks bombed out," Stephanie whispered, "like a war-torn country."

"Where'd all the people go?" Laney asked.

"Probably staying dry somewhere," Adelson replied. "There's got to be barns and farmhouses around, and some of these department stores are still standing. Maybe they're inside those."

The storefronts were dark and empty, with shapes moving behind them, shadows of people inside vast warehouses where families clung to the last few possessions they owned.

"If they can't find a FEMA camp around," Gress said, "small groups will form like they did at the Pentagon."

"I'd hardly call that a small group," Laney replied. "More like an army."

"Big groups like that can form with the right leadership."

Adelson shook his head. "We've gone back to the friggin' Stone Age."

"Stay on this road, Jamison."

"Yes, sir."

Stephanie shifted in her seat, watching miles slip by before something unusual came up on the left. A family stood on the left-hand side of the road, the parents waving with three children clinging to their legs. Jamison didn't even slow.

"Aren't we going to help them?" Laney asked, turning in her seat as they passed. "Looks like they're in trouble."

"Everyone's in trouble out here," Jamison said.

"Yeah, but we could drive them someplace safe, right? We could take them to a camp or something."

"Where will we put them, ma'am?" Gress asked. "Are they going to sit in your lap? It pains me to say it, but we've got our orders, and we have to keep moving."

Laney turned to Stephanie for help, but she only shook her head, guts churning in disgust. "He's right, Laney. We can't stop for anyone."

Laney faced forward with glassy eyes. "I thought we were supposed to be the good guys."

The Humvee fell quiet as guilt chewed away at them and the weather beat on them, gusts of sustained winds rocking the Humvee and causing it to shiver on its frame. When they came to a fallen tree blocking the road, Gress and Adelson got out and hooked the winch line around the trunk, and Jamison dragged it aside with a slow grind across the pavement. The soldiers got back inside, dripping onto the seat and floorboard, their breaths pluming frostily until the cabin warmed up again.

They entered the thickest part of Gainesville, dwarfed by industrial parks spread around them, rain-soaked warehouses and storage facilities surrounded by semi-truck trailers and rigs. A few idled in the parking lot, lined up in a neat row with their running lights on and glowing yellow in the darkness.

"Must be part of a convoy," Stephanie said, recognizing the door markers. "I wonder where they're headed?"

"They better be careful of that." Adelson nodded pointedly.

At first, Stephanie didn't know what he was talking about, and then lightning flickered to illuminate several hundred people standing in the next lot over. Rain glistened off their ponchos, faces covered with hoods as they walked toward the trucks.

Stephanie quickly reached between the seats. "Give me the radio."

"What's that, ma'am?" Gress asked.

"Give me the radio and turn it to channel fifty-two. There's a good chance those drivers will be on that channel, and we need to warn them."

"We're supposed to stay on —"

"Please, Sergeant."

Gress shrugged and handed her the radio mic, flipping it to fifty-two and turning it up to the chattering voices of the truck drivers.

"... that's right, Jersey Handler," someone said. "We're waiting on directions from central. Stand by."

"Roger that, Silverado. Standing by for instructions."

Stephanie cut in. "Hello, Jersey Handler and Silverado... to all the truckers parked in the Gainesville department store lot. You've got about a hundred people coming your way, and they don't look happy. Do you read me?"

There was a pause and then, "Who is this?"

"I'm Stephanie Lancaster, calling from the Humvee that just passed you. I worked with you two before when I was at the Pentagon."

"Yes, ma'am," Jersey Handler said. "You helped us avoid some pretty nasty storms back on I-75 last week. There's an angry crowd, you say?"

"They're west of you, and they'll be on you in less than a minute. Get out of there, guys."

Stephanie turned to watch the dark mob break into a jog, running toward the trucks as the drivers sat in silence. Finally, a reply came back over the radio. "Roger that, ma'am. We see them. Thanks for the heads up."

No sooner had the trucker stopped speaking than truck headlights flashed on along the entire line, and the big rigs kicked into gear and rolled off across the lot, heading for the exit lanes. The civilians sprinted toward them, brandishing weapons and hollering.

Stephanie handed the radio back to the Sergeant. "Thank you. We just saved those truckers' lives."

"Good work, Mrs. Lancaster," Adelson nodded.

"Again, guys. Just call me Stephanie."

They left the department stores and warehouses behind, the landscape turning into subdivisions with gas stations and mini-marts on every other corner. The darkness was complete, the moon hidden, their headlight beams paltry against the pressing night.

"So, Mrs. Lan... uh, Stephanie," Adelson said. "Are you some kind of big shot in the government?"

"Oh, hardly. I work for Shield Oil."

"What was your normal job?"

"I was in charge of getting permits to drill. Basically, I had to cut through a lot of red tape."

"Corporate lapdog, eh?"

"I studied environmentalism and climate change in college. I use science to explain why we can drill without harming the environment. A lot of people are against what we do, including my ex-husband. It's ironic that I spent the last few weeks working with his software to predict bad weather for the supply lines running out here. That's why I knew those truckers."

"So, you're some kind of genius?"

"Not even close. My ex-husband, Craig… he was the genius. He built the software, and he knows everything about weather."

"Where's your ex now?"

"Good question." Stephanie's heart stirred. "The last time I talked to him, he was leaving Fairbanks and coming home. I don't know where he is now."

"And he probably thinks you're at the Pentagon."

"Probably. But the second place he'll look is my house. That's where you boys come in."

Adelson chuckled softly. "We'll get you there, ma'am. You have kids and stuff?"

"Two college-age kids, Larkin and Amanda. How about you?"

Adelson shook his head to the gentle rocking of the Humvee. "I enlisted to get away from my family and haven't talked to them in a while. Pops and I had a falling out before I left, and I don't know what they're up to, or if they're even alive."

"I'm sure they're fine."

"No one knows that for sure, ma'am. But I appreciate your concern."

"Where are they now?"

"Destin, Florida. Lived there my whole life and thought the military would help me see the world. So far, I've only seen a couple of states and some ruins. Sergeant Gress promised to take me to Paris, but he hasn't made good yet."

"Pipe down, Adelson."

Stephanie rose in her seat and tapped on the window. "Hey, Jamison. Heads up!"

"I see them."

Two pale faces suddenly appeared out of the gloom. The truck rolled past, spraying an arc of water from their tires, drenching the two girls where they stood on the side of the road.

"Stop, Jamison!" Laney pulled herself between the seats.

"Sarge said not to stop for anything."

"Come on, Sergeant Gress," she begged. "That's two little girls by themselves. You can't just leave them!"

Something yanked Stephanie's heartstrings, and she turned to watch the two girls fade in the distance. "We should at least stop and make sure they're okay."

Jamison glanced sideways at the Sergeant. "What do you think, Sarge?"

Gress watched the girls in his side mirror before holding up his hand for Jamison to stop. The brakes squealed, and the Humvee pulled up short with the engine idling in the pattering rain, steam rolling off the warm hood.

When they didn't immediately back up, Laney slapped the seat. "Come on, Jamison! Go back!"

"I agree, Sergeant Gress," Stephanie said. "I know it's your call, but..."

Gress nodded. "We'll go back and make sure they're okay. We'll help them find shelter, but they're not riding with us."

Jamison reversed the Humvee in a high-gear grind, keeping the truck angled away from the little ones and avoiding splashing them a second time. The two girls were hugging in the icy rain, wearing simple purple and pink ponchos with comic book figures printed on them. Brown curls sprang from one hood while the other was light-haired with wisps of it lying flat and wet on her cheeks.

"I don't have a good feeling about this." Adelson squinted at the shivering forms.

"You never have a good feeling." Gress looked around.

The girls were standing between a pair of massive puddles with debris chunks strewn all around them. In the strip mall behind them, darkened windows stared back, empty and shattered with garbage and packaging spread everywhere. Signs sat crooked above the doors or had fallen off the facing, leaving sharp pieces of multi-colored glass scattered on the sidewalk.

"Oh, they're precious!" Laney reached for the door handle.

"Stay in the truck," Gress snapped. "I'll get out and talk to them."

"This is *definitely* a trap." Adelson craned his neck to see past Stephanie.

"Shut up, Adelson," Gress growled. "It's not a trap." He popped his door and let in the howling wind.

Stephanie caught him by the shoulder before he could get out. "I'll go, too."

"Sorry, ma'am. Stay inside."

"They'll never come to you, Sergeant. Not with all your equipment on and a gun in your hand."

Gress gave it a moment's thought and nodded. "Okay. You talk to them, and I'll keep an eye out. Ask them where their parents are and —"

"I know how to talk to children, Sergeant," Stephanie replied, popping her door and stepping into the rain.

Gress stayed by the Humvee while she gently shut her door and approached the kids, who watched her with wide, frightened eyes as she kneeled on the street a few feet away, pushed her hood back, and smiled.

"Hi, girls," she said. "What are you two doing out here by yourselves in the rain? It's pretty cold out here, huh?"

The pair were holding hands and trembling, breaths puffing in the frigid rain. A wind swept through, blowing garbage and debris across the parking lot and forcing them to take a step back.

"Where are your parents? Do you have a place to get out of the rain?" When they didn't reply, she scooted closer. "Are you hungry? Do you want something to eat?"

The two stepped back again, the light-haired girl gasping, shaking her head with fear-stricken eyes.

Stephanie chuckled warmly. "Oh, no. Don't be afraid... I won't hurt you, I swear." She made a sign on her chest. "Cross my heart and hope to die. Just let me —"

As she reached for them, they took a frightened step back, and the light-haired girl glanced at something on the opposite side of the road. A hot flash shot through Stephanie's chest, a shock of danger to her brain that left her feeling suddenly exposed.

She stood and pointed to where a shadow slipped through the fog. "Gress!"

"I've got them." Gress was already swinging his carbine up and tracking something through the gloom.

Stephanie turned to the girls, reaching to pull them out of harm's way when a woman streaked from behind a lump of debris and snatched the kids, dragging them back with her. In the store windows, shadows slipped toward the front where there hadn't been any before, brandishing weapons and aiming at them. Stephanie was torn between lunging for the girls and rushing back to the truck when a bullet hit the concrete next to her foot, bouncing up to strike the Humvee with a hard *clank*.

The girls screamed, and the mother covered them as muzzles flashed inside the store, rounds zipping past her ear and clinking off the truck. Turning too quickly, Stephanie tripped and fell into the puddle with a splash. Gress was returning fire, two bursts toward the opposite roadside, swinging back the other way to shoot over the heads of the mother and her girls at the shops. Someone cried out in pain, and the shapes dodged and dove for cover. Adelson raced up, firing his carbine, taking Stephanie by the arm, and hauling her back to the truck. He fell inside, dragging her behind him, her shins striking the step as she tumbled in. The Private reached across her, grabbed the door, and slammed it shut. The window came down, and Adelson stuck his weapon through the opening.

"Hold your ears!"

Stephanie slammed her hands over her ears as he rattled off shots, hot brass shooting around the inside the cabin. Gress jumped in, and the Humvee tore off in a spray of wet gravel, fishtailing as rounds struck the armor until they fled out of range.

Adelson pulled his rifle back and helped Stephanie into an upright position. "Sorry about that, ma'am."

"That's okay." She huffed hard, head ringing from the close shots and racing heart. "That was too close."

Adelson shook his head and ran his hand through his wet hair as they sped away. "I told you guys it was a trap."

CHAPTER FOUR

Morten Christensen, Pearisburg, Virginia

Morten held his hat on so it wouldn't be blown away by wind gusting through Smithson's fields. Alma pulled her black hood over her head and covered her golden hair and drawn features, locking arms with Morten and hugging him close against her. The entire family was with him, making the trek up the long gravel driveway to the Amish leader's homestead for another meeting with the community's elders.

Smithson's expanse of land stretched in all directions, illuminated by faint greenish moonlight that cut up the clouds in dabs of light. The families were gathering at the house, carrying umbrellas and tarps over their heads to stay dry. Women lifted their dresses and entered through the front door while the men went in the side, shedding their coats and hats.

"Do you think they'll discuss Wendy and the kids?" Alma murmured.

"Surely, they will," Morten replied. "And remember, we were never there. We didn't help them in any way."

"Yes, Father. But can you lie to Smithson's face when he confronts you directly?"

"At the risk of displeasing the Lord, yes."

"You're protecting our family," Alma whispered. "God will understand."

"We can't presume to know what God thinks."

"Agreed, Father."

"It pains me not knowing the whereabouts of my daughter-in-law and grandchildren."

Alma nodded and drew him closer, giving him one last hug before circling to the front door with Miriam and Lavinia. Samuel joined Morten at the side door to filter in with the rest of the men where they hung their hats, cloaks, and weapons in the entryway to drip on old rugs. The women greeted them at the end of the hallway with hot coffee, tea and honey, flaky biscuits, and fruit-filled pastries. Morten took a plate and stepped around Smithson's expansive living room with its roaring fire and tasteful Amish furniture spread throughout the place. Several men were already there, perusing the bookshelves, chatting quietly, or sitting alone. Smithson was seated in his regular recliner, a massive, cushioned chair with four plain but sturdy legs, his feet resting on a stool near the flickering flames. He nodded to Morten as he entered, and Morten raised his coffee cup to the Amish leader, working his way around with Samuel right behind him. They found a place off to the side, turning to face the center of the room, bathed in the warm hearth-glow.

"I haven't had such a treat in a long time," Morten said after he took the first bite of his pastry. "Mine's cherry."

Samuel raised his as he chewed. "Blueberry here. Delicious, though not as good as mother's."

With a sad smile, Morten nodded. "Your mother could bake. That's part of the reason my sons grew so tall and strong. She always made sure your bellies were full."

Samuel pulled a rare grin. "We were truly blessed. None of us ever wanted for a bite to eat or a snack... sometimes we sneaked them."

"Your mother always knew what you were doing."

"I don't doubt it. Mother was always on to us."

"Before falling asleep at night, she'd tell me all the trouble you young ones had gotten into."

More men filtered into the room, spreading out and filling the space. He recognized most and remembered Ray Glick and Liam Sweary from the gate. A pair of stout young men stood off to the side near Smithson, steely eyed with clean-shaven faces, cheeks chafed and pale with dots of color.

"Two of Smithson's guards, I'd warrant," Morten said with a nod.

"There're rumors of a man named McCallum sending his people to raid the barns."

"Aye, I heard the same, but with only partial success. We'll wait to see what Smithson has to say on the matter."

By the time Morten had finished his pastry and drunk half his cup of coffee, Smithson stood and spoke to two other elders before turning to get the group's attention. He held his hand up and snapped his fingers, and the men quickly quieted down, leaving only the clanking of utensils and plates in the kitchen and the soft sounds of the women talking.

"Welcome to my home and bless everyone who could attend. Let's all bow our heads in prayer."

The men fell quiet as Smithson spoke a few lines of prayer, ending in a collective, "*Amen!*"

"Again, thanks for coming. I find these daily meetings productive given the dark forces that test our faith here at the end of times. The first order of business is to talk about the sudden disappearance of some of our new friends." He shifted his attention to Morten, who felt himself shrink. "Wendy Christensen and her children, whom we'd placed out on the edge of town with some friends. They've vanished." The Amish leader studied Morten's face. "Does this not alarm you, brother Christensen?"

"The news is unsettling, though not surprising," Morten replied. "Considering the *friends* you sent were not friends at all."

Smithson let the insinuation pass. "You know nothing about this?"

"Alma and I dropped them off at the cottage two days ago, at your behest. We spoke for a short time. That is all."

Smithson stepped across the room with one thumb hooked into

his belt as he searched Morten's eyes. "You know that to lie to me is to denounce the people who have so graciously taken you in?"

"I know," Morten nodded. "I truly don't know where my daughter-in-law and grandchildren have gone."

"And you're not concerned about her being out there by herself with the likes of Oliver McCallum around?"

"Of course, I'm concerned," Morten huffed. "But our place is here with the enclave where we'll wait for the rest of our people to arrive."

Smithson stared at him a long time, leaving off with a heavy sigh. "Fair enough, brother Christensen. Your family's presence here has been a great boon for us all, and we look forward to the day your people arrive. It would be a shame if I found out you'd lied."

Morten stood six inches above the tallest man there, his massive shoulders square and strong. "You question my integrity, sir?"

"Not your integrity, Morten, but your loyalties. Let me know right away if you hear anything from them."

He gave a faint nod and stepped back into place, catching a warning look from Samuel, which he countered with a fierce glare. Smithson turned and continued to address the room as a handful of women walked through the crowd, refilling coffee cups and carrying around trays of pastries. Alma crossed to him and offered a pot, and Morten held out his cup for her to fill. Her expression was flat and unreadable, though her frown deepened as she met his eyes and moved on.

Smithson got a refill on his cup, took a sip, and grinned broadly. "This is wonderful, ladies. Thank you. Next order of business... a report from our scouts regarding Oliver McCallum's repeated attempts to cause us harm. And for that, I brought these two young men up. Most of you know Aaron Schrock and Levi Peachy. These are two young men who've proven themselves good with weapons and are avid hunters. They're yet to be married and with children, so I've chosen them to lead the patrol and keep an inventory of available weapons." He circled to stand between them, his hands resting on their shoulders. "Make no mistake. These are my generals, and they'll lead the defense of the enclave. Aaron, could you give us a quick report on what you've found over the past few days?"

The larger of the two stepped forward. He had a long square jaw and dank yellow curls framing his face. "Yes, sir. As Elder Smithson said, it's been a busy few weeks since the storms hit. I've divided our militia into patrol groups of twenty-five, and those are divided into teams of five. Aside from our alarm bells, we've made an exception and started using two-way radios in the event of an emergency." Mumbles rippled across the assembly, but Smithson stepped up to explain. "It's not something we wanted to do — believe me, the debate on it raged for four days — but desperate times require desperate measures. The radios will enable us to stay in contact with each other only when an attack occurs in our community. Only the patrol leaders are allowed to have them, and they're limited to ten sentences per day, each. Usage reports will be kept by John Hertz's wife." Smithson looked around the room until the murmurs settled. "Okay, Aaron, continue."

"Thank you, sir." Aaron stepped to the front and cleared his throat. "All of you know who Oliver McCallum is from his previous runs for mayor or from working with his construction company on projects around town. Most of you have had some pretty bad experiences with the man." Murmurs of affirmation rumbled through the room like low thunder. "You all know he's not very nice on a *good* day, and he bears a hatred for our community for owning the best land in town."

"The evil doer has had his eyes on our farmland for a long time," Smithson added. "He's tried to illegally build on it and get us kicked off. I guess he thought he could take full advantage of us when the weather changed and things broke down. Continue, son."

Aaron nodded. "The looting and thievery attempts have increased tenfold, and we heard from a couple of men around town that it was McCallum behind it. Apparently, he's been raising a small army to push us out of here."

Angry murmurs filled the room.

"How many does he have?" one man asked.

"We figure he's got at least eighty, and that number is growing daily. Our scouts tell us he's secured every large department store in town and has the support of the small business owners. I guess they think he can protect them."

"What about the local police?"

"The Pearisburg Police Force..." Aaron shook his head. "Most of them were ordered up to those government camps, and no one's seen a single cruiser since the weather got bad."

"We never needed them, anyway! We've always protected our own."

Smithson raised his hand. "There's a problem, gentlemen. With no one left in town to stop looting and thievery, everyone's taking the law into their own hands. It's left things wide open for McCallum to gather some people and declare Pearisburg *his* town. And while that might work with everyone else, it doesn't fly here in God's land."

"That's right."

"They try anything on us, they'll find out."

"They've already tried enough," Aaron spoke louder and more forcefully. "All the attacks that have happened—the assault of the Smucker girl, the thievery at the Kaufman barn, and the attempted burning of Liam Swarey's crops—all of it done by McCallum's people."

"How do you know?"

"We caught one of them."

"Where is he?"

"At the Hertz barn, which we're using as a temporary jail." Aaron stared solemnly across the group. "And while it doesn't please me to say it, we had to force the man to talk."

The men fell silent as the implications hung in the air, and Morten stepped forward. "They tried to take a girl from the enclave?"

"That's right, and God only knows what they wanted to do with her." Aaron shook his head. "And that's not all. We've had two patrols attacked, and three men suffered serious injuries. We used the radios to call for reinforcements and drove the attackers off. But they're getting bolder, so we're asking the older men to help us on patrols."

Morten nodded. "You can count me in, Aaron."

"And I," Samuel added.

"I'll see both of you up at the Hertz's barn as soon as you can get there."

The meeting covered a few more minor issues Morten wasn't concerned with, and he hung back with anxious thoughts. The news of McCallum and his evil actions were troubling, especially with Wendy and the kids out there on their own. Thirty minutes later, the meeting broke up, and he waited for the men to filter into the kitchen and hallway, seeking more refreshments.

"Are you okay, Father?" Samuel asked as they finished their coffee.

"I'm not okay, son. I'm worried about Wendy, David, and Charlie. They'll be staying close to wait for Zachary. What if McCallum finds them?"

Samuel shrugged. "Wendy chose to leave our community and our protection."

"That doesn't keep me from being concerned." He shook his head with a deepening frown. "I've got a good mind to go looking for them."

"Not a good idea, Father."

"Why's that?"

Samuel softened his tone, glancing at Smithson who was shaking hands with the other men as he made his way toward them. "We're already on shaky ground. Any transgressions against the community could get us all kicked out."

"Bah."

Samuel grabbed his arm firmly, voice dropping. "Promise me you won't go looking for them. It will only draw Smithson's ire."

Morten stared at the hand. "I won't make such a promise."

"Promise, Father," Samuel squeezed once and let him go. "Or you risk us all!"

By then, Smithson had gotten there and waited to shake Morten's hand. "I want to reiterate what a blessing you are to our community," he said. "Already, you've shown your commitment to doing the critical work needed for us to get through this. You and Samuel have volunteered to lay down your lives for this community."

Morten took his hand. "We serve this community, and the Lord, with pleasure. Thank you for taking us in."

"It's turning out to be quite a good decision, though I truly wish Wendy would have talked to us before leaving. If they did not like it here, we could have worked something out."

"It breaks my heart, but perhaps it was for the best."

"Perhaps." Smithson gave a strained smile and shifted to shake another elder's hand.

Outside, the families broke up and walked away to their homes and farms, the word spreading quickly about how dangerous the situation was becoming, whispers between parents as they cast worried looks at their children. The borders of their community were shrinking, the invisible walls that had kept them safe and happy for generations suddenly flimsy and weak. As Morten walked away, Alma strolled around the corner, opening her umbrella and locking arms with him.

"That went as well as it could have gone," he said.

"We heard everything."

He graced her with a slow smile. "Do the women of this enclave make a habit of listening in on the elders' conversations?"

"I'm pleased to say they do. The women here are wonderful."

Their long strides carried them through the rain, and soon they were out ahead of Samuel, Lavinia, and the rest of the Amish. "I wish I could say the same about all the men."

"Smithson again?"

"I'm more concerned about Samuel. He doesn't want me to look for Wendy and the children."

"Did you tell him you had no mind to go looking for them in this weather?"

"I told him no such thing."

Alma picked up the pace with her boots striking splashes through the puddles. "I'm proud of you, Father. I hope you find them."

CHAPTER FIVE

Zach Christensen, Klondike Highway, Yukon

"I've got a couple of these radio channels isolated." Craig leaned between the front seats with the radio pulled from its mooring and sitting on an ammunition box. "They're definitely Russian transmissions."

Gina held her rifle across her lap. "What do we do if we meet them on the road?"

"We keep going, no matter what," Zach replied as he checked his weapon. "It's not like there are many side roads to take."

"We run gauntlet," Grizzly said.

Zach nodded. "Something like that. Can any of you understand what they're saying?"

They were moving southbound on Highway 2, reaching a junction of roads called Carcross Cutoff. A sprawl of subdivisions, stores, and city buildings lined simple gravel streets, and a few cars roamed the neighborhoods lighting up the town, a quiet pall hanging over the city. The worst of the firestorms were behind them, though the sky still bubbled and fumed with fires and hydrocarbon currents, flashes of lightning and billowing flames. It was the Russian transmissions worrying him a little more.

Liza leaned forward and spoke over Grizzly's shoulder. It is military speak. "They are checking farmsteads... there was a brief altercation with the locals..." She settled back. "The rest is difficult to make out."

"They wouldn't be too clear over an open channel like this."

"They may be trying to trick everyone," Grizzly said with a shrug.

"Misdirection," Craig nodded. "But will our guys fall for it?"

"Probably not, but organized citizen groups might," Zach replied. "The signal is clear enough to tell me they're close by."

"Very close." Grizzly tilted his head to listen. "They have spotted highway. They are... how you say, approaching it?"

"Converging?" Craig asked. "They're converging on it."

"Yes, that is it."

"Is it *this* highway, or another?"

"Cannot say."

The wind howled through gaps in the windows and nicks in the armor, and the rain fell hard, the roads streaked with trickles and floods. Sometimes the temperature dropped, turning the shower into snowflakes and sleet, hail striking the road and clinking on the armored roof. Above them, the skies were plain gray storm clouds, much preferred over the tempestuous firestorms they were trying to leave behind. If not for the looming threat of Russians, it might have been a peaceful drive with the highway sweeping south around majestic spurs and through high hills filled with verdant green trees and snow caps.

The night wore on, and Grizzly kept a steady pace and pointed out things he heard in the Russian chatter, and by the time dawn broke, he flexed his hands on the wheel and checked the roadsides for signs of enemy troops.

Grizzly nodded to the radio as the voices picked up in clarity and volume. "I think Russian Captain is moving his men to this highway."

"How do you know?"

"They mention a place called *Lorne*."

"Lorne?"

Grizzly nodded to a green sign coming up.

Mount Lorne, 10 miles.

Zach stiffened and searched the hillsides for signs of movement. "Kill the headlamps."

"Done."

"Okay, everyone, keep an eye out. We're going to punch through any —"

"There!" Gina called from the back, tapping her finger against her passenger side window.

Figures were working their way down the hill, dark shapes in camouflage coming through the trees ahead and well off the road.

"Blow right past them, Grizzly."

"You bet," he replied, pushing their speed up to fifty and edging toward the left-hand side of the road.

The figures saw them and moved faster, slipping and sliding to reach the bottom. A few dropped into the ditch along the roadside, heads poking up, rifle barrels resting on the edges and pointed at the Humvee.

"They're going to open fire," Zach charged his gun. "Let's talk back."

Zach rolled down his window and stuck his carbine out as Russian muzzles flashed. The first shot glanced off the frame right by his head as he fired back in steady pops with the powerful rifle bucking against his shoulder. His rounds peppered the ground around the Russians, ricocheting and kicking up gravel as heads ducked. Gina joined him, cold wind screaming through the cabin as she shot several bursts to keep the Russians honest before they rushed by and took a sharp bend to the right. Soldiers jogged onto the highway wearing full tactical gear, raising their weapons to fire but lowering them when the Humvee drove out of range. One soldier spoke into his radio, his voice piping through the truck speakers.

"Is that them?" Zach asked.

"They are talking about us," Grizzly replied. "We have broken through this checkpoint, but there will be more."

"Did they say how many?"

"No, my friend, and I have heard no other towns mentioned except for Lorne."

"Which is ten miles away," Craig said. "Maybe they'll have a larger checkpoint there."

"We can probably count on it," Zach replied.

"How can they have a sizeable force already?" Craig asked. "We just saw them dropping troops a day ago."

"They're moving with a sense of purpose," Zach said grimly. "Everyone keep an eye out."

It wasn't long before they ran into another group of Russians behind a hastily constructed roadblock, pieces of rail fencing being dragged onto the highway with a squarish pile of rocks serving as a gunner's nest. Grizzly had been racing around a long bend when he caught sight of them building it, and he drove right at them, calling for Zach and Gina to cover him. Once again, they leaned out of the passenger side windows, firing on the Russian forces, bullets ricocheting off the barriers and sending a handful of soldiers scattering in every direction. They hit the rails, smashing over them in a blast of wood shards that rattled the undercarriage and spit out the back. The Russians were fast to return fire, hitting the Humvee's hatchback, one round striking the already worn glass and sending spiderweb cracks spreading across the surface. Zach pulled his weapon inside, and everyone ducked until they were out of range and racing south yet again.

"Another close one," Craig said, shaking his head at the ruined glass. "The next time, we might not be so lucky."

"Are they still talking about us, Grizzly?" Zach nodded at the radio.

Grizzly listened as he worked the wheel, driving them up a prominent ridge. "They have a description of our Humvee and want us stopped."

"That's not good," Zach frowned, "especially if we shot one of them."

"They will not be merciful," Liza said with a head shake.

"I know how Russian forces operate," Grizzly added. "They will terrorize the local population and not tolerate anyone fighting back."

"The five people in this Humvee have something to say about that." Gina sniffed.

"I'll bet they just want the roads," Zach said. "They want to block them and keep convoys from moving north."

Craig gripped his shoulder. "We're going south. Let the Marines and Army boys take care of them."

"We might not have a choice but to deal with them."

The cabin grew quiet as they ate up more highway, the road sweeping back and forth through pine-covered hills made of rich, brown earth. Sometimes the highway stretched straight and flat for miles with the dark shapes of mountain ranges rising in the distance. Telephone poles lined the roadsides with long, loping wires hanging between them. Dirt roads branched off to the east and west. Mount Lorne loomed two thousand feet tall on their left, visible above the tree line with peaks that touched the clouds. Dozens of spurs spread from several arcing ridgelines like a spine cutting across the landscape.

Grizzly slammed the brakes, tires sliding on the wet pavement as machine gun rounds spat at them from a hundred and fifty yards ahead, pinging off their armor, smacking the grill, and sending water droplets shivering off their metal sides. Zach cursed softly and rolled down his window to take aim, but Grizzly was already backing up, the wheels spinning as he got them out of danger quickly, and the shots stopped coming in.

"There." Grizzly drew his arm across his sweaty forehead. "We are out of range."

Zach held up his hand. "Who has the binoculars?"

"Right here." Craig gave them over.

Peeping over the dashboard, Zach searched the line of Russians standing in the road with their weapons up, a pair kneeling behind piles of logs.

"I see a half dozen and maybe some more off to the side in the trees."

"I guess that does it for us," Craig said disgustedly. "Can we go off road?"

"No place to go," Grizzly replied, gesturing to either side where the trees grew thick.

"We did it before."

"Yes, but this is not a horse. It is truck."

Zach made a cursory check around. "He's right. There's no other way to go but ahead, unless we take one of those side roads we passed a ways back."

"None of those are on a map," Craig said. "We have no idea where they lead."

"We'll have to take that chance," Zach said, "unless you want to try to run through those guys."

Craig glanced skeptically at the Russians. "Nah, you're right. Let's try to go around."

Grizzly got them turned around and headed back the other way while the Russians spread across the road, gesturing and speaking into their radios. That gnawing sense that they were going the wrong way again nagged at Zach, but there was no helping the change of direction, and he watched as they sped past the forestland, looking for a side road and a way out. A mile and a half later, a rutted, gravel road bent into the stands of firs and pines, weaving around the south edge of the hills.

"There it is," he said, pointing off to the left. "Let's give it a try."

Grizzly turned onto it in a spray of gravel, straightening the front end, and accelerated to forty, bumping over the tire-worn tract and kicking up a cloud of dust behind them.

"Think we can get around them?" Liza asked in a soft Russian voice.

"This road seems to skirt the south end of the hills," Craig said, "so maybe there are some connecting roads."

Keep an eye out for them," Zach replied.

The cabin got silent as Grizzly took them deeper into the Yukon woods until they passed a couple of dilapidated stores and a string of decent homes before reaching the first road pointing east. Grizzly turned onto it, the gravel and ruts getting worse, the truck holding together but clanking and rattling like a tin can.

"Bearville." Zach squinted at a crooked wooden sign coming up.

"That's not even on the map." Craig flicked the paper, folded it, and stuffed it in a pocket. "I don't even know why I'm looking at the map at this point."

"Just look for signs for the highway coming up."

The gravel road worsened, forcing Grizzly to slow as they bumped and bounced, entering a mobile home neighborhood with rundown houses, burn barrels smoking everywhere, and jacked-up cars in the yards with garbage floating across the road.

"Whoa, this place looks bad," Grizzly said as they cruised.

"Where is everyone?" Gina asked.

"There!" Grizzly slammed on the brakes as a group of people ran from behind a rusted van and crossed the road, wearing hunting jackets and caps, carrying rifles, shotguns, and duffel bags that dragged the ground. They moved north with focused intent, half-crouched like fighters. Two stopped to stare at them, and Zach raised his rifle to show they were armed. One man slapped his friend on the chest and gestured to the others, who were moving away, and they turned and jogged to catch up. Up the street, more people were crossing the road, sprinting into the north-side neighborhoods. Front doors flew open, and citizens by the handfuls joined them, only a few casting discerning glances toward the Humvee, measuring Zach's group before moving on.

Liza rolled down her window. "Are those gunshots?"

"Definitely," Zach replied as the distant pops of automatic machine gun fire echoed throughout the valley.

Grizzly moved forward slowly, stopping when people ran by. Zach waved casually at them, and they'd go on by, except for a man and woman he flagged down through his open window.

"Hello, there! Hey!"

The couple stopped in the middle of the road, shared an uncertain look, and slowly approached on Zach's side. Zach guessed they were in their thirties, dressed in jeans and winter boots, dark jackets with the hoods pushed back to reveal their rugged faces.

The woman held a shotgun and stopped a few feet away with errant strands of ash-blonde hair falling in her eyes. "Who are you?"

Zach jerked his thumb toward the north. "We're refugees from Fairbanks. Americans, trying to get home."

"You've come a long way." She didn't flinch when she saw the rifles resting in their laps. "And you've got a long way to go."

"Can I ask you what's going on here? Why is everyone running north?"

"Where've you been? Russians are everywhere. It's some kind of invasion force. Can you believe that?"

"We watched a lot of them fall out of the sky, and we met some on the highway north of here. Any idea how we can get around them and get back on the highway?

"If you stay on this main road, you can get there. If you're willing to stay and fight, we could certainly use the help."

Incoming rounds struck a nearby trailer, tearing through the flimsy walls and sending dust and dirt flying up in puffs of smoke, and the woman and her companion both ducked and gazed north with concern.

"We appreciate the offer," Zach said. "But good luck to you."

The woman nodded and raised from her crouch, backing away. "Good luck to you, too." She circled to the man, and together they sprinted off to the north to join the others.

"Good news," Zach said. "We can get to the highway from here. Let's go, Grizzly."

"Right on," Gina replied.

"Right on," Grizzly repeated and kicked the truck into gear.

An explosion ripped through the sky, and all eyes turned to the north, where a plume of fire and smoke rolled upward in a mushroom shape. The intense fighting drew closer, and civilians crouched between the houses and cars, shooting over the hoods and trunks, lying in wait around corners. Several flaming bottles arced through the air and landed in a junkyard, exploding in gouts of fire that enveloped the rusted-out car frames. Stripped-down mobile homes were peppered with rounds, and what remained of their walls were left smoking and falling in.

"What do the Russians possibly want with this place?" Craig asked. "I thought they wanted to take the roadways?"

"I don't know, Zach replied, "but we've got to get through before they take it."

They raced toward the town center, and a flurry of incoming fire pinged off their armor and sent everyone in the truck ducking. Grizzly hammered the gas, and they shot toward an intersection with a couple of stores, a gas station, and a small strip mall. A group of Russians had fought their way to the north side of the road and were gathered behind the strip mall, while the citizens occupied positions on the south side behind a van and a pickup in the gas station parking lot, gesturing for others to run up and help fortify their position. Grizzly eyed the crossfire as muzzles flashed, and he slowed before entering the blender of gunfire.

"We can't do anything here," Zach said, pointing to a road to the right. "Take that road, and we'll go around."

Grizzly slammed the accelerator and shot through the intersection, angling toward the right side of the road, throwing gravel and dirt off behind them.

"What the hell are you doing, Grizzly?" Zach said, sinking in his seat.

"Everyone get down!" Grizzly bellowed. "I go through... hang on."

Liza slammed her hands over her head, teeth clamped as they entered a blender of flying metal. Craig and Gina grabbed each other and ducked as low as they could go.

Grizzly aimed the grill at a group of Russians who'd flanked the citizens and were coming up out of the woods on the south side of the road. Rounds struck them on both sides as the Humvee bore down, the engine growling like a beast. Russians scattered or fired on the truck, but it was too late. Grizzly clipped one man, sending him rolling over the windshield with a thump, flying off the back to land in the gravel. The others spread out or leaped into the woods as the citizens turned their weapons on them. Grizzly tore through bushes and trees, ripping the wheel to the left to get them back on the road, swerving for a moment before bringing the vehicle under control. Zach rose in his seat, checking his side mirror to see the citizens overcoming the scattered Russians, guns spitting fire and smoke.

"Everyone okay?" he asked.

"Yeah," Craig replied. "Liza?"

"Ugh... yes, I am fine." She wiped tears off her cheeks.

"Just a couple more cracks in the window," Gina said, rubbing a new bullet indention and tracing a crack with her finger.

The gravel road narrowed into a single-lane path, barely wide enough for two cars to fit with driveways branching to either side into the woods, reaching dead ends where the wilderness encroached. The gunfire and explosions grew less distinct as they left the battle behind, though Zach was starting to doubt whether the woman was right about getting to the highway from there. Then they spotted an aged sign barely hanging from a pole, its surface marked and rusted, with *Highway 2* written in bold on the front.

"Here we go," Grizzly said with a grin that split his beard. "Right on."

"Right on," Gina chuckled with relief.

Zach stared at Grizzly. "Hey, man. I told you to take a right back there."

"I know. I saw the people were in trouble... I help them."

"Yeah, I know, man. But we've got to be more careful."

"Perhaps it was the old soldier in me."

"Right, but I'm in charge of this group. It's my responsibility to get us to that US border. You've got to listen to me if I ask you to do something, or at least let me know why not."

"No time for warning, Zach," Grizzly frowned in a pinched face. "I will do better next time, my friend. Is true."

Zach nodded, heart lifting when they came upon the entrance ramp and swung back on the highway with no signs of Russians anywhere. He patted Grizzly on the shoulder. "I know you were only concerned for those people back there, but this truck is taking a beating... *we're* taking a beating, and we can't stop to help everyone."

Grizzly nodded and eased into the left-hand lane.

"How many miles to Carcross?" Zach asked.

"Around ten." Craig spread the map on his lap with shaking hands. "Think the Russians will be there, too?"

"Count on it," Zach nodded. "How many roads branch off from there?"

Craig did a little tracing with his finger. "Carcross sits right on Nares Lake. Might be a good opportunity to refill our water bottles. Aside from that, there are two highways out. Highway 2 going south and Highway 8 that turns northwest."

"We'll approach the town cautiously," Zach said. "If there are no signs of Russians, we'll refill our bottles at the lake and hop back on Highway 2. We have to outrun them at some point."

"Let's hope so," Craig said. "I don't want to see another Russian as long as I live." He glanced apologetically at Liza. "Except for you and Grizzly, of course."

Liza smiled and patted his arm.

CHAPTER SIX

Wendy Christensen, Pearisburg, Virginia

Electric lantern light filled the room, and rain continued beating on the house. Wendy was sitting at the injured woman's bedside, stitching her left arm, drawing the needle through flesh, and tugging it tightly together. Blood seeped between the threads and ran down her arm until Wendy caught the runner with a bit of gauze.

"David, can you shine the flashlight right on this?" she asked, sitting back a few inches.

David stepped in behind her, looming tall and aiming light on the wound. Wendy leaned in, pressing around it, dabbing with the gauze before finally cutting the thread and tying it off so the knot held the stitches in place.

"I'm no EMT, but this will have to do." She clicked her tongue. "These stitches look terrible."

"I don't know anyone who could have done better," he replied, rubbing his head absently. "You did a pretty good job on my head. The hair's even growing back a little."

"It should cover any scars. This poor woman is probably going to have a pretty jagged one. Oh well, at least that takes care of the entry and exit wounds. The bullet didn't hit anything vital, so she won't bleed to death or anything. And I'm glad she didn't wake up in the middle of it."

"Lucky Charlie found that first aid kit in the laundry room, suture kit and all."

"Judging from all the projects out in the garage, whoever lived here did some woodworking and expected some cuts and scrapes. They were definitely prepared."

They had her in one of the guest bedrooms, light green walls with a twin bed, a simple nightstand at her side, and some plain paintings of mountains and forest scenes on the walls. The woman was tucked beneath the checkered bedspread with her arms resting by her sides. Wendy had done her best to clean her up, cutting off her shirt and bra and dabbing the smudges with baby wipes. Her pale skin glowed in the dim light, her cheeks were sallow and bloodless, crisp red hair with gray streaks brushed back from her forehead in a thick sweep. Clyde sat near the foot of the bed, watching curiously, his tail twitching back and forth.

"I'll work on some of these smaller cuts now."

David bit his lip. "She's pretty beat up, huh?"

"Yeah, whoever attacked her sure did a number on her. Those men we drove off, I guess." Wendy pulled the woman's blanket aside, keeping her breast covered but showing David an enormous bruise along her ribs on the left side.

"Wow, I can't believe she survived all that."

"She's a tough lady, for sure."

Footsteps approached and Charlie stepped in, tossing a handbag into a chair in the corner of the room and dropping a brown leather wallet on the bed. "Her name is Darla."

Wendy straightened. "How do you know that?"

Charlie flipped up a thin piece of plastic between her index and middle finger, showing a picture of the same woman in the bed, only cleaned up. "It says it right here on her driver's license."

Wendy frowned. "You didn't have to go out there and root around in the truck with that dead person right there."

"It's okay. I wanted to see who she was." Charlie stepped closer and held up the ID, comparing it to her bruised face. "To be honest, it could be either of them. They're both so beat up I can't tell."

Wendy shook her head and reached for a water bowl and a clean washrag. "Poor women." She wet the rag and wiped a smudge on Darla's right collarbone. "I can't tell what's dirt and what's a bruise. David, a little more light, please."

David swung his flashlight around, and Wendy continued gently wiping the smudge marks, lifting her right arm and getting beneath her elbow and forearm. She was skinny with thin cheeks and wiry arms and legs. When Wendy got to her face, Darla groaned, eyelashes fluttering open to reveal striking blue-green eyes.

Wendy backed up and smiled hesitantly. "Hi there."

"Where am I?"

"You're in a safe place right now... a bedroom. How are you feeling?"

Darla looked around dazedly. "I'm feeling okay, I guess... ouch." She'd tried to sit up but winced and laid flat again. "Ow, my arm."

"Just rest easy," Wendy said. "You got shot in the arm. You've got some bruises and scrapes, too, so you'll feel a little pain for a while. I've got some simple painkillers here if you want them..." Wendy picked up the pills and a glass of water from the nightstand and showed her.

Darla stared at the kids suspiciously.

"Oh, these are my kids, David and Charlie. They helped me bring you in–"

"Where *was* I?" Darla croaked.

"You drove up our driveway and wrecked into a tree outside our house."

"*Your* house?"

Wendy laughed nervously. "Well, not *ours*, but I guess you could say we moved in for the time being."

Anger flashed across Darla's face, and she tried to sit up again but winced and fell back in frustration. "No, this is *my* house."

"You're Darla, right?"

"Yeah, I'm Darla, and I live here."

Charlie took a second look at the ID. "She's right. It's the same house number out front."

Darla snatched Wendy's arm and lifted herself with a pained gasp. "My sister... Is she okay? Is she...?" Darla looked around the room. "Where...?" Fading, shivering, she fell back to the bed with a sigh.

"I'm sorry, Darla, but..." Wendy shared a concerned look with Charlie and David. "It's just that..."

Darla's eyelids fluttered shut, and she drew a deep breath, turned her cheek to the pillow, and released a quivering sigh.

Wendy dumped the last bucket into the sink with a splash, then turned to stare at the remaining drip on the ceiling. The circle of discoloration was only about six inches in diameter, though the leak had been substantial and had drenched the floor before they'd caught it. The storm continued to rage outside, but the tarps were holding.

"Looks like we fixed the problem," David said, stepping over to the cooking island and leaning there. An electric lantern stood on the table behind him, casting his thin features in shadows and giving him a haunted appearance.

"I sure hope so," Wendy replied. "I don't want to get on that roof again."

"I thought you guys were going to get blown off," Charlie said as she passed through from Darla's room with a plastic bag full of bloody rags.

"Especially when we dumped those bricks," David whistled low. "I felt like a scarecrow up there."

Wendy grinned and circled to the cooking island to sit at the kitchen table, shrugging off her sweater and pulling a notepad in front of her. She tapped on it with a pen. "Now that Darla is resting and stitched up, let's go over what we found in the house so far."

"The garage has the usual stuff," David said. "Sawhorses, regular tools; hammer, nails, screwdrivers, and stuff like that. There are even some power tools we could use..."

"If we ever figure out how to get the power on," Wendy said.

"The best thing out there is the other truck. It's older than the one Darla wrecked, but it looks like it runs."

"The keys are probably right there." Wendy nodded at a key rack on the wall next to the laundry room door.

"We've got transportation if we need it. Want me to start it?"

"When we're done here."

Charlie threw the bloody rags in the laundry room and sat at the head of the table to her right. David grabbed his bottled water and joined them, sitting across from Wendy.

"But we're not going anywhere," Charlie said. "We're waiting here for Dad, right?"

"Absolutely. We're waiting for your father right here."

"Darla might not be happy about that," David said. "She was pretty insistent about this being *her* place."

"It doesn't matter what Darla thinks." Wendy glanced toward Darla's room. "We're staying here no matter what she says."

"Even if she wants us to leave?"

"She's injured and needs our help, and she owes us for bringing her in and stitching her up."

"Not to mention protecting her from those men," Charlie said.

"That, too. After seeing what's out there, we won't find a better place than this."

"And what about the horses?" Charlie rolled her bottle cap around on the table. "If worse comes to worst, we can ride those and escape any trouble."

Wendy laughed. "You don't know how to ride. None of us do. Although it would be pretty comical to watch us try."

"Maybe Darla can teach us how, now. The point is, we've got horses."

Clyde came over, and Charlie patted him on the head, rubbing between his ears as he panted and lolled his tongue. He licked Charlie's hand and walked back into the living room to hop on the couch. The Gray Labrador was filling out well, gaining weight in his haunches and shoulders.

"Clyde is looking really good," Wendy said.

"Hard to believe he's the same scrawny dog we found under the porch."

"I must say, I'm glad we kept him. He's been pretty amazing."

"Thanks for letting me have him." Charlie's eyes turned glassy. "I don't know what I'd do without him. And we can finally afford to feed him with all the food out in the stables. Darla must have had a dog at one point."

"Strange, we haven't seen one around," Wendy said, "unless they had it with them when they went into town and it didn't make it back." She tapped her pen on the notepad. "So, what else have we found in the house?"

"Besides the bedroom Darla's in," Charlie said, "they've got another smaller bedroom and a big one."

"A master bedroom."

"Yeah. There's a bathroom in the master bedroom and in the hallway, and they've got several closets and all the rooms, which we haven't been through completely. It's a super nice place."

"Yes, it is. Have either of you been downstairs yet?"

"Not me," Charlie said.

"Or me." David nodded toward the sink. "The best part about this place is that they still have running water, but it doesn't get hot."

"All right." Wendy rested her palms lightly on the table. "And we've already taken inventory of the pantry."

It was a wide section of shelves between the refrigerator and hall to the laundry room. The top shelves had boxed meals, assorted chocolates, snack nuts, and two bins of whole coffee beans. On the middle shelves were wooden organizers with packs of powdered mixes; chili, broths, soups, and drinks. The canned goods were lower with the typical vegetables, tuna, and chicken brands.

"What we have in the pantry should last us a while," Wendy said, checking down her list. "A lot of the bins are half-empty, so maybe Darla wasn't stocking up so much anymore. But she's got a pressure canner and a bunch of canning jars, too."

"That's the cooker thing with the gauge on top."

"That would be it." Wendy tapped her chin with the pen. "Makes me wonder if she's growing food or buying it from the Amish. If we're out scavenging and happen to find some crops, we'll harvest them ourselves. It's something to think about when we start doing scavenging runs, which we may want to do sooner than later. There's bound to be a ton of abandoned farms and fields out there. Anything else good?"

"I was looking through the bedroom before we brought Darla in." Charlie nodded to a revolver on the cooking island. "I found that .357 in a drawer."

"Along with David's Springfield, your Ruger, and my Hellcat... plus my M&P 15, we'll have a decent little arsenal. With fifty rounds each, that would bring us to about two hundred and fifty rounds total. Not too shabby."

"Do you think Grandpa could get us back the rest of our guns and ammo?" David asked.

"I'm sure he'd love to, but he's dealing with Smithson and the elders. Once our weapons get on their inventory list, we'll never see them again."

Wendy stepped aside and nodded at the kitchen table. "What about that computer tablet there? I saw you messing with it, David. Were you able to get it going?"

"I can turn it on, but it's password protected. Darla probably knows what it is."

"I'm sure she does."

"Why would we need it anyway?" Charlie asked. "It's not like there's an internet anymore."

"That's true, but there might be some good information on it, and maybe there's something we can use to view the cameras."

"We'll have to ask Darla when she wakes up," David said.

"Okay, is there anything else we need to check?"

"Just the basement," Charlie said.

"All right, downstairs it is. I'll go first." Wendy grabbed her rifle off the table and carried it to the basement door.

"You really need that?" Charlie came on her heels.

"Someone could be down there."

"Wouldn't we know that by now?"

"Not necessarily. She could have a dog in one of the back rooms or something. All I'm saying is that we should be prepared for anything."

With her flashlight in her left hand and Charlie carrying an electric lantern, they stood at the top of a carpeted stairwell.

"It looks pretty nice," Wendy said, descending quietly to the bottom where she shined her light around.

It was set up like a living room with a bar in the back, fully stocked with whiskeys and vodkas. A flat-screen TV hung on the north wall with a leather couch facing it and rustic knickknacks on the end tables and shelves. Wendy might've expected sports memorabilia, but it was all framed pictures of electric motors, strange circuit board configurations, and science-related things.

"This is pretty cool," David whispered.

"Yeah, not exactly my style," Wendy replied, "but neat."

"I like it," Charlie said.

There were two doors on either side of the TV, plus a third built into the east wall. Wendy walked to the left-hand door with her rifle pointed down. She popped it open and stood back to let Charlie's light in.

"It's just a bathroom." She closed it and went to try the other one.

"I'll check this last door," David crossed to the east wall.

"Be careful," Wendy said before entering a storage room with furniture, more boxes and canning jars, bins marked as *Old Clothes* and *Dishes*.

"Mom! Charlie!"

Wendy turned on a dime, rushing to the east door with Charlie meeting her, pistol in her hand. She shoved the door open and found David standing in the middle of a workshop with technical diagrams and science fiction movie posters on the walls. A large workbench sat on the north side of the room with intricate parts and miniature car bodies strewn across it.

"Look at all this stuff," David said.

"What is it?" Charlie asked, stepping past Wendy.

David placed his pistol on the workbench and held up a model car for them. The frame was black and sleek, the wheels soft rubber, with a large antenna hanging from the top. "I think this is an RC car.

Yeah, here's the controller." He picked up a hand-sized remote controller with an antenna and switches, levers, and buttons on the front.

"There's more over here." Charlie stepped to a shelf on the right side where more RC vehicles were parked neatly in slots; boats, planes, cars and trucks, each about a foot long and nine inches wide with antennas rolled up and taped.

"And look at all these parts." David gestured to small boxes and bins on the bench and below it on shelves. "He's got wheels and the motor parts. This guy must've built them or fixed them."

"An RC car hobbyist," Wendy said. "Not exactly something we can use, but pretty cool."

"Not so fast, Mom." Charlie moved to another set of bins filled with odd spare parts. She dug into one box, shifted some things around, and pulled out two 2-way radios. "Do you think we can use these?"

"Well, heck yeah." She took one and flipped it on, listening to the static. When Charlie turned hers on, the feedback came through both speakers in a high-pitched noise that pierced their ears.

Wendy quickly snapped hers off. "Let's remember not to do that next time."

"Sorry," Charlie chuckled and perked up. "But at least they work."

"Don't we have to be on the same channel or something?"

"Yeah, but it's easy." David took Charlie's. "We switch it with these knobs. Should be able to talk to each other if we're both on the same one."

"I wonder what the range is on these?" Wendy bit her lip. "We can use them when we're on watch."

"Won't we be watching through the windows?" Charlie asked. "Why would we need radios for that?"

"For the most part, yes. But we'll have to put someone at the end of the driveway to watch the road. The radios will be *perfect* for that. If someone turns into the driveway, the person on duty can warn the rest of us."

"I'm sure they have enough range to cover us," David replied, "but I don't know how well they work in the rain."

Charlie frowned. "Do we seriously have to keep watch in all that rain and mud?"

"Absolutely, we do." Wendy held hers up and shook it. "We'll test them right now. I'll go down and pick us a spot."

"No, Mom," Charlie said. "You took first watch because I fell asleep, and you've been on more watch shifts than anyone. I'll come with you and help you find a good spot, then *I'll* take first watch."

"If you're up for it," Wendy agreed. "My eyelids are drooping shut, and I could use a couple of hours' rest."

"Are you kidding me?" David said. "The entire trip down here was crazy. I hardly slept."

Wendy took his arm and hugged him. "We could stand a couple of weeks of uninterrupted peace and quiet. The faster we get into a rotation, the faster we'll get caught up on rest."

Upstairs, they found their ponchos and started putting them on, when Clyde came over, wagging his tail with his ears perked up.

"You get to stay inside where it's warm, boy," Charlie said. When Clyde only whined and tilted his head, she chuckled. "Trust me, buddy. You don't want to go out in this mess. Stay here and wait for me. We'll be snuggling up on that couch pretty soon, okay?"

Clyde chuffed and danced a little on his front paws.

"Good boy." Charlie rubbed his head.

"We'll grab that brown tarp David and I brought from the stables, and I thought I saw some cushioned stadium seats that might come in handy. David, can you be ready up here with the radio?"

"Sure. What channel?"

"How about fourteen?"

"All right." David leaned on the cooking island and adjusted his channel. "I'm ready. Are we going to say 'over' and all that?"

"You don't have to say 'over,' but let's keep conversations short. I doubt many people in the area are using radios, but we don't want them listening in, anyway. Also, let's call each other by our initials. You're DC, Charlie is CC, and I'll be WC."

"Sounds good."

In the garage, Charlie picked up the tarp while Wendy grabbed the two cushioned seats off a shelf. "These look waterproof. Perfect for what we need."

They stepped through the garage and out into the rainy day. The skies were overcast with lighter wisps of clouds pushed by northeasterly winds. The trees leaned over, tired and bedraggled, leaves stripped off the top sections and mulched by the stinging rains. They circled the house and walked down the driveway, ponchos pulled tight as streams of water poured over their boots. About halfway down, Wendy stopped and searched into the woods for a spot out of the way where someone could keep watch.

"I think I see something up there."

She stepped off the driveway and climbed a short bank, grabbing saplings and brush to pull herself up, stopping at the top where it evened out. Streams cut through the soil and pooled in a trough at the bottom that flowed parallel to the highway. Twigs and sticks dropped from the upper boughs, falling softly onto the forest floor.

"How about this rock here?" Wendy gestured to a wide stone beneath a birch tree, its thick branches dripping slowly in big fat drops. "It's not perfectly dry but should be okay with your rain poncho. What do you think?"

Charlie blinked her wide blue eyes. "It's better than standing in the stinging rain."

Wendy put the cushioned seat on the rock and bade Charlie sit. She opened the tarp a couple of folds, laid it over Charlie's shoulders, and pulled it out to cover the top portion of her legs.

"How's that?"

"Seems okay for now." She drew the tarp tighter around her. "If I sit cross-legged, I can fit beneath it. I should be able to stay pretty warm and dry out here."

"Can you see the road, okay?"

"Yep."

"Okay, I'm going to try David now." Wendy turned her radio on to the soft sounds of static. She switched to channel fourteen and pressed the talk button. "DC, this is WC. Can you hear me?"

"WC, this is DC. I can hear you fine. Works great."

"Okay. I'm handing the radio over to CC." She gave Charlie the radio. "Give it a try."

The kids talked a moment before David signed off. "Stay frosty CC."

"There's no other way to be out here."

Wendy stood there another moment, not wanting to leave Charlie alone in the cold, rainy weather. She looked miserable sitting there with her shoulders slumped and the tarp drooped over her, rivulets of water dripping on her head.

"Are you going to be okay out here?"

"I'll be fine." Charlie smiled tiredly.

Wendy hugged her. "Okay, but I'll have the radio close. If you see anything on the road, call me. If someone comes up the driveway, let us know fast and follow them."

"Don't worry. I'll be your eyes and ears."

"Thanks, honey. I love you. See you soon."

"Love you, too, Mom. Get some rest."

After a brief embrace, Wendy walked back and leaped onto the driveway, coming up to pass the white truck with its grill still wrapped around the tree. Darla's sister was still inside, lying against the door with all that blood and mess, her cherry-blonde hair clinging to the passenger side glass. They'd have to bury her soon, and every hour they waited would only make the job harder. Plus, Darla wouldn't want her out there bloating and stinking and rotting away where she could see her.

Wendy sighed into the cold rain and went inside.

CHAPTER SEVEN

Zach Christensen, Carcross, Yukon

They rolled up to Carcross between a flat plain of fir trees and patches of wilderness, snow-crusted roadsides, telephone poles leaning with limp wires stretched thin beneath the high winds. It was close to dusk, flurries whipping through the air, with the town plopped down between Nares and Bennett Lakes, surrounded by a sprawl of bulging hills with pointed peaks and verdant green slopes. They came upon a trading post on the left, with roads and trails sprouting off in every direction. Small buildings and shacks lined the roadsides, some freshly painted with nice storefronts, others dilapidated and falling apart. They all had the same construction style. Low and long with a single peak running through the center, many with native symbols along the sides. Way back in the neighborhoods newer bi-level homes and two-story structures squatted in the lower hills, and rough gravel roads wound throughout the town.

"I hope we've outrun the Russians," Craig said.

"I wouldn't count on it," Zach replied with a wary eye on the road, scanning the buildings and empty streets. "Does anybody know anything about Carcross?"

Gina leaned in. "Hank and I went there a long time ago, maybe ten years ago. It's a huge tourist town. They've got bike trails, hotels, and shops in the center of town where Nares and Bennett Lakes meet. I remember it having fishing camps, bike trails, and a ton of annoying tourists. It was quaint enough, from what I remember. Got a rail line that goes right through the center and heads on south."

"It looks deserted," Craig leaned between the seats.

"Slow down a little, Grizzly," Zach said.

The diesel engine wound down as they cruised into town. The windows in every home and store were empty and dark, mailboxes lining the gravel roads with their doors flipped open. A few cars and trucks sat in the driveways or up on blocks, and yards were overgrown and messy with garbage. They cruised past a wood crafter's shop, a lonely diner with *Mel's* written in blue cursive across the window, and several bland buildings with faded paint. A newer building with native script on the dirty front window came up on the left with a few cars in the lot but darkness inside. Beyond that was another structure with stacks of car bodies surrounding a large building with closed bay doors.

"Stop here," Zach said. "Looks like a mechanic's shop."

"Lots of cars and trucks," Gina said. "We could fuel up."

"Absolutely. We'll refill the jerrycans and top off the Humvee."

Grizzly crept through the lot between stacks of junkers and crushed vehicles, scrap metal and rusted frames, searching for diesel trucks. When they got around back, Zach ordered him to stop next to a large Ford with a double-long cab.

Gina popped her door. "I'll get the siphoning gear. Meet you there."

Zach climbed out with his spear held loosely against his chest, immediately walking to the front of the truck and checking both directions. When he saw no other cars, he angled toward the shop and kept himself between the building and the Humvee where Grizzly and Gina were trying to open the Ford's gas cap. A brisk wind blew through, mixing antifreeze fumes and snowflakes that danced in front of him. He checked out another small junkyard where a handful of dogs watched him from the end of the row, their heads low as though looking for a weakness. Grabbing an empty jerrycan he found there, he brought it back to the others and tossed it to Grizzly.

"Fill this one up, too. We don't know how many opportunities we'll have once we get past Carcross."

Zach continued his watch for the next thirty minutes as they refilled, walking over to the next building and looking through the abandoned vehicles, finding a few bottled waters and assorted garbage. When the distant sounds of gunfire reached him, he made his way back to the group to see them packing their cans in the Humvee's cargo area.

"We heard gunshots." The big Russian waited with his door half open, hanging on it like a tired bear.

"So it wasn't just me?"

"No, we heard it loud and clear."

"Seems like they came from the west, but it's hard to tell."

"Should we find a different way?" Craig asked from the back seat.

"There are no more ways," Zach replied.

"There are some small roads that branch off the south shore." Craig had the map out. "Highway 2 goes right on through. That's what we want to be on if we want to move fast."

Zach got in. "We keep heading south on two and deal with the Russians as they come. If it looks like we're going to be caught, we'll turn the truck around, head back north, and find another way."

"Understood." Grizzly got in.

Loaded up and refueled, they jumped on the highway and headed south, sweeping past more evacuated homes and businesses.

"I guess they got out while the getting was good," Craig said.

"Or they're hunkered down like the people in Whitehorse," Zach replied. "Keep your eyes opened."

They reached the Carcross town center where it took on a touristy tone with gaudy storefronts and paved roads branching off to clusters of themed shops and restaurants to the east. Tightly packed houses lined the Bennett Lake shore to the west, and an airfield sat off to the northeast behind some woods.

"Grizzly, pull off between this big group of stores." Zach pointed to the left where seven buildings squatted along the Nares Lake north shoreline, including a learning center, administrative facilities, a short row of restaurants with bright red siding. They rolled up and squeezed between two stores, hiding themselves from prying eyes. Abandoned vehicles sat in the lot like orphans, and wind gusts played with pieces of garbage that tumbled across the parking lot. The land sloped down to the lake shore, where the remaining daylight shined off the quiet surface in shimmering waves. Zach got out first, circling to the rear of the truck and scanning the center of town, the neighborhoods, and both lakes which were split by a single bridge.

"Okay, you guys collect all the water bottles into one duffel bag? Throw the press filters in, too. I'll take them down and fill them up."

Craig circled to the rear of the Humvee and popped the hatch, rifling through their things for a duffel bag.

"That will take a lot of time." Liza's accent was thicker the more tired she became.

"No, I want you guys to stay together. If you want to check the back doors of these building, that's fine. As long as we all keep our heads down, we should be okay."

Distant gunfire rattled off, coming from the northeast past the airfield. Zach walked along the storefronts and checked in that direction but saw nothing conspicuous, merely the looming gray skies and small openings of light shining through.

Grizzly came up with a duffel bag bulging with water bottles. "I will go with you."

"No. Stay here and guard the truck with Gina. I'll be back in less than ten minutes, then we're out of here."

Zach accepted the duffel bag and reached inside the passenger side window for his binoculars. "Just holler if you see or hear anything, okay?"

"Yes."

With a nod to the others, Zach walked east toward the lake, checking both ways behind the buildings and jogged to the tree line with the duffel bag bouncing on his back. He picked his way down through the gently sloping woods to the shoreline, and the Humvee and his friends quickly fell out of sight. Nares Lake stretched to the southeast, a narrow body of water miles across.

Waves lapped against the rocky shore, making soft splashes that mirrored the turbulent skies. Placing his rifle and the duffel bag down, he took the two press filters out and straddled a pair of flat stones. He removed the filter tubes from each canister, filled them with lake water, and put the filter tubes back. With his palms against the tops, he began to slowly press the water through, and after ten seconds, he had thirty-two ounces of pure, clean water. He filled up two empty plastic bottles and stooped to get more, repeating the process until he had a neat line of bottles on a rock off to the side.

A diesel engine throttled up in the distance and grew louder as it approached. Zach scooped up his binoculars and strode halfway up the slope, scanning through the trees to the north, seeing a flash of vehicles moving between the buildings, no markings to tell if they were friends or foes. Dashing back to the shore, he started packing everything up when brakes squealed, doors slammed, and Russian voices belted commands.

"Drop your weapons!" one shouted in heavily accented Russian.

"Here, you, too! All of you. Put down!"

As Zach scooped up his rifle, more vehicles swept up and screeched to a halt in the gravel lot. Dropping everything, he sprinted up the hill and ducked behind a small cluster of bushes. A Russian truck raced along the rear of the stores, with two others already parked in front, penning in their Humvee. The armored trucks were large and unmarked, drab green and resembling stout SUVs. Two soldiers had Grizzly by the arms, and another had his weapon pointed at Liza and Gina, who seemed ready to fight.

A soldier slammed Craig against the hood, pressing his face to the warm metal as he protested. "Take it easy, assholes! Hey, you can't do that! We're Americans!"

The soldier punched Craig in the small of the back, causing him to arch in pain. Zach raised his weapon to shoot, but there was no way he could fire without risking the lives of his friends. Liza shrieked something in Russian and was shoved against a store wall and patted down, while Grizzly remained quiet with his hands up and seeming relaxed. Zach searched for a rock to throw as a distraction, but quickly gave up on the idea as the Russians herded his friends into a Russian vehicle while another soldier got behind the wheel of their Humvee. Raising his weapon, he put the passenger of the nearest truck in his sights, fingers slipping inside the trigger guard and ready to squeeze. Gina sat in the back seat, staring at him, her barely perceptible head shake warning him off. He could only watch as the Humvees kicked into gear, turned around, and sped off, circling east toward the airfield.

With a soft curse, Zach waited until the armored trucks had gotten a good distance away before he left his cover and jogged between the buildings to see where they were taking them. As he reached the paved sidewalk connecting the storefronts, the sound of running boots froze him in a crouch, listening, swinging his rifle up. He backed away as two Russians came around the corner, laden with backpacks, heavy weaponry, canteens, and ammunition packs strapped to their chests. Their eyes flew wide when they saw him, twisting simultaneously to fire from their hips. Zach was backpedaling, shooting at the foremost soldier, hitting his flak vest on the left-hand side, dropping him to the ground, causing Zach's second and third shots to fly high. Then he was cross-stepping to his right, swinging his rifle around to fire at the second Russian who was already sliding to the building on the left, shooting as he ran, missing badly but getting away as Zach's bullets chewed the corner brick to pieces.

He held his ground, circling to his right toward the wounded soldier who was on his knees and scrambling for the rifle he'd dropped. Zach zipped him up from hip to shoulder in a quick burst of rounds that sent him falling on his face in the gravel. A bullet flew past Zach's nose, fired from the second Russian, the round striking the building to his right. Instead of retreating, Zach shot back and closed in, spraying mortar everywhere and keeping the Russian at bay until he threw his left shoulder against the same corner. The Russian had to be right there, just a few feet away as his buddy moaned and writhed on the ground. Zach was a rod of muscle, tension gripping his body, rifle pointed at the corner. More gunfire would surely alert the other Russians, if it hadn't already, so he had to think of something quick.

"Put down your weapon!" Zach called. "Put it down, and I'll let you see to your friend. Can you understand me? Do you know what I am saying—?"

The Russian spun around the corner, rifle up and squeezing the trigger. Zach was ready for it, and he grabbed the hand guard, and shoved it up, sending a single round zipping past his head. He buried his boot in the soldier's chest, kicking him hard and ripping his rifle from his grip. The soldier staggered back and almost fell but kept his feet. Zach dropped his rifles and jerked a carbon blade from its sheath, lunging for the Russian as he went for his service pistol. He was smaller than Zach, but no quicker, and Zach grabbed his hand before he got the weapon out of its holster, swinging his blade and catching the soldier in the side where there was a gap in his flak armor. That drew a strained cry from the Russian as he struck Zach across the jaw with his free left fist, a firm blow that rocked Zach's head to the side, knees going weak as he staggered. The soldier ripped his gun hand back, but the pistol tumbled from its holster and clattered to the ground. Before he could get to it, Zach pressed forward with a sweep of the carbon blade, driving the soldier away from his weapon. Then Zach closed in, stepped on the gun, and kicked it backward.

The Russian threw a glance back through the trees where the airstrip was five hundred yards distant. Zach shook his head and grinned, daring him to run for it. Mirroring his smile, the soldier pulled his own knife free, a seven-inch blade to match Zach's. With a firmly set jaw, the Russian took a fighting stance and moved in with feints and stabs. While Zach had every advantage in height, reach, and speed, the Russian had desperate energy in his movements, and Zach couldn't find a way inside his guard. Sweat dripped down his temples. His neck and sides ached. The Russian's blade flashed in and caught Zach on the left hand, a tiny cut that brought a painful sting. Zach lunged and counterattacked, stabbing in high twice, barely getting out of the way before the Russian sliced his knife arm. It was the soldier's turn to grin, sensing Zach's lack of combat training and his awkwardness with the blade as he waved it around like someone from a movie.

Zach caught movement out of the corner of his eye. The wounded soldier, shot up the back, was crawling to his dropped rifle, falling on it, rolling over, and pointing the weapon in Zach's direction. With a desperate lurch, Zach grabbed the soldier in front of him and spun him toward his friend. The rifle rattled, and the Russian jerked in his grip. Zach shoved him forward with both hands as pain rippled across the soldier's face. In two steps, he threw the Russian over his wounded buddy, and he tripped and went down.

Zach flew to his knees beside the first Russian, left knee pinning the rifle as he stabbed him above his armor, burying the blade in his neck twice to finish him off. Then he calmly stood and marched to the second soldier, kneeling next to him and ready to do the same, but when he got there, the Russian only stared lifelessly at the sky, his fighting done.

Zach checked the tree line hiding the airstrip. No Russian vehicles were racing toward him, nor were there any troops pouring from the storefronts in west downtown. Zach grabbed the soldier by his feet and pulled him between the stores, groaning at a deep ache that radiated from his middle. He dropped the boots and put his hand to his belly, fingers coming up bloody-a *lot* of blood. With a disappointed grimace, Zach dragged the other soldier closer. Once he had both out of sight, he collected their weapons and took them around back, trying a few of the business's doors, finding one that was loose in its frame, easy to ram his shoulder against and break open. It was a supply room-kitchen, with a table and sink on the north wall and shelves of goods on the others. Throwing his weapons on the table, he returned for the Russians, dragging them around and into the shop, piling them together, shutting the door, and standing there in the darkness as a terrible stomachache gripped him and warm wetness seeped down his leg.

Kneeling next to one of the dead soldiers, Zach rifled through his backpack and found a first aid kit and a clean rag. He stripped off his jacket and undershirts to discover the last two layers were soaked in red. He pulled those off, tossed them aside, and dragged up a metal chair, sitting and leaning back to get a better view of the wound. Unbuckling his pants, he used the rag to dab around and found where the knife had pierced skin. The cut was about a half-inch long, two inches below his ribs on the left side. The way the blade had gone in, it seemed to have cut sideways beneath his flesh and into his muscle, but not very deep. Bruising and swelling spread from the entry point and into his lower abdomen and thighs, and blood bubbled up and overflowed whenever he pressed around the wound. Resting the first aid kit on his right leg, he unzipped it and was relieved to find several packages about six inches long with directions written in Russian. Still, he had an idea of what was inside, and he ripped one open and took out a syringe filled with white pellets. With a grunt of relief, he removed the blue tip cover and pressed the end into the cut, gently squeezing the plunger and injecting the pellets in the wound. He worked his way from one end of the cut to the other, blood smearing the tip as the pellets swelled and congealed into a gelatinous clot. Once the bleeding had stopped, he used a saline applicator to clean around the wound and placed a bandage on top.

He twisted at the hip to test the pain level, seeing he still had a decent range of movement to the right, but when he turned to the left, it was like a spear through his middle. Zach found a package of what he guessed were pain pills, though he couldn't read the label. Hoping it wasn't a heavy narcotic, he ripped it open, took two, and swallowed them with water from the soldier's canteen. With chills racing up his back and his breath pluming out in the frosty air, Zach measured up the soldiers' sizes. He rolled the larger of the two over and removed his backpack, filled with holes from where he'd shot it through, the jacket punctured several times and soaked with blood.

When he got the pack off, he unzipped it and searched for a change of clothes, finding some oversized undershirts that fit him snugly but were a bit short. Still, the garments were dry and soft against his skin, and he layered up and shrugged on his bloodstained jacket once more. Hands freezing, belly aching, Zach moved around a little and clapped to get warm. After a while, he left the building and returned to the lake shore, grabbing all the water bottles and carrying them back up to the storage room, drinking two right away to help replenish his fluids. On the shelves, Zach found containers of chocolate shavings and sugar toppings for ice cream cones, plastic spoons, paper cups, and two walk-in freezers at one end. Inside were gallons of ice cream, from double vanilla bean to chocolate mint to salted caramel swirl.

Zach slung his rifle on his shoulder and grabbed the tub of salted caramel and a large metal spoon from a drawer. He tore off the top and dug in, walking out on the floor where chairs had been turned up, and the wide glass storefront gave him a view of the street.

Violent skies approached, the same darkness that had chased them from Fairbanks, with streaks of lightning and green-gold currents that blossomed into fire, the hydrocarbons spreading farther and wider than he could've ever imagined, pushing out the snow clouds, creating havoc with the wind, and threatening to overtake them all.

There in the shadows, Zach watched and waited for more Russian troops to show up, and when they didn't, he put the ice cream down and returned to the rear of the store. He sorted the Russians' gear and threw together a light assault pack and an extra rifle and ammunition. When he was done, he exited through the back door and moved along the rear service lane to the north where he hoped to find his friends.

CHAPTER EIGHT

Wendy Christensen, Pearisburg, Virginia

The wind howled in a high tenor that shook the walls like a train rolling right beside the house. Rain crashed against the siding, another endless storm ripping over the hillside as the weather refused to end its obstinate behavior. The plants and vines shrouding the west end of the farmhouse dripped water, and gusts of wind thrashed the shingles. Despite the raging storm outside, it was warm and comfortable inside, a slight chill in the air forcing Wendy to put on a blue hoodie from Darla's closet. An electric lantern cast a soft glow through the room, and she kept the shades closed tight to prevent any light from leaking.

Darla moaned in her sleep, head turning back and forth as she murmured unintelligible words. All Wendy could do was have a wet cloth ready to wipe her sweaty-pale face and cracked lips. Clyde was curled up at the foot of the bed near Darla's feet, and Wendy smiled and got up to pet the dog, rubbing between his ears as he lay there dead to the world. She started to leave the room when Darla's eyes fluttered open.

"Oh, hey," Wendy said, coming back and sitting. "How are you feeling?"

"Like I ate a handful of sand," Darla rasped, reaching for the glass of water on the end table.

"I got it." Wendy helped guide it to Darla's lips, where she sipped hesitantly at first and then gulped the rest. "Very good. I'm sure you must've been thirsty. We've been trying to make sure you drink, but—"

"How long have I been out?"

"It's been two days, and you've been in and out the whole time. Do you remember anything? Do you remember *me*?"

Darla licked her cracked lips and tried to push herself up, wincing when the pain in her shoulder hit. "Ow, that hurts."

"Yeah, I don't recommend trying to use your left arm. You took a bullet there, but didn't hit anything vital. We stopped the bleeding and stitched you up."

"Thank you..."

"No problem. We didn't mean to sound rude before when you woke up. This is your house, and we appreciate having a roof over our heads."

"Least I can do. You've probably been eating my food, too."

"We've been eating a mix of our supplies and yours. Mostly sticking to stuff that doesn't need a fire. Like your beets and potatoes and stuff. Some snacks, too. The stove doesn't work, and it's impossible to build a fire outside. The wood is soaked, but my son put some out in the stables to dry. I imagine we'll have something usable in a couple of weeks." Wendy pulled a face. "I don't know, though. With all this rain, it may take forever to dry out. We don't have any electricity, but we can hear something rumbling down in the basement, and sometimes the generator kicks on outside. We found your breaker switches but were afraid to mess with anything."

"Don't touch *anything*." Darla shifted to her right and scooted higher on the pillows. "You'll end up blowing something, and I'll be shit out of luck."

"We haven't touched anything for that exact reason."

"Well, I don't need you blowing the circuit breakers."

"We're not stupid," Wendy cooled and sat back. "We stationed someone by the road in case those men come back."

"What men?"

Wendy quickly rehashed how they'd found Darla's place and were in the process of walking back from the stables when Darla drove up the driveway and crashed into the tree. Soon after, another truck had come up with armed men inside who'd shot at them, but Wendy and the kids had run them off.

"What did you run them off with?" Darla asked suspiciously.

"I've got a rifle, and my kids are armed with pistols. It was enough."

"Must've been if I'm still alive." She glanced toward the door. "Now, where's my sister? Send Melissa in here." .

"Well... that's the thing. Your sister, Melissa..." Wendy drew herself straight. "There's no easy way to say this, but she didn't make it, Darla."

"Didn't make it?"

"No. We –"

Darla grabbed Wendy's arm with her claw-like hand, and she rose with a twisted grimace. "What did you do to her? What did you do to my sister?"

"Nothing!" Wendy cried and jerked her arm free. "She was shot up when you came in. You *both* were."

"Why didn't you save her? Where is *she*?" She moaned the last word and fell back, gripping the covers and dragging them to her chin.

"I'm sorry," Wendy said, tears stinging her eyes. "If there was something we could've done, we would've."

"Where...?" Darla sobbed and twisted the covers. "Where *is* she?"

"We put her out in the barn with the horses. She's covered up... I figured you'd want to be there too, when we bury her."

Darla sucked a gout of air and released it in a low, mewling moan, twisting with the covers gripped in her hands, the tendons in her arms standing out.

Wendy reached for her arms. "Settle down, hon. Just... settle down. You're hurt, Darla, and moving around like this is only going to make it worse."

Darla knocked her hands away. "My sister is dead, and now strangers are in my home..." Darla rose and took a swing at her, but Wendy leaped up and knocked her chair over.

"Darla, stop it!"

"No! You get out of here!" Darla rose to grab her but fell sideways on the bed. Get out of my home!"

Wendy's lips drew into a fine line. "We're *staying*. We saved you from those men, brought you inside, and stitched you up. Seems like a fair trade, so far."

"I ain't trading. I ain't doing *nothing* with you." Darla's strength suddenly left her, and she curled up on the bed and pulled the covers to her face, crying, moaning, sobbing into them.

Wendy's chest tightened with sadness and regret, wanting to help her but not wanting to get her eyes clawed out. "I'm sorry, Darla. I really am. As long as we're here, we'll see to your recovery, but don't ask us to leave."

Darla cried for another thirty seconds before her grip on the sheets loosened, her breathing grew heavy, and she settled into a deep sleep.

Wendy retrieved the electric lantern, taking it with her out into the hallway, where it cast its light throughout the living room and kitchen. "David? David, are you around?"

When she didn't get a reply, Wendy crossed to the cooking island where the two-way radio stood. She had no idea how much life was left in the battery, and they'd have to figure out a way to recharge it soon. Being in passive mode helped to conserve power, but both radios would run out of juice sooner than later.

"CC, have you seen DC?"

Charlie's voice came back over the static-filled line, rain drizzling in the background. "Haven't seen him."

"Thanks."

Wendy put the radio down, turned back into the hall, and checked the other bedrooms in case he'd snuck off to get a nap. When she didn't find him there, she returned to the kitchen and took the electric lantern to the garage, holding it up to reveal the black truck and shelves of garden supplies and tools, flashlights and an AM/FM radio.

"David!"

Something bumped against the garage wall, and Wendy turned to the side door with her hand resting on her pistol, peering sidelong through the glass to see a shadow moving toward her. A tall shape strode into view, well over six feet, looming, wearing a poncho with the hood shrouding his face in darkness. Wendy leaped back with a gasp but relaxed when David held up a radio-controlled Jeep by its roll bars. Stepping forward, she unlocked the door and pulled it open, letting in the whipping rain.

"You scared the crap out of me, David. What in the world are you doing out here?"

"I was testing out this car. It got stuck in the driveway, so I went down to get it and bring it back. Anyway, let me in."

Wendy stepped back and let the dripping teenager into the garage where he set the car down and shook himself off.

"I figured you'd be sleeping. Or were you down in the workshop all day?"

"Yeah, just seeing if we can get any use out of anything down there. I can't charge anything, though, so none of it will run for long."

"I talked to Darla, and she more or less acknowledged the generator would help with that, then she passed out again."

"She looking any better?"

"A bit, but she needs to eat something."

"I hate this rain so much."

"It stinks, but there's nothing we can do about it."

"Does Darla know about her sister?"

"I told her, but she didn't take it very well."

David scoffed and shook his head. "Follow me. Let me show you something."

"Outside?"

"Yeah, outside. You have to see it for yourself."

"Well, I'm going on shift, anyway. Might as well get bundled up."

Wendy took her poncho off the hook, put it on, and cinched it tightly around her neck. She grabbed a big flashlight off another hook and nodded for David to go. They shut the door behind them and circled to the driveway and up toward the stables, with Wendy taking three steps to every one of his long strides. Once inside, he led her along the corridor, where the horses snorted softly in their stalls. In the barn section where the feed was kept, the usual grainy smells and hay aroma wafted past her head, but beneath that was a subtle scent of rot lingering in the air, offensive and gut-turning. David marched straight over to the north wall where they kept the body covered in a sheet and a plastic tarp, lifting one corner aside to reveal the woman's swollen feet. The toenails were perfectly black, the pale skin marbled with dark, broken lines. The rotten smell rolled from beneath the cover and washed over them, and Wendy turned her face to the side with a groan.

"Was that really necessary?"

"It was. She's been out here for two days."

"I know," Wendy frowned. "It's unpleasant."

"It's *more* than unpleasant. Charlie won't even come out here to help me feed the horses, and it's making them nervous, by the way."

"The horses?"

"Yeah. Can't you tell? They're acting all weird. We've got to do something sooner or later."

"Okay, okay. We will, but cover her up for now, please. I'm sure Darla would love to pay her respects before we put her in the ground, but she's not in her right mind."

"I get that, but if you think this is bad now, wait for another four days. She'll smell horrible." David's voice held a note of defiance she hadn't heard before. "And it'll probably start drawing some bigger animals. Darla wouldn't want her sister dragged across the woods and ripped apart."

"We'll bury her when I say it's time to bury her," Wendy snapped. "Until then, I'll talk to Charlie about bucking up and helping you with the chores out here."

David dropped the cover and threw up his hands in exasperation, striding down the central corridor, barely noticing the horses as he passed them. Wendy followed him, focused on his back, practically jogging to keep up. Outside, David strode faster, heading straight for the house and pulling quickly away. By the time she was halfway there, he'd already gone inside and slammed the door, leaving her standing alone in the yard. She sighed and took the driveway toward their lookout spot, climbing into the woods.

"Charlie!" she called. "It's me. I'm coming up."

"Okay!"

She found Charlie leaning back against the tree and sitting on the big stone. A brown tarp hung from limbs above her and was spiked to the ground, providing a teepee-like shelter from the storm, the structure holding strong despite the heavy winds threatening to tear it up. Around the stone, they'd placed cushions covered in plastic, and Charlie had one between the tree and her back. Water bottles were stacked neatly next to the trunk with a small bag for their garbage held down by a rock.

"Did you have a good shift?"

"Pretty easy, I guess. I hate the rain."

Wendy rolled her eyes. "Yeah, I'm getting a lot of complaints about it. Darla woke up, sort of."

Charlie collected the plastic bottles and stood, ducking low to avoid hitting the tarp. "How's she feeling?"

Wendy shrugged. "I'm not sure. She passed out again soon after. I think she'll make it if she stays awake long enough to eat. Can you check up on her when you go inside?"

"Sure. What do I feed her when she wakes up?"

"Open a can of chicken noodle soup and serve it to her cold. We could have electricity soon, but Darla's the only one who knows how to set the breaker box. I could probably figure it out myself, but I don't want to mess with anything."

"Don't blame you. Have a good shift. Love you."

They hugged, and Charlie walked back to the driveway through the dripping trees. Wendy sat to take her place, picking up a cover that hung from a hook on the tree above her head and drawing it under her poncho to keep her legs warm. The gray pavement of the highway was lonely below her, the rain splashing in puddles, the runoff washing over the road, creating gullies and small creeks that drained off to flood the fields in the valley. Wendy couldn't imagine what it was like for anyone trying to live down there. Hundreds of wet, moldy homes like the one Smithson had forced them to sleep in, and she shuddered to think what life would've been like if they'd stayed in the Amish community. Blowing a raspberry, she slouched and braced herself for a long, wet, eight-hour shift.

Wendy hugged herself tighter as the cold seeped into her skin, her teeth chattering at times, forcing her to stand up and move around a little to get warm. Her thoughts turned to David. While he'd been sharp and disrespectful with her before, she understood his frustration. The rain was incessant, a constant downpour and *drip, drip, drip* that could drive a person insane. Even beneath the tarp and with her poncho hood pulled over her face, the mist seeped into everything, making her miserable and tired. Nothing had moved on the road, no cars or trucks, not a single soul. They'd been busy a time or two over the past couple of days, Charlie once calling up to tell her a group of people were walking by and David spotting a man and his dog traveling west along the road.

If Zach were there with her, he'd wrap her up in his big arms and hold her until she was warm, the same as movie nights on the couch. Zach's chest was so big Wendy could wallow on him and stretch out against his tall, lean body. Every fiber in her being longed for him to be back, to hear his voice around the kitchen when they made dinner together, or talk to David and Charlie about their schoolwork. Despite his problems after leaving the police force, she still loved him with all her heart. Part of Wendy felt hopeless, so much nasty weather and three thousand miles of roads between them. The worst parts of the human race out there trying to stay fed and alive.

She took another deep, cold breath, catching it when the forest floor crackled behind her. After hours of listening to the wood's gentle rhythm, every raindrop and falling branch creating a language Wendy understood, the sound was off. Whatever had made that crackle wasn't natural... it was a footfall, someone moving up the hill a few feet away. If it was David or Charlie, they would've called out and let her know. It was their rule and something they'd stuck to coming on and off shifts. Wendy stood and leaned against the gnarly tree trunk, looking around it and up the hill as a shadow crept through the murky darkness and moved across the top. Wendy slipped her pistol out of her holster, and when the figure was far enough away, she lifted her radio.

"CC, this is WC. You're about to have some company. I see one guy creeping toward the house in front. Get some help and get ready. I'll be right there."

"Understood."

Tucking the radio back into her pocket, Wendy moved slowly and carefully behind the man, placing her foot down whenever he did, mirroring his noisy movements. Leaning forward, grasping saplings to help her balance, Wendy took longer strides, trying to catch up to him before he reached the driveway. He came to the brush line and disappeared in a blink, sending panic tap dancing across the back of Wendy's skull. With quicker steps, she ascended, not bothering to hide her footfalls, her heavy panting, or her sharp cry when she slipped and struck her knee on a rock. Crawling up to the brush line, she pushed through and jogged across the driveway. The figure was nowhere in sight, so Wendy circled the garage and came to the back, shoulder to the corner, peeking around, finally creeping along the wall to where the door stood wide open. She inhaled sharply, adjusted the grip on her weapon, and stepped in to the sounds of a scuffle in the laundry room. Fists flew, a man grunted, and someone slammed the dryer with a clang. Pivoting, Wendy rushed to the door, flashlight flipping on, gun held off to the side. Two figures fought violently, their shadows projected on the walls in sharp dimensions. David gripped a shorter man by the poncho, shoving him into the dryer again, water droplets flying everywhere. Then he drew back and swung, connecting with the man's jaw but slipping, both falling to the tiles in a heap.

"Mom!" Charlie cried from where she stood in the opposite doorway with her gun.

"Stay back!"

The man squirmed beneath David, kicked him in the head, then twisted quickly to get on top of him and wrap his hands around David's throat. David seized his wrists and tried to break his grasp, but he was too thin, didn't have the strength, and the man's thumbs pressed on his windpipe, driven by thick forearms and straining tendons. Wendy stepped in, snatched his hood back, and grabbed him by his curly hair, jerking him straight and jamming the gun barrel against his head. He was a young man but older than David, with a thin scruff of beard and desperate focus in his eyes.

"Let him go!"

The man only squeezed harder, and David's grimace widened, his breaths coming in ragged gasps as he tried to keep his windpipe from being crushed.

"Let him go," Wendy growled, jerking his head back and moving the barrel to his cheekbone so he could see the black steel.

Blinking in surprise, he relaxed his grip but didn't let go.

"Don't make me ask you again." She spoke in a cold, flat tone that must have got to him because he released David and held his hands up, still locked into claws. For a second, it seemed like he might go for David again, but she jerked him straight and shoved him against the wall, jamming the gun into his chest before jumping back. "David, are you okay?"

David was twisting and getting to his knees when he lunged at the man with a hard right that caught him in the cheek and rocked his head sideways. Wendy grabbed David and shoved him aside, taking her gun off the intruder for a moment. The man started to get up, but Charlie stepped in with her Ruger pointed at his face.

"Stop it!" she shrieked. "Don't be the second man I kill!"

Her barking tone froze the man long enough for Wendy to shove David out of the way and swing her weapon back in their attacker's direction.

David scrambled to his feet, glowering at the man, slamming his fist on the dryer with a bang of vibrating metal. Wendy shined her light in the face of their attacker, forcing him to wince, hands up and shaking imploringly.

"H-hey... just let me go, okay? I didn't mean to harm anyone."

"Didn't look that way to me," Wendy replied. "You tried to strangle my son."

"Look, I stumbled into the wrong house," he stammered. "This guy jumped on me and tackled me. I was just fighting back."

"You were creeping up to the house," Wendy scoffed. "I saw you in the front yard and followed you up."

He blew a frustrated breath. "Okay, so maybe I knew what I was doing, but I was just looking for food. I haven't eaten in days."

"Looks like you're eating pretty well to me."

"No way. I'm one of the last people in the camp that eats —" He cut himself off with a wince.

Wendy raised an eyebrow. "Camp? What camp?"

"Did I say that? No, I'm not from any camp. Just a loner trying to survive. Please, just let me go. I'll go away and won't come back."

"First chance you get, you'll attack us," David sneered.

"I swear I won't. I'm genuinely sorry for tangling with you. I just..." He shook his head with a helpless, drawn expression. "Like I said, I was hungry. I needed food!"

Wendy sighed and nodded at David, then rested her hand on her pistol. "Where's this camp of yours? And don't lie to me."

"It's a good ten miles east of here, *way* outside of downtown." He fidgeted and squinted into the light. "Let me go, and I swear I'll get out of here... you won't see me again."

"We can't believe him," David said. "He'll tell the people in his camp. They'll come here."

"I don't know..." Wendy shook her head, recalling everything the kids had been through since leaving Stamford. All that time on the road, shooting at people, their hearts turning colder after each consecutive firefight, witnessing death every step of the way. "Charlie, keep your gun on this guy. If he tries to attack you, you know what to do.. David, step into the garage with me."

When they were both standing by the black truck, Wendy said, "I'm all for doing what's necessary to survive, but keeping someone prisoner is stepping over the line."

"What line, Mom? The line everyone else crosses without a

thought?" David gestured at the man, voice rising. "This guy broke in and would have hurt us, and he knows *everything* about us now."

"Not really."

"He knows how many we are and what kind of weapons we have."

"I don't care about all that," the man said, overhearing them. "Please, just —"

"Shut up," Wendy snapped before turning back to David and lowering her voice. "What do you want to do, son? Take him hostage? Shoot him in cold blood right here? Will *you* do it?" Wendy held her pistol out. "My gun or yours?"

David's eyes dropped, then he shook his head and slammed his palm against the fender in frustration.

"I didn't think so," Wendy said, leading him back to the laundry room where the prisoner cowered. "What's your name?"

"Matt."

"Okay, Matt. I want you to promise you'll never come back here again."

"You've got it."

"You'll forget all about us, right?"

"Absolutely. I don't know any of your names, and I don't want to know them." He laughed nervously. "I don't want to die."

"Okay, then. You're going to leave and never come —"

"No!" someone barked. "We can't let him go."

Darla was standing in the doorway, wearing the pajama pants and T-shirt Wendy had put on her with a coverlet thrown over her shoulders. She leaned against the door frame with her right hand, her skinny arm quivering, legs shaking. She glared at Matt. "I know him. He's Matt Stegman, and he works for Oliver McCallum."

"Who's that?"

"He's the bastard I was messing with before his men chased me back to my house. They tried to kill me."

"Don't listen to her," Matt said.

"You damn well better listen to me, Wendy. Because if you let him go, he'll run straight back to McCallum and tell him all about this place." Darla fixed Wendy with a hard stare. "You let him go, you'll be writing a death sentence for your family."

Matt lunged forward, trying to crawl past David through the door, but David jumped in front of him and slammed the laundry room door shut, cutting off his escape.

Wendy snatched Matt by his poncho and held onto him, looking up at Darla and shaking her head with indecision. Finally, she gestured to David. . "David, hold him here while I get some rope from the garage. Matt, you'll stay here until we figure this out."

Matt craned his neck and begged. "Come on, lady. Please don't listen to her. She doesn't know what she's —"

"Shut up and sit your butt down against that wall."

CHAPTER NINE

Hanta, Selawik, Alaska

Hanta sat at the bottom of his basement stairs in a chair, elbows on his knees, stomach growling, clothes grubby as he waited in silence. Old fishing nets and line hung on the walls, oil containers and other repair equipment he used on his boat sat on shelves. A kerosene heater stood in the middle of the room, radiating constant dry heat, though he only had three more gallons of fuel left. It was warm enough, and they were alive, and that's what mattered. They'd stuffed towels and rags under the door, and he used industrial strength caulk to seal the cracks around the windows. Socks were plugged into any open pipe ends except for one he'd placed an air mask filter over, and they'd been relieving themselves in a bucket in the corner.

Alasie and the girls sat on a blanket in front of his tool bench among the jerrycans and work equipment, pulling down their masks long enough to eat their fish, greens, and berries. Sedna and Uki giggled at their mother's constant doting, blissfully unaware that there was almost nothing left and they'd soon starve. Hanta sat and breathed, still in shock from what had happened to their village. The flaming cyclones, the noxious air, the screams, the nightmare that had descended upon them days ago.

"When can we go up?" Alasie pulled down little Sedna's mask and fed her. The air was breathable in the basement, though he made the kids wear cloths over their faces, scarves, rags or whatever they could find.

"I don't know," Hanta replied, casting his eyes upward where the wind howled and shook the house. "I still hear the lightning that makes me think it's not safe."

"But —"

"We're alive for now."

"Husband..." Alasie said in a pained tone. "The food."

"Yes, I know. I'll go up soon and check." Hanta bit back his words, not wanting to sound so harsh but plagued with frustration.

Alasie nodded and continued feeding Sedna and Uki while they watched him with loving eyes. Hanta smiled and went back to staring at the door, wringing his fingers together, trying to excise the horrible images that played like a movie in his mind.

It had started with a rumbling in the sky, lightning cracking in long intervals of sound and light, followed by firestorms that hit the north side of Selawik first, windswept flames catching homes on fire and blowing cinders through town. Alasie had called him into the kitchen where she'd been cooking, their jaws dropping in amazement as the night sky glowed and flocks of birds fled in fear. They stepped outside with their neighbors, fathers and mothers pointing and shaking their heads, their curious confusion turned to panic when the fires began leaping from building to building, scalding winds blasting hot embers through the streets. While most stood in a daze, others tried to outrun it. Hanta grabbed Alasie and brought her inside, gathering the kids, throwing on their coats and boots, and ushering them out the door with a plan to reach his boat and drive away.

They were about to join a group of people running toward the docks in blind terror when green-gold air currents swept over them, foul-smelling winds that suffocated people where they stood. Many stopped to retch or choke, grasping their necks and trying to scream, only managing to gag and spit foam. Hanta grabbed his family and pulled them back inside, slamming the door shut and watching from the windows. He ordered Alasie and the children into the basement while he gathered as much food and water as he could. Since then, they'd been holed up, slowly running out of supplies but too afraid to go upstairs and risk breathing what was out there.

Innik ran over from the window where he'd been standing on a stool to see outside despite Hanta's constant orders for him to get down. "Daddy, Daddy! Outside!"

"Yes, son." Hanta took his arm and smiled. "It's very bad out, and I've told you many times to stay away from the window."

"I know, Dad. But I saw people!"

"People?"

Innik nodded vigorously and pointed. "Out there. Walking."

Hanta stood and crossed to the window, and Alasie joined him with Sedna in her arms. The glass was grubby, smeared with dirt except for a small spot Innik had wiped clean. Alasie held out an extra rag, and he used it to clear a bigger section so they could all see out. He had a view of the front yard and a couple of houses across the street. Past those were glimpses of other homes, still erect, bright pink and green siding standing out between the charred timbers where houses used to be. The once pristine, white snow and ice had melted and flash frozen again, transforming the landscape into a series of glassy bumps and ridges that sparkled beneath the bleak daylight. The surrounding waterways, lakes, tributaries, and marshes had polished surfaces, and most of the trees had been torched to the ground, leaving stumps or burned branches formed into the shapes of gnarled hands.

"I don't see anything, Innik," Hanta said, squinting and craning his neck. "Are you sure —"

Two people shuffled by in the street, locked arm in arm, their brown, wrinkled faces without masks as they looked skyward.

"It's John and Clarita!" Alasie exclaimed. "They're alive!"

Hanta put his hand against the window and beat on it until the pair stopped to look. He pointed to his mouth and back at them but wasn't sure they could see him through the smudged glass.

Finally, John saw him, smiling and waving as if that said it all. Hanta clapped once and rushed to the stairs, pausing long enough to gesture. "Come on. It must be safe!"

Pulling the towels from beneath the door, he threw it open and stood with one foot in the kitchen, tilting his head slowly and sniffing. There was the lingering scent of something, but it wasn't the noxious stomach turning fumes from before. He moved cautiously through the kitchen and stopped at the window, watching a couple of dozen people shuffle around with no facial protection. Hanta tore the cloth off his face and ran for the door, popping it, stepping outside into a gloriously cold wind that hit him like a splash of water. Hands on his hips, he stood and took in the destruction, his momentary sense of freedom crushed by the dead lying in the streets, dozens... no, hundreds, frozen and dusted with light snow. People they'd been neighbors with since he was a boy. He turned to Alasie who had tears in her eyes as she bounced Sedna in her arms, hugging her as if the act could somehow ease her own pain. Innik and Uki were holding hands and staring at the dead adults and the smaller bodies of their schoolmates and friends.

Everything was smoking and crackling, giving off the faint scent of burned wood and flesh, threatening to turn his stomach and make him retch onto the icy street like many others. A faint haze drifted over the community, blurring everyone like something from an impossible dream. Survivors stepped into the light, throwing up their hands and crying, holding each other, hugging and wailing in helplessness. Hanta drew Innik and Uki to him, pulling them close, trying to hide them from the aftermath but unsure how.

John and Clarita came over with streaming eyes and sad smiles. The pair were old and had been through lean times and tragedies, though nothing could've ever prepared them for what had happened to Selwik. Hanta nodded and patted John on the shoulder, bringing him closer in a hug while Clarita and Alasie embraced in a mixture of sadness and relief. They were alive and breathing, and the storms were gone... but so many had perished. Someone called out and pointed north, and all eyes turned to the big brick school building standing tall and immaculate, untouched by the firestorms. It was the newest structure in Selawik, with classrooms, a cafeteria, and a gymnasium that could hold the entire town.

"We've got nothing left," John said, shaking Hanta's hand and motioning to Clarita, "so we're going to the school."

"We'll share our home," Hanta countered, with Alasie nodding vigorously. "We still have food and supplies."

"That's very kind of you, and the town will need them soon. For now, we go to grieve with the others."

Hanta nodded as villagers gathered up their heartbroken family members, lifting them and guiding them up the street to meet those coming from other parts of the community. He recognized many fishermen and the town sheriff as well as the clergyman from the Selawik Church. "Perhaps we should go and offer our support."

Alasie nodded and handed Sedna over. "We'll gather some blankets and a sack of food."

"It could be spoiled by the foul air," Hanta replied, holding his daughter tight.

"It was in the pantry and wrapped up. It should be okay."

It wasn't long before they were marching up the street with blankets in their arms and a couple of sacks of food, joining what seemed like a flow of undead toward the gym's front doors where the town elders greeted people and welcomed them inside.

When they were almost there, Innik grabbed Hanta's coat sleeve and pointed up. "Look, Daddy. The sky. It's not angry anymore. Does this mean it's over?"

The blackness was gone, the lightning vanished, and the bubbling, roiling funnels of fire had settled into a harmless dark gray like a calm lake after a big splash. "I don't know, son. They look like normal clouds to me, but we won't know for a while. Let's just focus on being thankful and helping everyone else right now."

And while he'd spoken truthfully to Innik, he shared a smile with Alasie to give her hope that it actually *was* over and there'd be no additional suffering. As they crossed the main road leading north, the ground began to shake and rumble, window glass rattling, the entire crowd turning to look south where three massive black shapes trundled across the bridge, dragging sleds from the direction of Nglaktak

Lake. Guns and communication antennas sprouted from the tops, their tracks creaking and groaning and churning up snow and ice. The big diesel engines roared loud as they drove up the road toward the gaping villagers.

"Kids, get back." He nudged Innik and Uki far off the side of the roadside.

"What are they?" Alasie said, carrying Sedna far from harm.

"I don't know," he replied. "American armored tanks? What would they be doing out here?"

"We heard it on the radio," John said. "There are Russian troops who landed in Alaska."

"Russians?"

"That's what the radio said before the transmission broke. They must be going to fight them."

Hanta's legs shook as the massive P-10s trundled by in a sound like thunder, the squeaks and squeals of the moving parts shrieking into the darkened sky. And then they were gone, driving north toward the waterways surrounding Selawik Lake in a cloud of snow dust.

It was only when they were far away did Hanta's nerves settle. "We should wish them luck, then."

John shrugged. "I wish luck on *us* because we have many friends to mourn and much to rebuild."

Hanta sighed. "Agreed, my friend. Let us go inside and see what we can do."

Stillman crouched in the lead P-10, holding on to a handgrip on the ceiling to keep his balance as they drove quickly north, watching the external monitors as they plowed across the storm blown landscape.

"Did you see what I saw, sir?" the driver asked. "Those villagers weren't wearing facial protection."

"It looks that way," Stillman agreed.

"Does that mean we can go outside without ours?"

"We'll keep ours on for now until Callie gives us an update on the air quality readings."

"Yes, sir."

"Colonel Stillman. The message from Fairbanks got through."

Stillman turned toward the communication console beside the one Craig Sutton had used on the way to investigate the Alaskan Rift. Much of his Navpax equipment sat unused, though the screens were still on and the readings flashed across them.

"What is it, Cryer?" Captain Callie Cryer handed him a headset, and Stillman put it on.

"This is Colonel Stillman."

The voice from the other end was spotty but mostly got through. "Colonel Stillman, this is Sergeant Peters from Fairbanks."

"Good morning, Peters. How are things going at the base?"

"We're still looking for that beautiful weather so we can get more birds in the sky. In the meantime, we're taking some casualties, but NORTHCOM doesn't want us committing too much right now. The carrier groups are just about here, so I'd expect things to take a bad turn for the Russians when they do."

"We're playing it smart. We don't want to take the kind of losses the Russians are by trying to fly in these skies. What can we do for you?"

"NORTHCOM wants to know if Colonel Red Hawk still plans to pursue the Russian forces through Western Alaska?"

"Roger that, Fairbanks. The Colonel and I spoke a few minutes back, and he's determined to stay the course. He wants to run Commander Orlov out of the state. We're holding course. We've got enough supplies and…"

Static ripped across the line.

"Sergeant Peters? Are you still with me?"

When nothing came back, he shook his head at Cryer. "Connection dropped, Captain. Do your best to get it back."

"I'll try, sir," she said with an exasperated gesture, flicking two buttons and turning a dial as she listened. "But this sky is like static soup."

Stillman grinned. "I know you'll keep trying. First, get me the Colonel."

"Yes, sir."

A moment later, Red Hawk joined him on a much clearer connection. "What's up, Stillman?"

"Sir, just spoke with Fairbanks —"

"Yeah, we caught that, and you told them correctly. Sorry I didn't take the call, but we're working on triangulating the Russian positions."

"I understand, sir. Is there anything more I can do?"

"Get the scouts ready. We'll find a good place to stop and have a look around. Maybe we can find Orlov before he finds us."

"Yes, sir."

Four hours later, they sat idling, wedged in a shallow depression between converging ridge lines with slopes covered in cedar and shore pines, a part of the forest left unburned by the storms. The beautiful scenery filled the high-definition monitors inside the P-10 as if Stillman were watching from home and it wasn't just on the other side of the armor.

The Marines were seated in the troop cabin, repeatedly checking their equipment and whispering quietly. They'd been cooped up inside the vehicle for days, stopping only to stretch their legs and relieve themselves whenever they had to refuel. Through the internal speakers, the wind howled like a wolf as it tore into the tree lines where the P-10s sat idle and waited for the scouts to return. Stillman sat next to Cryer at the communication console, listening as Red Hawk went back and forth with the scouts, though they'd been searching for hours and there were no Russians around.

A woof of wind hit the line along with engines revving and purring in the background. "Colonel Red Hawk, this is Scout Leader One."

"Go ahead, Scout Leader One."

"Sir, we spotted Russians. Coordinates incoming."

There was a pause, and Red Hawk came back. "Scout Leader One, that's right on top of us."

"Yes, sir. We're on our way now."

"Were you seen?"

"I don't think so, sir. They didn't adjust their course or seem like they noticed."

"What are we looking at?"

"Four Russian BTRs and six assorted medium-armored vehicles."

"Roger that," Red Hawk replied with tension in his voice. "Come on home, Scout Leader. Stillman?"

"We're on it, sir," he raised an eyebrow to Cryer. "We'll make sure Fairbanks knows right away that we've got Russians incoming."

The Captain nodded and started sending a message on the encrypted channel. Whether Fairbanks would receive it or not remained to be seen, but Cryer would stick to it until it got through.

The static on the line died, and Red Hawk secured a connection between himself and Stillman. "That's too much armor for us to take on head-to-head."

"I agree with that assessment, sir. We're faster than them. We could potentially engage them in some hit-and-run maneuvers."

"Sure, but those medium units could be a problem. Let's just hope their scout teams don't find us first. Ah, here we come now."

Stillman turned back to the external monitors in time to see two snowmobiles fly over the ridge up ahead and shoot down into the valley. With their detection systems hampered by the static-filled air, they were relying solely on manual scouting units, eyes and ears, to get information about their enemies.

"Man the remote guns," Red Hawk commanded through the internal speakers, and a Marine squeezed past Stillman to sit at the weapons console on Cryer's left, engaging the remote guns to the sound of whining turret motors spinning to life. "Be ready to turn and burn if we've got to, Stillman."

"Yes, sir. We're ready."

A hush came over the cabin as the external monitors showed snow dust billowing up along the ridge line, and treetops on the opposite slope shivered and crashed. The top part of a BTR appeared, its wide squarish shape cresting the ridge line but not quite reaching the top. More units followed that one, and a diesel roar filled the speakers as the Russian armored column rolled by.

The cameras swept across the ridge line, tracking the vehicles as the Marines sat in tense silence. They stared up front, some with their heads down and whispering silent prayers, others tapping their knees and stewing in nervous tension. The noise and rumbling continued for another thirty seconds until the last of the medium-sized trucks passed, and Stillman released a quiet sigh of relief.

"That was close, Stillman," Red Hawk said on their private line.

"Yes, sir. They came within forty yards of us and didn't even see us. Orders, sir?"

"Let's get ready to move out. We'll give the Russians ten or fifteen minutes to get by, then we'll get back on the road."

"What if that was Orlov?"

"It's not him. Those were older model BTRs, and the markings weren't the same as the ones they were driving on the rift mission."

"Good eye, sir. I'll get us ready to move out."

As soon as the connection was cut, Cryer got his attention. "Colonel Stillman. A minute, please? You'll want to see this."

Cryer had been in the communication chair prior to the call with Red Hawk but had switched to Dr. Craig Sutton's console where she'd been watching the monitors with great interest.

"What is it, Cryer? What are we looking at here?"

"Well, something caught my eye while we were waiting for the Russians to pass. Dr. Sutton's Navpax readings went nuts when the Russian column was going by."

"What do you mean?"

"Well, we still have all the monitoring gear connected, so we've still been getting readings."

"We didn't remove any equipment before we left Fairbanks."

"Right, and I didn't think much of it before. But look at these heat signatures rising off the ridge line. See what I mean?" Cryer was pointing at the middle and right-hand screens, running her finger around areas that gave off a faint pink haze. "They were bright red before, sir. They made a perfect outline of the Russian equipment. I could've taken a picture. I wanted to say something, but I didn't want to interrupt you and the Colonel."

"Well, Cryer, I've got to say..." Stillman scratched his head and watched as the remaining pink signatures faded.

"Craig was using this to track the cyclonic firestorms we were experiencing on the way to the Alaskan Rift." She shook her head. "I wish I would've thought of it sooner... and I wish I would've asked him about the equipment and software, too. I'm kicking myself for that."

Stillman made a churning sign with his finger. "Sum it up for me, Cryer."

"Yes, sir. We were using our standard detection devices to try to keep up with the Russians, but the Navpax system is a thousand times more sensitive than the standard P-10 detection equipment, and we can track the Russians just like we did with those firestorms, and at a good distance, I'd wager."

"This is incredible," Stillman said with a firm nod. "Good work, Cryer. I'll tell Colonel Red Hawk right away. This will allow us to cover a hell of a lot more ground."

"Yes, sir," Cryer grinned.

"Do you think you can pull double duty on this console and keep up with communications?"

"I can do it."

"All right. Let's prepare to move out. And keep an eye on those screens... *after* you patch me through to Colonel Red Hawk."

A minute later, he'd finished explaining the concept to the Colonel, and he could feel Red Hawk beaming across the comms channel.

"This is great news, Stillman. It means we can drive deeper into enemy territory, maybe all the way to the coast and find out where they've been landing."

"It'll be risky, sir."

"Sure, but NORTHCOM would love to have those coordinates so they can bomb the hell out of them. Yeah, let's keep moving, Stillman. Let's go."

Stillman, Red Hawk, and a handful of Marines stomped up the hillside over the ice and snow, grabbing saplings to pull themselves up a steep incline. The air was quiet and still with only the sounds of their boots crunching in a staggered fashion. The Marines were working to refuel the P-10s, chattering in muffled voices through their air filtration masks, moving stiffly but with professional precision, seemingly happy to stretch their legs and see the Alaskan wilderness for a few precious minutes. A close contingent of troops spread out around them, forming a defensive line atop the ridge, lying flat and peering over, gesturing when the coast was clear. When Stillman and Red Hawk reached the ridge top, Stillman's jaw dropped at the sweeping view of snow-covered forests, parts of it burned away and layered with dead branches and pine needles like scabs. Pockets of reformed ice glistened across the valley, reflecting a swell of sunlight fighting to get through the cloud cover.

"Look at that sky, sir," Stillman said.

"Is it... clearing?"

"Looks that way, sir."

The angry clouds that had been spewing constant explosions, rippling lightning, and poisonous fumes had calmed to a low boil. They'd faded from black to a softer shade of gray, undulating and bubbling slowly, cold winds stretching them into thin streaks of white.

"It looks much better," Red Hawk said.

"Yes, sir."

"It could mean the Alaskan Rift is finally run out of gas, literally."

"It'll finally give us a chance to get some planes in the sky."

"Those carrier groups will tear the Russians apart if they catch them on our shores." Red Hawk clenched his fist and glared westward. "We need to keep up the pressure and keep them running. Their little landgrab is going to fail, and we are going to facilitate that."

Red Hawk started taking off his mask, but Stillman stopped him. "Not yet, sir. I've got Cryer running some air quality readings. Let me check in with her." He hit a switch on the side of his mask. "Cryer, how are those readings coming?"

"I've got them, sir. On my way."

Two minutes later, Cryer left the P-10's rear hatch and came tromping up the hill with a heavier coat and her air filtration mask on, though she held her monitoring device barehanded, waving it with a trace of a smile in her eyes.

When Cryer got to the top of the hill, she saluted and stood at attention.

"At ease, Captain," Red Hawk said. "What do you have for us?"

"The air quality index readings coming off the truck instruments are showing between seventy-five and a hundred and twenty-five, and my handheld is confirming that. We're still hitting some bad air pockets, but the air quality is *far* better overall than it's been in weeks. Most of us could go without our masks, but anyone with allergies might want to keep theirs on."

"What are you getting right here at the top of this hill?"

"We are at the low end, sir. Right at seventy-seven AQI."

Red Hawk and Stillman exchanged a look before Stillman removed his mask and took an experimental breath. The brisk wind hit his face like a delicious splash of water, instantly waking him up and drying the sweat beneath the rubber seal. The air was cold in his lungs with a faint hint of something smoky, like a distant campfire or cookout. Underlying that was the sharp scent of pine and fir trees sweet in his nose.

He nodded and grinned. "It smells pretty damn good."

Red Hawk removed his, took a deep breath, and let it out with a relieved sigh. "Captain Cryer, go ahead."

"Thank you, sir." She threw her mask off and let her light brown hair tumble across her shoulders. Face turned to the sky, she stepped to the highest part of the ridge, clenched her fists at her side, and breathed deeply several times, finally smiling wide."

Red Hawk chuckled and gestured toward the P-10s. "Captain, go tell the Marines they can take off their masks, provided they don't have allergies. And if they have any issues to put their air filtration masks on right away. That goes for you, too. Then I want you on the horn to Fairbanks. Let them know first, then try to reach as many tank groups as you can. If this has truly ended, we can forget these low altitude battles and get the carrier strike groups and long-range fighters involved. Go on."

"Yes, sir!" Cryer gave a brief salute and took off down the hill, leaving the two standing beneath the brightening gray skies.

Stillman shielded his eyes as the thin streaks of white spread and stretched, the sun breaking through and touching the ground with its golden rays. "Now that's a beautiful sky."

Red Hawk stared upward with half-lidded eyes, basking in the streaming light, holding out his hands to take it in, voice choked with emotion. "It's the most beautiful thing I've ever seen."

"Yes, sir. What are you thinking we do now, sir?" Stillman asked.

The Colonel raised his field glasses and swept them across the wild Alaskan landscape. "I can't help but think, where is Commander Orlov?"

"I'd expect the Russians to put the operation into overdrive, landing as many troops as they can to secure their positions before we hit them from the sky. My guess is that he's somewhere on the Alaskan shoreline, running the show, getting troops off boats and helping them drive inland."

"They know our reinforcements will hit them in a big way."

"I could be wrong, too. The clearing skies could encourage them to give up the pursuit and head home."

Red Hawk shook his head. "No. They'll try to hold key spots and keep pushing until they have a big chunk of our country. Their officials have been talking about it for years."

"Do you want to hold here and wait to hear back from Fairbanks?"

Red Hawk lowered the binoculars and squinted into the distance. "No, we keep moving. We keep pressing on. We're going to find Orlov and cut the head off the snake. Let's mount up."

"Yes, sir!"

CHAPTER TEN

Stephanie Lancaster, the Virginia highways...

Jamison spun the wheel, boots slamming the gas and brake alternately as he drove the Humvee into the mudslide. The entire hill had collapsed across the highway, thin mud gushing over the pavement, gobs of it spraying backward off the tires in a high arc as they plowed through. The truck slewed sideways, its tail end sliding off to the left, the frame rattling when they hit a piece of deadfall. The right front end bounced up and over the rotting log in a jarring collision, wood splintering everywhere as Sergeant Gress voiced his displeasure.

"Sorry about that." Jamison hunched against the steering wheel, leaning forward as he eyed the road through the rain-splashed windshield. The wipers were turned to high but not improving their visibility by much. Stephanie held on to the armrests, sweating nervously as the truck shifted and moved beneath her in sudden swerves that weren't conducive to keeping the tires gripped to the pavement. On the other side of Adelson, Laney kept her head down, eyes clamped as she whispered a prayer.

Stephanie reached across Adelson and grabbed her hand, squeezing it tightly. "Are you okay, Laney?"

Laney half smiled. "I always got a little carsick, but this…"

"Don't worry," Jamison called, "we'll be out of this slick in a minute. I just —"

The truck rocked again, jolting everyone forward, Jamison cursing and whipping the wheel, accelerating with a punch of the gas pedal, sweeping to the left side of the road before cutting back the other way. Laney started to finish her sentence but only shook her head and bowed it.

"Hang in there, hon," Stephanie said. "Just hang on."

Laney nodded and grabbed the handle on the back of Jamison's seat, gripping it for dear life. Adelson had his feet set apart, bracing himself for balance as they shifted and moved over the lumpy terrain, finally busting free from the thick mud, gaining traction with a jolt and a high rev as the big truck accelerated through the storm. The Virginia back roads were a mess of roughshod pavement and floods, Stephanie figuring the rains were doing a hundred years' worth of erosion in a short few days.

"According to the map, we should be about past Sperryville and coming up on Luray." Gress shined a flashlight at the map in his lap. "Judging from the signs I've seen, we have about twelve miles to go."

"Twelve miles in this might as well be a thousand," Adelson snorted. When Laney sighed nervously, he corrected himself. "But Jamison is a *great* driver. He'll get us there in one piece."

"There isn't a road I can't keep four wheels on or an obstacle I can't get around," Jamison replied as he worked the steering. "The suspension on this puppy is a modified double A-arm independent build. It has double-acting shock absorbers and sixteen-inch ground clearance."

"There was the incident on our way to Stamford," Gress reminded him. "You took out that mailbox."

"The roads were icy," he replied defensively. "We were sliding around, sir, but I kept the wheels on the road."

"Just keeping you honest, soldier."

"Hang on!" Jamison called.

They were cutting down a straightaway into a dip in the road and coming up on a set of train tracks ahead. The Humvee plowed into the trough of water with a heavy impact that threw Stephanie forward, and the truck displaced thousands of gallons of water with a *shhhhhh* sound. The brown sludge ran over the Humvee's hood and up the front windshield, blinding them for a moment before they climbed free and shot past the train tracks. Stephanie swallowed dry and relaxed her arms and shoulders, settling back with relief.

"So, um, Laney..." Adelson said. "We know what Stephanie did at the Pentagon. What about you? What were you doing there?"

"Just food service," Laney replied. "Nothing nearly as important as what she was doing."

"Food service is cool," Adelson nodded. "That's what I did before I got into this outfit."

"He's talking about his time in *fast* food," Jamison snickered. "He can flip burgers a lot better than he can soldier."

"Can it, man," Adelson replied. "For your information, I was the best fry cook on third shift."

Laney chuckled, and Stephanie smiled.

"Seriously, I did what I had to do. I was young, looking for my true self, stuff like that. And look where I ended up."

"In the Army," Gress answered. "For what it's worth, you soldier just fine, soldier."

"Thanks, Sarge," Adelson laughed and kept talking to Laney. "It must be pretty cool working at the Pentagon."

Laney shrugged but turned slightly to face him. "I guess it's okay. I got to meet some cool people. Senators, congressmen... the President, even."

"I'll bet a lot of world leaders, too."

"Oh, sure. I met a few, but I can't tell you who they were. It's top secret."

"And if you told me, you'd have to kill me."

"Exactly."

By then, Laney was smiling wider, her attention taken off the dangerous road. As the two conversed, Stephanie took in the drab environment, the endless dark skies displaying varied shades of gray, sometimes deeper clusters lumped in that moved swiftly to the northeast. Between the sheets of rain in the rivulets trickling down her window, she could make out next to nothing, only the sharp edges of buildings, lumps of cars and trucks, distant campfire lights, and flashes of headlamps in the maelstrom.

Gress traced lines on the map. "According to this, you'll need to take a left up here, Jamison,"

"Yes, sir." He turned at the intersection and swept out past squarish homes on the hillsides, corners broken off and gnawed on by the winds. A front door rested in a ditch, and rail fences had washed up to the shoulders. Off to the left was another lake field with a dozen round car roofs splitting the surface.

"The flooding is off the charts," Stephanie said. "This is something no one could have planned for, not even Craig. I'll bet this weather would have him curious."

"I wonder where he is now?" Laney asked.

"No clue. I just have to believe he can take care of himself and that he's in good hands."

"Is he a science, uh, type, like you?" Adelson asked.

"A nerd, you mean?"

He chuckled. "Yeah, I guess that's what I meant."

"He's a lot nerdier than I am. That's part of why we didn't stay together... he couldn't pull himself away from his work. Kept his nose buried in his computer and his simulations. I'm glad he did it now because his programs saved a lot of lives, but at the time, it was tough."

"Okay, take a right up here," Gress said. "We should be getting close, but with all the signs knocked down, I can't tell where we are. Laney, does any of this look familiar to you?"

Laney leaned forward between the seats, squinting into the rain, checking both sides. "It looks kind of familiar, but everything's changed. We lived in a little subdivision on the north side of town, if that helps."

"We should be passing through the south side soon," Gress said with a head shake. "Keep looking. If you see something familiar, let me know. Jamison, keep driving, but take it a little slower."

"Yes, sir."

Everyone joined in the search, every brightly colored barn and silo brought into question, every street marker they came to called out by the Sergeant, asking whether Laney recognized the landmarks. They tried for a solid hour to locate anything that would pinpoint them in relation to the town center. Gress ordered Jamison to turn right at some point, feeling like they'd overshot the mark and had passed the town completely. Another mile later, more mudslides had washed out the roads, and then Jamison slapped his hands on the steering wheel in frustration.

"Go easy, soldier," Gress said. "Find us a way around."

"I'll have to take us off road, sir."

"Do what you need to do. You're thinking up through those yards?"

"Yes, sir."

"Make it so."

The next few minutes were a blur of bumps and knocks as Jamison drove up the driveway between two houses and plunged through the backyards, crashing over a wooden fence and circling way around with the tires perpetually spinning. Mud splattered the back window as they swerved in a pointless direction. Stephanie caught flashes of lights behind glass, shadows moving, then gone. Jamison spun them to the right, the rear end clipping a swing set and sending metal poles and plastic flying. Stephanie's teeth rattled in her head, and she was about to beg them to stop when the Humvee slid onto a driveway and slowed to the end in a shockingly smooth finish.

Jamison wiped his forehead with his sleeve. "Looks like we're back on the highway, but I don't know if it's the same one. Any clue, Sarge?"

Gress was pouring over his maps again, seemingly out of ideas, when Laney pointed excitedly at something directly across from them. "That's the grade school!"

"Grade school?"

"Yeah. They built it a few years back. It's on the west edge of town. I used to drive past it all the time."

"Okay, that's something." Gress lifted the map and ran his finger along the west side of town. "There's a road here called. Reynolds? Sound familiar?"

"Oh yeah. That's an easy one." Laney brimmed with excitement. "Go right here... Reynolds will be a half mile straight ahead."

"Excellent. We'll have you home soon. Hit it, Jamison."

"Yes, sir."

Soon, they were racing north and took a right on Reynolds, Laney with both hands on Jamison's seat as she recognized more landmarks, taking over the directions and guiding them like she was home again. There were several turns, working their way into the subdivisions that were like war zones. The rains had washed out entire sections, blocks of houses swept free of their foundations, mixed in a sludge that seeped into the street, clogging the sewers and low points in the road with layers of mud and building materials. One dip was filled with tilted, half-buried cars Jamison had to punch through to keep going.

Laney put her hand to her mouth. "I hope everyone's okay. I don't see anyone around."

"If they haven't evacuated," Gress said, "they're hiding, but it won't be for long with all these foundations washing out. I've never seen rain like this in my entire life."

"There hasn't been rain like this... ever," Stephanie said, swallowing hard as she looked for signs of life in the sprawling subdivision with its crumbling homes and destruction.

"Just two more streets... take a right up here, then the next left."

"These roads." Jamison shook his head. "They're buckling all over the place. Soft spots and —"

They struck another pothole, a deep one that sent a jolt up through Stephanie's spine to her jaw. "I'd be happy not to hit any more of those."

"Here it is coming up on the left." Laney was grinning as she shifted to her window, the vehicle rolling to the top of a hill where most of the houses still stood, their foundations solid with no cracks in the brick or parts falling off.

"These houses look pretty good, Laney," Stephanie said.

"Yeah. They were always up a little higher and never flooded. I just hope they're home."

"Which one is it?" Jamison asked.

"Near the top... the one with the red shutters. I guess you can't tell so well in this light. Third one up."

"Gotcha."

The darkened two-story house sat still, silhouetted against the dark skies, light brick with slipping shutters, and a single peak on one side. It appeared to be in good shape but for the porch, which was skewed to the left. Above the front door was a large window, the glass still intact but dark inside. The rest of the windows were okay except for one in the upper left-hand corner with cardboard taped over it.

Stephanie tapped Gress on the shoulder. "Sergeant Gress, do you see the broken window up there?"

"Yeah. Not sure it means anything."

"It could mean they're home," Laney said, reaching for the door handle to get out. "Maybe that window got broken and my sister put the cardboard over it."

"Hold on... get her, Adelson."

Adelson gently grabbed her arm. "Wait a second, Laney."

She pushed outside. "Let me go!"

Adelson kept his grip but gave her some slack. "Let us check it out first. We don't know who's inside or who's wandering around out here. We don't want you to get hurt."

She studied Adelson's face for a moment but finally nodded and got back in, pulling the door shut quietly behind her.

"Thank you, Laney," Gress said. "This won't take long, I promise. Jamison, you stay here. Adelson, with me."

"Yes, sir."

Stephanie popped her door and stepped back to let the soldier out. "Be careful," she told them before getting in and holding Laney's hand.

The two soldiers stood beside the Humvee for a long moment, speaking briefly, their words whipped away by the wind. After some time, they began walking toward the house, keeping ten yards between them and carrying their rifles loosely at chest level. The tall, lanky Adelson moved off to the left and peeked around the house while Gress did the same on the right, and they came together in the middle, checking the darkened windows as they went. Gress paused at the living room bay window, shined his flashlight inside, and said something to Adelson. The Private tensed and moved with brisker footsteps, leaping up on the porch and resting his shoulder on the door. He seemed about to take the doorknob in hand but nudged it wide instead.

"Oh, no." Laney's voice trembled. "Why would they leave their door unlocked?"

"For a lot of reasons." Stephanie gripped her hand harder. "They might've left and gone somewhere else, or..." Nothing came to mind. Heart thudding, a hot sense of dread filling her chest, she scooted closer to Laney as Gress slipped in on Adelson's heels, the soldiers consumed by the darkness as they moved deeper into the lower floor. They stopped in the back near the kitchen, the flashlight beam remaining stationary for a good minute before shifting to what Stephanie suspected was a hallway. The light shined faintly into the first-floor bedroom windows and then moved slowly upstairs, stirring up the gloom.

"I'm about to jump out and go in." Laney pulled her arm away and popped the door.

"I wouldn't do that," Jamison shot over his shoulder. "If the Sergeant says to stay in the truck, best to stay in the truck. Let them check it out and make sure it's safe before we go —"

Gress stepped outside with Adelson behind him. The Sergeant held his helmet tucked under one arm while drawing his other across his forehead. He flicked his flashlight beam toward the Humvee before turning it off and strolling down. Laney shoved her door open and flew out with Stephanie on her heels.

"Laney, hold up a second. Wait!"

But Laney was running through the yard, splashing in the spongy grass, sprinting as the wind tossed her hair around. She stopped a few paces from Gress, who held out his hand, face drawn and pale in the half light, eyes hollow and sad. It hit Laney like a punch to the gut.

She slumped, and stumbled to the right, legs starting to buckle before Adelson reached out and caught her.

"What is it, Gress?" Stephanie asked as she came up.

"Something happened." Laney sobbed and rolled in Adelson's arms. "He said I can't go in."

"Why not, Sergeant? What happened in there?"

"It's just not a good idea," he replied with a sad head shake. "Trust me. It's not a pretty scene —"

"What's wrong? Tell me!" Laney shrieked in a quivering falsetto filled with misery and fear. Her body stiffened, and she pushed against Adelson repeatedly, harder, finally punching him in the chest and thrusting him away. Adelson let her go, but Gress stepped in front of her.

"We should probably get back in the truck and leave," he said.

"I'm not going anywhere until I see my family."

"I'm sorry. I can't let you go in."

"Oh yeah? Try to stop me." Before anyone could grab her, Laney tensed like a cat, crouching, sidestepping the reaching Sergeant and bolting past him, darting for the door. Gress took two steps in pursuit but pulled up with his fists on his hips. She was already there, scrambling up the steps and disappearing inside. Stephanie came forward and ripped the flashlight out of Gress' hand.

"Laney, hold on! I'm coming with a flashlight."

She met her in the foyer, where Laney was standing with her shoulders slumped, fists gripped in front of her, terror scrawled across her face. Like a deer trapped in the headlights, she stood frozen, too scared to go on but unable to turn back. The smell had been unnoticeable outside but was pungent inside, stinging her nose in the confined space, a cloying reek that wrapped around her head and curled her stomach. Stephanie took one of Laney's hands and gripped it tight, pulling it against her with a sobering shake.

"Are you ready?"

Laney nodded and whispered. "Yes. Thank you."

Stephanie turned to the living room, shining the flashlight around at the wet puddles glistening on the carpet, the constant drip from above setting her nerves on edge. Pieces of the ceiling had fallen in, large chunks hanging there as water leaked down the walls. When Stephanie stepped into the living room and shined light across the waterlogged furniture into the kitchen, Laney's expression lit up, and she rushed straight over. Stephanie followed her as she fell to her knees next to a bloated, stinking corpse of an older man with a stained T-shirt and a tussle of salt-and-pepper hair. His head was turned toward a cracked window where the wind howled through tiny punctures. Judging by the swollen shape and glazed eyes, he'd been dead for many days. Laney was sobbing, shaking her head, reaching to touch him but unable to bring herself to do it. Then she gestured to several holes in his chest marked by old stains on his shirt.

"Somebody shot my dad..." she cried, her words slow and muddled like she had a mouth full of cotton. "Can you believe that? Why would they shoot him? Why?"

Stephanie blinked back tears and rested her hand on Laney's shoulder. "I don't know, honey. The world's upside down..."

"Upside down? It's totally screwed!" As if remembering something, Laney leaped to her feet and rushed through the kitchen, stopping in front of a trail of blood drops spreading from the tile to the carpeted hallway. Bloody handprints streaked the walls, smears and splotches of it all around them.

"What the hell happened here?" Laney's chest hitched, and she hurried ahead before Stephanie could hold her back, turning up a set of stairs and disappearing from her sight.

Stephanie raced up after her, following the bloody boot prints, more crimson smears, and huge, round stains of it on the first landing.

"Someone was chased up here," she whispered, swallowing hard with growing horror. At the top of the stairs, she stopped and caught her breath. "Laney, where are you!"

Receiving no response, she followed the bloody tracks with her eyes down a long hallway, not wanting to see what was at the end. Laney's fevered wails from a bedroom sent a chill up Stephanie's spine, her knees weakening, forcing her to hold on to the balustrade to keep her feet. With a deep breath of resolve, she crept along the hall, following Laney's erratic sobbing, finding her in the last room on the left, the one with the covered window. She was kneeling in the darkness next to a dead girl who was slumped against the wall beneath a long streak of blood, her face hidden by a length of curly brown hair, not unlike Laney's but hanging lank and wet on her cheeks.

"Laney?" Stephanie crossed quickly and kneeled next to her. "Laney, are you okay, hon?"

"No," Laney sobbed, slouching, seeming to compress in on herself. "That's my little sister. How can I be okay?"

Stephanie tore down her emotional walls and pulled Laney tight, averting her face and holding her breath against the stench. As she held her shaking form, she looked around at the rock posters and girly decorations on the walls; her favorite colors seemed to be purple and gold. The soggy bedspread and pillows were lying in a mess on the mattress and spilling onto the floor. The stars on the ceiling were bathed in a flood of water that built up and dripped.

"I'm so sorry, Laney. This is terrible."

She nodded against Stephanie's chest, turning slightly, and hugging her back. "She was just about to start college. What kind of animals would do this?"

"The worst possible kind. The kind who don't deserve any mercy at all."

Laney's body turned rigid, hands clenching, squeezing her so hard it hurt. "I want to *kill* them. I hate them so much. I hate all of this."

"I know you do... I do, too. What about the rest of your family, Laney? Would they be in the house, too?"

"Yes, but I'm afraid to look. I don't want to see my mom..." she sobbed again, her sudden anger draining into defeat.

"It's okay. Do you want to stay here with your sister while I go check?"

She nodded and squeezed Stephanie one more time before letting go, hands falling into her lap as she stared at the dead form in front of her.

"I have to take the flashlight, okay? It's going to be dark for a minute."

When she didn't reply, Stephanie got up and left the room, walking into the master bedroom where she found a woman sprawled in the bathroom, a hammer in her hand as if she'd put up a fight. The floor was coated with bloody water and towels, shampoo bottles and soap knocked everywhere. For some reason, the scene hit her hardest, and she stood there for a long moment with the flashlight shaking in her hand. Her lips trembled, and she squeezed out tears and leaned on the sink.

"Stephanie, are you okay?" Laney called from the other room.

"Yeah, I'm fine." She wiped the wetness off her cheeks. "I'm coming."

Laney was standing in the middle of her sister's bedroom when she got there, one arm full of picture frames and a couple of shirts, a silver bracelet in her left hand.

"What's that?" she asked, nodding to the jewelry.

"It's my sister's friendship bracelet. We both have one, see?" Laney held her hand up to show a jangling twin.

"I'm so sorry about your sister. I see you got some pictures?"

"Yes..." She blinked at Stephanie expectantly. "Mom?"

"She's dead. She put up a fight, but she was shot, too."

Laney's expression turned anguished, like she was drowning in a nightmare but had nowhere to run. Finally, she raised her chin and walked past her with staggering, drunken steps. Stephanie was right behind her and lighting the way ahead as they shuffled downstairs and into the foyer. Outside, Gress and Adelson stood with rain dripping off their helmets, shining enough light in their direction to illuminate the front stoop. Laney stumbled off the crooked steps, and Adelson flew in to catch her, lifting her and helping her back to the Humvee.

Stephanie stopped before Gress, flipped off her flashlight, and crossed her arms. "That was tough," she rasped.

"I tried to warn you."

"I know. I appreciate that, Sergeant. Thank you. But she needed to see them to put them to rest. Could we do something...?"

"Bury them?"

"Yeah."

"We've got protocols for handling dead bodies, and these have been dead so long..." He shook his head. "There is a serious risk of catching tuberculosis or contamination by handling the bodies. And with the wind and rain blowing around, it only makes things worse. I'd be putting everyone at risk."

"No, I understand," Stephanie started to move past him. "We'll make her understand."

"Now what?" Gress asked.

Stephanie paused. "What do you mean?"

"Well, this was Laney's stop, but I doubt she'll want to stay here. We can take her to a camp —"

"No, she can come with me. She can stay at my place."

"Are you sure?"

Adelson put Laney into the Humvee and quietly shut the door, hurrying around to the other side to get in.

Stephanie nodded. "Yeah. If she wants to. We're probably the closest thing to a family she has left. I won't send her off to some camp. We should have enough supplies at my place."

She walked past him, oblivious to the wind buffeting her, drying the tears on her cheeks and replacing them with a stinging drizzle she hardly felt. Garbage blew by in a wasteland of precious things left behind. When they returned to the truck and shut the doors against the storm's howling noise, Laney sat slouched over, sniffling, with the family pictures in her lap.

"Where to now?" Jamison asked.

Stephanie reached across and took Laney's hand. "No change in plans. We're going to my house next. Laney's coming home with me."

CHAPTER ELEVEN

Morten Christensen, Pearisburg, Virginia

Morten sat heavily at the kitchen table, its simple cherry wood design perfect for the cottage they'd settled in. After several days, and multiple visits from locals, they had just about everything they needed. A fire crackling in the hearth, adequate space for himself and Alma, tables and chairs donated from warehouses stocked with handcrafted Amish goods, and a well-equipped kitchen with a bread box, cast-iron pans, a small butter churner, and enough stores in their pantry to get them through the next couple of weeks. It was still raining, the downpour an incessant rattling at the edges of his sanity. It stopped occasionally but for only two or three hours before starting up again, the clouds always gray and drab like a sea of expanding putty.

He reached for a plate of freshly baked bread, cutting off a chunk and slathering butter on top as the fire in the great room crackled and spat. Alma came around the table with two cups of coffee, placing one in front of him before she sat with hers. She spooned in a bit of sugar and fresh cream from a decanter, stirring it with a clank of tin, staring at him with a faint smile.

"It's been half a day since the meeting at Smithson's," she said, "and already the scouts are reporting sightings of McCallum's men on the bordering fields."

"I hadn't heard that. Who told you —"

"I was over at Miriam's earlier, and one of the guards' wives came over to trade goods. I heard everything there."

Morten shook his head and blew a thin wisp of air. "News flies fast in this community. If only the men could be so open about things."

"The men are doing what they're supposed to do, protecting us and giving us hope. We all have vital tasks and duties." Alma leaned back and sipped her coffee. "I'll give it to the folks here. They're far more organized and capable than we were at Fort Plain."

"I've noticed that. In this cottage..." Morten gestured around. "It's a beautiful place and placed perfectly on the hillside with Samuel's and Uri's cottages close by."

"And we have everything we need here. Food, fresh water, warmth, and even hot baths. They have enough stores in the community barns to feed everyone for a couple of years, even after our people show up. That will be plenty of time to get the crops going again."

"Provided we hold out against those who would harm us. With the new volunteers, the older men like myself, we're over a hundred and fifty strong."

"And from what I've seen, the women here can fight if they need to."

Morten reached across the table and patted her hand. "We have everything we need except for Wendy and the kids."

There came a brief knock on the door, and Miriam pushed it open and stepped inside with a broad smile, holding up a basket as she shed her cloak and hat and hung them in the entryway. "Fresh bread from the Donaldson's. Tessa makes so much that their larders are overflowing with it."

"Set it down with the loaf we haven't finished," Morten chuckled.

"Oh, we have extra?" Miriam circled and sat by Alma, uncovering the loaf of bread in the basket. She grabbed a slice of Morten's, slathered butter across the top, and bit in with satisfaction. "Mmm. We are truly so blessed to be here. I'm worried about our Fort Plain brothers and sisters. Do you think they'll ever arrive?"

"We can only pray to God that they make it."

"And focus on the things we can control," Alma added.

"We fit in well with the community," Miriam shrugged. "What more can we do?" She looked back and forth between Morten and Alma, the two suddenly gone quiet as they chewed bread and sipped their coffee. "What is up with you two?"

Alma leaned forward with her elbows on the table, tossing a piece of bread in her mouth and talking brightly around her food. "Father is going searching for Wendy, David, and Charlie."

"I said no such thing."

"But it's been in your heart since you helped them escape," Alma said, "and I can see it in your eyes."

Miriam leveled a flat stare at them both. "Should we be risking our position in the enclave by doing odd things? And what if you were to get hurt, Father? I don't understand it. Wendy left on her own accord. Uri is much better now, thanks to Lavinia's good care and the comfort of the cottages Smithson has provided. Should we be forced out..."

"If you'd seen where Smithson wanted them to live," Alma said, "you would've left, too."

"I don't blame them for that," Miriam countered. "My concern is the depth of *our* involvement in it. I love Wendy and the children as much as you do, but we risk a lot by Father going out and putting to question our loyalties."

Morten swallowed his bread and rested his hands on the table, wrapped around the warm coffee cup, not enthusiastic about riding in the rain but feeling himself pulled inexorably into the storm. "I will always hold your advice in the highest regard. I can't deny there is truth to what you say. The last thing I want is to cast ourselves in doubt and give the citizens of the community cause to mistrust or reject us. I would regret putting my family here at risk, especially as vulnerable as we are with Uri. Our flock is still missing. But I think of what your brother would say if he saw us sitting here doing nothing."

Miriam stared at the table, cheeks red as she picked at her fingers. "So, you're going out then?"

"I would be lying if I said no. My plan would be to do this after my first shift with Samuel. He'll return to Lavinia tired and ready for a night's rest. I'll ride to the western outskirts, greet the guards as usual, and tell them I'm patrolling there for a few hours. It won't be far from the truth, and they likely won't question it."

Miriam reached and covered his hands. "You must be careful, Father. It's dangerous out there."

"That's precisely why I go," Morten nodded. "Don't worry. I'll be fine. We dealt with much worse on our way here." Lowering his voice, he leaned in. "We must be cautious to whom we speak of this. No one else should know, aside from the people in this room."

Miriam blinked with wide eyes. "Do you think Samuel would tell Smithson?"

"I don't know, but I'd rather not deal with that until I know Wendy and the kids are okay. Is that understood —"

Light footsteps came from the back hallway, and Mara stepped into the great room with a wide smile. "Hello, Grandfather, aunties."

"Hello, child." Morten shared a surprised look with Alma. "We didn't hear you knock."

"I came through the back door," she said cheerily. "I didn't think you'd mind."

"Our doors are always open." Miriam smiled, holding her arms out to Mara and hugging her when she reached the table. "But it's always polite to knock, anyway."

"You're right, Aunt Miriam. I'll remember next time."

"What do you have for us today?" She took the basket and rested it in her lap.

"My mother sends over some jams she received after trading some of your apple cider, Aunt Alma. She said you deserved your fair share of the takings."

Alma put the basket down and lifted the cloth covering to reveal several jars of gold and raspberry-colored jams. "Well, isn't that fair of her?"

"Lavinia has always been a stickler for accountability," Morten said approvingly. "Tell your mother we are very grateful for this, and we'll have some right away."

Morten removed a jar from the basket and pulled off the top carefully, filling the room with the scent of sugary fruit. With his butter knife, he slathered some on his bread and took a big bite, grinning at the burst of flavor in his mouth.

"Absolutely delightful," he said, chewing around his words. "I'm blessed to have such daughters and granddaughters surrounding me, feeding me, and making me fat." He patted his belly.

"Mother would approve," Miriam said.

The mention of Elvesta filled him with sudden sorrow, and he choked as he swallowed, coughing into his hands and blinking back watery eyes.

"I'm sorry," Miriam said, reaching with a napkin. "I didn't mean to upset you."

"I'm okay, dear daughter." He coughed several more times, put the bread down, and slumped. "I'm not sad, Miriam. I'm happy you remember our Elvesta fondly, though it breaks my heart knowing she's no longer with us. We could use her loving hand and words of hope." When Alma averted her eyes, he quickly added. "Luckily, my daughters have taken after her and fill my heart with joy by the hour."

"That's why we stay dedicated to our families," Mara said as she took a half piece of bread and pulled the butter and jelly closer. "No matter what."

"It *is* very simple, and God's love shines throughout every part of us. That's why we pray for each other. Yet, our actions speak louder than words, and that is how we show our love for each other and God; being kind yet firm, doing and not sitting, encouraging rather than tearing down, and protecting each other from harm. Sometimes it can be hard when family members disagree, but in the end, we all love each other, and we find a way to work together in the light of God's love."

"Disagree? You mean like with you and Papa?"

Morten chose his words carefully. "Your father and I disagree on many things, but I love him more than anything in the world, as I love your Uncle Zachary. As the patriarch of this family, I divide my love equally amongst my children and grandchildren, even when they have a multitude of questions that weigh down my ears."

He reached across the table and pinched her hand, making her giggle.

Fitzpatrick bore Morten through another spitting squall, the angry weather battering him with winds and rain, soaking his underclothes no matter how tightly he cinched his poncho and hood. His wide-brimmed hat sat low over his face, dripping water into his gray beard and down his front. He was somewhere west of the Pearisburg enclave, working his way around Buck Hill, sticking to the back roads and highways, which were becoming unrecognizable, the pavement giving way to buckling concrete and massive potholes. Before long, driving vehicles on it would be impossible. When the roads became too rough, or he needed to search a string of farmsteads along the hillside, Morten guided Fitzpatrick carefully, the mud squelching beneath the horse's hooves, the treacherous landscape ten times worse than when they'd arrived in town. When he didn't find Wendy and the kids up on a high ridge, he came off to check some properties on the lower western slopes where the fields were nothing but massive flood plains and the roads were simply gone. Water had risen to cover the bottom halves of trees, and ducks swam through the branches. A squirrel scrambled up in the higher boughs, leaping from one to the next until he found an elevated place to land and scramble past them in a frantic rush. Houses stood on raised ground, surrounded by two or three feet of water. Morten walked the horse around the edges, calling out for Wendy, Charlie, or David to answer. He passed homes flooded to the second levels with barns and sheds half submerged in lakes. In the distance, a group of people floated in a boat, moving from home to home, drifting inside wide-open barn doors or crawling through upper windows to presumably scavenge.

"Solid thinking there," Morten mumbled to the rain, and he raised his binoculars to get a better view. "Wendy, you'd be smart enough to think of that. Please let it be you." But the figures on the boat were unrecognizable, one watching him back with field glasses, and Morten lowered his and waved before moving on.

He ran across a handful of horses stranded on an island with a few trees and enough grass to graze, and he promised himself to pick them up on the way back. "It will be tough to explain to the elders, but it would be a dire shame to leave those beauties standing out there by themselves."

Morning turned to midday, and exhaustion wore him to the bone. After sweeping the western side of Buck Hill, Morten started back up again, riding endless slopes and roads that curved upward at twisted angles. Slumped over in his saddle, he pressed on, climbing up to the next ridge and walking Fitzpatrick across it, peering down into the southwestern valley until the forest and mist obscured his view.

"I reckon it's time to turn back, boy," he told Fitzpatrick, and he guided him off the ridge toward a flat indentation in the side of the hill, whatever was behind it hidden by trees. Revving car engines reached him, echoing through the valley and coming from the east in the direction he was heading. And while he didn't know if the people were friends or foes, there was a chance Wendy and the kids could be with them. Morten descended a steep incline with a soft crunch of horse hooves on the wet, mulched-up debris. They stepped out of the dense and dripping tree line a short time later, and Morten drew Fitzpatrick up with a soft "Whoa."

He stood on the west side of a large gravel lot with at least a dozen cars and trucks parked there. A long, black barn with Native American symbols written in bright white paint squatted in the center, its doors open about a foot and a man standing in front of it with a rifle. People came and went from the building, guided by folks wearing orange ponchos and latex gloves. A man limped outside along with a woman wearing a fresh sling on her arm. Others were brought in with bloodstained pants, head wounds, hands wrapped in thick white gauze, faces twisted in pain. A little girl in pajamas held her belly and cried while her father carried her inside. Those leaving smiled and thanked the workers before they got into their vehicles and pulled out, joining a road that dipped off the ridge and out of sight. A plain farmstead was perched on the slope above the barn, surrounded by trees, its bright red siding standing out in the rain. There were no signs of Amish, and the other guards in the lot regarded Morten with flat stares as he guided Fitzpatrick forward. One man in hunters' attire and an orange vest stepped over quickly to cut him off with a raised hand. "Hang on there, man. Who are you, and what are you doing here?"

Morten touched the brim of his hat. "Sorry for the intrusion, friend. My name is Morten Christensen, and I'm from the Amish settlement east of Buck Hill."

"I figured as much," he replied. Straight brown hair stuck out from his hunter's cap, and he wore a broom handle mustache, his eyes deep-set and dark. "You're a good way from home. What are you doing out here, Morten?"

"If I'm to call you friend, I'd like to know your name, sir."

"I'm Silas Toomer, in charge of security here at Nance Barn."

"Nance Barn? Looks like a hospital to me."

"That's right. Owned and operated by Fred Nance and his wife. With all the rain and weather, and most of the roads being washed out, people are having difficulty getting to the local hospital north of Pearisburg, so we set something up here for them."

Morten was nodding. "Makes sense to me. The lower valley is a floodplain, and people are out in boats going from house to house and looting."

"No kidding?"

"That's right. A few houses down there are still standing, but that's all."

Silas relaxed and let his rifle rest against his ample middle, the husky physique mirrored in his wide, clean-shaven jawline. "Can't fault them for trying."

"I guess not."

Silas raised his chin. "Who are you looking for, Morten?"

Morten walked Fitzpatrick a couple of steps, reaching into his coat slowly, pulling out an old picture, and holding it up. "This is my son Zach, his wife Wendy, and their kids Charlie and David. Zach isn't around right now, but Wendy and the kids live somewhere around Buck Hill. Have you seen them?"

Silas studied the image. "The Amish don't like taking pictures."

"My daughter-in-law and grandchildren aren't Amish. They don't practice the religion or live with us in the enclave."

"Oh, I see." Silas studied the picture for another moment before shaking his head. "I can't say I've seen any of these folks or heard their names. You get separated from them?"

"Something like that."

"If they come in, want me to let them know you asked for them?"

"Yep, and I'd trade you some supplies if you got word to me, too. Just be careful around the outskirts of our land. There's a bit of a war brewing on the east side of Amish territory, and my people are a little jumpy. Just come to to the front gate and wait for someone to greet you. Tell them you've got news for one of their people."

"What if I wave a white flag and tell them Morten sent me?"

"That might get you through," he laughed. "Well, Silas, this looks like a wonderful place, and I'm glad you're helping people. The Nance's seem like good people."

"We wouldn't be here spending our time guarding the place if they weren't," Silas said, nodding at the other armed men walking through the lots and patrolling at the edge of the tree line. "This is one of the few places folks can count on to get help, and we'll defend it with everything we've got."

"I'll bet you would," Morten said with the tip of his hat. "I'll be heading out now. Good luck to you and yours."

"Good luck to you, too." Silas watched him walk Fitzpatrick across the front lot, folks staring at them and glancing hesitantly in his direction, murmuring and whispering.

Morten tipped his hat to everyone, catching their eyes, holding out the image of Wendy and the kids, and receiving head shakes and dark looks in response. When he reached the edge of the tree line, he put the picture away and kicked Fitzpatrick a little harder, galloping into a thin spread of woods and weaving him back and forth to rejuvenate their energy. The afternoon grew darker, doubly so beneath the trees, the cloud cover crushing his visibility. He found paved roads and stuck to them, only going up driveways when he thought there might be a chance Wendy and the kids were there. Whenever he saw signs of human activity, he called out, hoping they were inside and had forgotten to mark their initials on something like they'd planned. Mostly, Morten's calls went unanswered, though one man came out on the porch with a shotgun, so he'd turned Fitzpatrick around and galloped away.

Eventually, the cold and exhaustion won out, and he grew tired and sore in the saddle. Soon, he was swaying, once jerking himself awake to find that Fitzpatrick had stopped at the edge of the woods with a stormy hillside rolling off to the right and pitch-black skies shivering with lightning and thunder. With a flick of the reins, he got them moving again, though it had turned dark, forcing him to use his flashlight to light their way. He picked his way down into the valley and waded across three feet of water to tether the trapped horses on the island and lead them back to solid ground. By then, his hips throbbed, his pants were soaked through, and his hands were frozen from the cold, but he clung to the ropes and guided them around Buck Hill to Amish territory. He met a pair of guards standing drenched in a field, their eyes wide and staring as he towed five horses out of the gloom. They raised their weapons for a moment, then recognized the tall figure with the broad shoulders and a drooping black hat.

"Here, take these," Morten said, holding out the tethers.

"These are fine beasts." A rosy-cheeked young man took them. "Where did you find them?"

"In a field just at the edge of our territory, trapped by high waters. They just needed someone to bring them back across."

"Are they ours?"

"I doubt it, son. Consider it a gift of God."

"A tremendous gift, indeed," the young man scoffed in admiration. "You'll be praised by the elders for this, surely."

"I seek not the attention of men, only the light of God's gaze. Take the horses yourselves, if you want, and tell the elders you brought them in. There is no need to mention seeing me this evening."

The guards shared looks of disbelief, and the one holding the tethers waved to him as he went by.

"Thank you, sir! God be with you."

"And may God walk with you, too, my friends." Grinning tiredly, Morten circled through the camp in search of their cottage, a set of dry clothes, and a hearth to warm his aching bones.

CHAPTER TWELVE

Zach Christensen, Carcross, Yukon

With hand warmers in his gloves, pockets, and boots, Zach waited until night came, filling up on a Russian MRE and topping it off with more ice cream, feeling his energy return tenfold, stopping only when he was too stuffed to move. As snowflakes glanced off the parlor's front glass, Zach watched the distant woods and airfield where headlamps flickered on the tarmac. The Russians were spreading their camp, though only a spattering of trucks had driven past him into Carcross proper and back again. Blossoming explosions and battles raged to the north, the sounds of gunfire fierce as the Russians tried to hold on to their position.

When a large cargo plane teetered in from the west and landed on the airfield, Zach stood and readied himself to go. He grabbed his assault pack, which held a small amount of food and water, first aid kits, extra pistols, rifle ammunition, and a few pieces of survival gear. An all-purpose ax, a pair of carbon blades, and a bedroll and covers fleshed out his equipment. He started to leave his air filtration mask but grabbed it at the last second and hung it from his belt.

Approaching midnight, Zach pushed open the front door and

stepped out into the cold, moving along the storefronts to the north, roughly parallel to the shoreline until he reached the end of the row of markets and stores where a dead-end cut him off. Jogging west across the street, he scrambled up the tree-covered slope to the edge of the tarmac. He crept parallel to the airstrip, moving steadily north with his Russian rifle ready, studying several large hangers and supply sheds three hundred yards to the north. Troops milled around or unloaded the massive cargo plane that had landed earlier, carrying crates from its open belly. It squatted on the airfield with its running lights off but its turboprop engines still going. To the west of the tarmac and supply plane was the Russian camp, a wide gravel area with dark buildings and service roads. A few hollow bulbs burned in the windows, lanterns dotting the camp edges, dozens of troops marching or jogging across the grounds.

Using night vision binoculars he'd taken off the dead soldiers, Zach scanned to the right where a hundred vehicles were parked in a wide gravel lot. The dark shapes were hard to make out, though the slanted rear end of their Humvee stuck out like a sore thumb. The brunt of the Russian troops were opposite him on the north and northwest edges of the camp behind makeshift barricades made from smoking vehicles. Mounted machine guns pointed into the woods, and at least one large piece of artillery cast an ominous shape in the darkness.

"How long do you plan on staying here?" Zach asked no one as he slipped along the tree line, heading for the hangars and maintenance buildings where some Russian armored vehicles were parked. Frigid air stung his nostrils, the skies spitting flames, with snow and ash drifting through the air. Russian voices reached him way before he got there, words he couldn't understand carried on the wind. Soldiers were pulling long hoses from fuel tanks and filling up their vehicles. Six guards stood around with rifles, watching the tree line and looking in Zach's general direction, forcing him to stay low in the brush. More Russian voices sounded behind him, and he craned his neck as a half-dozen soldiers leaving camp, adjusting their backpacks as they jogged past him toward the shops he'd just come from.

He slunk away, circling the building and leaving the fueling stations behind, walking to the beat of his own pounding heart with no particular plan in mind but to find his friends and set them free. A pair of flashlight beams cut through the woods, two soldiers standing up top, hands thrust into their pockets, shoulders hunched in the cold as they checked the area. Zach retreated to the bottom of the slope, running into walls of thick brush and tangle. He climbed over them or swam through sticker bushes that clung to his jacket, staying out of the light's reach. After the guards left, he climbed back to the top and kept moving, and another fifty yards took him past the airfield to the motor pool where he set his eyes on their Humvee. Off to the northwest, flames spat up, and distant gunfire crackled like bubble wrap squeezed in his fists, the treetops swaying with combustion winds and sometimes toppling over.

The guards were thicker, walking the service roads in disciplined shifts and crunching through the woods below him. Zach was nestled between them like a splinter, crouched in the shadows, counting the minutes as they passed. Figuring out their timing, he charged across and reached the lot, slipping among the civilian cars and a few CAF vehicles with bullet holes and blood frozen to the armor, fractured glass, and a few with flat tires. The second set of buildings and sheds were just to his west, whispering with troop movements and orders, Russian voices so alien they made him feel alone. His heart raced faster until he leaned against the truck fender and took a deep breath, letting it escape slowly along with his useless anxiety.

He got up and moving again, slipping between the rigid metal frames to reach their Humvee, its familiar shape comforting beneath his hands as he slid along its side. Zach tried the door, popped it open, and felt around the seat for the keys. If he found them, he could climb in and pull away, lights off and driving to the service road, past the guards and machine gun fire, making a lucky escape to the highway and heading south, another mile closer to Wendy and the kids. Then he imagined Wendy crouched beside him, one arm around his waist, clinging to him with her lips near his ear and her golden curls falling across his neck.

"They are your *friends*, Zach. You can't leave them behind. Even if you made it past the guards and sharpshooters, their grenades and missiles, you need them, and they need you. You can't turn your back on them."

"I know," Zach reached in and flipped the starter switch to the run position and watched the battery light come on, then quickly flipped it off again. "They haven't disabled the vehicle.."

Wendy whispered in his head. "You'll get your friends out of here first."

"Right. I just wanted to make certain the keys were here, that's all."

Zach left the keys and gently shut the door, Wendy's ghost vanishing as he stood. A pair of guards marched down the central aisle, forcing him to lean against the fender, roll, and slip to the vehicle's rear where he crouched and waited. After they passed, he moved to the edge of the motor pool, catching his breath and rising to look through the windows. More soldiers were heading in his direction, forcing him to abandon the lot and dive into a ditch that ran along a service road. Curled up with his cheek pressed to the cold mud, he waited for the boots to go away. When he raised up to see, a dozen Russian troops jogged from between the car frames right at him, rifles rattling against their flak vest. Zach pinned himself to the ground, trying to stay small and undetectable as they leaped the ditch and flew over him. The troops kept their heads up and ran toward the woods, disappearing in the direction of the stores where he was sure someone would soon find the dead soldiers.

The lot was buzzing with guards, a pair of spotlights shining from makeshift towers, tracing over the cold ground and sweeping the woods. Zach got up and retreated eastward across the service road, squeezing through a thicket, sliding backward but falling forward on his elbows and knees with a soft curse. As the spotlights swept overhead, he kept to the edge of the camp, circling to the north and finally jumping into a tangled clutch of deadfall. A tree had spilled on the forest floor, bringing saplings and vines down around it, old logs covered with cold moss and sharp offshoots. He squatted, waiting for the camp to settle and the spotlights to move in a different direction with the sounds of fighting even closer.

After an hour, he climbed the half-fallen tree, which rested at a forty-five-degree angle. When he'd gotten ten feet high, he used his binoculars to scan the camp through a gap in the brush. His position afforded him a clear view of the motor pool off to his left and the smaller sheds and buildings directly ahead. Off to his right where the fighting was fierce, a roadway cut into the woods and bustled with military vehicles, the soldiers thickest at the entrance where they crouched behind sandbags and old cars.

Two hastily constructed towers made of plywood and stripped materials were held together by two-by-four crossbeams. One soldier balanced precariously atop each, machine guns somehow mounted to the shaky rails, spotlights glaring down like bright eyes. He followed the troop movements, watching as positions shifted and changed, finally locating what he estimated was the camp center. They were using part of a school bus and several vans to shield their command center with tables dragged out and maps thrown across them. Zach turned the field glasses slowly to the left and spotted a building about thirty yards long constructed in that same classic lodge style. Faint lights glowed from the windows, and a pair of guards stood at the doors. A woman sat in a chair with her knees together, fists clenched beneath her chin, a Russian coat thrown over her shoulders.

"Liza," Zach whispered.

She remained seated until a Russian officer arrived from the command center and stepped up on the porch, gesturing to a guard and then at Liza. The guard took her by the arm and guided her inside the long building with the officer. Their shadows shifted in the windows, though he couldn't tell what they were doing. The pitched battles simmering to the north picked up with crackles of gunfire and another thump of an explosion he took as a mortar. There was no way to count the movements of troops buzzing around the area with boots running everywhere. Zach slid off the tree into the clutch of deadfall, backing out through the snags, turning to his right, and creeping away as the footfalls closed in on his position. Zach moved faster, crouching, weaving between vine-twisted saplings, leaping logs, and slipping on shredded leaves, leery of the firefights somewhere ahead of him. He'd be driven right into them if he kept going, herded into a kill zone, and cut to pieces by one or both sides if he didn't do something fast.

The spotlight skipped across the treetops, giving him a little light to see by, and that's when a dark gully appeared lower on the hill, partially hidden by a fallen tree. Flowing toward the gully, Zach kicked his feet out and slid, flipping on his belly, riding the loose leaves, and slipping under the tree to crash in the gully with his face pressed to the cool mud. The rushing footfalls moved by, one above him, the other below, and Zach made himself invisible, sliding deeper, curling up, and playing dead.

He released the breath he'd been holding and panted softly until his wind returned. His wound was leaking, the warm wetness seeping into his belt line, making him painfully aware of the cool ground and the wet, stinking leaves he was lying on.

"I'll never get past the guards," he whispered.

Something shifted to his right, the briefest hint of movement, the silhouette of a rifle barrel and a figure crouched behind it. Zach started to swing his gun around when a voice froze him.

"Stop it," a man hissed, spitting the consonants into the cool night air. "No sudden moves, or you'll die before your Russian buddies know what happened. If you can even understand me, commie."

Zach nodded and rested his weapon against the muddy wall, shifting a little and raising his hands to show they were empty. "I'm not Russian."

"CAF? American?"

"American."

"Marines?"

"American."

The man grunted and flipped on a flashlight for an instant before snapping off again, followed by scoffing and then full-on laughter, muffled into his sleeve.

"What's so funny?" Zach asked, not bothering to hide his confusion.

"Never in a million years would I have thought to see you again."

"Again?"

"Yeah, remember me?" The flashlight flipped on briefly and pointed back at its wielder. Laser gray eyes stared at him, a mouth smirked above a thin brown goatee, and mud and blood smeared his gaunt cheeks. He held a Russian machine gun with the barrel aimed at Zach's chest. The light snapped off.

"Scotty?"

"In the flesh. Think you'd see me again?"

"I'd hoped not. Where's Sandy?"

"I'm the guy with the gun. How about answering my questions first?"

"Fair enough."

"Where's your crew?"

"We pulled into Carcross this morning and got picked up by the Russians. Fought a couple and killed them. Dragged them into an ice cream parlor on the other side of the airfield. Ate several scoops of salted caramel, and here I am."

"Now, that's an adventure. As for my group, we arrived two nights ago and were making out pretty good. The place was nearly abandoned, so we stayed a little longer to pick up some supplies. The Russians landed soon after, killed my whole crew except for Sandy and me."

"I've been scouting around, and I know where they're keeping the prisoners." Zach nodded at the gun. "Are you going to shoot me or what?"

Scotty shook his head and lowered the weapon. "Nah, we've got Russians to deal with now. I think we can put aside our differences for a while." He laughed snidely. "I can't believe we ended up together again."

"Yeah, some luck."

"How did we even get past you?"

"We stopped to help some folks along the way, and you probably passed us at some point."

Russians shouted close by, and Zach grabbed his rifle and stayed low until the voices faded and the soldiers moved off.

"I've been trying to get closer, but it's just no good."

"Doesn't help that we can't see much from here." Scotty lowered himself into the gully and squatted with one leg extended, rifle in his lap. "Yeah, things are looking pretty grim. But just to be clear, I don't have a beef with you anymore, man. It was rough for Sandy and me after you ditched us at Deadhorse. I guess I sort of lost my mind a bit. I should've just given you the damn radio."

"I guess we got started off on the wrong foot."

"Yeah, sorry about that. Everything sort of clicked for me when I realized the Russians were standing on my home soil." Scotty grimaced and clenched his fist. "Guess I did some pretty bad things to get here."

"I had to make some pretty tough decisions myself. It hasn't been easy for any of us." Zach jerked his head to the northwest. "Do you know who the Russians are fighting out there?"

"I stumbled on some CAF bodies earlier. The fighting was pretty intense at first but seems to have leveled off. I escaped while they were trying to relocate us, barely made it to the woods and hid here." His grim expression was readable in the dark. "I'm not leaving without her."

"You have any sort of plan?"

"Well, I would have except for this..." He used the flashlight to show Zach his left leg, the pants cut away, a thick bloody bandage wrapped around his knee and calf. "Got shot."

The light winked out again, leaving Zach's eyes confused as they tried to adjust. "Well, that limits our options. Guess, I'll be going it alone on this one."

Scotty grinned wide. "The Russians have everything locked down over here, and the CAF hasn't made any progress in two days. Dead soldiers ain't the only thing I stumbled on out there." He nodded toward a long, dark shape at the bottom of the gully.

Zach crouched and crawled to the crate, running his hand across the edge and opening the top. He took out his flashlight and flicked it on to get a snapshot of several grenades and a long shoulder launcher packed neatly inside. "That's a Javelin missile launcher. What's it doing in Canadian hands?"

Scotty shrugged. "Who cares? US forces have been showing up more and more, bringing supplies and heavy armor. This might've been one of those drops. We can use it to break our people out. Now that you're here, I don't have to be the big hero."

"Lucky me."

"What's that mean?"

"I don't know... something that happened a long time ago..." He stared toward the Russian encampment. "Hostage situation gone wrong back when I worked for the NYPD."

Scotty turned from where he was counting the grenades. "What happened?"

"We had the hostage takers dead to rights, but we delayed too long and ended up getting almost all the hostages killed before we could stop them."

"How many?"

"Fourteen. Fourteen people died."

"Oh, man. I'm sorry. Really, I am. You followed orders to the letter?"

"Yeah."

"Then it's not your fault. You have to know that."

"It's my fault for *not* going with my gut. All those people died because we didn't take action. They needed a hero that day, and we... we screwed up."

"If you don't want to go, we can find another way."

A shudder of weakness passed through him, but he locked his jaw tight. "No, this time it's different."

"How do you know?"

"There are no safety ambassadors or red tape to screw me up."

"Safety ambassadors?" Scotty scratched his head. "What's a safety ambassador?"

"They were supposed to monitor, observe, and report public safety conditions during hostage situations and standoffs. Mostly, they just got in the way. To us officers, they were an unnecessary, just another piece of bureaucracy created by people who never understood how criminals think or operate."

"Was one there at the hostage situation you were involved in?"

"We were ordered to wait for them, but they never showed up. The delay... my *hesitation*, caused people to die."

Scotty shook his head. "Well, I'm no safety ambassador. Let's tear them up."

"I wish I would've paid attention and learned some Russian from Eliza or Grizzly." Zach had partially climbed out of the ditch, peering over the brush and deadfall to check for guards. Vehicles drove the side lanes and service roads, headlamps off, and shadow shapes strode between the buildings. "I could've used one of those Russian uniforms to fake my way through."

"Are you kidding me?" Scotty laughed as he sorted the crate's contents, setting grenades on the edge of the ditch and counting them. "You'd never find anything in your size."

"Probably right."

"You about ready to go?"

"Yeah, let's go over it one more time. I'll circle back around to the lot and get in around the cars. I'll toss a grenade to signal you. You launch the Javelin at the west side of the camp and take something out. The soldiers should be drawn that way, and I'll have a shot at the prisoner building. After I get them out, we'll rendezvous at the ice cream parlor. Second rendezvous point is the bridge."

Scotty nodded, hefted the Javelin missile, and placed it with the other equipment.

"Do you know how to shoot that thing?"

"Had a brief stint in the military before I started trucking, so I have some basic weapons skills. They make these things so grandmothers in Western European nations can fire them. I think I can handle it."

"Great. I didn't know you were former military."

"Too bad we don't have time for a couple of beers."

Zach laughed. "We'll save the beers for later. For now, let's make this happen before morning. How about a grenade?"

Scotty handed one over. "You know how those work?"

"Pull the pin and throw?"

"Hold the grenade in your throwing hand with the clip covered.

Pull the pin with your off hand, draw back, and throw. You'll have a few seconds to duck before it goes off."

"Sounds easy enough."

"Just be careful and don't blow your arm off."

"If this thing goes off in my hand, my arm will be the least of my problems." Zach lowered himself. "Will you be able to fire the Javelin and get to the rendezvous point with your leg like that?"

"I can walk well enough, and I've got a stick I've been using as a crutch." Scotty's expression hardened. "I'll evade the Russians well enough. Give me fifteen or twenty minutes to get there."

"That's a long time. They'll be crawling all over the place. I was thinking ten minutes, tops."

Scotty shook his head. "They'll think it's a CAF attack from the east and head in my direction. I'll already be gone and circling to the south right behind you. Hell, I might even beat you there."

"Challenge accepted."

Scotty reached out. "Good luck, man."

Zach gave him a firm handshake. "You, too. Shoot straight."

With his pack strapped on and his rifle in hand, Zach hugged the side of the gully and edged up over the log. Russians moved through the camp, headlamps flickering in the motor pool and blinking off again, the spotlights still scanning the woods in big sweeps. The prisoner building was almost dead ahead and to his left, the long shape barely visible in the shifting shadows. His friends were waiting for him to break them out, but he couldn't move, staying rooted in the soft earth and dead leaves, head shaking, eyes glassy as his knife wound slowly leaked.

"Are you okay?" Scotty asked.

"Yeah, I'm good…" Zach crawled from the gully, climbed from the ditch, and slipped into the woods toward the south side of camp.

Senses buzzing, adrenaline pumping steadily through his limbs, Zach made good progress through the dense foliage and tricky terrain, avoiding the guards up on the service road and the ones creeping on the lower slope. Before he knew it, he was back on the northeast side of camp, at the edge of the woods, scanning the motor pool. A few vehicles had moved since the last time he was there, though their Humvee remained in the same spot in the center row. The faint sounds of generators graced his ears, lights popping on sporadically throughout the camp and snapping off again.

He ducked as the spotlight swept by and moved off, then sprinted across the service road, barely making a sound as he reached the rear of a sedan with its trunk open and a few crates of military supplies packed in the back. Rising to see through the windows, Zach spotted more cars with their trunks raised, a few soldiers filling them with goods, slamming them shut, and moving to the next. Footsteps crunched near the front of the sedan. He guessed which direction to go, rolling around to the driver's side and crouch-walking to the front as the Russians reached his previous position and threw more gear into the trunk. Zach cut back to the left, away from the other vehicles he'd seen being loaded, slipping past bullet-ridden fenders, crunching on broken glass and gravel, the scents of leaking fuel and antifreeze wafting under his nose.

Soon, he'd passed their Humvee and was working his way toward the sheds on the west side of the lot. The larger prisoner building was just past those with soft light seeping from the windows and door cracks. Zach was about to creep that way, but a patrol turned him around and forced him to head south and east again with a string of quiet curses. There was no way he'd get closer without the distraction. Finding a pickup truck with fat wheels and a raised suspension, he stopped next to the passenger side door and felt inside his coat for his grenade. He quickly went over the plan in his head; pull the pin, throw it as far as he could, and dive beneath the vehicle until the Russians cleared. By then, Scotty would've fired the Javelin missile to draw the soldiers even farther away, giving him the time he needed to break toward the prisoner building.

Grenade in hand, he put his thumb in the pin ring and started to pull when a Russian came around the front of the vehicle, stopped cold, frozen for a split second before realizing Zach wasn't a comrade. He raised this rifle, screaming at the top of his lungs in Russian, jamming his gun barrel at him with a clear message.

"Okay, man! Whoa!" Zach kept his voice steady to keep the

Russian from pulling the trigger, slowly taking his thumb off the grenade pin and lowering it to the ground.

The Russian was shouting, calling over his shoulder to alert his comrades. Zach stared at the weapon with dread, the AK-74 jabbing at him, the soldier's finger inside the trigger guard as he scowled and screamed. Heart pounding in his chest, Zach caught flashes of Wendy and the kids. Charlie and David taking after him in their own ways. The intense struggles he'd faced trying to get out of the north, the small victories and frozen miles, sunken by the jutting barrel and spittle flying from the Russian's lips.

Something glinted in the night air, a glimmer of green-gold captured in the residual spotlight beams and the shed lights. A gust of sparkling wind swept over them, and Zach caught the foul scent of old oil, a greasy odor that swirled around his head, forcing him to avert his face, remembering the herd of dead moose and the wolves feeding on them, the groups of suffocated people they'd found on the roadsides. The soldier sniffed and snorted, confused as he caught the same corrosive reek. The smell got suddenly worse, and he snapped his head as it stung his nose.

Hydrocarbon bursts rolled over them, flattening, curling, corkscrewing through the air, drifting into the spotlight beam and rippling with strange colors. It was fairy dust, incandescent and glowing, growing thicker by the second until the Russian finally stopped hollering and began to choke. He grabbed his throat with one hand, gasping, neck tendons straining in agony. His tongue jutted out, and he made a smacking sound as if trying to clear peanut butter from the roof of his mouth. Gagging and spitting, he fell to one knee, the AK-74 dropping as he clenched his neck with both hands. Zach rose from his kneeling position and planted the heel of his boot in the Russian's chest, launching him through the air and dumping him on his backside where he writhed on the ground. Zach grabbed the air filtration mask off his belt, slipped it over his face, and exhaled to clear the air. His first breath was fresh enough, and every subsequent one came easier as he leaned against the truck and listened to the world fly to pieces.

Soldiers screamed and gagged. An order was shouted but died

with a throaty bellow. Shadows stumbled in the darkness, fell to their knees, and tore at their faces as they inhaled the hydrocarbon poison. Some Russians kept calm, shedding their backpacks and rifling inside for air filtration masks. They fumbled and stretched the tangled straps to get them in place, one soldier falling over dead before he could get his on. Others were recovering, breathing, leaning forward on their hands and knees with foam dripping from their chins. Zach stooped and picked up the grenade, prepared to tug the pin free. A hiss of sound zipped overhead, followed by smoke and a flaming streak from the northeast. The Javelin shot through the center of camp, sending Russians diving out of the way before it struck a building and blossomed in an explosive flash that rocked the ground. Debris blasted skyward, chunks corkscrewing and arcing through the sky a hundred yards in every direction with pebble-sized pieces spraying the vehicles with sharp pings. A second detonation shook the air, a ball of light and heat that tore up even more hunks, streaks of flames riding hydrocarbon drifts, capturing Russians and scattering them with their arms waving, heads on fire as hot bits of buildings rained down.

"Damn it. Too soon, Scotty!"

Zach pulled the grenade pin and reached back, hurling it high and far and hoping he could drop it near the center of camp and take out a couple of Russian officers. The projectile disappeared into the darkness, and Zach didn't wait to see where it landed. Gun gripped tightly against his chest, he ran to the first guard shed, slipped around it, and found the long prisoner building just forty yards away. The patrols were shattered, soldiers running everywhere but regrouping, rallying, helping their comrades, dragging them up by the arms, and rushing to the north side of camp.

With the way clear, Zach put his head down and ran, hoping he wasn't too late to keep his friends from suffocating on the poisonous fumes. Gunfire rattled off on the north side of camp, but no bullets flew his way as he crossed the forty yards and put his shoulder against the back wall, quick-stepping to the rear corner. He rounded it, creeping along the side, suddenly freezing and ducking when boots pounded on the gravel and two long shadows swept up.

Zach raised his gun to fire, but the soldiers didn't see him and sprinted by.

With a relieved sigh, Zach slipped around to the porch, glancing through a window on his way. Two rows of prisoners faced each other along the walls, sitting with their hands tied behind them. A guard stood in the middle of the row, fitting air filtration masks over their heads. Zach moved to the door, shoulder against it, stepping back and launching forward, slamming it open with a crack and splinter of wood. The guard was putting the last mask on a prisoner, strapping it over his head as Zach broke in. A dozen faces turned his way at once; CAF soldiers, civilians, and his friends. Craig was two seats from the guard, eyes wide and flicking at something off to Zach's left.

Zach started to turn, but it was too late, and a second guard tackled him from behind, knocking his weapon from his hands. He twisted, grabbed the soldier by the jacket in a two-fisted grip, and swung him down the aisle where he banged the prisoners' knees, staggered, and slammed into the first guard before dropping to the floor. Zach ran over him, left forearm out to ram the other Russian, hitting him full on, driving him to the rear of the building where they hit with a thud that shook the walls. Zach grabbed his coat and twisted at the hip, hurling him to the floor where he hit with a vicious crunch and cracked his head against the wooden slats. Kneeling over him, Zach drew his pistol, but the door swung open, the frame filled with two more Russian soldiers who spread to either side with their weapons leveled at him. Between them stepped a big officer with markings on his chest and shoulder, his steely blue eyes glaring from beneath short-cropped black hair. The officer snarled something in Russian, voice muffled from the old-style gas mask he wore. With the guns on him, Zach froze over the panting guard, tensing to make a move. The officer shouted over his shoulder, and Liza stepped around him, wearing an air filtration mask and a Russian military coat. Recognition flashed in her eyes before they turned flat again.

She spoke in heavily accented English. "If you shoot that man, you will die. Put the weapon down."

The officer snarled again, jabbing his finger hard at Zach.

"He says for you to put your weapon down and give up," Liza translated. "He says for you not to be a fool."

The faces of his friends stared back at him in a mix of admiration and fear. Gina sat near Grizzly on his right, shaking her head slowly, pleading to him with her eyes. Zach took his finger off the trigger, letting the gun dangle.

"Okay," he said. "I'm done."

Liza briefly translated, and the officer nodded. The soldier he'd bowled over kicked him off, stood, and snatched up a rifle, panting hard, eyes filled with hot scorn. He grabbed Zach's pistol and stuffed it into his waistline, then drew back his rifle with a furious glare. Zach winced and turned away as the butt of the weapon rushed toward him in swift retribution.

CHAPTER THIRTEEN

Wendy Christensen, Pearisburg, Virginia

"You're going to have to kill him." Darla was sitting across from Wendy with her crutch leaning against the table.

She'd pulled her dark red hair back and pinned it behind her head, and while her cheeks were still pale, some color had returned along with a fierce spark in her eyes. Darla hadn't mentioned Melissa since Wendy had broken the bad news to her, though her eyes held a haunted look where the burden weighed heavy. Water steamed from a kettle on a camping stove on the counter, and the scent of instant coffee filled the room. They'd turned on a second electric lantern to bring a gentle warmth to the space, driving away the cold rain that pounded the house relentlessly, creaks and moans shivering through the walls every time a hard gust blew.

Wendy faced Darla across the table, their steaming cups and a lantern between them. "Why don't we talk about getting some electricity in here first? We know you've got a furnace and a generator. It would be nice to cook off the stove for once. Not to mention this chill..." She shivered in her blue hoodie. "Let's get some heat in here, huh?"

Darla leaned in, her hands still a little shaky, bone-thin finger pressing on the table. "We'll get to that soon enough. You've got to take care of him first."

"Are you serious?" Charlie asked where she sat on Wendy's left. Her golden hair spilled over the thermal underwear top she had on, her hands tucked into the sleeves as she gripped her coffee cup. "He doesn't seem like a bad guy, and he apologized for breaking in."

Darla scoffed and took a long, audible sip of her coffee. "You don't know anything about Matt Stegmann or who he associates with. If you did, you'd rethink that." She gestured to the big bandage around her left arm. "Unless you want to end up with one of these, or worse."

"You act like *he* did something to you," David said from where he sat across from Charlie, still dressed in layers but holding off on his guard shift until they finished discussing the prisoner.

"Not directly, no," Darla admitted, "but he means no good being here all the same."

"He didn't come here armed," Wendy said. "That tells me right there he was probably telling the truth."

Darla blew a long, doubtful gust of air. "You folks don't know what you're dealing with. I've lived here my whole life, and I know this town very well. It had a corrupt underbelly even before everything went to hell."

"Well, I'm not going to kill a man in cold blood." Wendy replied flatly and took another sip.

"What are you going to do? Watch him day and night? There's already enough to do, watching the road and keeping up on things here. Took all three of you to patch the roof, didn't it?"

"You're welcome for that," Wendy replied, though she saw the truth in Darla's words. They had plenty to do and were already bone weary. There were the horses to take care of and scavenging runs to make if they wanted to survive long-term. The thought of watching a prisoner day and night exhausted her. "I'm thinking about letting him go. He didn't do anything to us, and if he's got any beef, I guess it's with you."

135

Darla scoffed with disdain. "You let him go unarmed now, you'll see him later with the gun in his hand and pointed right back at you."

"Why don't *you* kill him?" Charlie said. "If you think it's so easy, do it."

Darla stared at Charlie a second before setting her coffee cup down and reaching across to grab Charlie's Ruger where it sat in front of her on the table. She rose and took her crutch, thrusting herself to a standing position with her shaking arm and kicking the chair back. Grunting and hobbling, she got around Charlie and moved toward the laundry room door faster than they expected. Wendy was out of her seat just as quickly, rushing over and taking her firmly by the arm.

"Wait a second," she hissed, conscious that Matt could likely hear them through the door. "Sit down and let's talk about this."

Darla stood there shaking, her jaw clenched tight, eyes hard as diamonds. Her toughness faltered, and Wendy seized the pistol from the top and ripped it from her hand, squeezing her arm and drawing her away from the door.

"Let's just... talk through this." Wendy repeated, an order more than a request, and Darla slumped and allowed herself to be led away.

Charlie had watched the exchange with an anxious expression, but David had come halfway out of his seat, Springfield in his hand. As Wendy guided Darla back to the table, she gave him a head shake, and he sat but left the gun next to his coffee cup.

"Thank you." Wendy sat Darla before giving the Ruger to Charlie. "Holster that, please."

"Yes, ma'am."

Wendy swung around and sat, staring at Darla intently as she sipped her coffee. "What's this all about? Why are you so hell-bent on taking this man's life?"

Darla self-consciously pushed a strand of hair behind her ear. "All right, I'll tell you why I don't like Matt Stegmann and the man he works for, Oliver McCallum. I don't imagine you know that name."

"Doesn't ring a bell. We're from Stamford, Connecticut."

Darla scoffed. "North Easterners, huh? How did you end up down here?"

"You first."

"All right then. You don't know this, but I had a husband named Ron, and he ran a construction company with a couple of other guys in the area."

"Is he the guy with all the cool RC cars and stuff?" David asked.

"One and the same. He loved that stuff... built all kinds of different ones. Maintained them and fixed them for free. It was a big hobby of his."

"It's super cool," David said. "I've been playing with a few of them, if that's okay."

"I reckon it won't hurt anything," she replied with a half-smile. "Anyway, everyone knows everyone in this town, and your livelihood depends on your reputation. It's important to keep it clean, work hard, and be honest."

"I understand that," Wendy said. "My dad owned a construction company. I did the paperwork and set up jobs with contractors."

Darla gave an admiring nod. "Well, Ron contracted about a half a million dollars worth of work for Oliver McCallum up on the hill past where the Amish folks live. Some big fancy place."

"And who is this Oliver McCallum?" Charlie asked.

"He's a big wig investor around here. His family owns a few businesses and are respected by the community, if begrudgingly."

"Why begrudgingly?"

"The McCallums weren't always on the up and up."

"You just said people's reputation depended on them being straight up."

"While McCallum was a sketchy character — the whole family was — they gave back quite a bit to the community and had a lot of friends. They took care of people, depending on how well you played along. Well, Ron was in McCallum's good graces for years and had no reason to doubt any business dealings with him." Darla paused to sip her coffee. "That's why he volunteered to pick up the supplies and do the work without upfront payment. But at the last second, McCallum pulled out of the deal to move his investment money elsewhere. Of course, that pissed Ron off... we were stuck with this house

Ron had just remodeled, and he'd dipped deep into his credit lines to get the materials he needed."

"I know how some of these deals go," Wendy said. "My dad always asked for at least half upfront, no matter what."

"I told him that," Darla waved her hand, "but he insisted McCallum was good for it. Anyway, Oliver didn't seem too worried about it, saying we could sell the house at a profit, but the housing market wasn't so good at the time."

"You lost money on it?"

"We were stuck with the house. Lost a hundred thousand dollars and a lot of other work we could have been doing."

"Did you sue him?"

"We tried to, but McCallum owns most of the town, and he's been a big dog around here for a while. You know how it goes... a lot of buddies washing each other's backs."

"I've heard of that," Wendy nodded. "Never seen it played out in such a way, but I believe it."

"So, after about five years caught up in legal battles, draining most of our savings, Ron finally gave up, and we focused on getting back on our feet. We recovered and were doing all right. A lot of people sympathized with Ron and gave him more work than he could handle, allowing us to expand our crew to a dozen people."

"Small blessings," Wendy said.

"Praise God. I, for one, was glad Ron had quit fighting that uphill battle."

Charlie had gotten up and brought the jar of instant coffee and the kettle of hot water over, waiting for Darla to give herself a scoop before pouring the water in.

"Thank you, young lady."

"You're welcome."

"Things went fine for a while until McCallum finally bucked up the courage to run for mayor. I didn't see it at first, but I soon realized Ron was using it as an opportunity to get McCallum back. Started as little things like taking down his posters and elevating the shit-talking around town, then it escalated to ripping signs out of other people's yards. I put my foot down and told Ron that if you want to get McCallum back, he should make it official and join the opposition. He took my advice and joined the other side, doing email campaigns and knocking on doors for the other party. I thought things would be settled again, but that's when the real war began. They went back and forth for a while, mainly over social media and stuff like that."

Wendy snorted dryly. "You'd think they could sort it out over a beer."

"As far as I know, they never talked face to face again. Ron was all about social media and had a bunch of burner accounts he used to troll McCallum. By then, I'd had enough of it and was trying to get on with life, taking care of the house and our fields out back."

Wendy's question about Darla having crops was answered. "That sounds like the sensible thing to do."

"It was. Then Ron got sick. Wasn't long before he passed away, probably the worst year of my life... and now Melissa." Her head sunk, and she gripped the coffee cup as if her life depended on it.

"I'm so sorry to hear that," Wendy said, surprised at her own quivering voice. "And I'm sorry about Melissa, too. I couldn't imagine losing my husband."

"You're not with him now," Darla replied, her tone heavy with sadness or regret. "It's kind of like that, but forever."

"He's stuck somewhere else, but he's coming home."

Darla started to say something but left it alone.

"That really stinks, Mrs. Goodhew," Charlie said. "I'm sorry for your losses. It must be incredibly hard."

"I appreciate that," she replied with a reluctant smile. "I'm sure it's tough for all of you, too. Where *is* your daddy?"

"He was in Alaska working on the oil rigs when they blew up," Charlie answered. "I know people died up there, but Dad called us from Fairbanks, so we know he made it that far. Now he's on his way home..." Charlie stared at the table.

"I'd seen the news about the rig explosions. Terrible. Good to know your father made it out okay. How do you expect he'll find you down here? Pearisburg is a long way from Stamford."

"We've got family down here." Wendy squeezed her coffee cup.

"Zach knows roughly where we are. Unfortunately, we had a falling out with our people and couldn't stay there permanently. But Zach will know how to find us when he gets here. So, tell us how you ended up getting shot up."

"After the rigs blew up and the weather went nuts, I saw the writing on the wall." Darla scoffed knowingly. "Ron and I had always been part-time homesteaders and had some supplies down in the basement and the pantry."

"We saw those," Wendy nodded.

"But in the year Ron was sick, we slacked off and ran through them pretty quick. My sister was living with us by then, figuring we could stick together and get through it. She's been divorced for years..." Darla shook her head and rubbed one eye. "Anyway, we got in the truck and went into town just as things worsened and the storms were picking up. There was a stillness about things, and all the smiles I was used to seeing were gone. The usual places we got goods locally were shut down, and a farmer we used to get eggs from didn't have any, but there were no police or authorities taking control. Turned out Oliver McCallum had been around gathering supplies, convincing people he was doing it for the good of the town, hoarding and stocking warehouses around the department store and promising to protect our things in the name of law and order. You know, for the sake of the town?"

"Yeah, I think I know where this is going," Wendy replied.

"Melissa and I could smell bullshit a mile away, so we drove into town to see what was happening. True enough, McCallum and a bunch of his men—a small army—had taken over the industrial park on the east side of town. They had a lot of supplies, fresh crops they'd pulled up quickly, took over farms, and hoarding all the cold weather gear people needed to survive." A sudden tear flew down Darla's cheek, but she swiped it away. "I've never seen anything like it. Two thousand people lined up in front of the department store as McCallum's people wrote down what they needed and gave out only a portion. The kids from the apartment complex got coats and ponchos, their families given boxes of food and other supplies. It seemed fair enough until they shut the doors, claiming they needed to ration. Melissa and I had just come from around back, and we'd seen what they were doing. Some of McCallum's people were divvying things up amongst themselves. It seemed like a little thing, but some of them dug in deep, hauling stuff away in trucks. That's when Melissa and I stepped in."

"You caused some trouble," Charlie whispered.

"Darn right, we did," Darla smirked. "We went around front and raised hell to the townsfolk in line. They turned against McCallum's people, started pushing and shoving. One of the locals got the guards to give up the store. It looked like we'd get some fair distribution of goods when McCallum regrouped and sent some men back to the store with guns and weapons. People got knocked around, and fistfights broke out. He tried to grab me and Melissa. When we resisted, one of McCallum's men pulled a gun on me. That rubbed some locals the wrong way, and before we knew it, shots were fired. We tried to stop it, but someone fired at us, too, so I grabbed my sister and ran."

"Sounds like you got some people killed," David said flatly.

Darla turned her hot stare on him. "We were trying to help people, son. People deserved to know what McCallum was *really* doing. I'm sorry people got shot, but I'm not sorry McCallum got found out." Her expression softened. "His men started shooting at us as we were pulling out. I made it home, but not Melissa." Darla's face twisted up, miserable and ugly in the soft kitchen light, tears streaming, sorrow and fear reflected in her eyes.

Charlie started to get up but settled back.

"This McCallum guy has all the power in town?" Wendy asked. "He just owns a construction company. How can he command all these people?"

"He's a convincing character," Darla sniffed. "He had real estate and dealings all through Blacksburg and Christiansburg and a lot of the small towns around here. Most people know not to mess with him, but it's elevated to another level now. When the police went off to handle some flooding situations with the county and never returned, I guess McCallum figured he could do whatever he wanted."

Wendy glanced toward the laundry room. "You think he sent Matt Stegmanm up here, don't you?"

"Yeah, it probably freaked him out when his men followed me back here and got shot up by you guys. Sent Matt to see who he was dealing with. That's why you don't want to let him go. He knows how many of us are here. One skinny boy and three women, one of whom is injured. Maybe he'll be too busy with other things for a while..."

Darla shrugged. "It's a matter of time before he comes to deal with us. And after he cleans us out, he'll install his people here and take the horses and all the feed."

"How many will he send?" David asked.

"Who knows? He had a hundred people or more last time I checked. The only thing that might slow him down are the Amish up on the hill."

"What about the Amish?" Charlie asked.

"He doesn't get along well with them, either. Been wanting their land forever. Tried to rezone big parts of it a dozen times or more, and I heard through the grapevine about all the legal cases they were fighting in town. The Amish were the only people who could stand up to him, but he'll take them out for sure now... by force."

"How could anyone do that?" Charlie asked emphatically. "It just sounds... *evil*."

"Evil runs deep in certain men, and McCallum is like that." Darla fixed Wendy with a pointed stare. "Now you know why I feel the way I do about Matt. I'm not strong enough to force you to leave... and I owe you for getting me inside and keeping me alive, fair enough. But going light on Matt will get us all killed. If you won't do what needs to be done, then this would be your chance to get out of here while you can. Just go and leave me alone. I'll spend my last days in this house, and I'll take out a few of those bastards with me before I die."

Wendy scoffed. "We're *here*, Darla, and we're not leaving. At least not until my husband comes. Besides, you're in no position to take care of yourself. You're shot up and lost a lot of blood. We'll need to shore up our supplies and keep a steady guard rotation going. I wouldn't expect you to jump in right away, but if there's something you can do in the meantime, I'd imagine you'd be willing to do it."

Darla looked over them skeptically. "Have it your way, but don't tell me I didn't warn you about Matt. Best you get out of my way and let me end him if you're not serious about defending this property."

"We *are* serious," Charlie whispered determinedly. "Can't you see that?"

"We already set up a guard schedule," Wendy said, "and we have weapons and ammunition to protect this place. You've got a solid house, a generator, and enough food to get us by for a while. But we can do more than that. We can start gathering any crops that haven't rotted and scavenge some empty homes around here. If you've got land out back, we'll plant and work it. It's something we can carry forward as long as we need to. When my husband gets here, he'll help work it, too."

Darla shook her head and grinned sadly. "By then, Matt will have squirmed out of here, or you'll have let him go, and we'll be dead."

"You say we're not serious," David rested his hand on his Springfield, "but we've defended ourselves already. Shot people when we had to. The people who tried to kill us back in Stamford failed because we stood up for ourselves. This McCallum guy might be tough, but we're not afraid."

"Well, Matt Stegman won't be the only one he'll send. There'll be more, and we need to treat them like murderers at our doorstep."

"Should we just shoot him in the head or something?" Charlie spread her hands on the table helplessly.

"I don't see how killing an innocent man will help the situation," Wendy agreed.

"I'm with Darla on this one," David said with a head shake. "It stinks, but it's no worse than what we've already had to do. Look, they'll get to us if we don't get to them first."

"There's only one answer here," Darla said. "One solution."

"No, I'm not convinced we need to kill the guy. We'll keep him here, tied up for now. Yes, Darla, we *will*. Before we do anything else, we need to get some things working around here, like the electric."

"And we want you to teach us how to ride the horses," Charlie grinned.

The mention of the horses brought out a faint hint of a smile in Darla. "So you've met the family pets, huh?"

"Yeah. They're beautiful. Darwin is such a ditz."

Darla's smile widened. "We named him that because he was an awkward colt. Ron always said he'd win the Darwin award, and the name stuck."

Wendy chuckled. "We've been taking good care of them with feed and water, and Charlie figured if worst came to worst, we could take them out into the fields and let them graze. There is certainly no lack of water. You've practically got a lake in your backyard. Now, let's get some electricity on."

Darla leaned back and sighed. "Okay."

"Ron suggested putting in that monster of a generator a few years ago," Darla said. "I would've been happy with something much smaller. Guess I can't complain now."

"Something kicks on every now and again." David gestured to the basement door. "There's a strange vibration that runs through the house about the same time. What's that?"

"What you're hearing is the pump and purification system. See, we're running off an underwater well down inside the hillside, and a lot of folks are pulling off it, too. Or at least, they were. Anyway, that's why you been getting water pressure but nothing else. That was the one thing Ron set to automatically fail over should the power go down."

"That explains it," Wendy nodded.

"You'd of been right. Now, it's time to manually switch some of the other stuff." Darla grabbed her cane and started to get up, but her arm was shaky, and she immediately slid back into her seat with a soft curse. "Dammit. I can't do it. I'm going to need one of you."

"David," Wendy said.

"Which ones?" David asked, standing and leaning over a notebook with a pen in his hand.

"What you want to do is go down to the breaker panel, switch the main controller from breaker one to breaker two, then flip off switches one, three, and five. That should give us all the power we need for now."

David nodded and tossed the pen down before heading for the basement door.

"Won't the generator be noisy?" Charlie asked. "I mean, Matt found us, so couldn't others?"

"The generator is less noisy than the storm, but I guess we'll deal with it. You want hot showers, don't you?"

"A hot shower would be amazing right now." Charlie leaned forward with her hands clenched as if begging for relief. "I feel like I have ten layers of sludge on me."

"We do need to think about hygiene," Wendy agreed. "I can't remember when any of us took a hot shower. And that reminds me, I need to check my shoulder wound, too."

"I almost forgot. Sorry. Does it hurt?"

"It's still sore, but not like it's infected or anything."

"What kind of wound?" Darla asked, seeming curious about someone else's welfare for the first time.

"Gunshot." Wendy went on to explain what had happened back in Stamford during their last few days there. Charlie, Lionell, and Ms. Cheney, all turning on Wendy's family and attacking them in the end. For the first time, she took pleasure recalling how they'd stayed smart about the weather and avoided the flash freezing. And there was the final battle with the teachers and how Morten and his sons and daughter had swooped in to drive them away. By that time, the lights came on, dimmed, and then went out.

"That's normal," Darla explained. "I had him turn off the switches for the lights, but the refrigerator and stove should be fine."

Wendy got up and opened the refrigerator excitedly, having forgotten about the rotten food they'd found inside, getting hit square in the face with a stench and reeling backwards.

"Oh, geez. That's terrible." She pointed to Charlie. "The first thing we're going to do before you go on shift is get some garbage bags and clean this refrigerator out. We'll find other things to put inside." Wendy moved to the stove, turned the burner on, and watched as the flattop began to glow. "Oh, darling. This is wonderful. We need to cook something right away. A real good, home-cooked meal."

Darla smiled faintly. "It'll take a little time for the water heater to warm up, but after about an hour or so, we can start to take some showers. Doesn't mean we can take them every day, but maybe every third day, and we'll turn the temperature down in between."

David's thundering footsteps came up the stairs, and he burst into the room. "Did it work?"

"It sure did." Wendy gestured to the stove but turned off the burner. "We'll have hot water soon and some home-cooked food."

"That's awesome."

"One more thing. I got about a hundred gallons worth of gas in a transfer tank near the generator. You'll need to go around somewhere and scavenge some fuel."

"You mean suck it out?" Charlie asked.

"Siphon is the word. If you don't know how to do it, I'll show you. I've got some five-gallon jerrycans we can attach to the horses, then we can have you kids go fetch it for us on a regular basis."

Charlie clapped and then sobered with a glance at Wendy. "We don't know how to ride, Darla. Could you teach us?"

"Do I have a choice?"

"You *do* have a choice," Wendy replied, feeling like she was talking to a brick wall. "We're here because we have to be... there's nowhere else for us to go. And *you* need our help. So, while you might not like some of our decisions, it would benefit us to work together." When Darla didn't respond either way, Wendy leaned across the table and took her hand. "Look, we're not animals or we wouldn't have bothered saving you. We need each other, and you know it, and we could sit here and argue about every little thing, but let's just agree to get along for now, huh?"

Darla stared at Wendy's hand covering hers and slumped with sudden weariness. "Sure, I'll try to teach you, if that's what you want."

Charlie pumped her fist.

"I'll think about it," Wendy replied pointedly.

"Don't think too long. Pretty soon, that fuels gonna run out, and you'll wish these kids were ready to ride."

"We can do it," Charlie implored Wendy. "We're already doing guard duty, and we can handle guns and —"

"Of course, you can," Wendy covered Charlie's hand with hers. "You may be right on this. We've got horses, and if Darla is willing to teach us, we should learn. Especially as the roads get worse, the pickup truck won't be of much use out there."

"Speaking of pickup trucks," Darla said, stiffening. "You said you took my sister out to the barn?"

"That's right. She's covered up. I thought I'd give you the option of when to bury her"

"She'll be attracting animals and everything else."

"That's what David said." Wendy drew her hand back from Charlie's.

"Told you," David murmured.

Darla sighed with resignation, and her voice softened.. "It's okay. I... I honestly appreciate the thought, but I'd like to see her. I'd like to do it now if you'll help me."

Wendy shared a glance with David. "We'll help you. We will."

"Thank you," Darla said but didn't move.

Wendy gestured to the kids. "Okay, then. Let's get our ponchos."

The rain poured on them as David and Wendy carried Melissa's body from the garage out into the backyard behind the sheds. Charlie helped Darla, holding her shot arm while she shuffled through the slop and mess with the tip of her crutch sinking in the mud. She slipped a handful of times but kept her balance and continued on to the spot she wanted to put her sister to rest. They carried Melissa to a muddy rise and got to work with shovels and hoes. Water filled the hole as they scooped out mud, and soon they stood in a knee-high pool, tossing slop to the side as rain soaked them to the skin. After an hour, Wendy was shivering and aggravated, back aching and toes frozen with cold.

"That's okay," Darla waved. "I figure you got down about three feet. That's enough."

"It's barely rectangular," Wendy said. "Not much of a grave."

"It don't matter," Darla snapped, then her voice softened. "That's fine, thank you."

Wendy and David picked up Melissa by her shoulders and feet, her skin loose and fleshy as the tendons, ligaments, and muscles became detached in the first stages of liquefaction. As gently as they could, they dropped her into the hole, and she sank to the bottom, leaving the plastic sheet floating on top. Wendy stuck the tip of her spade into it and jabbed it down, and David joined her until it went under. In a tired, drab daze, they begin scooping in the mud and rocks, making splashes as water drained past them into the low part of the yard. Soon, the hole was filled with mud, and David and Wendy patted and stomped on it to form an oblong shape. Darla had been standing there through it all but stepped forward, leaning on her crutch with a trembling arm, clutching Charlie in a vice grip.

Darla cleared her throat, lifting her chiseled face, drawn with a mixture of emotions, from resolute to anguished. Finally, she gathered herself and began. "Sissy, I'm going to miss you plain and simple, and there's no two ways about it. We were two peas in a pod since we were kids, and I'll never forget the crazy times we had at the park, getting drunk and singing songs. There are too many times to count, though I will forever miss them. I won't forget how you lived life with grace and humility, and sometimes a middle finger when you needed to. When we were little girls, the world was ours, and we didn't shy away from anything. I only wish we had more time together. I guess the way the world's going, I'll probably be right behind you."

Thunder cracked overhead, lighting up Charlie's face, her chin trembling as she held on to Darla and kept her upright. Wendy bowed her head, unable to imagine what it would be like losing Zach, Morten, or her precious children. Dragging her shovel over, she wrapped her arm around Darla, who stiffened and punched the end of her crutch into the ground.

"I'll miss you, Melissa. You were beautiful inside and out, and you deserved way better than this. I promise if I get the chance — and I ain't saying I will — I'll give McCallum and his men something real hard to think about. Bye for now, until we see each other again in the Lord's arms."

Wendy stood there with tears streaming, eyes burning, wind whipping around her legs and until they were numb. Darla was quiet and still for a long moment before she finally nodded and pushed Charlie toward the house.

"Let's get on inside. You ladies can take a shower while I show David how to work the security cameras."

They went in through the garage door, dripping and muddy, exhausted, past Matt who sat in the laundry room with his hands tied behind his back. A gag kept him from talking, but he followed Wendy with plaintive eyes.

"I'll bring you out some food in a minute," she said. "Just give me a minute to get cleaned up and dry."

He sighed through his nose and nodded, and they took off their shoes and socks and hung their cloaks on hooks above mats to capture the dripping water. In the kitchen, Wendy rolled up their pant legs and shivered.

"Charlie, you're up first," Darla announced as she collapsed into a chair with a soft gasp, slumping and resting her crutch against the table.

"Why don't you go first, Darla?" Wendy asked "It's your house, and you deserve it."

"I need to rest first," she waved. "I couldn't beat a skunk in an alley fight right now."

"I bet you could," David murmured as he took his usual chair and pulled up the PC tablet that had been sitting in the middle of the table. "Want to show me how this works now while Charlie gets cleaned up?"

"Turn it on and I'll give you the password."

Wendy came around and rubbed his shoulders. "Why don't you change into some dry clothes, son?"

"I'm okay. I'm a little soggy, but I want to get these cameras up. Should help us keep an eye on things with a lot less effort."

"Well, okay."

"How do you find the IPs on this thing?" David asked.

"Hell if I know. I can show you how the app works and that's about it. Ron did all that other stuff."

With a thin grin, Wendy got an MRE from a cabinet, tore it open, and placed the barbecue patty into the heating element, adding a little water and shaking it up. She set it aside and poured water and powdered orange mix into a glass and mixed it. There was a cold rice package, a cookie, a piece of soft candy, and crackers to top off the meal. Wendy was starting to understand what Darla meant about watching a prisoner day and night. Every time she removed his bonds to eat or use the restroom, they'd be risking him escaping or attacking them. Not to mention the drain on their supplies. The grim reality settled on her shoulders, an uneasy feeling that something would have to give; either her reluctance to do what needed to be done or throwing caution to the wind and letting him go.

"This is so cool," David said, holding up the tablet. "Mom, there are seven cameras around the property. One on every corner and above each door plus a few out at the barns. They're all coming through clear except... wait, there's a problem with camera number seven. Looks like there's some mud on it or something. I'll go out and clear it later."

"Look at you go, boy." Darla sat back with an admiring smirk. "You work those cameras like you've done this a million times."

David shrugged. "I guess playing a lot of video games helps."

Wendy rolled her eyes. "Finally, the video games pay off."

"I don't know anything about that," Darla stated flatly, "but these cameras are great. You can set them for motion detect, and they even worked pretty good at night. At the very least, we should be able to see people creeping up on the house. Best of all, I can do it sitting right here at the table, which means we just need one person watching the road at all times."

"Actually, I am working on something," David said. "Something with your husband's RC cars and a camera. I've been testing things out, and I think I can mount a network camera on the car and send it down to the road to watch. Maybe we don't even need to be down there at all."

Darla slapped her hand on the table. "Now, that's thinking, son."

"I'm going in to feed Matt now," Wendy told them as she plated his food and got a plastic fork from a cabinet. "I'll need to release his hands so he can eat. Be listening if I need some help."

Darla gave an absent wave as she poured over the tablet with David. While they went on, Wendy took the plate into the laundry room, keeping her pistol hip turned away from Matt. He blinked at her with relief as she put the plate down and removed the gag from his mouth, dropping it around his neck.

He gasped and took a deep breath. "Thanks, lady... uh, *Wendy*. Thank you, thank you. That feels amazing."

"Just so you know, my people are right in the other room, and I've got my gun. If you try to hurt me or escape, it'll just give me a reason to use it on you."

"Yeah, no problem. I'm starving. Is that barbecue?"

Leaving his feet tied, Wendy undid his hands and stepped back, waiting for him to do something stupid. When he only sat in expectation of the plate, she picked it up and set it on his knees. He dove in eagerly, mixing the barbecue with the rice and shoving forkfuls in his mouth.

"Slow down. You act like we didn't just feed you this morning."

"Never know when it'll be my last meal."

"Stop with that." Wendy turned away and stepped toward the door.

"Well, that's what you're going to do, isn't it? Shoot me out back or something? Kill me in cold blood?"

"That's not been decided yet."

"You don't have to do it, you know."

"You didn't have to break into our house."

"Fair enough," Matt talked around his food. "I wish I'd never come here, but the food's a heck of a lot better than what McCallum's feeding us."

"So you admit you work for him?"

"Never denied it."

Wendy squatted and put her back against the wall, took out her Hellcat pistol and held it loosely. "What does he have you doing, this McCallum guy?"

Matt shoveled in barbecue and rice and took a bite of his cookie. "Darla hates McCallum, and they've got some kind of past, but he's not such a bad guy. He's just trying to get control of the town and make sure everyone gets through this."

"Darla said he was hoarding resources. You agree with that?"

He shrugged. "Somebody's got to take charge of things, you know? That's going to be the difference between yesterday and the new world."

Wendy cocked an eyebrow. "What do you mean by that?"

"Like McCallum says, the new world's going to need some leadership, and he's stepping up to do it."

"Darla says he's a cheat and can prove it. He ripped off her husband."

Matt shrugged again. "He said, she said."

Wendy nodded slowly. "Is the food good? Like you said, it might be your last meal."

He stopped eating and gawked at her, then grinned. "You'll come to your senses and let me go." He waved his fork at her. "None of you are killers. Well, maybe Darla, but not you or David, definitely not Charlie."

"We've killed people," Wendy said pointedly. "That should worry you."

"Yeah, because people were trying to kill you. *I* wasn't trying to kill you." He put his fork down, and Wendy handed him his orange drink, which he drank in three gulps.

"But if you go back to McCallum and tell him what we have here, he'll come to take us out. Might as well be trying to kill us."

"I already told you I wouldn't do that." Matt shook his head. "There's a few hundred farms right around here. He's got a lot more to worry about than y'all."

"But eventually."

"What if I told him this house had collapsed, fell in, and wasn't worth a spit? Maybe the barn got washed out, and the horses ran free, and nobody was even living here anymore."

"That would take trust, Matt. And that's not something I can afford to give freely right now."

"Mom?" David stood in the doorway, long arms pressed against the frame. "Are you okay in here?"

"Yeah. Matt?"

"Just let me finish this drink real quick." When he was done, he handed her the plate and cup and nodded toward the garage door. "I've got to go pee."

"All right. David, you ready?"

"Let's do this."

With David holding his Springfield on him, Wendy untied his feet and gestured at the door, careful not to get in between them. The pair went outside along the garage, and David stood behind him as he relieved himself beneath the eaves. Matt dutifully returned to the garage and stepped up to retake his seat in the laundry room where Wendy trussed him up again.

"Please, not the gag," Matt implored her.

Wendy put the gag in place, making sure it was tight before gesturing for David to go back to the kitchen.

Charlie was coming down the hall, fresh out of the shower, her hair up in a towel, steam rolling off her, bare legs sticking out from a long white robe.

"That was amazing," she said. "Thank you so much, Darla. I feel like a new girl."

"I see you borrowed one of my robes."

Charlie stopped and gasped. "Sorry. I grabbed whatever was in the closet. Want me to put it back?"

"No, child. You're fine. Use whatever you want."

Charlie clasped the robe tight around her. "Thank you. This is *so* soft. You've got a good taste in robes."

"If you say so... Wendy, you're up next."

"I don't think so, Darla. It's your house and your shower. Plus, someone needs to go down and watch the road until Charlie's ready."

"I want to take Clyde with me." Clyde raised his head at the mention of his name. "I want to train him to help me on shift."

"Sure, honey." Wendy picked up the PC tablet. "Can you guys watch the cameras while I go down to the road?"

"That's all you, David." Darla rose shakily from her seat. "I'll lie down for a minute while the water heats up. If you need anything, let me know."

"Do you need some help?" Wendy started to go over.

"No, no. I can do it on my own. I trust you folks to keep an eye on things while I get cleaned up." She paused and fell somber. "I'll miss Melissa. She was a great sister and a source of strength for me through the years."

"I've never lost a sibling," Wendy said. "I can't imagine how you feel. And... Darla... we hardly know each other, but if you want to talk, I'll be here."

Darla nodded and hobbled past Charlie to the master bedroom where the door shut with the soft squeal of hinges.

"Is she going to be okay?" Charlie removed her towel and let her wet hair fall around her shoulders.

"I think so." Wendy nodded. "Do any of us have any other choice but to be okay?"

"I guess not."

Wendy kissed Charlie on the forehead, loving the scent of her fresh, clean hair. "I'll tell you what, why don't you take your time and take a little nap. I'll stay down at the road for a while and keep an eye on things."

"Don't you want to shower soon?"

Wendy chuckled and held her cheek. "I will. Right now I'll change into something a little drier before I head down."

Back in one of the side bedrooms Wendy found a pair of jeans, some socks, and undershirts they'd left to dry on the furniture. Everything was days old, dirty, and threadbare in spots, and until they could get the washer and dryer going, she'd alternate between the two stale outfits. From Darla's closet, she took a hoodie with a high school emblem on it, hoping she wouldn't mind. The bedroom had a set of drawers with some old sweaters and T-shirts she'd ask Darla about later. Until then, it was probably best not to take it for granted and start wearing too many of her things. She clipped her pistol on her hip, stuffed an extra magazine of ammunition in her back pocket, and slung her rifle. In the hall, Wendy peeked into the room Darla had been using. The bed was made, the sheets tucked in, and a half-empty glass of water sat next to a box of bandages and folded washcloths on the nightstand.

Back in the kitchen, the kids were sitting around the table with fresh coffee at hand, checking the cameras and talking softly.

"I think Darla wants to move to the master bedroom, so why don't you guys plan on taking the room she was in. You can share the bed, or alternate sleeping on the floor and bed. I'll leave that up to you."

"No problem," David replied.

"Sure thing."

"David, you're on guard duty while Charlie rests." She took one of the two radios off the kitchen table. "Check on Matt every fifteen minutes, okay?"

"You got it."

Wendy stood by the laundry room door for another moment, watching them talk and enjoying their camaraderie. After slipping on her poncho and boots, she walked by Matt without a glance, stepping through the garage and out into the cold with a huge weight on her shoulders and a big decision to make.

CHAPTER FOURTEEN

Oliver McCallum, Pearisburg, Virginia

The small group gathered in the hastily constructed, twenty-by-thirty-foot shed. The rain was constant, and Oliver McCallum was numb to it. It gusted against the walls in rhythmic splatters as the sky panted with windy breaths, making him tap irritably on his knee beneath the table.

His daughter TJ sat to his left, tall and lean with her dark hair pulled back and a couple of strands framing her hawkish face. Roy was in attendance, too, his son, sitting at his right hand and trying to scowl at Teresa Alcott who sat across from him rifling through a stack of papers. Roy was a burly, teddy bear of a man with thick brown hair and a medium-length, neatly trimmed beard.

Teresa pushed a thin dreadlock behind her ear and regarded him with deep brown eyes. "We can't live on this," she said, sliding some papers to McCallum. "A family of five on three cans a day?"

Roy took the sheets and pulled them closer, reading them for a moment before huffing his reply. "Remember, we're rationing. They've got odds and ends to fill out the rest."

"Being rationed to *death*," Teresa shot back.

"It's a community pool," Roy said and leaned in. "That's how it works."

Teresa stiffened and crossed her arms in her gray waterproof jacket. "People ain't going to stay."

"No one's stopping them from leaving." TJ gripped the table and raised one bold, arching eyebrow. "They can go whenever they want."

"Some of them have, but they've returned. It's bad out there, guys. Hundreds of thousands of people running the streets with complete lawlessness. It's my job to make the folks *here* want to stay, which means loosening up on the supplies."

"And in two months, we'll be staring down the barrel of starvation," TJ sneered.

Roy glanced annoyingly at his sister and shifted in his seat. "Teresa, Your job is to keep the people in line. Make them understand the situation and help us help them."

Teresa scoffed. "That's hard to do after they watched some of your guards pull off with a good helping of their supplies. Supplies *they* put into this. They trusted you to distribute things as needed for the betterment of the community."

"And I punished those men myself!"

"A slap on the wrist," Teresa laughed. "They didn't even have to give the stuff back. What a joke."

"Let me see the sheets," McCallum said gruffly and held out his hand.

Roy slid the papers in front of him. Rubbing the scruff on his chin, McCallum reviewed the line items and lifted one page to compare it to their current inventory. We can work something out."

"No, Dad," Roy said. "We can't give them any more —"

"Hush, son," he replied and held up a finger. "I've got this now."

Teresa shifted back to McCallum with a nod. "You better work *something* out, or people might not leave... they might rebel."

"Is that a threat?"

"Not at all. I'm giving you the community's pulse. That's why you assigned me this role."

"Yeah, I know, and you've been doing a good job of it. But this ain't no union, and workers' rights… well, those aren't a thing right now."

"All right, let me approach it another way," Teresa said. "You've got your soldiers out there —"

"They're just guards," McCallum replied simply.

"Okay, guards," Teresa smirked, "out there working to consolidate the farms and neighborhoods around here, hoping to get others still in their homes to contribute. But what about the two thousand homeless people in that parking lot relying on you for food? What happens when they start fighting amongst themselves and stealing from each other? You can't keep the peace if things go south. Your only option is to make people happy and keep them that way."

"I've got a force of over a hundred men and women now," McCallum countered, "able-bodied fighters who are loyal to the cause. They'll guard the supplies tighter, and people who steal will be punished even harder."

Teresa stared at McCallum for a long moment, her jaw working back and forth. "I believe you *want* it to go that way, but actions speak louder than words."

McCallum leveled a lead-gray stare at her and nodded appreciatively. "You know what, Teresa? You're right. People won't respect us if we can't put our money where our mouth is. I thought my reputation would proceed me, but it's clear we're still a little rough around the edges and people are having trouble believing in the process. What do you say we rectify that right now?"

"How?"

"Follow me."

McCallum pushed the papers back to her and stood, gesturing for everyone to follow him outside where winds swept in and blew sideways rain at them. A pair of his guards armed with rifles stood nearby and held their weapons casually.

Surrounding them was a sea of sheds and shacks behind the massive two hundred thousand square-foot Big Bargain department store. The temporary buildings came from a nearby warehouse filled with prefab materials, which McCallum had commandeered for the town's use, driven up and assembled in about a day by all of his men.

A fence encircled the encampment, a combination of chain-link and wooden rails with two gates built in, large enough to drive out the tractors, earth movers, and mini excavators parked against the building. Next to those were five massive fuel tanks, side-by-side, storing diesel, gas, and kerosene. A huge propane tank topped off their energy supplies, and they used that to run the camping stoves and heaters. Along the eastern fence line stood a set of temporary stables filled with horses they'd collected from the farms east of town where McCallum's people roamed with impunity. Pairs of guards patrolled the grounds, and a woman armed with a rifle walked her horse on the ridge line.

McCallum strode past his guards and angled toward a dock area where workers loaded in truckloads of goods. He jogged up a set of stairs where a guard nodded and opened the door for him. Dripping wet, they crossed the warehouse floor where racks of non-essential supplies were being replaced with high-value goods. Forty people worked there, carrying clipboards and wearing hard hats as they stared up into the racks and checked things off. Many waved or nodded at McCallum as he passed into the main department store through a pair of swinging double doors.

The space was massive with white tiles and hanging lights, voices echoing, and a couple of birds who'd gotten in flitting through the rafters. People rearranged shelves and moved boxes of goods with electric pallet jacks, shopping carts, or two-wheeled dollies. Price tags were cut off, and bins and boxes were stacked in neat rows the entire length of the building. McCallum strode briskly between skids of paper towels and toiletries and stepped outside past more guards, finally stopping with his hands on his hips. Two thousand people occupied a sea of tents in Big Bargain's main lot, every conceivable color of vinyl and canvas thrown up and tied to bricks and stones to keep them from blowing away.

They'd pulled in RVs and pickups, tarps strung between them with rope to cover the truck beds in a hodgepodge of creative constructions. An area in the center jutted upward like a tent in a patchwork circus. The parking lot flowed with water, and people had put in drainage pipes and barriers to redirect the streams to the edges or down the main aisles. It was dry enough, but nothing like the homes they used to have. Bedraggled people stopped what they were doing, tired and wary eyes watching him from beneath dripping cowls. Ponchos hung off thinning shoulders, and tattered shoes covered sore feet as they repaired holes in their walls or found better ways to reroute the ever-flowing water.

"These people have nothing left," he told Teresa, who'd stepped up beside him, "and it's up to us to be a point of confidence and light in all this mess."

"I couldn't agree with you more," she replied, "and that's why you should listen when I say —"

"That means we're law and order, too. People don't respect law and order if it has no teeth."

"What's *that* mean?"

"It means the laws aren't being respected." McCallum gestured around the camp. "We must do a better job securing our supplies"

Teresa stared at him as the rain continued to pour.

McCallum looked up and let the rain splash across his cheeks, filling the wrinkles etched into his fifty-two-year-old face. "Now, I want you to follow me up here and watch how we put things in order again."

Without checking to see if anyone was coming, McCallum walked off to his right and up a set of stairs to a flatbed trailer, striding across it and nodding to a guard who handed him a bullhorn. Teresa and Roy came up haltingly while TJ was curious and stood behind them, biting her lip like she'd always done since she was a little girl.

McCallum lifted the bullhorn and pressed the talk button to a squelch of feedback. "Hello, folks! I'd like you to gather around if you don't mind. I have a couple of things I want to say. Come on, now! Don't be shy. I think you're going to like this."

People dropped what they were doing, confused but curious as they filtered up to the front. A few stepped from their tents and came up, and McCallum encouraged them with gestures and a big, convincing smile. "That's right. Come on up. There we go. That's at least a couple hundred of you, and that's enough for what I need to say." He chuckled. "They say news travels quickly in this town, even more so today."

The crowd loosened up, and a few laughed.

McCallum paused and let his eyes roam casually over the group, picking out the faces of people he knew and some he didn't.

"You folks have heard me talk about staying strong in this time of crisis and how we need to stick together and back each other up. We don't want people coming from outside and hurting us or taking what we have until the government figures things out."

"What's the governor say?" someone shouted from the crowd.

"That's a good question," McCallum pointed. "Nothing! We've heard nothing from the Governor's Office or even the county, and our officers were pulled out of town to handle crises in other areas. I guess they knew we were strong enough to make it and didn't need much help."

A few people nodded and crossed their arms proudly.

"But that means we're on our own, and I couldn't tell you if the government even exists anymore. Last radio message we got said the Pentagon was overrun, and the President was hiding in some bunker in a mountain." McCallum waved absently while murmurs of disapproval ran through the crowd.

"That means we're on our own, and we need to start following the rules I stated at the start of this whole thing." McCallum held up two fingers and ticked one down with each point. "One, respect the members of your community. That means don't fight them, steal from them, or cause them any more grief than what they're already going through. Second, take only what you need. That means when we give out something from storage, don't try to take more to trade it or tuck it away somewhere. Remember, these are community goods supplied by you as a tax for living here under our protection. Safety in numbers. Everyone gets to eat. Et cetera, et cetera."

Those who stood proudly nodded in agreement while others held mixed expressions, and McCallum marked them in his mind.

"The rules protect all of us and will see us through this. Soon, we'll have the entire eastern part of town and be moving on Buck

Hill in no time. That opens things up to getting folks re-homed and ready to settle in for a long winter."

More people nodded and filtered up to the front, some still with sacks slung over their shoulders or holding tools they were using to make repairs. McCallum caught a few smiles and knowing grins.

"The last thing we want is infighting to make things harder on ourselves. We've already got the rains and bad weather while those damn Amish sit up on Buck Hill and laugh. Am I right?"

The smiles grew bolder with some scowls sprinkled in for the Amish, nods of affirmation as he drew out the emotions they'd had pent-up inside.

"Now, there's a third rule I didn't mention before, but I should have. I just... I don't know... figured it was an unspoken understanding we had with each other. The third rule is..." He made a sweeping gesture behind him. "You don't steal from the Big Bargain."

The crowd grew hushed as a question lingered in the air.

"That's right, someone did it. Someone stole from the Big Bargain. They stole from me, and they stole from *you*. Now, it's time to set things right. Come on, boys. Bring them on up here."

A pair of hard-looking guards dragged a man and woman around the corner of the building, their hands tied behind their backs with black hoods on. The crowd murmured as the guards pulled them roughly up the stairs and past McCallum where they were forced to their knees and their hoods whipped off to reveal their confused, scared faces. Their clothes were dirty, cheeks pale and brushed with dirt, hair greasy and tangled.

Teresa stepped up behind him. "What are you doing?"

McCallum took on an innocent tone. "Why, they'll be punished for stealing from the Big Bargain." He raised the bullhorn again. "What I told Ms. Alcott here is that these two will be punished for stealing from the Big Bargain. This is Thomas Lansing and his wife, Macy. My guards caught them out in the stables trying to get away with a horse, and they had about a week's supply of food and water with them."

"That was *my* horse," Thomas said in a ragged voice, straining against his bonds. "The horse *I* threw in, thinking you were going to do something good here."

"You mean the *community's* horse," McCallum corrected him pointedly. "One someone else might've needed to travel to get more supplies or help defend our borders."

Teresa grabbed his arm and raised her voice. "You'd punish a couple of half-starving people for stealing when your men have been doing it this entire time?"

"Hold on now, Teresa." McCallum stared at her hand. "I hear what you're saying, and you're right. I'd be a hypocrite if I didn't discipline my own guards. Boys, bring them up."

A second pair of guards dragged two more men around the corner, huskier than the civilians, straining and jerking as they were shoved up the stairs and pushed to their knees. When their hoods were ripped off, they looked dazed and skeptical, one sneering when he saw where he was.

"What the hell is this?" he asked, and a guard slapped him across the head and told him to shut up.

"These two men were caught with two truckloads of goods, things that belong to you, that you contributed to this cause." McCallum shot Roy a dark look. "And I'm embarrassed to say that one of my own people let it happen."

The murmurings grew, a mixture of resentment and agitation, but judging by some satisfied faces, a few knew what was coming.

McCallum urged Teresa to step up. "Come on up and be strong. We're going to do this together."

Teresa pulled back with a horrified look. "I won't punish these people."

McCallum threw his hands out in mock exasperation. "This is what you wanted. You wanted to see the people who stole receive some punishment. A reprimand. More than a slap on the wrist."

When she only stared at him, he held out his hand, and a guard slapped a police baton in it, which he strode over and tried to give to Roy.

"Okay, son," he said softly. "You're up."

Roy's face lit up with fear, but he quickly buried it with an embarrassed smile. "What's this?"

"I judge that these folks here did us wrong, and you're my executioner, son. You're going to carry out the punishment."

Roy stared at the baton, shiny and black with marks and notches, some stained red. "What do you want me to do with that?"

McCallum shrugged. "Don't matter to me what you do with it, as long as you do it with authority and make everyone understand there'll be no getting away with thievery around here."

Roy started to reach for the weapon but glanced at the prisoners on their knees and pulled back. "I don't know, Dad. This seems —"

"I'll do it." TJ had a gleam in her eyes.

"I know you would, darling," he replied, "but I need your brother to do this for me."

"Why me?"

"Because you put us in this situation."

"Yeah, but —"

"You're lucky it's not *you* on your knees right now," McCallum said with a note of finality. "Now, take it."

Roy took the baton and walked over to stand behind Thomas, looking from him to his weapon with disgust and uncertainty. He glanced at McCallum, who urged him on with a fierce nod, but Roy just stood there with emotions clashing on his face, one second mean and nasty, the next soft and frightened like a little boy. Thomas bowed his head, sniveling and sniffing while Macy glared at the crowd and then at Roy, almost daring him to do something. When he raised the baton, everyone gasped, and Thomas cringed. Roy started to swing but couldn't do it, couldn't bring it down with the swift hand of justice.

McCallum had been watching and waiting for his son to have the guts and show some leadership, and the sight of him standing there with a dumb, scared expression brought heat bubbling up inside him.

"You can't do this!" Macy screamed at Roy, capitalizing on his hesitation and pleading with the crowd. "Are you people going to stand here and let this happen? This is cruel and unfair. We just took a few things and —"

McCallum stalked over and snatched the baton out of Roy's hand, turning on the thief and bringing it down on his shoulders once, twice, a third time with brute force, bending him forward with each heavy blow until the last one cracked him across the back of the head and pitched him onto the trailer bed. Macy wailed, an earsplitting sound that shot up McCallum's spine and pushed his anger past the point of no return. With a growl, he brought the baton around in a backhanded sweep at Macy's jaw, wood hitting bone, striking her so hard she twisted on her knees and fell limp, knocked out with one hit. McCallum went in for another blow but scoffed and backed off when she didn't move.

The crowd gasped, but McCallum turned on them. "This is what you wanted, right? Fair and equal laws? Punishment for the wicked? You want peace and security but get mad when somebody steps up to do it." He pointed the baton at them and scowled. "The rules apply to everyone, even my own men. I'm no hypocrite."

Cross-stepping to his right, McCallum wailed on the first guard, fury fueling his thick arms as he swung the baton repeatedly with heavy thuds on the guard's neck and shoulders. The man grunted with every strike, bowing forward, finally falling and curling up on the trailer bed, using his feet to kick McCallum away. That only enraged him further, and he beat his legs until he was crying and begging for him to stop. The last guard was crawling away on his knees, but with his hands tied behind his back, he didn't make it far. McCallum was on him in a second, his vision filled with red rage, striking his head and neck, two cracks across his skull, splattering the trailer bed with blood. McCallum ignored the guard's pleading cries as he stood over him, raining blows until he lay there curled up and writhing in pain.

In a flush of emotion, the anger drained from McCallum's body, and he stood there, chest heaving, panting, sweating in the cool afternoon air. The crowd was silent, watching him with shocked expressions, others nodding and in agreement with what he'd done. Either way, it was respect, and that's what he wanted to see. When he reeled and pointed the baton at Roy, his son backed up as if he was about to take a beating.

"Get control of your guards, son. If you catch any of them stealing again, they'll get this. If you can't do it, you'll join them. Is that clear?"

Roy wiped the fear off his face and stood straighter with his chest out. "Yeah, I got it. I understand."

TJ watched Roy and McCallum with an unreadable expression, but Teresa... Teresa stood there horrified and stared at the blood pooling on the trailer bed, the moaning guards, and the two civilians beaten within an inch of their lives.

"You're insane," she whispered.

"You think this is bad? It'll get worse before it gets better, believe me. Now, get these people some medical attention. I want them back to work as soon as they're able. Nobody floats around here." He reeled on the crowd and swept the bloody baton across the lot of them, growling in a gruff voice. "Nobody *floats* around here. We *all* swim. We survive."

Taking silence as agreement, McCallum marched over to Roy and jammed the baton into his chest. Roy stared at the bloody end, the crimson-stained nicks and scratches, and lifted his eyes to his father with a hint of disgust and regret.

"One way or another, son," he said, "you'll swim, or you'll drown. Now, take it."

Roy did.

TJ fixed Roy with narrow eyes and a sideways grin.

CHAPTER FIFTEEN

Stephanie Lancaster, Roanoke, Virginia

Jamison drove the Humvee up to a washed-out overpass with big concrete blocks that had slipped off the rebar strands and dropped to the road below. The cars trapped on it when it had collapsed lay amidst the chunky rubble, pitched atop one another, smashed grill-first into the ground. Blood painted the insides of the windshields, and the glass was cracked into spiderwebs. The expressway above them was falling to pieces, pavement slipping off to pile up at the bottom of the embankments.

"We'll have to turn around," Jamison said with a frustrated slap on the wheel.

"You don't see a way through this, Specialist?" Gress asked.

"Not from where I'm sitting, but we could get out and look around. Might be a way through."

"Let's do it. Adelson? Why don't you get out and watch the truck while we look for a way through."

"Yes, sir." Adelson turned to Stephanie because Laney had been slouched and miserable the past several hours, not speaking a word to anyone nor inviting conversation, and so he'd left her alone.

Stephanie popped the door and climbed outside into the rain, letting the Private out where he moved to the front of the Humvee and stood guard. She got back inside, wiping the moisture off her face and watching as Jamison and Gress walked off into the mist which shrouded the stone overpass like an ancient ruin, the lichen-covered slabs cracked and leaning.

She turned to Laney. "Are you okay, hon? I guess that's a dumb question."

"It's fine." She shrugged. "I can't think of anything but the past right now. We just had dinner last week. You know, a *real* family dinner? Usually, everyone's so busy that we hardly have time to say hi. My sister used to text me even when she was sleeping in the other room."

"My kids are the same way," Stephanie chuckled. "They can't be bothered to get off their butts and go into the next room. It's strange. I guess we would've done it when I was a kid, if we'd had cell phones."

"My sister and I will never grow old together." The darkness outside drew Laney's eyes, the wavering trees with branches sweeping to the sides and undulating like they were alive. "I hadn't thought about it much, but we always talked about marriage and families and all that. Taking it for granted we'd have a million more days together, thousands of Christmases and birthdays. Life really is short, like they say."

Stephanie frowned. "We all take things for granted, even me. I'm grateful for what time I had with my family, and I'm happy to be going home to Amanda and Larkin, but who knows how the world will be next week or even tomorrow?"

Laney smiled wanly. "I was just thinking... maybe my family were the lucky ones. Everything's so miserable now. All the people we've seen struggling, wet, homeless, dying slow. That would be us if we didn't work at the Pentagon. At first, I thought *we* were lucky, but I'm not so sure anymore..."

"That crossed my mind, too. But I *must* go on for my kids, and Craig." Stephanie reached for Laney's hand and squeezed it hard enough to draw her attention. "And *you*. You're part of my family now, more or less." She laughed. "It sounds weird, but it's true. We'll do what we can to protect each other, but the rest is out of our hands."

Laney was nodding and wiping away tears. "Thank you so much. I hate to be so ungrateful, especially when you've offered me so much."

"Don't worry about it. You just took a huge loss, and I can't imagine how you must feel. I'll do my best to make you feel at home, and I can't wait for you to meet Larkin and Amanda. They're bright, beautiful kids who'll love you."

Laney nodded and wiped her sleeve across her eyes, and the door popped open again with the soldiers getting in. Adelson waited for Stephanie to switch with him so he could sit beneath the turret. The soldiers got in and shook themselves off, the Sergeant getting out the maps while Jamison put the Humvee in drive and pulled forward.

Gress turned his chiseled chin back. "We found a way through and can keep moving ahead on this highway. Hang tight in case we hit some rough ground."

Stephanie nodded and hung on as Jamison guided them between chunks of concrete and smashed vehicles, lightning flashing to illuminate pulverized bodies trapped in the cars, faces turned up in frozen screams. Thankfully, most were covered by lank wet hair or hidden in shadows like sleeping ghouls beneath an unholy light. The Humvee gently rocked as they hit divots and potholes, bumped over chunks of debris, and nudged aside a small sedan standing in their way. They angled toward the left-hand shoulder and up the steep concrete embankment to get past a jam, then dropped and drove free.

It was clear highway for a while except for the torrential downpour and slippery pavement that constantly shifted beneath their tires. Sewage drains overflowed, and dead animals lay in the streets next to their human companions. The wind whispered and suddenly sprang up in a howl, branches glancing off the roof, pebbles and mud spraying the windows. After another quarter mile, Gress grabbed Jamison's arm and pointed to a massive sinkhole in the middle of the road with a car buried nose-down in it.

"Got it, Sarge."

They drove through yards before joining an old country back road, avoiding strip malls, department stores, gas stations, and people. Gress directed the specialist, pointing where to turn, his path to Stephanie's house highlighted in yellow sharpie. And while the Sergeant had called in a few times on his radio, it was silent except for a soft crackle of static and the occasional voices of soldiers talking from miles away.

"Don't worry, Stephanie," Gress said. "We're on track and will have you home in a few hours."

Stephanie nodded. "Thank you, Sergeant. I'm grateful to you men and Colonel Davies for getting us out of the Pentagon. I can't wait to see my kids." A grin slipped out. "They'll think I'm royalty with soldiers escorting me to my doorstep."

"We'll do our best to look impressive."

"What will you men do after you drop me off?"

"We're not supposed to talk about it," Gress replied, "but I can't see what it would hurt. We'll meet up with another firing team and move on to Knoxville to protect some civilian leadership there. Just your usual group of senators and congresspeople."

"If I'm not mistaken, Jack Stanwyck is the leader of that camp. They're good people there. Competent and smart, and they've held it together pretty well."

"That's good to know," Gress replied. "I've been in contact with the camp, and they're still there. Let me know if you want to talk to anyone there before we drop you off."

Stephanie was already shaking her head. "My government work is done for now, and I'll focus on my family from here on out. Are you guys going home at some —"

In the dark, swirling mist, a bright color caught her eye. They were rounding a bend in the hill with flatlands off to the right, slopes to the left, driveways flanked by trees and more fog, cutting visibility to forty or fifty yards, tops. Through the wound-up trees came a streak of yellow, the long, trundling vehicle with black lettering along its sides, catching a flash of ...*County Schools*... as it raced to cut them off. "Jamison, the bus —"

"I see it!"

The Humvee lurched forward, trying to beat it, but Jamison saw they wouldn't and slammed the brakes. The driverless school bus came barreling down the hidden driveway, trailing ropes and chains, rushing across the road to smash into the guard rail on the other side and completely block their path. With a crunch of sliding tires, they stopped ten yards away, a sudden rush of shapes lunging toward them, crowbars and bats cracking against the bullet-resistant windows, Laney crying out and cringing while Stephanie winced as the blows rang off the sides.

She pounded on the back of Jamison's seat. "Get us out of here!"

"Knock it off!" He jammed the truck into reverse and slammed the accelerator.

Suddenly, Stephanie was lurching forward as the Humvee shot backward, bumping bodies and knocking them away with heavy thuds and screams. Someone ran up to Stephanie's window with a pistol, firing point-blank into the glass. She'd held her hands up to block the bullet somehow, but the round only bounced off, leaving spiderweb cracks from one corner to the other. Jamison hit the brake, and they stopped in a spray of gravel, everyone in the backseat thrown around and covering up except for Adelson, who grabbed the hatch handle.

"Want me in the turret, Sarge?"

"Not yet," Gress grunted. "Hang tight."

Figures ran up, shouting for them to stop, pounding the sides and windows, firing more rounds and trying to break the glass, the ricocheted shrapnel tearing through those standing nearby, heads snapping, bodies falling. The next moment, Jamison hit the gas, and they rocketed forward, aiming for the back of the bus where it was lighter. They smashed into it, a shatter of glass and thin metal, shoving it through the loose mud and gravel with a low grinding sound that reverberated up the Humvee chassis and into Stephanie's bones.

They hit a shallow embankment, the entire right side of the Humvee lifting high, hitting the dirt, spraying grass and turf on the people chasing them. Others fell on top of the truck from tree branches, grabbing handholds, trying to hang on as the Humvee ground to a crawl, fighting the loose soil as it pushed the massive bus aside. For a moment, Stephanie thought they'd be stuck, sitting ducks for the violent mob who were back, wailing on the truck with everything they had, twisted faces framed in the windows, shouting and cursing them, ordering them to stop. Jamison whipped the wheel to the right and left again, and the Humvee suddenly broke free, sending people falling off the back and rolling down the road behind them.

"Now, Adelson!" Gress called.

Adelson snapped the latch and threw the hatch up, climbing up in one motion, grabbing the big caliber machine gun, and spinning in the turret to send a burst of rounds back down the road. Red tracers spat through the air as the bullets sliced people like butter. Stephanie turned to see the bloody scene illuminated by a long slash of lightning that swept the sky from east to west.

"That's enough, Adelson!" Gress shouted, slapping the soldier in the leg.

Adelson secured something up top, then fell back through the hatch with rain and wind getting in and going everywhere. The hatch slammed shut, and the soldier sat hard, the faint hint of gun smoke and oil wafting off him.

"I could've taken them all out, sir!"

"Nah, save the ammunition."

As they wove down the road, Jamison slapped his palm on the steering wheel. "Damn, sir. They got one of my headlights."

The right headlamp was strong and cut through the darkness, while the left was angled toward the ground, dim and useless for the hazardous road ahead.

"Try the brights," Gress said.

There was a click, and the right headlamp kicked brighter, but the left one remained dead, leaving them half-blinded.

"Sorry, sir."

"Don't be sorry, soldier. That was some great driving. I'm glad you're behind the wheel."

"Thank you, sir."

"Are you okay, Laney?" Stephanie said, leaning forward. "None of those rounds got through and hit you, did they?"

"I'm fine." Laney nodded.

The diesel roared as they kicked to a higher gear, plowing them ahead through the dreary haze, the endless country road that seemed to go nowhere, but Sergeant Gress had it mapped out in yellow highlighter, and she believed he'd get them home.

The Humvee trundled down a long entry road to Stephanie's subdivision, pulling slowly to a stop in front of the neighborhood entrance sign that read *Appleton Acres*. It was deep night by then, and the homes were dark shapes on a road that swept up to the right. The streets began branching off into the straight and narrow lines one would expect in a quiet neighborhood.

"This is it, Sergeant Gress. Does it look okay to you?"

"We won't know until we get further in, but no one's shooting at us yet, so I think it's safe to proceed." He waved Jamison forward.

As they wove up to the first crest, a shallow valley of working-class homes stretched as far as they could see: bi-level models, long, squat ranches, massive two-story mansions, and everything in between. It was a mix of brick and vinyl siding, high peaks, and open foyers with big lightless windows. Each one they passed was dead with no signs of families inside. Stephanie started to point to shadows moving up the driveway and between the houses, but they were gone by the time they drove by.

"Just tell us where to turn from here," Gress said.

Stephanie nodded slowly, gaping at the dark streets. "I can't believe there's no one home. It doesn't look like much has washed out, does it?"

"I saw two or three on the edge of the lake we passed. They looked like they were slipping toward the water, but it could just be a trick of the light."

The streets sulked in pitch darkness with no streetlamps or porch lights to give it life. There were a few cars parked curbside or in driveways, several collisions littering the road and sidewalk, one vehicle having driven straight into a home, leaving deep tire tracks in the yard and the front end buried in the bay window. The familiar shapes Stephanie expected to see had become alien to her, unrecognizable without TVs flickering in the windows or people walking the neighborhood for exercise. Whatever they'd had before was dead and gone, and images of Laney's father and sister flashed through her mind, murdered in their own homes, left to rot in the cold moisture.

Tears streaked to her chin and dripped off. A hand covered hers, Laney's. "It's going to be fine," she said. "It won't be like at my house."

Stephanie nodded and swiped at her tears. "Take a left up here, then the first right. That'll be my road."

"Yes, ma'am," Jamison replied, turning slowly around some old wreckage with no signs of people anywhere.

"I was expecting it to be a little more... *safe*. Larkin and Amanda told me they had neighborhood watches, and there was some organization, but it doesn't look like it."

"Don't judge too quickly. If you were protecting your house, you wouldn't leave any lights on, would you?"

Stephanie was shaking her head, trying to make herself believe.

"It would be like fireflies at night," Adelson agreed with the Sergeant. "Would draw everyone within miles. No, the darkness is good. They could be hiding."

"I hope so." Stephanie locked onto their two-story structure with a foyer peak, two dormer windows, and forest green shutters. Like the other homes in the neighborhood, the windows were pitch black, and water dripped down the brick in long stains. The yard was full of shingles and garbage, branches of trees and leaves strewn about. She pointed as they drove up. "It's right here on the right, Jamison. The tallest one there."

"Got it," he replied, pulling over to that side and coming to a slow stop. He put the truck in park and looked everywhere else but at the house, his hand drifting slowly to his rifle.

She grabbed the door handle, but Adelson held it shut, giving her a slow head shake. "We need to check the area out, Stephanie. You know the drill."

"Can I just get out and go?" she begged, trembling and on the verge of tears. "I want to get this over with. I want them to be alive. Please, let them be alive."

"Hang on." Gress held up his hand and kept it raised for a full minute before dropping it. "Okay. Adelson, with me. Jamison..."

"I've got the wheel, Sarge." The specialist rolled down his window. "I'll keep an eye up and down the road and let you know if I see anything."

Doors popped open, and Stephanie got out, turning to face her house as Adelson slipped up to her and held something out. "Here, take this."

"What is it?"

"My service pistol. For any close encounters. Can you shoot it?"

"Of course," Stephanie replied, taking the weapon and holding it at her side.

Adelson slid to the rear of the Humvee with his head on a swivel. Gress moved to the front with the same posture, tension captured in his shoulders as he stood there checking the shadows. A cold breeze blew through, and Stephanie hugged herself tighter, unable to take her eyes off the front door, wanting to shout, hoping the porch light would come on and Larkin would fly out with a big smile.

"Can I go up now?"

Gress turned and rechecked the area, rolling his shoulders and lifting his rifle to a firing position.

"What's wrong, Sergeant?"

"I'm not sure, but I thought I saw movement along the row of cars. Adelson?"

"I caught movement on this side as well, sir. Right down — Wait! Hey! Show yourself!" Adelson swung his rifle up to the right, aiming between the next door houses. "Sarge!"

"Steady, soldier," the Sergeant shot back. "Jamison, out. Adelson, get in the —"

As Jamison popped his door and got out, shadows swept in from different directions, creeping around the corner of every house, hunkering down behind vehicles parked in the streets and driveways, silently surrounding their little band.

Laney reached across and pushed open the door. "Get in!" she hissed.

While it made perfect sense, Stephanie couldn't make herself do it. The house was right there, everything she knew in the world and maybe her kids, too. She shook her head and stayed outside as more footsteps came out of the darkness, whispers carried by the wind and dozens of eyes on them.

Gress was tracking several shapes converging on a pair of cars up ahead, the dark forms slipping behind the bumpers and keeping low.

"We're United States Army," he bellowed. "We're heavily armed and will not hesitate to shoot you if you attempt to engage us. Stand down or die!"

Stephanie broke toward the front of the Humvee, shouldering past Gress, waving her weapon, and shouting at the top of her lungs. "This is Stephanie Lancaster, and I'm here to check on my children. If any of you stand in the way... believe the Sergeant... you'll definitely *die!*" She was panting, holding back brimming tears, shaking her head as a pair of shadows slipped closer with weapons in their hand.

"Stephanie, get back in the Humvee," Gress said, raising his rifle to his shoulder and getting a bead on the figures. "Do it now before all hell breaks loose. Adelson, how are you on that turret?"

"I'm there." He climbed through the hatch, gripping the Browning's handles and swinging it around almost full circle to cover their rear. Jamison was just beneath him, slipping past Laney's door to crouch in a firing position at the back fender. The wind kicked up, blowing garbage across the street, followed by a bullhorn's piercing feedback as it flicked on.

"Stephanie Lancaster?" came the distorted voice. "This is Zeke Morris. Is that really you?"

Heart leaping out of her chest, Stephanie rushed forward and waved. "That's right, Zeke! It's Stephanie Lancaster. I'm here! I'm home!" She grabbed Gress' arm and pulled his weapon down. "It's Zeke. He's one of my neighbors. Don't shoot."

Stephanie slipped past Gress, hands waving, smile widening as a burly man in a black rain poncho stepped from behind the car.

A flashlight flipped on and shined right on her. "It *is* you, Stephanie. We've been waiting for you."

"Where are my kids, Zeke?" She asked in a trembling voice, the emotion she'd been holding in finally bubbling over. "I want to see my kids."

Zeke laughed with relief, turning the beam down. "They're in the house and fine." Raising the bullhorn, he bellowed to everyone within earshot. "Neighborhood watch, stand down! It's Stephanie Lancaster and some Army boys. Everything's okay. I repeat, stand down!" He held a radio high, showing it to Sergeant Gress before speaking into it.

The lurking shadows slipped into the open, holstering their weapons, shouldering their rifles, and waving faintly at the Humvee and the soldiers.

"Stand down, men," Gress ordered.

Jamison stood from his crouch, and Adelson let go of the machine gun handles and held his hands up. Stephanie turned to Gress with her eyebrows raised.

He smiled and nodded toward the house. "Go ahead, Stephanie, go see your kids."

She tore around the Humvee and was off through the debris-strewn yard, hitting the walkway at a dead run. She was about to grab the doorknob when the door flew open, and light poured from the entrance. Larkin was standing there with a shotgun in his hand, the barrel lowered, a sideways grin on his boyish face that widened with surprise and joy.

"Mom! You made it. I can't believe you made it! How did you —"

Stephanie rushed forward and grabbed him, squeezing as hard as she could, hard enough to hurt him. Tears finally broke free, flowing unbidden as she hugged and shook him until he laughed.

"Okay, Mom! I love you, too."

Amanda leaped out behind him, squealing with joy as she threw her arms around both of them and hung on, knocking heads with Stephanie. "Sorry, Mom!"

"I don't care!"

The scent of Amanda's freshly washed hair wafted past her nose and brought a flood of memories. Stephanie choked back a sob and grabbed her, clutching her shirt and pulling her tight, burying her face in her shoulder.

"I missed you guys so much," she sobbed. "I didn't think we would make it. It's crazy out there."

"Zeke and the neighbors really helped us." Amanda nodded

toward a few dozen people who'd come into the yard, grinning, pointing, and crossing their arms with broad smiles. "We've been on patrol and everything. We saw you guys coming from a mile away, but we didn't know it was you. We didn't expect you... oh, Mom." Amanda leaped into her arms again, on her tiptoes and squeezing harder. "We didn't know if you'd *ever* make it."

Letting Amanda go, Stephanie wiped tears off her cheeks and turned to the approaching soldiers. "I made it thanks to these brave men who brought me home."

Larkin gaped at Gress, Adelson, and Jamison as they came up with slung rifles and thick flak vests, helmets pulled low over their faces. He hesitantly held out his hand. "Thanks for bringing my mom home."

"No problem, man." Adelson stepped forward and slapped Larkin's hand. "We were bringing her home if it was the last thing we ever did. She's a great mom."

"And these guys... amazing," Stephanie squeezed Gress' arm. "They drove me all the way from DC. Can you believe that?"

"That's a long drive," Amanda said. "Thanks again."

Laney stepped from behind Adelson, her dark curls clinging to her face, water dripping down her cheeks, a hesitant smile breaking through the shadow that had plagued her. "Hi, guys."

"This is Laney, kids. She'll be staying with us if that's okay?"

"Where'd you find her?" Larkin asked.

"I work with her. She's good people."

"Okay then, sure."

"Are you kidding?" Amanda stepped forward and reached for Laney's hand, drawing her closer to the porch. Stephanie noticed she was wearing her thick, fuzzy slippers. "I've been dying to have someone else to talk to in this house. Larkin is such a nerd."

"It's good to have you home," Larkin said and threw his arm over her shoulder for an extra hug.

Stephanie drew Laney and Amanda onto the porch, putting them behind her as she turned to face the soldiers. "Why don't you guys come in for a minute? Let us make you some coffee or have a meal or something."

"We appreciate that, Stephanie," Gress said. "But we've got another mission, and we can't delay. Again, we appreciate the offer."

Her gut twisted, and the tears rose again, but she wiped them away and stood firm in front of the soldiers. "I understand," she nodded. "You've got orders. But if you ever come back this way, please stop in. You'd be more than welcome."

"We'll do that, ma'am." Gress tipped his helmet to her, followed by Jamison and Adelson.

As they started to turn away, Laney leaped off the porch and took Adelson by the elbow, jumping into his arms, clinging to him, hanging there, and kissing his cheek. He sputtered and grinned, face flushing red as he hugged her back and let her go. Amanda took her hand and led her inside without another word. Adelson touched his face and smiled with a mixture of sadness and surprise, shaking his head and following Gress and Jamison to the Humvee. As they packed to leave, Zeke came up and gave her a brief but warm hug.

"Good to have you back in town, Steph. You'd be proud of your kids. They did amazing. Real contributors. The best scavengers we've got."

Stephanie nodded with a gush of pride. "Well, none of this would be here if you hadn't stepped in and taken charge. Thank you, Zeke. I'll never forget it."

"Don't mention it. Now, why don't you have dinner with your kids, then come talk to me about taking a shift with the watch? There's a lot to do, and we all like to stay pretty busy."

"Sounds good. Talk to you soon."

Stephanie shut the door behind her and stood in the foyer, letting the familiar sights and smells soak in. The reason for the dark windows was the tight black coverings they'd put over the glass, sealing in every speck of light. A row of four candles stood on the mantle, giving off a cozy ambiance, and the scent of cooking filled the air.

Amanda peeked into the hallway from the kitchen. "Mom, you want me to put on some coffee for us?"

"That's the best thing I've heard all day." She sighed and looked around. "Home sweet home."

CHAPTER SIXTEEN

Morten Christensen, Pearisburg, Virginia

The Christensen's quaint cottages had stone walkways that cut between flooded gardens and converged into a lane that led toward the center of the Amish community. Behind the cottages stood a small stable structure where they stored the horses and wagons with a little room left for feed and supplies. And beyond that were three acres of beautiful fields they could farm as soon as the rains stopped, which seemed a distant hope.

Morten finished his jam-covered bread and coffee, taking in the warm room before heading out the back door with his heavy coat and hat on, stepping into a wash of instant rain. The area between the cottages was filled with herbal plants and small tomato gardens, most of it washed out from the water, though they'd found several ripe ones to pick that morning and were scavenging every bit of food they could from the flooded fields. Cutting behind Uri and Miriam's place, Morten made a beeline for the stables, entering through a side door and lighting a nearby lantern. The soft glow revealed ten stalls, a loft, and several workbenches and storage shelves in the back. With a smile, he circled to Fitzpatrick, patting the white patch on the horse's nose, kissing his snout, and slapping his neck firmly.

"Thatta boy. Want to go out for a ride?"

Fitzpatrick snorted and tossed his head.

"I thought you might want to. I know it's still raining, but you're probably bored senseless standing in this stall all day. I pray to God for the sun to come out and for God's light to finally shine on us."

He quickly saddled Fitzpatrick, took his rifle where it hung on a nearby hook next to his backpack, and shrugged them both on. Back at Fitzpatrick's stall, he was about to lead the horse out when the door behind him slammed shut, and Lavinia walked in, dripping rainwater and shaking her umbrella out on the plywood floor. Morten put his hand on Fitzpatrick's chest and held the horse.

"Lavinia, good to see you. What brings you to the stables?"

Lavinia leaned the umbrella against the stall wall and stepped back with her hands on her hips. "I should ask you the same thing, Father. I've watched you come out here for two days, saddle up Fitzpatrick, and ride out after only a few hours of sleep."

Morten could have lied to her but only nodded. "Why I come and go are none of your business."

She clicked her tongue. "I respect that. You're a grown man, and mother has been gone a long time."

Morten scowled. "Your mother would have respected me enough not to question my choice to ride out, trusting in the reasoning of it."

"And that's where we've reached an impasse, for I know why you go out, and it's not for our good or the good of this enclave."

"Tell me then." Morten leaned forward, his scowl deepening. "Why do I go out in this mess when I don't need to? What could possibly draw me out of the comfort of my beautiful cottage if not for the sake of something good."

Lavinia was at least a foot shorter than Morten, and his imposing stature cast a shadow over her, forcing her to step sideways into the soft barn light. She swallowed hard but held firm. "You're going to look for Wendy and her children."

"Well, at least you know my heart, daughter. Or perhaps a little bird sent by you to eavesdrop."

Lavinia scoffed. "It hardly matters what Mara saw and heard, and what she told me only reinforced what we'd already known. That you're going outside the enclave in a fruitless endeavor that only serves to weaken us."

"And how does it weaken us?"

Lavinia crossed her arms, her dress hitching sideways as she shifted her hip. "I'm assuming Smithson doesn't know what you're doing, which will put you at odds with him... and that will put *him* at odds with *us*."

"It's no one's business what I do when I'm not fulfilling my primary duties." The same anger he'd had for Samuel's defiance on the road boiled up inside him. "Smithson himself said what a difference we've all made here, and he looks forward to us being a big part of this place."

"That's wonderful to hear, but we must adhere to the laws Smithson and the elders have put down. We have to think about what they'd say knowing you were going out each night, putting yourself in danger for people who do not belong with us."

Morten's chest swelled, and he flexed his fist at his side but quickly relaxed and remembered his patience. "Whether you think they belong with us or not, they are our family, and I do God's work when I look for them. No one will stand in the way of that." He shook his head, hand opening as he tried to explain. "You know about McCallum and the dangers surrounding us."

Lavinia nodded.

"Well, Wendy and the kids face that every day without the protection of men on horseback armed with shotguns. Every moment I can't prove they are safe drives a spear through my heart. What will it take for you to understand that?"

"I only understand what you taught me, Father." Lavinia fixed her jaw. "Loyalty to God and my people."

"Which doesn't extend to Wendy or her kids." Morten nodded knowingly.

"I will always wish them well," she replied with a hint of defiance, "and part of me feels guilty for judging them, but I have my son and daughter to think about. I have a husband to whom I must be a wife, and I can't afford to ride alone without caring for what my spouse thinks..." She shook her head and averted her eyes. "Sorry, Father."

Morten forcibly relaxed his jaw and stared at her, hating how defiant he'd taught her to be. "Yes, I'm afforded that *luxury* because of the passing of my wife, your mother. But you'd do well not to bring that up too often, daughter. In fact, I'd advise that be the last time you throw her in my face."

Lavinia stepped forward, her expression softening. "Before these hard times, I might've been willing to take them in, to do everything I could to help and protect them, but I can't even ensure that for my own children. Everything I do, every sentence I utter, is to keep us in good standing here, to earn our place until the rest of our people arrive. The world squeezes us like a fist, trying to extract every last drop of blood from us. We can't afford to go out of the way for people who don't fit in here."

"How can you feel nothing for them? This is Zach's family. This is *our* family."

Lavinia stiffened, her cheeks growing rigid again, the ice in her eyes hardening. "I'd hoped it wouldn't come to this, Father, but I think Smithson should know what you're doing. I think you should tell him or else..."

"Or else, what? You'll do it?"

"Do not accuse me for what might happen, Father. You're the one who risks getting us expelled from this place, which is Eden compared to what's out there."

He took Fitzpatrick's reins and led him out of the stall. "Go to Smithson. I care not. But make sure Samuel is with you when you go to betray me. Don't allow him to hide behind your convictions. Make it known to all!"

If she replied, he didn't hear because he was already guiding the horse outside. He slammed the door behind him, climbed into the stirrup, and threw his leg over the saddle, settling back beneath a gentle pelting of rain.

For the second time in as many days, Morten traversed the rugged countryside, made worse by the loose soil and toppling trees, roots wiggling free, unable to hold their weight. Especially on the steeper slopes, where the thick trees leaned together, the lower branches interlocked in a precarious balance like drunkards coming back from a bar. He traced the path he'd taken before but used roads wherever he could. While it was afternoon, the silty shadows and mist cut his visibility to about sixty yards, gusts of gray fog moving in and sweeping over him. Fitzpatrick's short coat beaded with water that dripped down his sides.

"It's okay, boy," he said, wiping the rain off his neck. "We'll make short work of it today. I'm dead beat."

Defeat settled on his shoulders as the valleys and hills kept Wendy and the kids hidden. "I need a search party of two hundred people to cover all this land."

He shook his head, recalling the last conversation with Lavinia and the things she'd said... always the daughter-in-law who knew how to bring out the pain in his heart. Still, he loved her with all his being, as stubborn and forthright as she was.

Fitzpatrick slipped a little on a hillside, and Morten gripped hard with his knees, imagining tumbling down over the deadfall and debris, breaking his bones on heavy stones, piercing his side with offshoots of branches as sharp as daggers. With a flick of his reins, he gently guided Fitzpatrick until he got his hooves beneath him and they were steady again.

"Excellent, Fitzpatrick, but I get your point. This is far too treacherous for us this day. Let us seek easier terrain."

They'd been moving parallel to a highway on his right, and he turned Fitzpatrick carefully down to it, picking his way over forest debris and logs, finally surging up a shallow ditch to reach the left shoulder where he stopped to take a deep breath. Then slowly, they walked across the buckled pavement, circling ponds that had formed, slipping past broken-down cars that had rolled off the side or had gotten their wheels stuck in cracks.

One stranded SUV had its hatch thrown up, and he dismounted to collect some child's clothes from a pink suitcase there, gathering a few bottled waters they'd left behind, a backpack, and several cans of food. It wasn't much, but it was something to show he was working for the community as well as for Wendy and the kids. With those things packed up, Morten mounted Fitzpatrick and hit the highway again, heading west, away from the enclave, skirting Buck Hill's lower base.

Coming around a bend where lake waters lapped at the shoulder, and the dark shapes of trees stood off in the murky gloom, Morten got the impression that someone was watching him. Off to the right, twigs crunched on the hillside, and eyes crawled over him as he approached a driveway partially hidden by brush and trees. He reached inside his coat for his revolver, drawing it slowly from its holster and slowing Fitzpatrick to a halt. With a quick turn, he caught a figure standing on the hillside twenty yards behind him, wearing a dark poncho and boots and holding onto a sapling for balance. "Whoever you are," Morten growled, raising and cocking the gun. "Step back or be delivered to God."

"Grandpa?" The figure threw back her hood, and a tumble of golden hair fell around her shoulders. Piercing blue eyes stared at him through the gloom, and when she smiled, it lit up her face and his heart simultaneously.

"Charlie?" He was breathless, shaking, and he cursed softly and de-cocked his weapon, turning the barrel away from her. "Oh, dear child. I could've shot you."

"I would've shouted, but I didn't know if it was you. I thought it was, but I had to be sure."

"It's okay, girl." Morten swung out of the saddle and strode over, but the ditch was filled with rushing water like river rapids between them.

"Follow me this way," Charlie said, gesturing and moving west through the woods. "We'll meet on the driveway."

Nodding, his heart jumping in his chest, Morten went back for Fitzpatrick, took his reins, and led him over just as Charlie was climbing through the shallow, debris-covered hillside, leaping a short trench to land with both boots in the driveway. She ran at him with a broad grin, throwing herself into his arms and nearly knocking him over.

"Whoa, girl! Go easy on your old grandpa."

"Sorry, I'm just so excited to see you." Charlie practically sang, backing away but clinging to his coat sleeve. "And Mom's going to be so happy, too."

Morten gestured up the driveway. "So, you found a safe place to live."

"Yes and *no*." Charlie dragged out the last part. "We found a nice house, but there is a little drama to go with it if you know what I mean."

"I don't, but I soon hope to find out. Where's your mother?"

"She's up at the house..." Charlie gasped softly as she pulled a radio from her pocket. "I almost forgot to call her. WC? Are you there, WC?"

There was a moment's pause before Wendy replied through the radio speaker. "I'm here. Is something wrong?"

"No, not at all. We've got a visitor. Tall, wide hat..."

"Meet me at the top of the hill."

Charlie put her radio away and trudged up the driveway. "Come on. We'll take Fitzpatrick to the stables to meet the horses."

"You got stables and horses?"

"Oh, yeah. We got lucky finding this place, but trouble found us right back pretty quick. We'd only been here about a day when the owner came home being chased by a bunch of thugs..."

"What?" Morten replied with a grunt. "Were you forced to use your weapons?"

"Yeah, but it's okay, Grandpa. We drove them off and saved the women, at least one of them; the owner's sister died. Anyway, here's Mom. She'll tell you everything."

Wendy came around the back of the house and stepped onto the driveway, her slender frame swimming in the jacket and poncho she wore, skinny yet shapely legs tucked into a pair of waterproof boots, ringlet curls falling from the cowl.

"Dad!" She rushed over with beaming eyes, leaping into his arms with such force that he had to swing her around or stumble back down the driveway.

"I'm so glad you found us."

"It took me two days." He held her at arm's length to get a good look at her. "I scoured Buck Hill, high and low. You traveled a lot farther than I thought you would."

Wendy shrugged and smiled. "It was tough to find something warm and dry that didn't have a roof filled with holes. Plus, we ran into some trouble on the road and went an extra mile or two to get away."

"I'd expected as much. Lord, I can barely keep from grinning. To see you two alive... and David?"

"Oh, he's fine. Inside and resting. We've been taking turns watching the road and making sure no one comes up the driveway like they did the other day."

"Charlie was just telling me about that."

"And I'll fill you in on everything once we get inside, but first let's put Fitzpatrick away."

As they strolled up the hill, Morten marveled at the place, the bright white siding standing out in the gloom, the darkened windows, and the small backyard that rose to Buck Hill's high ridges. The curved gravel lane swept around to a combination stable-barn. The only strange thing was the white pickup with its front end smashed into the tree, and he'd let Wendy tell him all about it in good time.

"You've got a beautiful place here."

"Not ours, of course, but the woman who owns it came home. She was a little beat up when we found her. She's not complaining too much about us staying."

"Not after we patched her up," Charlie added.

"Showing her gratitude, huh?"

"Darla is a handful, but she's a good person."

By then, they'd reached the stables and took Fitzpatrick inside, walking him down the main corridor where Darwin, Ginger, and Sassafras stood with their ears perked up, snorting and sniffing.

Morten brought him up for an introduction. "These are some beautiful animals." He reached toward Ginger to let her smell him. "Well taken care of, too."

"The kids have been taking great care of them," Wendy said. "But they weren't in bad shape when we got here."

As the horses sniffed each other, Charlie introduced them. "Fitzpatrick? This is Darwin, Ginger, and Sassafras. I call her Sassy. Guys, this is Fitzpatrick. He's a good old guy who brought us all the way from Stamford. Show him some respect."

"Mind if I put him in this last stall here?" Morten asked.

"Oh, of course," Wendy said, moving past the horses to the empty stall on the right, unlocking it, and throwing the door open.

Morten led Fitzpatrick inside, turned him around, and left him alone. "By the way, what's that smell?" He'd gotten a whiff of something strong, sweet decay mixed with fresh rain, stuffing up his nose enough to make him nauseous.

"Oh, that's the sister I was telling you about," Charlie said. "We buried her and all, but the smell just won't go away."

"I'm sorry to hear that, but at least she's resting at peace now."

"It's been a hard few days for Darla, but she's strong..."

"That's good."

"Can you show me how to unsaddle Fitzpatrick?" Charlie asked. "David and I want to learn how to ride now that we've got horses. It only makes sense since the roads are messed up and all."

"Worse than they were when we started," Morten confirmed, then shook his head. "Let's leave Fitzpatrick saddled. I'll need to be getting home soon. I have a feeling Smithson will be looking for me."

"He doesn't approve of you looking for us?" Wendy asked.

"He wasn't aware of it, though something tells me he knows now." Lhe two stared at each other for a long moment before they both said, "*Lavinia.*"

Wendy chuckled. "That woman can't leave well enough alone, and she hates us."

"She doesn't hate you," he corrected. "She's frightened, and she's just trying to protect her little ones."

"She's not wrong."

"No, she isn't, but she could learn to be more understanding. I'm afraid I failed at teaching Samuel that, and it's showing through Lavinia now. I hope she comes around before it's too late."

"Let's get inside. I've got coffee on the stove."

"Never were better words spoken. Please, lead on."

They returned to the house and circled toward the front door, and Wendy turned to explain. "I'm bringing you through the front because we have a guest in the laundry room. I'd rather him not see you."

Morten shook his head. "This is getting more interesting by the minute."

Wendy let them in and motioned at a trio of large mats in the living room. They stood there and dripped, taking off their boots and ponchos and hanging them on a nearby hook. The lights were on, and the faint sounds of running appliances touched his ears. The air was filled with the smells of cooking, shampoo, and the stronger aroma of freshly brewed coffee. David came in from the laundry room and smiled.

"Grandpa! Yes!" He rushed over, and they clasped hands and embraced, pounding each other on the backs. David stood a few inches shorter than his grandfather with some years left to grow. "Come in, Grandpa. We've got coffee ready."

Morten followed David over unable to keep the smile off his face despite his aching bones and weary body. It was a quaint place with modest, functional furniture and warm lighting, with a couple of lamps in the living room and a single electric lantern on the kitchen table. A woman sat with her back to him, slick red hair and a thick bandage on her upper left arm. Her crutch leaned against the table, but she didn't turn.

"How do you like the place?" Wendy locked arms with him and guided him to a chair.

"Could use a crucifix or two, but it's cozy."

Darla looked up with ice-blue eyes. "My husband Ron picked most of the decoration. He was into new tech stuff and didn't think much about religion. Same goes for me."

"That's too bad," Morten said, standing at the head of the table to Darla's right. He held out his hand. "I'm Morten. I'm Wendy's father-in-law."

She took his hand and shook. "Up at the Amish place, right?"

"We don't officially belong to the enclave but came from another Amish community in Fort Plain, New York." Morten pulled out his chair and sat, resting his hands on the table. "In fact, we're still waiting for our people to get here. Hopefully, we'll join ranks with Smithson's people. Double our size."

"Wendy told me a little about your adventures from Stamford. Sounds like it was a tough ride."

"It was that and more. Almost lost my son."

"Sorry to hear that."

"How is Uri?" Wendy asked as she poured coffee, and Charlie brought over an extra chair to sit on Morten's right.

"Uri is doing very well," he said. "With Miriam, Lavinia, and all the kids doting over him, he'll be fine."

"That's great. Cream? All we have is powdered."

"Perfect, Wendy. Thanks." With a stirring in his heart, he leaned toward Darla. "And I heard you lost a sister just the other day. I am so sorry to hear that, and I'll pray for you both."

Darla stared at him like a stone, though her voice was soft when she responded. "Your prayers won't do jack for us, but I appreciate them all the same. Thank you."

Wendy brought the coffee and placed the cup in front of him, the steaming aroma drifting past his nose. He sipped. "This is greatly appreciated. It's been a cold, wet couple of days out searching for you, but I've found you by the Lord's good graces."

David sat across from him. "So, did Smithson pitch a fit when he found out we left?"

Morten laughed, recalling Smithson's face when the guards told him the news. "He was surprised you got away, but he doesn't suspect I was involved, and I'd like to keep it that way, but I'm afraid Lavinia will say different." He shook his head sadly. "Unfortunately, I was forced to skirt the truth to keep from being discovered, and I feel the Lord's eyes on me for the indiscretion."

"What are you afraid of?" Darla asked.

"Lying is a terrible sin in our community, especially if it's to an elder or a leader of an enclave. Being new to the community, a simple lie could get us thrown out on the street..."

"Kind of like what happened to us." Wendy took her usual seat with her coffee.

"My will has been tested these days, and I pray to make the right decisions. I pray for forgiveness every day."

Darla scoffed but didn't say anything.

"Enough of sad subjects," Morten said. "How about you? Tell me what happened after you left me on that rainy highway so many days ago."

As they sipped coffee in the warm light, Wendy recalled everything they'd done since going out on the road, walking the rainy streets searching for a home, finding nothing but washed out, leaking houses. There was the family with the insistent father Charlie had to shoot. Finally, she told him about stumbling upon Darla's place and settling in, then Darla crashing into the tree.

"We brought her in and patched her up," Wendy finished. "Good as new."

Darla scoffed but nodded. "I'm feeling better, and I appreciate what Wendy and your grandchildren did for me, Morten."

"How's Aunt Alma?" Charlie asked.

"Alma is, as always, a bright light on any day. She reminds me so much of Zachary."

"As tall as a tree," Wendy nodded, then fell dark. "Will you get in trouble for being here?"

Morten shrugged and leaned his big frame back so the seat squeaked. "The worst he can do is kick us out, but I'd beg for my family to stay first."

"And you'd come right here," Wendy said with a fierce glint in her eye. "Promise me you'll come straight here if they try anything on you."

"I promise I will," he conceded, "but it would break Miriam's and Lavinia's hearts to be away from the others. Already, they've made friends with the women of the Pearisburg community, and I'd hate to see them lose that."

"Well, I'm glad they found a place they fit in. Were your homes any better than the ones they gave us?"

Charlie snickered. "I'll bet you couldn't beat us when it came to holes in the roof."

Morten laughed at her sing-song voice. "Actually, they gave us some nice cottages right next to each other at the end of a lane, and we received some farmland to work and a place to keep the horses and wagons. The differences in how they treated us compared to you encouraged me to help you leave, and I'm glad you found such a good place."

"That's because the Amish are hypocrites," Darla said with a slight curl of her lip. "They preach a big game, but when it comes time to be merciful, they save their own hides first."

Morten shifted uncomfortably. "There is some wisdom in your words, but if the world wasn't so harsh, Smithson and his people would open their arms to refugees."

"It's when things get tough that people are tested," Darla replied. "Their true colors shine right through."

Morten gave a faint nod and a tired sigh. "And this is causing a rift between us. Lavinia and Samuel... I can't trust them. I fear they would forsake Wendy and the kids to remain in the enclave, and they have their own children to think about." He took a deep breath. "While I came to see that you were okay, I also bring ominous tidings."

Wendy leaned forward. "What is it, Dad?"

"Our people at the enclave have been facing attacks and looting."

"We were hoping it wouldn't be that way here, but there are still dangerous people on the highways."

Morten shook his head. "It goes beyond a few citizens looking for a scrap of bread. There are forces organized in town, led by a man named Oliver McCallum."

Darla grinned across the table.

"This man has organized attacks on the Amish, forcing us to form regular patrols, heavy ones, constantly circling the Amish lands and communicating emergencies by radio."

"Well, I'll be." Wendy cocked an eyebrow. "Smithson agreed to use radios?"

"Yes, but in a limited capacity. A few sentences at a time."

Darla snorted.

Morten ignored her and continued. "There've been shootings, barns robbed, and at least one female molested by the group. Our people have taken our share of flesh from them, and we've fought them to a standstill."

"Doesn't sound much safer where you are."

"We are well protected, and you're not. That's one reason I wanted to find you. They have dozens of men, probably over a hundred by now, armed and able to fight. We've heard they're taking over just about everything in town, trying to reorganize and ration things —"

"The thing is," Darla snarled, "they're taking supplies from everyone else and putting them into their *own* sheds and barns. And the damn sheep in this town are willingly giving up their possessions for safety they'll never truly have."

"That's exactly right," Morten agreed. "When they see this place here... the horses and feed supplies, they'll want the things you have."

Wendy shot Darla a knowing look. "Actually, Dad. We've had a run-in with McCallum already."

"What do you mean?" Morten said with a twisting stomach.

Wendy glanced at the laundry room door. "Yesterday, we caught someone trying to get in the house. David tackled him, and we were able to subdue him and tie him up. I was going to let him go, but —"

"He needs to be taken care of," Darla broke in.

"What do you mean, taken care of?" Morten asked.

"He needs to be taken out back and shot. It's the only way to handle the situation, if we want to stay here. We have to be strong... can't show any weakness. Wendy and these youngins need to wake up to the reality of —"

"It's not like we didn't shoot people." Charlie had a heated stare.

Wendy held her hands out for calm. "We've done terrible things to stay alive out here, more than you, Darla. But you're talking about putting a gun to someone's head and shooting them for no good reason."

"Not for *no* reason," David replied.

"For what you *think* he's going to do," Wendy said. "You can't assume people are trying to kill you at every turn."

"Aren't they?" David challenged her.

"Darla didn't shoot at us," Charlie gestured.

"Because we dragged her half dead butt from her truck! If we'd come walking up that driveway while she was home, she would've shot us."

Darla shrugged. "That's true."

"We're not going to shoot him," Charlie hissed as she leaned over the table. "I can't believe you guys are even thinking about it."

"What do you think, Dad? We've got this guy who's associated with McCallum, and if we let him go, he might bring back more."

"Ain't no might about it," Darla said.

Morten took a long sip of his cooling coffee. "McCallum will get around to this place sooner or later, no matter what you do with your prisoner. The real question is whether to even stay here or not." Morten pushed his cup around. "It would be much easier to pick up and leave. Perhaps a place higher up on the hill or up by this barn I found... a hospital of sorts."

"The Nance's," Darla nodded. "I know them well. Good people, but even they'll fall under McCallum's rule at some point. And you're right about him getting out here, eventually. But if we let that prisoner go, he'll tell McCallum there's just three women and a string bean of a kid out here. Best to lie low leave them a corpse to find in the woods. Make them think twice about trying us. Give us... give *me* some time to heal." Darla nodded at Morten. "Luckily, he doesn't know you're associated with us. If he did, he'd really want to hurt them. Maybe even try to use them against you. Another reason not to let our prisoner go."

"He wouldn't do that, would he?" Charlie asked.

"Yes, he would. The actual real question is..." Darla stared at Wendy. "Are you people going to stay or go? I don't care either way. But either way, I'm taking care of Matt."

"You could all go," Morten suggested. "Then you wouldn't have to deal with him at all."

"She won't leave her home, Grandpa," Charlie frowned.

"Ron and I lived here for a long time," Darla said, "and I've got a lot of good memories tied up in this place. Leaving would just about kill me, I reckon."

The table fell silent, only more questions rolling around in

Morten's head as he finished his coffee. "Well, I should probably be getting back now."

"Won't you stay and have another cup?" Wendy asked, already standing and moving to the counter.

"No, I'm afraid not. I've got my problems to deal with back in the enclave. I can't tell you what to do, Wendy, but a part of me agrees with Darla and David."

"Grandpa —" Charlie started.

"No, Charlie," Morten raised his hand. "There is truth to what they're saying, and I've seen the damage Oliver McCallum can do firsthand. I've seen the bullet holes in Amish homes, entire barns half burned, and shelves empty of supplies. He's an evil man, and you can't forget that. You can't afford to give anyone the benefit of the doubt." Quiet filled the room, everyone pondering Morten's words until he concluded it was time to go. Standing, pushing back his chair, he reached to shake Darla's hand. "Thank you for the hospitality. You have a lovely home, and I wish you a speedy recovery."

Darla grasped his larger hand with a nod. "All right. Have a safe trip home."

Morten went to the door and put his boots and coat on, then turned to hug David and Charlie.

"When will you be back?" Charlie asked. "And can you bring Alma next time?"

"We'll see. I hope it's soon. Now that I know where you are, I can get here pretty quickly, even with that mess out there."

"Be safe, Grandpa," David said, clasping his hand one final time before letting him go.

"Take care of everyone and remain vigilant."

"I will."

Wendy approached with glassy eyes and wet cheeks, and he let her guide him to the door. "I'm sorry you're in this position. You should be with us in the cottages under our safety and care."

Wendy was already shaking her head. "It's just not meant to be, Dad. And don't worry, when Zach gets home..." Wendy crossed her arms and averted her eyes. "I'll hold out as long as I can, but I really need Zach here with me."

"There, there," he said, wrapping his arms around her, feeling her slim shoulders against him, strong yet defiant, as rigid as steel when she wanted to be. Emotions clashed inside him, and his voice wavered. "Zach will make it home, one way or another. I know this in my heart. I know my son. You only need to stay strong for him and for yourselves."

David and Charlie stood by the table, smiling and tearing up. Darla half turned and watched them with curiosity.

"And you're not alone," Morten continued. "You've got the kids, and this woman… Darla… she's special, I can feel it. God has touched her in a way I can't explain. While I can't tell you what to do, you might be wise to listen to her."

"I promise I will." She backed away, smiling. "Thanks for checking on us. I can always count on you."

"And I on you. You've done a wonderful job. You've protected these kids so well, and I've no doubt you'll make the right decision regarding the prisoner." He held her hands, waiting for her to ask him to decide for them, to carry out the execution himself. When she didn't, he nodded, smiled, and took his rifle off the peg, slinging it on his shoulder and standing by the door. "Bye, Wendy. I'll see you soon."

She grabbed his hands one more time. "See you soon. Be careful."

Morten left and heard the door shut behind him, closing his eyes to keep his heart from bursting, to keep from turning around and staying there, to take care of all their problems and see them through the troubled times. But he had a whole other family back in the enclave who were depending on him as well. Like Wendy and the kids, Smithson would kick them out without their supplies, wagons, and horses and call it retribution for disobeying God. He entered the stables and guided Fitzpatrick away from the lingering corpse stench and into the rain. Mounted up, Morten rode down the gravel driveway to the highway and took the shortest way home, praying for Wendy's heart to be light whatever decision she made.

CHAPTER SEVENTEEN

Zach Christensen, Carcross, Yukon

Zach came awake in the prisoner building, his air filtration mask still on but skewed on his face, breathing more sawdust than anything. Squirming and straining against his bonds, he expected the poisonous fumes to kill him, but when the air seemed normal, he settled down and took in the room. He was seated between Gina and Grizzly with Craig across from them next to the CAF troops. The soldiers were beat up pretty good, their noses bloodied, lips busted, eyes blackened, with cuts on their scalps. Zach met their eyes one by one, saw the bedraggled resentment of capture, the weariness, and an underlying tone of anger. The officer of the group raised an eyebrow and nodded to Zach.

Craig leaned in and whispered. "It was a nice try, man. I didn't think..."

"You didn't think what?" Zach said gruffly.

The Russian guard was taking his pack and rifles outside while a second guard shut the door behind him and cut off the cold.

"I thought maybe you'd bug out and leave us," Craig shrugged. "And I wouldn't have blamed you, wanting to get home and all."

Zach shook his head. "Would never happen."

Gina gave him a half smile. "I knew you'd come. I had zero doubts."

"Thanks for the faith. How are you?"

"None the worse for wear. They're feeding us basic rations. Splitting them between three or four of us. It doesn't seem like they want to keep us alive for long."

"What's the guard rotation look like?"

"Same two guys most of the time, but sometimes they switch them out. We call them Boris and Rubles." She nodded toward the remaining guard, a burly man who stood by the wood-burning stove in the front corner, bending and warming his hands. "That's Rubles. Mostly, they stay up in pairs, but they rotate out to sleep sometimes. Doesn't seem to be a regular rotation."

"Makes sense. The rest of them are out fighting. Feels like they tied us up with rope."

"Some with rope, others with vinyl straps. Now, those guys..." Gina nodded to the CAF soldiers. "They've been taking a little extra abuse."

"As long as they're not hurting you." He turned to Grizzly on his left. "How about you? Doing okay?"

"Arms stiff." The big Russian shifted uncomfortably, beard resting on his ample chest. "Hungry. Not happy."

"Where's Liza?"

"She is translating for Russian commander. He is not so nice."

"Yeah, I wouldn't expect him to be, this far from home and surrounded by enemy troops. We have to be —"

"Shut up," Rubles said, staring at them from the furnace. "Quiet."

"What if those gases come through again?" Craig asked him, nodding to the air filtration masks hanging from hooks by the door. "Will you be able to get our masks on fast enough? You almost didn't before."

The Russian backed away from the stove and walked down the aisle, stopping in front of Craig. "Do not worry. If air turns bad, I will put your masks on, but you..." He plucked Craig's nose with his finger. "You, I will take time. Maybe not get on before you choke."

"But I'm a hostage, you have to treat me with —"

The Russian's hand swept in and struck Craig across the face, rocking his head sideways. "I would save *them* before I save you." He gestured to the Canadian soldiers. "Those are my orders."

Grizzly was glaring at Rubles, wanting to say something but holding back.

Zach leaned closer, whispering. "Don't."

The guard reeled, and his grin turned ghoulish at the sight of Zach's bruised face. "You have something to add?"

Zach shook his head, licking the blood off his lip and staring at the floor.

Rubles stepped closer, his voice cold. "You killed two of my comrades. It will give me great pleasure to see you die, American."

Sitting there helpless, Zach involuntarily tugged at his bonds and tilted away from the leering face, putting as much distance between them as he could.

"Try to escape," Rubles shrugged. "Rope will only grew tighter around your swollen hands." He leaned closer, and Zach smelled his foul breath. "I wish you break free. Then I have excuse to shoot."

Shaking his head, averting his eyes, and after a moment, Rubles returned to the stove, warming his hands and fussing with a tin pot he assumed was full of coffee or tea.

"Have you tried to break out?" Zach whispered from the side of his mouth to Gina, his tone lower than a breath of air. "Anyone make any attempts yet?"

"No. I was waiting for you. Or Liza..."

"Liza?"

"She's been following the Russian commander around camp. They've been in here a few times to question us."

"About what?"

"Troop positions. Asking us what we're doing here in an American Humvee. I just told him we were fleeing Fairbanks like everyone else, and they seemed to believe that."

The CAF soldiers had been studying Zach since he'd come in, the officer speaking volumes with his stoic expression, his attention shifting to the door whenever an exceedingly loud explosion went off outside camp.

Zach licked his busted lip. "He's waiting for an attack."

"Couldn't come soon enough. Save us the trouble of trying to break out." Gina lowered her voice even more. "We're going to break out, right?"

"I'm open to a plan if you got one, but I can't..." Zach strained slightly, the raw rope cutting against his wrists. "Whoever tied these is a pro."

"So we're down to Liza."

"Not if she's working with them now." Craig spoke a little too loudly.

"Shut up!" Rubles called. "Once more, and I will come!"

Craig clamped his mouth and stared at the floor. At that moment, Boris came back, pushed inside, and slammed the door behind him, stamping his feet and clapping his hands to get warm, joining his comrade at the stove where they spoke Russian.

Twisting back the other way, Zach said, "Do they know you're Russian?"

Grizzly shook his head.

"That means Liza's not working for them." He spoke loud enough for Craig to hear. "If she was, they'd know."

"They'd treat me as traitor," Grizzly finished.

Rubles spun with his fist clenched, glaring heatedly. After a moment, he stalked down the aisle with his eyes on Craig, the scientist cringing in his seat and preparing for the blow that was about to come.

Zach turned to Gina, whispering loudly. "These guys keep hitting Craig, but I'm the one they need to worry about. Idiots."

Rubles changed direction, and Zach rolled with the blow when it came, allowing his head to rock backward, jaw stinging with the openhanded slap but not absorbing the full strength of the strike.

"One more time... we will take you outside to ditch."

"I'd like to see you try," Zach snapped back with the growl.

"Stop it," Gina whispered harshly, but Rubles raised his hand to hit him again.

The front door flew open, and a huge officer stormed inside to freeze Rubles with a steely stare, barking something that snapped him to attention. Rubles replied in Russian, his tone respectful but with a hint of fear. Nodding, he stepped aside and swept his arm toward the Americans. Liza appeared from behind him, half the officer's size and wearing Russian fatigues buttoned up tight to her neck. She regarded Zach and his companions with cold eyes beneath her short-cropped hair, a contemptuous stare that bore into them as if they were sworn enemies. The commander murmured something, and she strode forward to stand in front of Zach with her hands on her hips.

"This is Lieutenant Egorov. He would like to know your name and rank?"

Zach squinted. "What?"

"Your name and rank!"

"I don't..." Zach shook his head, then nodded with understanding. "Ah, my name and rank. I don't have the name and rank. I'm not a soldier."

Liza relayed the information to Egorov, who gestured and said something else.

"Then why are you dressed in military clothing?" Liza lifted her eyebrows. "And how is it you could kill two of his men?"

"I'm a former New York City police officer. I have some training and combat skills."

Egorov nodded at the translation.

"What were you doing in this area?"

"I was coming south like everyone else, escaping the storms... and Russians. I was hoping to get across the bridge and far away from here. I'd only stopped at the lake to refill my water."

"And where is your transportation?"

"A truck that's parked on the other side of the lake."

"You could have filled your water up there."

"Yes, but I wanted to sneak into town to see if there was any food. Turned out there was some ice cream."

Egorov frowned and crossed his arms, resting his flat stare on Zach. "And how did you get those military fatigues? They match what that man is wearing there." He flicked his eyes toward Grizzly.

"The Army was giving out food and clothing in Fairbanks," Zach said firmly, confidently, as if he believed it. "They forced everyone on buses to go south. Ours wrecked and I found a new truck. Drove south for my life, like a lot of people. At least until we ran into you."

The Lieutenant paused and nodded. "As civilians, you will be treated fairly and in accordance with international law. You will not be prisoners of war like the man behind me, but you will come with us to the next location as soon as we are ready to move."

Zach stiffened. "What do you mean moving? Why would we be moving? Where to?"

"To the next tactical objective. A word of warning. Do not attempt to escape or attack any of my soldiers. You will be fired upon and killed. Do you understand?"

Zach nodded slowly, catching Liza's soft expression that went suddenly hard again. She stepped behind the Lieutenant with her hands clasped behind her back and head bowed. Egorov walked to the door, talking with Rubles and Boris and gesturing repeatedly to the CAF soldiers. Something he said turned Liza's face white, but she quickly hid her fear and remained in the shadows. After a moment of back and forth, the Lieutenant exited with Liza fast on his heel. The guards returned to their kettle, brewing coffee that filled the cold room with a strong, burned almond smell.

Craig waited until the guards were preoccupied before he leaned forward and whispered. "I don't like what Liza is doing. She's practically working with them."

"She's not working with them," Zach replied softly. "I saw it in her eyes. She's protecting us more than we know. Grizzly, how did she explain why she was with you?"

"She said she was part of Orlov's team, and the bastard Americans captured her, and we were transporting her to states. They think I am American soldier. I did not deny it."

"Good. It's important we keep them thinking that."

"One more thing. Something Egorov told the guards." Grizzly's expression was grim.

"What?"

"If Canadians breach the defenses before big move, they will eliminate CAF prisoners, strip uniforms, and put in barrels to burn."

CHAPTER EIGHTEEN

Wendy Christensen, Pearisburg, Virginia

"Love you, Mom," Charlie said, and Wendy accepted a peck on the cheek from Charlie who was bundled up in warm clothes and a poncho, her hair pulled back inside the hood with clips and a ponytail holder.

They switched positions in the kitchen, ready to trade shifts, Wendy just coming in from hers, soaking wet and chilled to the bone.

Charlie gripped her face. "Gosh, you're cold."

Wendy smiled tiredly and shivered. "It's getting chillier out. If it gets below zero, it's going to present a lot of problems for us." She held out the radio. "Call up if it gets too cold, and we'll switch again."

"You get a shower and get warm." Charlie put her hand on the laundry room door handle.

"You got your gun?"

"Yep."

"Okay, be careful. And leave Matt alone out there. We put him in the stables for good reason."

"I won't talk to Matt. I swear." Charlie left and shut the door quietly behind her.

Wendy strode to the kitchen table and picked up the PC tablet to watch her walk down the stone path to the driveway, switching to the next camera view as she passed out of sight. It had been a full day since Morten had swung by, and his words resonated in her mind.

"Cup of coffee?" David asked where he stood by the counter in a loose T-shirt and jeans, his longish hair swept back.

"I'd love a cup," Wendy agreed. "And you need a haircut."

David brought the coffee over and put it down in front of her, taking a seat at the end of the table. He let her have one warm sip before he started in on her. "Have you thought about it?"

"How can I *not* think about it?"

"So."

"What do you want, David?"

"We've got all the proof we need to... to do what we have to do. This guy will be nothing but trouble. Even Grandpa said so. The Amish are having trouble with that whole group."

"But Matt doesn't know we're connected to them."

David sighed exasperatedly and started to say something, but Wendy cut him off. "I know you don't like him, but we moved him out to the stables. Isn't that enough?"

"You only did that so Darla wouldn't shoot him herself."

"And to put him safely apart from us where we could keep an eye on him." Wendy glanced at the PC tablet where Matt sat in his chair between the skids of feed. David had screwed a camera to the barn wall before they brought him in and sat him where he couldn't see it.

"And now we're just torturing him out there," David pointed out. "It's cold as hell, and he can't be comfortable sitting like that. Every second he sits there will only make him angrier. If he gets away, he'll do what Darla says."

"He doesn't seem angry when I talk to him," Wendy replied, though the answer was halfhearted. "He seems to be a nice young man."

"That's what he wants you to think." David leaned forward and whispered in a low voice. "Earlier today, I was watching him on the camera and saw him fidgeting and doing something weird. I suited up and went out there, sneaking in through the back door where he couldn't see me. He was trying to get free. I came in to let him know we could see him, then I tied him up even tighter."

"Oh, no." Wendy shook her head as her worst fears came true. "I'm sorry, David."

"None of this is your fault, but we have to do something. If he gets loose..." David shook his head, and a lock of hair fell forward. "Who knows what would happen? What would Grandpa do, or even Dad? You know they wouldn't let Matt hang around. They would've done something by now —"

Wendy slammed her palm on the table and rattled the cups and spoons. "I know he's a threat to us here, and the fact that he tried to get away..." Wendy shook her head, a wellspring of emotion flooding through her, tears stinging her eyes. "But I'm not your father or grandfather, and I'm not sure if I can..."

"I'll do it for you... for us."

"No," Wendy replied emphatically. "I won't let you carry that guilt with you the rest of your life. Look, I know we shot people before, but they were attacking us and meant us immediate harm. My conscious is clear in that regard, but if we take someone's life when we don't have to... how can we justify that?"

"I know what you're saying, but if you can't do it, then it's either me or Darla. She hates the guy anyway."

"Where is she now?"

"She's back in her bedroom resting. Said she'd be out there later to help monitor the cameras. And, Mom..." David raised his eyebrows. "She's got the revolver, and I'm pretty sure she's not as weak as she looks."

"How do you know?"

"Earlier, when she was moving into her bedroom, I saw her carrying some blankets and things from the drawers, using her good arm and walking just fine."

"Without her cane?" Wendy gasped softly.

"Yeah. She wasn't shuffling or shaking like she normally does. To be honest, I thought it was Charlie at first, but when I looked again, it was definitely Darla. She's fooling us, and one day soon you'll wake up and Matt will be dead. It's inevitable."

"We'll keep an eye on her," Wendy said.

"Great, me, you, and Charlie will keep an eye on the highway, the house, and make sure Darla doesn't shoot our prisoner, a guy we don't want around, anyway. Sounds like a great way for one of us to get hurt."

A sick heat built up in Wendy's chest as emotions warred for control of her conscience. If Zach were there, he'd say the hardest decisions came before a situation got out of control, not after. The best decisions *prevented* bad things from happening. She hadn't wanted to believe it at first, but Zach would agree with David and Darla, though it didn't mean he'd be right. Tired of worrying, sickened by the corner she'd backed herself into, she finally snapped.

"Fine," she said, pushing her coffee cup away so the lukewarm liquid splashed on the table. "I'll deal with the situation right now."

She took her rifle off the back of the chair and marched into the laundry room, stuffing her feet into her boots with David following behind her.

"What are you doing?"

"Just come with me. We'll handle this now."

Wordlessly, they laced up, put their ponchos on, and stepped out into the rain, marching out to the barn. It was Wendy's turn to outpace David, her strides quickly putting her ahead of him, plumes of breath breaking around her hood. When they reached the barn, she went in and stopped, the main corridor suddenly elongating as her anxiety level rocketed. With her feet rooted to the floor, Wendy waited for David to catch up, close the door softly, and come to her side.

"What are you going to do?"

"I'm letting him go, and I don't want to hear any more arguments about it. It might not be the right strategic decision, and it might not be what your father or grandfather would do, but it's what feels right in my heart. I just need you..." She balled her fist and gently punched David's chest. "I just need you to have my back in case he tries something. I know he won't, but if he does..."

"Sure, Mom," David replied without further argument. "Darla will be pissed, but I've got your back on this."

"Thank you, son."

Wendy walked the long corridor, ducking away from Darwin as he tried to nudge her, coming to a stop at the supply side where Matt sat facing the door in the same clothes he'd been wearing since his capture. She circled to stand in front of him, and he watched her with flat, expressionless eyes that shifted doubtfully from Wendy to her rifle. She slipped it off and handed it to David.

"You know what to do if he tries anything."

"Absolutely." David accepted the weapon and stepped back.

Wendy paused a moment, checking her heart once more before she leaned forward and pulled his gag down. "I'm letting you go."

Matt dropped his head, sighing with relief. "Oh, that's great news. I knew you'd come around."

"But I need you to make a promise."

"Anything." He nodded and squirmed in the chair.

"You have to promise that you leave here and not bring anyone back."

"I swear I won't."

"If anyone asks what's out here, you tell them you found Darla dead. The people who shot at McCallum's men are gone, and the place was looted clean."

"I swear I will."

"And there're holes in the roof and whatever else you can think of to dissuade anyone from coming out here. In return, I promise to not only let you go but help you out if you need anything."

"Mom, what are you doing?"

She raised her hand to shush David. "What I mean is that we could help you with food and shelter if you need it. You have a spot here to crash for a day or two or whatever you need."

"I appreciate that, ma'am," he replied gratefully, nodding vigorously. "And I might take you up on that offer. Despite everything, y'all treated me well, and I'll remember that."

"We didn't treat you all that well." Wendy gestured to the shiner David had given him.

"I got what I deserved for trying to break in."

Wendy circled to untie him, tugging at the ropes, the knots so tight it was hard to tell where to begin. "How do you figure we were so nice when you knew Darla wanted to kill you, and David didn't like you much either?"

Matt stammered. "Well, it was Charlie really."

"Charlie?" She stopped untying him and moved back around to face him. "What about Charlie?"

"Well, she was nice to me. Brought me extra snacks and even sat and talked to me a couple times."

"What did you talk about?"

"Just passing things, really." Matt flashed her a hesitant smile, glancing back toward his bound wrists as he rushed his explanation. "She... she told me a little about how you got here, traveling with the Amish folks and —" Matt winced and shook his head tersely. "I mean, she told me you went through hell getting down here and that it was a pretty tough road."

Wendy's stomach dropped, and she exchanged a sour look with David. "What else did Charlie tell you?"

"Nothing. We just talked about the road, and the horses, and all the refugees. She said there were thousands of refugees out there."

Wendy held up her radio. "I can call Charlie right now and ask her what you talked about. You know more than anyone she's an honest girl, maybe a little too honest."

Matt squeezed out a tear, started to talk, then clamped his mouth shut again. Finally, under Wendy's scrutinizing gaze, he nodded. "She told me her grandfather, aunts, and cousins are at the Amish community. The one Smithson is running."

"The one with whom your boss is in a direct war."

"Yeah, he is, but I'm not. I like the Amish, bought stuff off them all the time. Tools and work coveralls. The women make a hell of a fruitcake..." When all he received was Wendy's flat expression and a solemn head shake, he broke down in stuttering worry, another tear racing to his scruffy beard. "Ah, dang. I swear I won't tell anyone you're related to them. I promise... I already told you I'd keep people away from here. And... and, you said you'd help me if I needed it. We had a deal, didn't we?"

"Shut up. David, come here."

She led him toward the barn doors where the rain was pounding outside, and the wind howled through the cracks loud enough to mask their whispers.

"This is bad," David said. "Charlie talked to him. He knows everything about us now."

"Weren't you watching?"

"Yeah, but I couldn't watch them every second." David kicked the ground sheepishly. "When Charlie went on shift yesterday, I took a little nap. Couldn't keep my eyes open, I was so tired. That's probably when she talked to him, and when he was in the laundry room, too."

Wendy bit her lip and put her hands on her hips. Matt was squirming in his seat, shifting his shoulders, beads of sweat glistening on his brow as he watched them fearfully.

"Sorry. I should have stayed awake."

"It's okay." Wendy tried to breathe calmly. "We just have to figure out what to do with this new information."

"Isn't it obvious?" David hissed. "We can't just let him go now. We're way more valuable to this McCallum guy now."

"I don't think so."

"We know about the Amish patrols, the bell... the crappy cottages they put us in on the west side of the property. That would be an easy target for them if they knew it was there."

"What you're saying is crazy, David. They wouldn't come out here and torture us for information, would they?"

"I don't know, and I don't want to find out. Do you?"

Wendy turned toward the barn doors, shaking her head, fists clenched tight. Hand slipping to her pistol, her knees melted, and she put her arm against the cold wooden slats to steady herself.

"Are you okay? Do you want to sit down?"

"No, I'm going to do it, David. I swear I am. Just give me a second, okay?" Drawing shallow breaths to pluck up her courage, she imagined how it could be done. A quick turn, a handful of strides to Matt, the gun against his head, then a squeeze of the trigger. Or she could fire from where she stood, but that wouldn't be nearly as certain, and Lord knew she didn't want to injure him and have to shoot again. It was no different than what she'd had to do in Stamford, firing at old acquaintances, Turley and the others, people who'd turned on her in the end and tried to hurt her family. Matt would do the same thing, he'd —

The chair fell over with a clatter, followed by the sound of running feet. They spun to see Matt sprinting down the corridor, one rope lying on the floor, the other tangled in his legs, making him stagger against the stalls.

"Get him, David!"

He raised the rifle, but Matt had already reached the horses and was ducking beneath their necks. David thrust the rifle into Wendy's arms and took off after him. While he had a head start, Matt ran stiffly like his legs were asleep, and he didn't get far before David caught him, grabbing him by the shoulders and dragging him down. Matt hit the dirt face first with a heavy grunt, then he was crawling, kicking, and fighting to get away. Wendy was right behind them with the rifle, trying to aim at Matt but drawing the barrel up so she didn't accidentally shoot her son. "David, get him up!"

"I'm try —"

David took an elbow to the jaw, rocking his head backward, almost knocking him off. But the tall boy lunged and wrapped his arm around Matt's neck, twisting and choking him. Matt grabbed David's arm where it was locked on his throat, fighting hard, throwing his head back to crack David in the chin. David's hold loosened enough for Matt to shove him off, then he was half crawling and stumbling to his feet, scrambling for the barn door.

Wendy pressed the rifle against the back of his head. "Stop."

Matt froze and held his hands out, swallowing hard. "You just going to shoot me dead? Hey, I've got friends and family, too. I've got people counting on me."

Wendy was trying to tune him out, sweat trickling down her face despite the cold. Her tongue slipped out to lick her upper lip, gripping the rifle so hard her hands felt like stones.

"Please don't. Please. I'll stick to my promises. I'll do it right by you guys. I swear —"

"Shut up." Her finger slipped beneath the trigger guard and rested on the curve of metal. It would only take a hair's breadth of pressure to eliminate the problem. She shifted the barrel, sliding the hard steel from the middle of his head to behind his ear, relaxing her hands, gripping the weapon again as the world tilted.

The stable door came open with a clatter, and Charlie stepped in, water dripping from her poncho, the smile on her face melting when she saw Wendy with a rifle to Matt's head. "What's going on, Mom? David?"

"Mom's taking care of this," David stated flatly. "Leave."

"Taking care of what?" Charlie took another step in, her face suddenly horrified. "Wait, Mom. No!"

"Charlie..." Wendy tried to order her outside, but she couldn't bring herself to do it. Instead, she shook her head and bumped the rifle barrel into Matt's skull, but it didn't help her squeeze the trigger. Finally, she swung the barrel away with one hand and grabbed Matt by the back of his coat, jerking him upright until he got his feet beneath him and stood, gasping in astonishment as Wendy shoved him toward the door.

"Get out of here and stick to your promises. Do you understand me?"

"Yeah, I get it. I will. Thank you!"

"Shut up and go." Wendy shoved him forward with her rifle barrel.

Matt stumbled out into the mud and rain, throwing a lingering glance at Charlie before sprinting around the stables. Wendy followed him around the corner, standing on the gravel driveway and watching him disappear into the trees, swimming through the low brush until he was gone.

"Were you really going to shoot him?" Charlie came up huffing with her fists clenched at her sides.

"She was going to," David said, coming around, "until you showed up. What's the idea of telling him where we came from?"

"What do you mean?"

"Matt and his people are practically at war with Smithson, and that means *us*, now. You weren't supposed to talk to him..."

"I felt bad for him," Charlie sniffed. "He was out here by himself in the cold, and I brought him an extra snack or two. It wasn't a big deal."

"It was!" David rubbed his jaw with a wince. "The dude hit me."

"Well, you were trying to kill him." Charlie pointed out. "You've had it in for Matt the whole time! He's no different from us."

"Oh, he's way different from us. And now we're going to find out."

Wendy straightened and then deflated with a heavy sigh. "*No.*"

David and Charlie stopped arguing.

"What did you say?"

"I said no. To answer your question, Charlie, no. I wasn't about to shoot Matt because I couldn't squeeze the damn trigger. I couldn't do it... I couldn't shoot." She grabbed Charlie and hugged her. "But what's done is done, and he's gone. Best case, he keeps his promises. Worst... we'll have to deal with it." Letting Charlie go, she shook her head. "I just don't know how he got away."

"This." David held up a sharp piece of metal. "He must have had it on him or picked it up somewhere."

Wendy sighed. "Okay, let's get inside and talk about what we're going to do now."

Wordlessly, they marched back to the garage and slipped through the door where Darla stepped from the darkness. She'd replaced her crutch with her revolver and held it tightly in her right hand.

"I saw most of it on the cameras," she said. "Did he get away, or did you let him go?"

Wendy raised her hand and dropped it weakly. "I let him go. I couldn't pull the trigger, and I'm not going to apologize for it."

"I'm not surprised." Darla shook her head. "You're one dumb bitch. Now they're coming for sure."

CHAPTER NINETEEN

Zach Christensen, Carcross, Yukon

The cold winds howled, the building shook, and the Russian camp came to life. The sounds of battle had faded for the past twenty-four hours, and the soldiers were marching and driving around with haste. Headlamps flashed through the windows, and shouts echoed throughout the camp. A big plane took off while another landed, and by the sound of the engines, it was an even larger transport than the first. Heavy equipment was moved to the road in what Zach suspected was the big push to the north, which meant they'd be driven in the opposite direction, that much farther from Wendy and the kids.

They were fed whatever the Russians could find: MREs, snacks from the local stores, or scavenged canned goods. The guards entertained themselves by poorly feeding the prisoners, spilling food on their chins and shirts, smearing their faces with it. Rubles loved tormenting them the most, Craig first, then Zach for tackling and almost killing him.

Rubles stood in front of Sandy, who sat a few seats down on Zach's left between a pair of Canadian refugees, grinning as he fed her baked beans. He forced her to chase the spoon with her mouth, only to draw it away at the last second. She'd been crying a lot, especially after what Zach had told her about Scotty and how he'd pulled the trigger on the Javelin missile too soon, leaving a question if he was alive or not. Zach couldn't say for sure if he had an air filtration mask in the ditch with him when they'd started the engagement.

"You son of a bitch, just let her eat," Craig snarled and bristled in his chair.

Rubles stuffed the beans in Sandy's mouth before she was ready, spoon clicking on her teeth as he jerked it out, causing her to choke and spit brown sauce down her chin. Sandy turned her head away and almost knocked the spoon out of Ruble's hand when he snatched her chin, squeezed it, raised it, and shoved it aside. Then he strolled to Craig and sized him up for some retaliation.

The other guards were okay, feeding them regularly, more nervous about the forces closing in on them judging by the discussions Grizzly translated. But not Rubles. He seemed perfectly content with being surrounded by the enemy, as long as he could torment the prisoners. Being the main guard in charge, Rubles spent the most time with them, getting their meals and having their air filtration masks at the ready should the hydrocarbon fumes return.

The slap hit with a crack, Craig wincing, face turned aside as his cheek burned red. Rubles chuckled and held up a spoonful of beans. When Craig only shook his head, the guard laughed harder and walked away, saying something to Boris who stood by the wood-burning stove.

"He said Craig may have an accident soon," Grizzly whispered in his thick accent.

"You should quit provoking them," Zach told Craig.

"I'm just trying to keep their minds off the women," he replied. The scientist had thinned even more over the past few days, beard grown out to give him a roundish Viking appearance, dark eyes standing out in anger. "I'm really worried about Rubles getting one of the women alone at the latrine."

"You and me both," Zach nodded, straining for the hundredth

time against his bonds, his wrists beyond sore, chafed and bleeding, scabs sticking to the ropes.

"Don't worry about me." Gina's dark, greasy hair hung in her eyes. "I can handle myself. I've got the knife."

Sometime the day before, Gina had returned from the latrine and told him she'd liberated a small blade from a compartment in her belt buckle and planned on freeing herself the first good chance she got. Since then, she'd been holding it, even falling asleep with it clutched tightly in her fist.

"It's a last resort," Zach replied. "If we give them a single excuse to shoot us, they will."

"We need a bargaining chip," Craig said. "Could we tell them we're with the US military and promise them information to let us go?'"

"We don't have any information."

"*Bogus* information."

"That would make things worse for us," Zach said. "We'd be lumped in the bucket with the Canadians."

Zach glanced at Captain Sterling as Rubles opened the door and stepped out into the howling wind on some errand.

"What are you planning?" Sterling mouthed.

"Knife," Zach replied and leaned toward Gina, who grinned.

Boris looked up for a moment, causing the group to quiet down, then turned back to the stove to warm his hands. Sterling shook his head and raised his eyebrows, and Zach agreed with a nod. They'd never get the ropes cut before the Russians blew them away with Rubles laughing as he painted the walls with their blood.

"I was hoping the CAF guys had some ideas," he told Grizzly.

"We are not close enough to speak freely." He rolled his large shoulders.

"We need these guards to beat it for five minutes so we can talk."

"I can make that happen," Gina whispered from the side of her mouth.

"And how will you do that?"

"I'll get them outside. Just leave it to me."

"What about your knife?"

Her dark eyes shifted to Boris as Rubles re-entered, slammed the door shut, and stomped his feet. Gina's chest rose as if she was working up to something. "Don't worry. I'll handle it."

"You're a strong woman, but don't push your luck with them. If you screw up, you'll be shot on sight. Promise me you won't try anything... extra."

Gina kept her chin low and stayed focused on the guards. "I promise to be careful. Be ready."

"What?"

"Just be ready."

"Okay."

"Hey, Rubles! Over here." Gina's voice was deep and bellowing. "I have to use the pisser." While the Russians spoke halting English, they knew what the word *pisser* meant.

"Hold it," Rubles called back.

"I can't." Gina shook in her chair with a clatter. "I've been holding it all morning. I'll go right here in my chair if you don't let me up."

Rubles shrugged.

"What will Egorov think when the prisoner shack starts to smell? Come on, Rubles. Take me to the latrine."

Rubles cursed, pointed at Boris, then jerked his thumb at Gina. Boris shook his head, and the two argued for a few moments before Rubles poked him in the arm hard and repeated the order. Boris frowned but left the stove's warmth to untie her. Kneeling and pulling at her bonds, he worked the ends loose and stood.

"Get up."

As he slid between the chairs, Gina stretched her right elbow out and bumped him off balance. He cursed and slapped her in the back of the head, and she leaned into Zach dramatically, grabbing her head with one hand while slipping the two-inch saw blade into his palm. The guard seized Gina by her coat and lifted her from her chair, escorting her roughly to the front of the shack where Rubles waited with a sneer and an open door. Gina struggled, fussed, and elbowed to get free, but Boris pushed her through the door and shoved her outside before she could cause any more trouble.

Rubles started to shut the door behind them, but Sandy straightened in her chair. "Hey, guys! I've got to go, too. I've been holding it twice as long as her."

Rubles glared at Sandy like she was a plague-ridden rat. "No. You wait."

"Just take us out at the same time. More for you to watch."

Craig shook his head in warning, but Sandy ignored him. "That's right. I'll give you a show, and maybe you'll feed me right without spilling it down my shirt, huh?"

Ruble's glare turned into a leer, and he hurried down the aisle to untie her. Zach's insides squirmed as he undid her bonds and dragged her to her feet, shoving her toward the front of the building. He gave one look back at the two rows of prisoners before forcing her outside and slamming the door shut behind him.

He caught Sterling's eye. "My name is Zach. The man across from me is Craig Sutton, and the man to my left is a Russian trucker we call Grizzly; he understands what the Russians are saying, which has been a big help already. I know both ladies who went out to the bathroom. It's part of a distraction to give us some time to plan an escape. Also, it may be important that you know the Russian translator... the woman named Liza. She's with us as well, and I'm a hundred percent sure she's playing along with the Russians."

"Good to meet you, Zach. I'm Captain Sterling."

"Do you have any ideas how we can escape?"

"We were hoping you had some. You mentioned Liza. Do you think she can find a way to get us out of here?"

"She'll try, but obviously I haven't been able to speak with her yet."

"You mentioned before that Gina had a knife."

"I've got it now," Zach said, checking the door.

"How did you come up with that?"

"She got it into my hand when the guard wasn't looking."

"Good. Can you cut yourself free?"

"Unsure... probably. The blade is pretty small, and I have big hands. But even if I could get free, I'd have to get to the guards before they blew me away."

"They're not the smartest soldiers I've ever seen, but they're competent enough. I'm not sure it's even worth a try."

"I've been keeping it as a last resort, but I may have to try it sooner because..."

"What is it, Zach?" The Captain glanced at the door. "Be brief. We don't have much time."

"We overheard the Russians speaking earlier. They mentioned something about moving the camp soon and taking us civilians with them. The only thing is, they plan on eliminating you and your men."

Sterling shook his head in confusion. "Why would they do that? It would be a major war crime."

"They do not care," Grizzly said. "Cruel Russian regime will not take chance moving military prisoners if they do not have to. It is waste of resources. And I do not believe them when they say they will take citizens with them. I believe..." He swallowed hard. "I believe we will be eliminated as well."

"Why haven't they wasted us already?" Sterling asked.

"They thought we knew things," Zach replied with a shudder at Grizzly's revelation, "so they kept us alive for a while."

"Egorov is not patient man," Grizzly said. "I have seen this many times as young soldier in Russian Army."

The Captain fixed Grizzly with a hard stare but nodded that he believed him. "We'll have to wait until they take us outside or attempt to move us. It will give us a few moments to stand up, stretch our legs, and try to fight." He glanced at his men. "On my mark, myself and Leroux will create a diversion, and the rest of you will try to get your hands in front of you. Grab the first weapon you can get your hands on."

The half-dozen soldiers in the room nodded their bruised and bloodied faces.

"I'll use the knife," Zach said. "Try to saw through as fast as I can, provided I don't drop the damn thing first."

Boots thudded across the wooden planks outside, followed by cruel laughter and Gina's angry bark at the Russians. The door flung open, hitting the wall with a crash, and Gina and Sandy were shoved inside with the guards coming right after them. Rubles gave her another hard push, and she flew forward, stumbled, and fell to her knees. He was on her in a second, grabbing her hair and practically dragging her back to her seat, throwing her roughly into it and circling behind her to redo her bonds. Her lip was cut, smeared with bright blood that dripped to her chin, and when Rubles jerked the ropes tighter, he rocked her in her chair. Boris brought Sandy up and shoved her hard into her seat, her reddish hair tussled around her shoulders, grimacing as the guard bound her and joined Rubles at the stove.

"Did they hurt you?" Zach whispered.

"Just the usual. But we gave them some bruises, too. Lucky for us it's still daylight."

"Bastards," Zach said a little too loud.

With an angry huff, Rubles strode down the aisle to stand in front of Zach, where he drew back his fist and cracked him across the jaw, twice. "Shut. *Up!*"

The blows were hard, flooding his mouth with the iron taste of blood and sparking his anger. Zach stared at the guard's boots and raised his eyes slowly to meet his, forcing the Russian to take a step back and bristle. When Zach remained defiant with his square chin held high and firm, Rubles shook his head and returned to the warm stove.

"They took us to the latrines and tried to rough us up." Gina's voice was soft beneath the howling winds that rattled the walls. "Rubles wanted to do more but there were officers around, and they don't want to screw up with them, yet."

"I'm going to kill that guy before this is said and done."

"If I don't get to him first. Still have the knife?"

"I've got it, and we have a tentative plan. We'll make our move the second they transport us somewhere."

"You mean when they're walking us to our mass grave?"

Zach nodded. "I'll saw like hell and hope I can get through these bonds and join the fight."

"You could start sawing now."

Zach shook his head slowly. "What if we don't move for another day? They'll check my ropes and see I tried to cut them. No, I'll have to do it hard and fast while they're fighting Sterling and his men. Let's just hope I'm fast enough."

The afternoon stretched on, and the patrol activities increased, shapes and shadows running by the windows as hard snowflakes struck the glass. Natural winds pushed back the hydrocarbon flood flowing in from the north, the skies still occasionally brightened with orange blossoms and angry light. Trucks growled through the parking lots with a squeak of wheels and shocks, fading as they were pulled off to the south, likely to the far end of the tarmac.

Messengers visited Rubles and Boris more often, letting in the cold, gesturing to different parts of the camp as they gave instructions in excited voices. Each time, Zach held the serrated knife against the ropes, figuring it was the moment they'd be led off and shot in cold blood.

"What are they saying?" Zach asked Grizzly.

The Russian leaned close while keeping an eye on Boris and Rubles. "Supplies move to tarmac. Plane will lift off to another base. They plan on jumping over CAF forces."

"Leapfrogging," Zach nodded. "Can you tell if they're going to take us with them on the plane, or driving? Or... something else?"

"Not yet, but I sense it will be soon. I will follow your lead. Tell me what to do when time comes."

Zach nodded slowly, running through the possible scenarios for the hundredth time but falling short of good outcomes, wanting to talk to Sterling but unwilling to raise his voice.

"If I get my hands free," he said, "I'll give you the knife. Best thing you can do is protect our people. If we have to run, send them into the woods on the northeast side of the camp. Keep going until you reach the CAF forces."

"Will do best I can. I want to say..." Grizzly's eyes turned glassy, his voice pitching deeper. "It has been good fighting with you, Zach. You always strong as Russian bear. If something happens... I say thank you now."

"Nothing will happen. We'll get out of this."

Grizzly only nodded and sat back, resting his shoulders for a fight they never asked for. Zach took a deep breath and tried to relax while his body thrummed with restless energy. Craig was watching him with flat determination and a glimmer of hope. He bowed his head once, slowly, and Craig nodded back, and they waited for night to come.

With the slow passing of hours, and the wind and snow blowing against the window, Zach drifted off, the foggy haze of sleeplessness gripping him and pulling him down where memories of Wendy and the kids waited. While he was glad Morten was looking after them, not hearing their voices, their laughter, the little things he loved about them, brought dreadful feelings that nagged at his mind.

His sleep was fitful, filled with uncertainties and restless fears. All he could do was hold on tightly to the knife, the blade biting into his palm and drawing blood. The bustle had increased tenfold, officers shouting orders, spotlights whipping across the edges of the woods, the windows projecting moving shadows like movies on the walls. The low rumbling of the big plane parked out there reached them, turbine driven propellers spinning up and collecting wind.

When heavy boots thudded on the porch outside, it jolted Zach awake in confusion, part of him thinking they were still on the road in the Humvee, heading south with Grizzly behind the wheel. The door flung open and crashed back, and a Russian soldier stood silhouetted there with wind whistling and soft snowflakes dancing around his shoulders. Rubles and Boris met him, already bundled up in their hats and gloves, rifles slung, flanking the soldier and whispering. Zach checked with Grizzly, but the Russian only shook his head.

"This is it," Zach uttered with a sudden stomach drop, bringing Gina awake from her dozing.

Shifting his hold on the sweaty, bloody knife, wiggling his wrists back and forth, he managed to place the blade against the thick ropey fibers and started sawing carefully.

By then, the Russian guards had stopped talking, and the one who'd come in turned and exited the building, pulling the door shut behind him. Boris and Rubles stood facing the rows of prisoners with a dozen anxious faces raised and staring back. Boris was ashen, the color drained from his cheeks, visibly shaking as he held his rifle against his chest. Rubles grinned slowly across the group, mouth stretching into a leer when he met Craig's eyes. He took the safety off his weapon and charged it with a *clack* that caused everyone to jump. A civilian at the end of the row struggled frantically to get out of his bonds and a woman dropped her chin to her chest and cried.

Rubles elbowed Boris and indicated he should take the left side while he got the right, and he lifted his rifle and aimed it at the CAF soldier on Captain Sterling's left. Boris started to raise his weapon but made a frustrated sound and turned to Rubles with a plaintiff gesture. Rubles grunted angrily and slapped him on the chest, motioning impatiently.

"Boris does not want to do it," Grizzly whispered in awe.

"Well, Rubles seems pretty excited about it," Zach replied, sawing harder.

"Please tell me you're close," Gina said. "You've got less than thirty seconds."

"Trying," Zach hissed.

The serrated blade was efficient and cut through the fibers swiftly, but the ropes were a good half inch thick, and Zach's wrists were already sore and aching before he'd even started. The blade was slippery, blood and sweat slicking the metal, the teeth catching his skin sometimes if he didn't angle it right. Rubles said something, and Boris shoved him in the shoulder and gestured around, spitting and complaining. Rubles grabbed him by his coat, teeth bared and snarling into his face, letting go and punching him in the chest, motioning to the door, and ordering him outside.

Boris stared down the rows of prisoners with regret, then he turned and stomped outside, slamming the door so hard that it popped open a couple of inches and hung there.

Rubles stood in the center of the aisle, chest out and shoulders straight, his ghoulish expression wrapped in a veneer of death. He scanned Zach's row and stopped on Gina, but when he got to Craig on the other side, he practically beamed. Stepping back, locking his weapon at his shoulder, he took aim at the first soldier again, the Canadian with his head bowed, grimacing, whispering a prayer.

Sterling said something to his man and then turned his glare on

Rubles. "No you commie bastard! Start with me! Shoot *me* first... shoot me first, I say!"

Rubles paused long enough to grin at the Captain before returning to his sights. The door came open another few inches, and a slim, female shape slipped through, diminutive compared to the guard, lithe and quiet as she snuck in behind Rubles with a long knife in her hand. The short-cropped hair gave Liza away, the whites of her eyes gleaming with feral intensity as she approached. Zach's blood hammered along to his frantic, rhythmic sawing, the tiny knife almost slipping from his fingers. Biting his lip, he forced himself to focus harder.

Liza moved in with the blade pointed down, started to attack, but paused and flipped the weapon so the tip was pointed up. She took two steps back and then ran forward and leaped onto Ruble's back, knocking him off balance, arm slinking around his neck and whipping the knife across his throat, slicing him from ear to ear in a spray of blood that hit the walls. Rubles fired, and the Canadian soldier jerked and screamed in his seat, red gushing from the wound in his chest. Sterling and the rest of his men hollered and cursed Rubles furiously, urging Liza on as the pair staggered backward into the door, slamming it shut and pinning her there. Ruble's gun went off twice more, striking another CAF soldier and hitting the roof in a trickle of dust. He screamed, dropped his rifle, and grabbed Liza's sawing wrist with one hand while elbowing her repeatedly. Rubles was gurgling blood, bubbles forming around his torn trachea and soaking his fatigues, one thin line spurting out in a sudden gush as his carotid artery pulsed.

"Zach!" Gina was kicking in her seat and trying desperately to get up, but the way they had her hands tied behind her, she could barely move.

"Almost got it!" Zach said sawing harder until...

The blade slipped from his fingers and hit the floor.

Zach cursed softly, drawing stares from everyone who'd known what he was doing. Squeezing his bloody fists together, he jerked against his bonds, but the remaining half inch of rope wouldn't break. Teeth bared, shoulders rippling with muscle, he tried again. At first, all Zach heard were the urgent whispers of his friends, the blood pulsing in his head, the bumping and knocking as Liza and Rubles fought, and Boris pounding on the door to get in. Then came the soft tear of rope fibers, a slow ripping sound as each strand was shred into wild hairs by Zach's strength. Finally, his hands popped free, and he swung himself forward out of his seat, staggered a step, and lunged for the door.

Liza and Rubles were crumpled against the door, the Russian spitting and gurgling, slowly dying in a pool of his own blood, teeth bared and bloodstained as he smashed his head into Liza's face. Liza had turned away, absorbing the blows, her skull striking the door even as Boris shoved it from the other side. Zach dove in and snatched up Ruble's rifle, took him by the hair, and rolled him to the side. Then he grabbed Liza's desperate, reaching hand and dragged her away as rounds punched through the wood in splinters and hot lead. It flew open and Boris jumped in with a mean grimace, gun swinging toward Liza who was sprawled on the floor. Zach took his gun's handgrip and forced it upward while jamming his own rifle barrel into the man's chest and firing two quick shots that went clean through him and struck the wall. Grabbing him in a death embrace, spinning in a circle, Zach threw his back against the door and slammed it shut.

He held him there for a moment, eyes squeezed tight and waiting for more soldiers to come, but the camp continued its bustling, ignoring whatever horrors were happening in the prisoner's building.

"We've only got a few minutes," Zach whispered.

Rubles groaned and gurgled again, clutching his throat. Liza growled low and feral, grabbed her dropped blade, and threw herself on him, stabbing him repeatedly, each strike bringing an animal grunt from her throat. Zach put Boris down, slammed the door latch with his elbow, and took Liza by the shoulder, pulling her off the Russian where she fell back and glared up at him, her pale face smeared with blood, teeth still bared and growling.

"Liza, start cutting them free." When she didn't immediately respond, he grabbed her by the wrist and shook her. "Start with the Canadians. Come on, cut them free."

He let her go, knelt by Rubles, and found a knife sheathed on his belt. Zach cut Gina loose first, then Grizzly and Craig. In minutes, the CAF troops were free, Captain Sterling grabbing a rifle and moving to the back of the building. He stood there, measuring the wall first before pointing the gun at the floor.

Zach tossed some cut rope aside and came up. "What are you doing, Sterling?"

"The guards are supposed to be killing us, but there were only a few shots. Someone might get curious."

"Good thinking, Captain. Everyone hold your ears."

The freed prisoners threw their hands over their ears, and the Captain emptied the entire clip into the floor in single shots, one and two at a time, simulating a soldier walking down the row and killing captives. Zach and Sterling returned to the dead Russians and relieved them of their magazines and any other weapons they had on them. A medic knelt by the wounded CAF soldier and tried to dress the gunshot in his chest, finally shaking his head at the Captain.

Sterling glared at the floor in disappointment, then addressed the group. "Great work people. Now, here's what we're going to do —"

Something exploded in the distance, and the usual shouts of Russian officers became more distinct as the camp stirred like a hornet's nest.

Zach moved to a window and scanned the grounds. "Sterling, looks like your buddies are back. I'm seeing some explosions and gunfire on the northwest part of the camp. An attack?"

Sterling circled to join him at the window, taking a look for himself. "We've got several units in the area. We were captured waiting for reinforcements, so maybe that's them."

"I assume you want to join them?"

"That's right. We've got a score to settle with these Russians."

"And kick their asses out of our country," added another who stood by the door with a pistol.

The CAF soldiers had stripped the dead Russians of their guns and knives, and Grizzly had torn off a chair leg and hefted it like a club. Liza was crouched in the center of the room surrounded by Craig and Gina, who were wiping the blood off her face and checking her for other injuries.

"I need to take my people south under orders from Colonel Red

Hawk in Fairbanks. That means we're heading to the motor pool and bugging out."

"You sure you don't want to join us? Might be able to find you a better ride once we hook up with our people."

"No can do," Zach shook his head firmly. "We'd love to help, but we've got to get on the road. Sorry, Captain."

"No apologies necessary." Sterling peeked out the window again to the sight of Russians dropping what they were carrying and sprinting to the northwest. Mortars launched in high arcs and exploded in the woods. The sky lit up with bursts of tracers. The incoming fire was brutal, striking the wall of vehicles the Russians had placed on the edge of camp, heavy rounds cutting through metal like tin cans, sparks and pieces of dangerous shrapnel flying off.

"Sounds like your boys are talking louder now," Zach said.

"Perfect timing." Sterling turned away from the window and faced his men. "Now that I think about it, it might be a better idea to go for the air field. Maybe we can cause a little havoc."

"They've got a big cargo plane out there," Zach said. "Maybe more by now."

"Just tell us where you want us to go, sir." A soldier hefted his pistol. "We're with you."

"You saw the plane out on the tarmac?"

"That's right." Zach gestured toward the southeast. "Big turbo prop plane dropping off supplies. There were maybe twenty-five guards around it. Going to be a tough proposition for you guys, but I wish you luck."

"Same to you." The Captain held out his hand. "Thanks again."

They shook and lined up at the door with the soldiers first and Zach's people coming behind them, followed by the rest of the civilians. While the Canadians had most of the guns, Zach held one of the AK-74s, and he checked it over to ensure the weapon was ready to fire. A civilian brought an arm full of air filtration masks and handed them out, and he hooked one on his belt.

Grizzly stood next to him, brandishing his club, his accent growing thicker with anger. "I am ready to fight again."

"The plan still stands." Zach looked across his group as they huddled close. "Work with Gina and protect Liza and Craig. I'll do the heavy fighting."

Grizzly nodded as Sandy came up with a somber, expression. "Tell me where you last saw Scotty?"

Zach stood straighter, orienting himself and finally pointing to the north and a little west. "About twenty yards inside the tree line inside a gully. He was hunkered down there but I didn't see an air filtration mask. I'm not sure if he survived the hydrocarbons."

"Thanks." Sandy had scavenged the piece of wood from the chair Grizzly had torn apart and held like a club, shifting from one foot to the other and staring at the door.

Zach rested his hand on her shoulder. "You can come with us if you want. We started off on the wrong foot back in Deadhorse, but Scotty and I... we let bygones be bygones."

Sandy nodded as Sterling popped the door and led his men to the right along the front of the building. The nearby lights were flickering, bathing the area in a strobe storm, and Sterling and his men squatted for a moment before taking off, leaving Zach with a momentary sense of panic. He raced to the corner of the building and checked for Russian guards, then sprinted toward the motor pool fifty yards away. The shadows of the CAF soldiers continued on to the right, splitting from Zach's group and disappearing into the night. A moment later, a machine gun ripped off, followed by shouts and screams.

With a silent prayer for them, Zach focused on the light glinting off the windows and chrome bumpers ahead, running as fast as he could but slowing when the others started falling behind. Besides his people, and Sandy, there were three civilians tagging along, but he didn't stop until they reached the first row of cars, slipping between a pair of sedans. He crouched there and waved for everyone to squat. Once they were accounted for, he peeked over the hood toward the north, then crept to the other side and checked south and east. All the guards were gone, likely run off to join the fighting, and the motor pool was half as full as it was before. Their Humvee stood out in the shadows, looming larger than most of the other vehicles around except for the SUVs and vans.

He leaned toward Grizzly. "The truck's there, and the keys are on the seat."

"Good. I am ready to drive."

"Okay. Let's go."

Without waiting for a response, Zach slipped from between the sedans and made his way to the right, rifle up and ready to fire should he meet a soldier. Footsteps crunched on the gravel behind him, and the air screamed with the battle's growing intensity and the *rat-a-tat* of guns carrying on. Tracers shifted toward one of the spotlight towers, raking across it and cutting the Russian controller to pieces.

They reached the truck and Zach directed everyone in behind them while Grizzly went for the door and squeezed his big body inside. Zach moved to the back of the line, speaking to the three civilians who crouched there, a man, woman, and teenager doing their best to wear brave faces amidst the flashing guns and combat sounds. Sandy crouched there, too, quiet with a knife in her hand.

"There's only so much room in the Humvee," Zach said. "I'm sorry, but we can't take all of you. Just Sandy, like I promised."

The mother and father shared a look, before the father kneeled close. "I didn't figure you would, but I don't know what else to do. We were snatched out of our store when everyone else ran. We're not soldiers... this is my wife and kid we're talking about here. Help me out, man."

The Humvee rumbled to life, and Grizzly waved for them to get in. Gina jumped in back, while Craig helped Liza through the other door so she sat in between them, leaving the family of three and Sandy crouched by the Humvee's rear fender.

Zach checked around. "Okay, wait here."

He slipped between the rows, ducking when tracers ripped across the center of the camp and flew over their heads, crawling on his hands and knees past a van and reaching a newer black four-wheel-drive. Climbing in the driver's side, he checked beneath the seats, flipped down the sun visor, and finally struck gold in the glove compartment where he pulled out a set of keys.

Back at the Humvee, he held the keys up to the father. "There's a nice four-wheel-drive over there. Take that."

He accepted them with a nod of thanks. "I appreciate this, man. But we don't have any protection, either. I don't have —"

Zach circled to the Humvee's rear hatch and popped it open to find their weapons tossed inside with their backpacks. Zach shoved the Kalashnikov into the father's hands and took up his own spear, checking the load and digging beneath their equipment to find the extra ammo he'd packed.

"They left us our weapons?" Gina asked, reaching from the back seat to grab her AR-15 and check that it was loaded.

"They probably thought our weapons were junk." Zach searched his pockets for the extra magazines he'd taken off Boris and handed them to the father. "Do you know how to shoot a rifle?"

"A hunting rifle, yes. Never fired one of these." He held the gun out and stared blankly at some of the switches.

Zach slammed the hatch and looked for Sandy, but she wasn't where she'd been crouched, and when he stood tall enough to see over the Humvee, he spotted her running off to the north toward the woods there. With a sad head shake, Zach brought the family to the passenger door. "You'll have to figure the weapon out on your own."

"How are you getting out of here? I mean, are you going south?"

"With haste." Zach threw open his door and put one leg in.

"But there are Russians on the airfield, and that's the only way to get to the service road out."

"Captain Sterling and his soldiers will be down there fighting them about now, if the fight isn't over already."

The mother's and son's faces were etched with fear, holding hands and crouched behind the Humvee's armored protection. The boy swallowed hard and stared at Zach as if he was their only chance, face lit up by the distant explosions.

"I'll tell you what. Get the Jeep started and wait for us to pull out. Stay right on our tails, and we'll make a run for it together. But you gotta stay on us. We're not slowing down for you, got it?"

"Yeah, I got it. Stay on your tail. I can do that. Thank you."

"Thank me if you live through this. Ready?"

"Yeah, give me one minute." The man gave a terse nod and turned to herd his family around the Humvee toward the black Jeep.

Zach climbed in, slammed the door shut behind him, and sat in the comfortable rumbling vehicle, surrounded by armor and bullet-resistant glass, a thin veil of protection against the chaos. Sweat trickled down his back, and the pain in his stomach had returned, the encrusted bandage broken and leaking blood again. As they waited for the family, he held up his wrist to measure the rope burns and cuts on his hand. Then a shadow moved a few yards ahead of them, and he gripped his weapon and reached for the door handle. But they were gone, disappeared into the night, no one noticing the idling Humvee at all.

"Ready to drive?"

Grizzly sat calmly with both hands on the wheel, his seat pushed forward, belly rubbing against it. "Always ready to drive."

Gina reached into the front with some bottled waters. "Drink up. Rubles was pretty stingy."

"And he got what came to him." Craig tilted up a bottle and drank greedily.

Liza was leaning forward, elbows on her knees and touching her face with shaking hands. Her cuts stood out of the darkness, deep gashes on her forehead and mouth, blood smeared across her skin. The swelling around her left cheek was easily visible, and Gina wetted a rag from the cargo area and handed it to her. Bright lights whipped through the parking lot and pinned them, the Jeep pulling up, and Zach rolled his window down and waved. A moment later, the headlamps went off, and he gave the thumbs-up sign, then turned to Grizzly with a nod.

"Okay, man. Drive us out of here. We're heading back along the tarmac, past the big turboprop plane, and onto the service road. Don't stop for anyone."

"No problem."

The Humvee kicked into gear and tore off, shedding gravel and stiff grass as they shot down the central row and took a hard right at the entrance, whipping onto the service road. The big turboprop plane sat about two hundred yards ahead in the middle of the tarmac with running figures illuminated by the flashing belly lights. Gunfire popped off all around the aircraft, Russians trading fire with what he presumed were Sterling's men.

"Looks like they found a couple more guns," Zach commented as Grizzly hit a bump and landed on the tarmac with a jolt and squeal of tires. "Stay to the left, Grizzly. We don't want to get in the middle of that fight."

"No problem."

They swept hard to the left, edging up to the shoulder, as far away from the crates and equipment behind which the Russians were hiding. The Jeep was right behind them, keeping up with Grizzly's crazy cuts, bumper-to-bumper as they rushed toward the plane. A pair of Russians saw them coming and broke cover, cross-stepping and firing. Rounds pinged off the Humvee as everyone instinctively ducked. Bullets struck them hard, and Zach started to roll his window down and fire back when Grizzly gave him an offhanded wave.

"Stay down, Zach. I will take care of."

The Russian was calm as he whipped the wheel to the right, Humvee tires screeching horribly, vibrations rippling through suspension to rattle his legs. Zach was thrown to the left as a sudden barrage of rounds struck the front of the vehicle. The soldiers' eyes flew wide as the truck banked toward them, clipping one man and hitting the other full on, rifle flying, arms waving as he rolled over the hood and windshield, then tumbled off the back. Everyone twisted in their seat, watching as the Jeep swerved to one side, missed the men, and barreled ahead to get right back on their tail.

"Nice driving," Grizzly said, "but not as good as the Grizzly."

Zach chuckled nervously and shook his head as the wind pushed blood up his side of the windshield in reverse streaks, another couple of cracks running along the bottom edge. Behind them, a small battle played out with more gunfire flashes as Sterling's men moved in from the shoulder and bodies fell. A pair of grenades went off near the loading area at the back of the plane, but that's all they saw as Grizzly reached a paved road that led to the highway, past the long Yukon First Nation style buildings they'd seen throughout the town.

Grizzly turned them south onto the highway in a squeal of tires, pressing the accelerator to the floor and grinding the diesel harder. They passed the ice cream parlor and the rest of downtown on the left, hitting the scenic bridge where abandoned Russian barricades were set up in the form of logs and broken-down vehicles. Grizzly edged up to an SUV and nudged it aside, making way for them to reach the south shore with the Jeep right behind them.

Clinging tightly to Klondike Highway, they drove southeast along Grayling Bay. Grizzly flipped on his headlamps, cutting through the gloom, bathing the road in stark light, and illuminating the soft snow whipped up by the turbulence of their passing.

CHAPTER TWENTY

Wendy Christensen, Pearisburg, Virginia

Wendy was in the middle of a beautiful dream where Zach was just getting home from work and the smells of a smoking grill filled the air. Charlie was at the kitchen table doing homework as always and David was messing around with something upstairs, probably video games. She greeted him at the door, tall and handsome in his NYPD uniform, clean-shaven face, a short crop of blonde hair, and blue eyes. Despite how hard her day was at work, she tried to greet him with a smile and a hug, and she loved when he picked her up and spun her in a circle.

"We're so silly," she'd said. "We're like a couple of people in a movie. Dumb and happy."

"It's easy to be happy when I have you to come home to."

It had gone that way a thousand times, though the exact words were always a little different. Some days were worse than others, though most turned out happy... nothing they couldn't handle, nothing they couldn't work through. Before the brutal hostage situation, Zach had been a different person, loving and attentive, putting those around him first. Afterwards, he'd gone quiet, a dark cloud looming over him, like he'd put his spirit in a bottle and corked it tight. But his last phone call had changed all that. Something in his voice was different: the concern, the hope, and the love, wrapped up in the promise he'd made to come home to them.

Lightning cracked, and a dog whined with worry, tail thumping against the floor. Wendy opened her eyes and shook off the grogginess, leaning forward and remembering she was sleeping in one of the backyard sheds facing the rear of the house. It was small and dusty with oil containers on shelves, gardening tools, and a couple of jerrycans of gasoline tucked beneath an old table. David sat on a stool in front of a four pane window built into the wall, giving him a great view of the house. He gripped Clyde's collar to keep him in place, and Charlie had her hand over his muzzle.

He glanced back. "They're here."

Wendy got up from the stool she'd been dozing on and approached from the side, putting her shoulder against the door and looking through the window into the rain. Dark figures crept along the side of the garage, one stopping beneath the camera and spray-painting it black. Two others worked at the door handle until it popped open, and they slipped inside.

"Darla was right," Wendy whispered. "Are you guys ready?"

"I am," Charlie nodded.

"Me too," David released Clyde's collar and checked his weapon.

"You guys know the plan. Charlie, head out toward the stables and guard the horses in case someone else comes around. David and I are going to do our thing." David put his hand on the doorknob, but Wendy took him by the arm. "Remember what I said, kids. Shoot first and ask questions later."

They stepped through the door into the stinging rain.

Something was buzzing next to Darla's hand, drawing her from a horrible dream about the last three years of Ron's life, a dark cloud of illness that had haunted them like a nightmare. The change from living at home to spending hours at the hospital, then hospice, had filled her heart with a permanent hole, breaking it many times over, so much that the scars had grown tough and thick over the wounds. She shifted and coughed softly, and the PC tablet buzzed again. Wiping crust from her eyes, she blinked at the generic set of drawers and random wall decorations in the room, bathed in a soft candle glow. She lifted the tablet in time to see someone raise and spray paint over the camera lens by the back door.

"They're here, Darla." Wendy's voice popped from the radio on the nightstand. "Five of them."

"Just like I figured." She sneered and pushed her hair out of her eyes.

Lifting the shotgun from beside her with her right hand, she spread her knees and used her feet to pull a wooden crate closer, resting the barrel on it and sprawling her legs to aim at the door without shooting her foot off. The silence sank in, nothing but the sound of her shallow breathing and the heartbeat in her chest. Something rattled in the kitchen, doors opening and shutting, footsteps creaking on the tiles, growing softer when they reached the carpeted areas. She picked out one, two... more than that. They were the intruders, the killers, strangers in her home.

It was as good a time as any to turn the war with McCallum bloody.

Whispers graced her ears, and she tracked them on the other side of the wall as they stopped at the other spare bedroom, grabbing the doorknob and whipping it open, rushing inside with swift footsteps. There came more soft voices, drawers sliding, cloths and extra bedding tossed on the floor. Then they were in the hall again, peeking into the bathroom before gathering right outside her door. Holding the shotgun one-handed, she raised the stock and came forward to put her shoulder against it, keeping her wounded arm close to her side. She half expected the door to open slowly, but it flew wide fast and banged the wall. A man charged in with a weapon drawn. Darla was already tracking him, squeezing the trigger before he fully left her sights, the shotgun blast like thunder in the room. Crimson color splashed the wall, and the man flew back, his right shoulder blown half off, flesh and wet jacket flying off in pieces. The next man entered behind him, firing wildly over her head. Darla was already cocking the shotgun, leaning hard right and firing the second shell with a kick that nearly shook the weapon from her hands. The man took it full in the chest, hitting the wall and going down. Another man appeared in the door frame but leaped back into the hallway with a curse.Darla cocked the rifle with a clack, kicking the box away and rolling off the side of the bed, landing with a pained grunt. A second later, two gunshots struck the wall where she'd been sitting, and she somehow got her legs beneath her, lifting and dropping the shotgun across the bed. She fired at the door, but the men were gone, their footsteps fading as they fled.

Darla cackled like a witch with a sandpaper voice. "Let that be a lesson to you, dipshits! Don't come into my house and shoot at me, boys! No, sir! Don't even try it!"

The two muffled shotgun blasts sent a shift through Wendy's body, and she spread her legs and stood fifteen yards from the garage door, her rifle aimed dead center, finger on the trigger and ready to shoot at the first signs of movement. David was off to the left, holding his Springfield in his thin arms, prepared to catch anyone Wendy missed. While she'd been unable to kill Matt Stegmann, she held her rifle relaxed against her shoulder, leaning into it, breathing steady in the dripping rain. She wouldn't have problems making up for her mistake.

The first intruder appeared in the frame, and she squeezed off two quick shots, catching him in the midsection and left side as he slid sideways and down along the wall, dropping his weapon and clutching his stomach. The second man came right behind the first, but the kick from Wendy's first two shots had put her off target, and the man squeezed beneath them to get away, flying past David as his Springfield popped to life, sharp flares in the late evening gloom. The third man appeared for a moment and then retreated out of sight.

"Damn!" Wendy shifted her barrel a foot to the right and fired three shots at an angle into the siding. The man on the other side cursed and charged through the doorway holding his hip and shooting wildly in Wendy's direction. She ducked, slipped, and fell in a splash as David exchanged a brief round of gunfire with him. He hobbled quickly away, heading for the stables. David started to go after him but paused and ran back to Wendy.

"Are you okay, Mom?"

"Yeah." She shook him off and jogged toward the stables. "Go inside and check on Darla. I'll run them off."

Charlie had been waiting for something to happen, standing at the rear by the supply side entrance after locking the main doors on the stable side. It was almost pitch dark except for a dim exterior floodlight above her, creating raindrop shadows on the ground as a misty haze burned off. She was dry, but the rain hit so hard it splashed a good foot inside the building, dousing her boots and making her feet cold. They'd been waiting for hours in that shed, hoping the promise Darla had made wouldn't come true. She'd been happy to spend the time with Clyde, kneeling on the blanket and play-wrestling with him, finally lying next to him and nodding off. The time passed in waves of rain, which meant an eternity of minutes that never ended. But when the men came, Charlie had done as she was told and took Clyde out to the stables with a dreadful uneasiness growing in her stomach.

When the shotgun blasts went off, she swallowed hard, took her pistol in hand, and stepped out with Clyde into the rain. At the corner of the barn, she looked back west toward the house but could only see the far corner. With her shoulder against the wall, she stuck beneath the eaves to stay somewhat dry. It didn't take long for more shots to follow, two quick ones, then another, then too many to count as the air erupted with firing.

A man hobbled out of the mist, staggering and cursing, something wrong with his hip. He had a pistol in his hand, and Charlie stepped onto the gravel lane and held her pistol pointed at his chest.

"Hold it right there, mister!" she shouted. "I said *stop!*" The commands sounded high-pitched and feeble, voice shaking, surprised when the man stopped and held both hands in the air. Clyde growled and tugged at the end of his leash, but Charlie gave it a jerk to keep him there. "Get down on your knees, now!"

"I can't get down." He kept coming, his face strained and wincing, gasps spitting from his mouth. "Got shot in the... hip. Just let me by. Let me go..."

"I said *stop*!" Charlie took a step back, drawing Clyde with her.

Clyde hung from the end of his leash, straining forward, raising on his haunches, suddenly pivoting to his left and charging someone coming from the corner where she'd been standing. A boot flew in and kicked Clyde in the side, and he yelped and rolled away. Charlie reeled, gun up as a man stepped up, grabbed her gun, and tried to tear it from her hands. When she wouldn't let go, he shoved her hard, but Charlie clung to the weapon, teeth bared, lunging and clawing at his face with her left hand. Furrows ripped down his cheek, skin beneath her fingernails as she went full wildcat on him and reached to take another chunk.

"Agh!" he cried, twisting the gun upward out of her hand and punching her in the temple so hard she fell backward, staggering, tripping, and hitting the gravel.

She blinked up at him, head ringing, the world going fuzzy around the edges. The man tried to turn the gun on her, but Clyde flew up and locked his jaws on his arm, the dog's body swinging as his momentum carried him by. Then he landed on his rear legs and pulled, lurching backward, jerking, snarling and ripping back and forth as the man screamed and punched at him. The limping man strode past Charlie with a sneer and grabbed Clyde by his collar, pistol-whipping him in the head. Clyde let the second man's arm go with a yelp and tried to slink away, but the injured man clung to his collar and jerked him backward.

The second man was holding his wrist against his chest, sizing up Clyde, charging in and kicking him in the side again. Clyde flew from the first man's grasp and rolled across the gravel with a pained yelp.

Charlie screamed as both men raised their guns to fire. "*Nooooo!*"

Wendy came around the side of the barn to see figures pushing and shoving at the far end at the edge of the light. Rifle raised, she closed in on them but couldn't tell them apart in the shadows. Then Charlie flew out of the group and staggered backwards, windmilling and landing on her backside with a sharp cry. One of the men turned to fire on her, but Clyde sprinted in and hit him, grabbing his arm, shaking, snarling, pulling him away. The man she'd shot earlier hobbled up and pistol-whipped Clyde with his gun, another man kicked him away. Wendy was twenty-five yards off, teeth bared and fury coursing through her veins. She struggled to see but aimed dead center at the two men who were about to shoot Clyde.

As soon as Charlie yelled "Nooooo!" she fired on the wounded man, five staccato shots that bucked the weapon against her shoulder. The man slumped forward like he'd been shoved, firing into the gravel at Clyde's paws. He half turned to get a bead on her, but his strength gave out, and he dropped the gun and fell. By the time she switched targets, the second man was stumbling away and firing back at her, bright flashes of his gunfire, the smaller .380 lacking the power and distance of her rifle but dangerous all the same. She took an extra breath to get him centered, tracking him as he retreated, then emptying the rest of her magazine on him, each bullet hitting him like a punch until he finally dropped and lay dead in the driveway.

Wendy released the breath she'd been holding and jogged toward Charlie, lifting her to her feet and dragging her into the light. Charlie was crying and reaching for Clyde as he ran up and licked her hands. Wendy had slung her rifle and was checking Charlie's arms and face, blood smears all over her cheeks but unable to tell where she was hurt.

"Are you okay, honey? I think you're bleeding, but I can't tell from where."

Charlie felt her chest and arms, then shook her head. "I'm fine. Just got hit in the side of the head... wait, Mom!" Charlie grabbed Wendy's hands and held them up, wide-eyed at all the blood on her fingers. "Your stomach. You're shot!"

Wendy stared at herself in disbelief, laughing nervously at first but noticing a slow ache developing in her midsection, a sharp twisting of her insides like hands wringing her bowels.

"What?" She pushed at the hole in her poncho where red stained the edges. "I can't be shot," she said, suddenly breathless as her wind was stolen.

One second Wendy was standing, then she was on her knees, barely feeling the sharp rocks through her jeans. Images flashed in her mind... Zach coming home to find her gone and the kids struggling or dead because she'd made one simple mistake and not shot a man. Charlie fell to her knees in front of her, grabbing her wrists and trying to get her to her feet, eyes wide with breathless panic.

"Get up, Mom. Please. You've got to get up. We've got to get you inside..."

Wendy blinked as pain and darkness grew together in black vines that entwined her consciousness and dragged her into oblivion to the soft sounds of pattering rain.

"I'm sorry, honey," she whispered and fell into Charlie's arms.

CHAPTER TWENTY-ONE

David Christensen, Pearisburg, Virginia

David moved through the house quickly and quietly, down the laundry room hallway and into the kitchen, gun raised in both hands like the cops did in the movies, following a trail of blood to the back hallway. Light spilled from the open bedroom door and illuminated swirling smoke. Holes peppered the opposite wall, and the door frame was chipped up and splintered.

He started down it but paused. "Darla? Darla, are you down there?"

"Yeah, I'm down here, boy. I got 'em."

David rushed to the room and entered where Darla was sitting at the foot of the bed, a dead man at her feet, another in front of David, both sprawled on the bloodstained carpet. Splatters covered the walls and ceiling, pieces of flesh splattered there.

"Are you okay?" David asked.

"Yeah, I'm fine. These guys..." She gestured with her good arm. "Dead as door nails."

"I guess so," David chuckled uncertainly. "We, uh, got one guy outside, and Mom's out there chasing the other two away."

"I hope she gets them." Darla's eyes were intent. "The less McCallum has to send back here, the better. Now, you better —"

Gunshots reached them through the house, muffled but unmistakable as the powerful pops of Wendy's rifle he'd come to know so well.

"That came from the stables." He turned and rushed down the hallway as fast as he could, bumping off the laundry room door frame and leaping into the garage. He was out the back door in a second, sprinting through the rain to the side of the stables where Charlie and Wendy were kneeling on the gravel lane. Clyde was beside them, sniffing at Wendy's hands as she held them up and stared at her blood-slicked fingers. Two dead men lay nearby, unmoving, their chests filled with holes, turning the gravel red.

"Mom?" he whispered, rushing over as Wendy collapsed on her side into a puddle. David dropped to his knees, and he and Charlie rolled her onto her back.

"What happened?"

"We fought with those two men, and one of them took my gun and shot Mom… oh, no, I got her killed!"

"No you didn't." David holstered his weapon and felt her wrist and neck at the same time, fingers searching her cold, clammy skin for a pulse. He didn't feel one at first, and a flare of dread and panic surged through his body. Letting go of her wrist, he turned her head to the side and made sure he had his fingers on the artery. He closed his eyes and waited, Charlie saying something he ignored, and there it was, a faint bump against his fingertips, the beating of his mother's heart… a sign of life.

"Come on, Charlie. We need to get her inside."

"You mean carry her?"

"Yeah. You grab her feet, and I'll grab her shoulders. She doesn't weigh much."

Charlie faltered and wiped her eyes, staring at her mother's blank face, golden curls lying flat against her cheeks. David had already gotten to her shoulders and slipped his hands beneath her arms.

"Come on, Charlie! Get her feet!" He kicked a puddle, splashing water into her face for good measure.

"Okay..."

She kneeled between Wendy's feet and got a good grip. David counted to three, and they lifted her off the ground so she swung easily between them. It was still more than Charlie was used to, dead weight, too. Wendy started to slip from her hands, but she adjusted her grip and held on, nodding for him to go.

David led the way and walked backwards, focused on staying on his feet and not tripping. "We'll take her into the garage and get Darla. She'll know what to do."

Slowly but surely, and without dropping her once, they squelched through the wet yard toward the wide-open garage entrance with Clyde trotting next to them, sniffing at Wendy before Charlie shooed him away. Fears flashed in David's mind, the sick, dismal sense that he might lose his mother. But it only made him grip her harder, lift her higher, and grit his teeth against the crippling emotions. Soon, they had her inside and placed her on the garage floor where Charlie fell to one knee and started to lift her jacket and undershirts.

"We need more light," David said, crashing through the laundry room into the kitchen where he grabbed the lantern.

Darla was standing at the end of the hallway, her good arm braced against the wall. "What happened?"

"Mom got shot!" Racing back to the garage, he set the lantern nearby and cranked it to high. "What can you see?"

Charlie had lifted up her shirts to show a very tiny bullet hole almost dead center in her stomach, blood pulsing from the wound with every breath Wendy took.

She held up an oily rag. "I've got an old rag here, but it's dirty —"

"Here, take these," Darla was coming down the stairs, holding the door frame with one hand and a stack of clean rags in the other. "You need something relatively clean, girl, or you'll infect that."

Darla shuffled closer and leaned in. "David, press a rag on top and then put some pressure on it. Charlie, go get the first aid kits where your mama lined them up on the kitchen counter. We'll need some gauze, and I think one of them has some coagulant and maybe even some hemostatic sponges."

Charlie nodded and took off while David folded the rag neatly with shaking hands and pressed it to the wound. A ripple of shudders passed through his body, and his teeth chattered uncontrollably, a belated twister of emotions churning inside him. Tears sprang from his eyes and he tensed to keep from losing control of the already soaked rag.

A scrawny claw landed on his shoulder and squeezed hard. Darla's gaunt face hovered over him, a corner of her mouth lifted in a sneer. "Listen, boy. You better get a hold of yourself or you're going to lose your mama. You understand that?"

Gritting his teeth and shaking the indecision from his mind, he held the rag over the wound with one hand, folded a new rag, and swapped them quickly, tossing the old one aside. "Charlie!"

"I'm coming!" Charlie flew out of the laundry room and fell to her knees opposite him, slamming down three first aid kits and looking up at Darla for a decision.

She was circling around to Wendy's head and shoulders, pointing to one of the bigger kits in the middle, unmarked but neatly bound with a leather strap. "Try that one. I think that might have some of those sponges."

"What do they look like?" Charlie asked as she rifled through the contents, putting aside big roles of gauze and tape.

"It will be a big syringe filled with these little pellets."

Charlie shook her head. "I don't see them anywhere. There's nothing like that at all, just a bunch of gauze."

"Dang it," Darla snapped, glancing back into the kitchen. "He might've switched them around or something. I know what we can do. Pull out a roll of gauze, cut a piece off, then roll it up good and tight. That's it, Charlie. Now, do two or three more."

Charlie's fingers worked swiftly, cutting big pieces with her teeth, ripping them, and rolling them up into two-inch long cylinder shapes. "Okay, what now?"

"I want David to pull off the rag and for Charlie to stuff those roles of gauze into the bullet hole as deep down as you can get them, got it? Get them good and deep so it presses against whatever's gushing down there."

"Okay," Charlie's voice shook.

"On three," David said. "One, two... three!"

They swapped positions, Charlie shoving one of the gauze roles down into the tiny hole as blood pulsed between her fingers. Then she stuck another one in, then another, five more until the hole was plugged tight.

"I think that worked." Charlie held her hands over the wound as if it might explode in a geyser. When it didn't, she grabbed a rag and began wiping blood from around it.

"Now, David. Keep pressure on it. There you go. Check her pulse and breathing, Charlie."

Charlie switched positions and put her fingers over Wendy's neck, nodding and smiling. "I've got a pulse."

"Is it strong?"

"What's strong?"

"I wish I still had my blood pressure cuff..." Darla looked around. "I know it's in the house somewhere, but it's been a long time. Charlie, see what you can do to make her comfortable."

Charlie stood and dashed into the laundry room, coming back with a pillow and slipping it beneath Wendy's head. "We let Matt use this to sit on when we had him in the laundry room."

"I'll bet she wishes she would've shot him now," Darla said. "What gun did they shoot her with?"

"My Ruger .380."

"Well, maybe it won't be so bad then."

Charlie pounded her fist on her knee. "He took it from me, then shot Mom. It's my damn fault!"

"It's not your fault," David snapped. "Now shut up about that. We have to help Mom."

"What's not your fault?" Wendy asked with a slurred voice, head turning in slow confusion on the pillow.

"Mom!" Charlie cried. "How do you feel?"

"Stomach... agh!" She tried to touch it, tried to hold herself up and see.

"You got shot, Mom," David said and eased her back. "We got you inside the garage and stopped the bleeding, but we don't know what to do now."

"The men...?"

"You got them both. They're dead."

"And you're okay?"

"We're fine, but you lost a lot of blood. What should we do next?"

Wendy tried to see her belly wound again but couldn't lift her head very far. She found the kids' hands and squeezed them. "Good, kids. Good..." She grimaced and clenched in pain. "*Argh*... good job. I love you guys."

"We love you, too," David said. "Just... tell us what to do."

"As long as the bleeding's stopped," Wendy winced, "I should be fine. Can you get me into one of the bedrooms? Maybe a couple of pain pills?"

Darla leaned in with a hushed tone. "Now, Wendy. That's a belly wound. Albeit not from a high caliber weapon, but tricky all the same. You could pull out of this. Then again, you might not. I've seen my share of belly wounds, and you really need to get that looked at. I know a guy up around the hill. We can prep you for travel and take you in my truck. You could risk it staying here, but you need his help —"

Wendy waved her off. "I'll be fine. I just need to rest."

Charlie had been watching the exchange with growing anxiety. "Maybe we should listen to her. If there's someone close by who can help better than us, we should do it."

"Is it a hospital?" David asked.

"Not a hospital exactly, but the best place to take your mother right now."

David took Wendy's hand in both of his. "We should do it. It's just a drive away."

"It'll be a bumpy ride, and we'll have to make sure to keep the bleeding under control, monitor her blood pressure and all, but —"

"We just got here... got settled in... I ruined it," Wendy gasped in pain, pausing to let it pass. "It's my fault. I should've shot that rat when I had the chance."

"No," Charlie said. "I'm the one they took the gun from. You said to shoot first and ask questions later, and I didn't. I didn't do what you said and now —"

David grabbed her arm and squeezed it, giving her a slow but certain head shake. "We should stop blaming ourselves right now. I'm just as guilty as anyone."

"But you agreed with Darla," Charlie replied with pitiful self-scorn. "You were right. I should have listened to you, but I was a baby."

"I couldn't even do it." David squeezed harder. "All I did was talk about it, but I couldn't pull the trigger either. That's all behind us now. We've got to help Mom. She's..."

Wendy's expression had fallen slack again, her eyes shutting, breathing going shallow.

"Mom?" Charlie shook David off and stroked Wendy's hair, lying forward so her ear was resting on her chest. The world grew smaller and David's mind, pressing in from all sides, threatening to crush him. Nothing mattered. Not the rain nor the wind. Not Clyde's baleful eyes as he stood behind Charlie with his tail wagging slowly. All that mattered was his mother's life, her being able to take another breath.

"Son?" Darla placed her hand on David's shoulder and leaned most of her fragile weight on him. "Yeah?"

"You're going to have to make a decision. The faster the better. You want to keep your mama here or take her to a doctor?"

"How am I supposed to decide that? I'm just a teenager."

"Life hits all of us hard, and it don't care about your age or your social status or if you are on Santa's naughty list. The important thing is that when it hits us, we make the right decisions. Now, I'm too weak to lift Wendy or drive, and she's not my mother. This one's squarely on your head."

David and Charlie shared an uncertain look, and he saw strength in her, the way she held herself straight and confident despite the uncertainty. David was the same way, but the fragility inside him was hardening and holding resolutely against the weight of the world.

"We'll take her," he said. "Darla, get the keys. Charlie, let's get Mom in the back seat, and remember to be super careful."

"First, we've got to stabilize her a little better," Darla gestured to the first aid kits. "Get her coat off and let's get a bandage wrapped around her waist. One of those elastic ones that sticks".

David and Charlie worked together to get her jacket off, but she still had several layers. "Should we cut these off?"

"No, just pull the shirts up. David, lift your mother... *gently*. Charlie, did you find a bandage?"

Charlie held up a thick roll. "Got it right here."

Darla nodded. "Okay, do it."

David leaned over Wendy and grabbed her by her waist, lifting the small of her back so Charlie could get her thinner arm through. Charlie dropped the end of the bandage roll, pulled her arm out, then reached over the top to grab it, wrapping it three times around her waist to seal the bandage and gauze roles tight.

She cut the roll and pressed the self-adhering end down, smoothing it out. "That's it," she said.

Darla nodded and started to shuffle back into the laundry room. "Okay. Now I'll get the keys."

"I've got her feet." Charlie went and waited.

David walked to the truck cab and opened the back door, sizing up the distance they'd have to carry her. "Okay, we'll go legs first. Just get her feet into the seat, then climb in and pull her the rest of the way."

"Got it. I'm ready."

David returned to Wendy's shoulders, slipping his hands beneath her and lifting by her armpits high enough so his elbows were locked like he was doing a dumbbell curl. Another three count, and they had her off the floor, the pair circling to the door, Charlie sliding in on her backside and pulling Wendy's legs with her, wiggling and kicking until Wendy was almost inside.

"Good job, Charlie." David strained to keep her elevated, putting one foot on the edge of the door frame to support her with his knee. "I've got her. Can you pull her legs in the rest of the way?"

"Yeah, one second." Charlie moved deeper in, grabbed her boots, and hauled her all the way in.

"Okay, awesome," David rested her on the seat with a grunt. "She fits inside pretty well, but we'll need to make sure the door doesn't close on her."

"I'll tuck her legs." Charlie manipulated her legs until her knees were bent.

"Great work, Charlie. Stay in there. I'll grab the blanket and the pillow."

David circled to pick them up as Darla was coming out of the laundry room with a set of keys and an automatic blood pressure cuff in her hand. She tossed the keys to David and shuffled toward the passenger door, calling back to Charlie. "Do you know how to take blood pressure?"

"No."

"Okay, I'll show you."

David got in the driver's side and gave Charlie the blanket and pillow, then climbed behind the wheel and started the truck up on the first try.

"You've got to open the garage door, son. It's not on electric, so you'll have to pull the cord."

"Right." David hustled to do that, and a blast of wind and rain rushed inside, cooling his burning face and frantic emotions.

Back behind the wheel, he pulled out and came to a stop behind the white pickup, getting out and running to the garage where Clyde was waiting, confused and whining.

"It'll be okay, boy," David said as he closed the side door, locked it, and walked to the roll down door. "We're just taking my mom to the hospital, but we'll be back soon. You've got food and water in your bowls."

Clyde's tail wagged a little harder, and he licked his jaws and whined higher.

"I know you'll miss Charlie, but we'll be back, I swear."

The door lowered with a rolling clatter and fell shut. Twisting the handle to lock it, he ran to the truck and got in, easing down the steep driveway with water running between the tires and the windshield wipers cranked to high. They reached the bottom of the driveway where the flooding was worse and the pavement was cracked to pieces.

"Go right out of here," Darla pointed. "Take it slow. We'll get there."

"How's that blood pressure coming, hon?"

"Looks like about one seventeen over seventy-six. Is that good?"

"Not too bad. I figure she might have lost twenty-five ounces of blood or so, give or take. Blood pressure should still be okay. How's her pulse rate?"

"Ninety-four."

Darla kept her eyes on the road, pointing out obstructions and slippages to David, but he was already on it, braking and accelerating to get around obstacles and bumps.

"Ninety-four isn't too bad, either. Take a new reading every few minutes or so and remember them. That heart rate will go up the more blood she loses, and it's a good way to tell if we sealed up that wound good and tight."

"Got it."

"We'll want to tell the doctor that when we get there."

"Okay."

"I just hope he's still there and has enough beds."

"Who is this guy?"

"Just a friend of mine who comes down to take care of the horses every now and again."

David shook his head in confusion. "The horses?"

"Yeah. Doc Nance is a veterinarian."

"What?" David slammed his palm on the steering wheel. "We're taking my mom to a vet? What can he do?"

"More than you think," Darla snapped back with a glare. "What you need to do is keep your eyes on the road and get us there alive. Go up this hill here."

David approached a sharp right that cut straight up the hill, one of those patched up roads with barely any shoulders, drowning in waves of water in a glistening layer. The angle to get on it seemed ridiculous, the cracked pavement on a sharp slope. Up higher, some sections were broken off and would still require him to ride on the banks and put one or two tires in the grass to get past them.

"What are you waiting for?"

"You want me to drive up that?"

"Unless you want to carry your mother up that hill and have her die on the way, best hit the gas. Don't worry, this has got four-wheel-drive, and it's a V-8 diesel. Ron's pride and joy. He gave it some stupid name like Joy or Bertha or something... seemed to change it all the time. Bottom line, don't be afraid of a few potholes, but don't slide off the sides either."

David shook his head. "Thanks for the driving advice."

He eased one tire onto the incline, and gravity pulled him back down almost immediately. With a little more gas and a throaty bellow of diesel power, he got both tires on it and had the grill pointed up, but he pounded the break and held them there.

Darla started to snap at him but took a deep breath and addressed him in a quiet tone. "I know it looks dangerous as all get out, and I hated driving up there myself, but the only other way is around the other side of Buck Hill, and I can't promise those roads will be any better. This one here... it will take you straight up in just a couple of minutes. It's really your mom's best bet."

She peered harder through the window with a look of gritty determination. "Hit the gas and hold it down. Don't let up or stop. If you go off the side and get stuck, put the emergency brake on. We can try to carry your mother up the rest of the way." She grabbed his arm in that claw-like grip of hers and raised one thin eyebrow. "You can do this, David."

David swallowed hard. "Okay. Ready back there, Charlie? It's going to be a bumpy ride."

Charlie gave him a thumbs up.

"Here goes."

David marked the path up to the top, noting the twists and turns, making mental guesses and calculations on which angles to take. Wendy's groans from the backseat terrified him, like someone was ripping her insides apart. Her breathing finally tapered off into shallow gasps that settled into a steady rhythm again.

"Go, David," Charlie said, her face pale and frightened in the rearview. "Just go!"

David switched from brake to gas and launched the big diesel truck up the hill with a lurch that pinned him back to the seat, arms stretched, hands white knuckling the wheel. The first pothole sent them rocking forward, the front of the truck jumping a few inches off the road, tires spinning, spitting it off to the sides. The rear tires gripped pavement and launched them forward again, ripping up the hill as they were bumped and jostled around. David reached a swath of concrete that had cracked off and sat at an angle, spilling water back into the woods where it had eroded into a shallow trough. When he hit it, the truck lurched to the right, tires spinning as they banked hard. With another twist of the wheel, he got them straightened out, grinding over sediment and more potholes, hitting one that bounced him across the front seat, his foot coming off the gas for a split second until he could lurch back the other way.

"Mom!?" David glanced in the rearview.

"I've got her!" Charlie said.

Darla threw herself over him, grimacing as she lay on her wounded arm, reaching across him, and snatching his seatbelt. She pulled it over his arms, and David lifted his hands off the wheel momentarily so the strap could properly stretch across his body. He grabbed the wheel as he hit another string of potholes, one so deep it was like running over a concrete parking bump, nearly stopping them in their tracks. But the tires spun, catching the edge of the hole, rocketing them over pieces of deadfall and leaves, dragging it with them with heavy scraping sounds. The trees made a tunnel over the road, branches stretching upward, some leaning in too far and scratching the black paint job. Something clattered on the roof and fell into the truck bed with a thump.

"Almost there," Darla said, clutching a handle above her head.

David slammed the gas pedal, shooting them to the top where they swerved onto a level road that wrapped around the hill.

"Hang on, David! Stop!"

He yanked the wheel to the left and pounded the brakes, sending them skidding sideways into a rocky embankment where the ground was soft and muddy, the truck lurching to a dead stop. With the engine still idling, David sat there panting with his hands frozen on the wheel. Darla was leaning forward and pinching the bridge of her nose, shaking her head slowly but then offering David and admiring nod.

"Good driving, kid. I couldn't have done it better myself. You okay?"

"Yeah," he said and glanced in the rearview. "How's Mom?"

"She's okay," Charlie replied breathlessly. "It knocked her around a bit, but I pulled the seatbelts over her and held her with both hands. The bleeding's fine."

"Take her blood pressure again, would you?"

There was a pause of about thirty seconds before Charlie came back. "The machine says her heart rate is a hundred and five, and her blood pressure is a little lower."

"Well, good thing we made it to the top of the hill." Darla nodded. "Doc Nash's place is just up ahead. A couple more turns."

"Any more hills like that one?"

Darla shrugged. "No hills like that, but you never know these days. We may still have a little four-wheel driving to do." She glanced back. "We won't know till we see it. Best get driving, son."

Heartbeat racing, pulse out of control, David grinned. When he lifted his hands off the wheel, they weren't shaking anymore. They weren't shaking at all.

CHAPTER TWENTY-TWO

Morten Christensen, Pearisburg, Virginia

Morten walked arm in arm with Alma, umbrellas in hand as they trudged up to the Caldersons' for that family's turn at holding service. The elder's home was expansive, nestled into the hillside with other massive farmsteads, each one large and immaculate, with living rooms the size of a church hall and perfect white siding that glowed in the gloom and rain. Despite the terrible weather, the hillside was a vibrant smudge of trees standing tall against the constant storms.

"It's picturesque, wouldn't you say, Father?" Alma asked.

"It is a picture painted by God." Morten agreed. "It is God's work."

"It truly is," Alma replied. "Do you think Samuel and Lavinia think so?"

The rest of the family came behind them, Samuel and Lavinia with their children, and Miriam helping Uri along as he strode slowly, slightly stooped and favoring his wounded stomach. Little Lena and Esther walked on his other side, both girls holding his arm and smiling so bright they blotted out the murky weather. Morten drew

Alma off to the side, and they allowed Samuel and his family to walk by, stepping back when Miriam and Uri came up.

"You should have stayed in bed another few days, son."

"I won't tolerate another day of sloth, Father," Uri replied in a strained tone. "Missing service leaves an emptiness inside me, and I'm rather anxious to give back to the enclave as they've given to us."

"Admirable, son. I look forward to being on guard duty with you as you know we must all contribute there as well."

"Yes, sir. I'll gladly do my best to protect the community. But I'd like to help with repairing the damaged homes as soon as I can. Especially after what you told me about the home Wendy had to live in."

"You love home building, but you'll not be back working until you're fully healed. For the most part, Smithson's people have built strong, sturdy foundations. That part of the property was unusually neglected."

"But even the sturdiest homes have splits and cracks in them, and one completely washed out on the east side. They'll need men like me to rebuild and reinforce them, especially if this dastardly rain keeps up."

"Let's hope it doesn't." Morten started to pat him heavily on the back but simply rested his hand on his neck and gave it a gentle squeeze. "In the meantime, be happy with coming to regular service and getting yourself in working shape."

"Aye, Father. I will."

They marched down a winding lane of red maples that crowded over them and kept the worst of the rain off, the gravel path joined by other families coming out of their homes or side streets from parts of the community, the elderly on horseback while the younger folk guided them. Children laughed and played as much as they could before their parents brought them back in line with warm reprimands that had few teeth. The women wore fresh white bonnets and colored dresses, grays and blues and greens, and the men wore heavy coats and hats, holding umbrellas or covers over their wives and families. Morten noticed their crowds' happiness had grown as time for service approached, and he took that as a sign of a healthy community, one he could be proud to be part of. He locked Alma's arm tighter and gave her a smile, and she graced him with one in return. Smithson walked well ahead with Mary but turned to wave, and Morten waved back as they left the cover of the trees and strolled across a wide bridge with pristine white rails, the waters flooding almost to the deck.

Halfway up the hill, Morten was enjoying the array of gardens and stunning rock walls that surrounded parts of the community when a disturbance broke out behind them. Most of them ignored it and kept walking, then shouts rang out, calls for Smithson to come down off the hill. People stopped and turned, pale faces staring toward the bottom. Alma released his arm and stepped one way than the other, trying to get a better view.

"What is it, girl? What do you see?"

"Two riders... one with an extra man behind him. A man wearing an orange vest."

"Orange?" Morten turned.

The crowd parted to let the horses through, and Morten started working his way down with Smithson and several elders. Near the bottom by the bridge, a man wearing an orange vest tapped his Amish rider on the shoulder and pointed directly at Morten, who waved his hat and met them halfway.

Morten nodded. "Silas Toomer."

"Morten Christensen." Silas got off the horse and glanced nervously at the Amish pressing in around him. "Sorry if I, um, interrupted something."

"Not at all. We were just on our way to service. It can wait a few minutes. I can only assume you're here because of the picture I showed you."

"That's right, I am—"

"What is the meaning of this?" Smithson pushed through the crowd in a huff.

Morten cut him off. "Venerable Smithson, this is Silas Toomer from over at Nance's Barn."

"I know Fred Nance and his family." Smithson addressed Silas directly. "If Fred's begging for help, you can turn right around and tell him we've got our own troubles here."

Silas stammered. "No, sir. I'm not here to deliver any message from the Nance's. I'm actually here to see Morten."

"Morten?" Smithson appeared even more confused. "But he's only been in town a few days. How would he know about Fred Nance's place?"

Alma, Uri, and Miriam stood side-by-side with the children behind them, and Samuel and Lavinia pressed closer with anxious eyes.

"Is something wrong?" Morten asked, ignoring Smithson. "Is my family okay?"

"They're fine," Silas assured him. "But Wendy is wounded. Shot by one of McCallum's people."

"Follow me back to my cottage," Morten said urgently. "We'll ride out together."

Smithson took him by the arm. "How do you know Silas?"

"I can explain," Morten said. "I was out patrolling one day when I came across Fred Nance's barn. I stopped and talked to the people there, and that's how I met Silas here."

"But none of the patrols would've taken you that far from our community. Unless you were..." Smithson's confusion transformed into anger. "You've been out looking for Wendy and your grandchildren. That's why you were on the west side of Buck Hill."

Morten replied with soft defiance. "I went in search of my family but did not neglect my responsibilities to the community. I've kept up with all my duties and —"

"You were not given permission to go looking for outsiders," Smithson snapped and stepped forward with his chest out, chin raised in fury. "Perhaps I wasn't clear in our *many* meetings, but anyone leaving the community must get permission from myself and at least two other elders. That goes for trading goods outside the enclave or working in town. Not long after you and your people arrived, we removed that privilege entirely. You're aware of that."

"Aye, I am."

"You know the consequences for going against the community mandates, yet you defied them anyway."

Morten ground his teeth and averted his eyes or risked shoving the man into the mud.

"Does your family feel the same way?" Smithson turned and gestured to Miriam, Alma, and the others.

"We do not, Elder Smithson," Samuel said. "We told my father not to leave the boundaries of the community, but he wouldn't listen."

Smithson fixed Morten with a heated glare. "I'm afraid you'll be missing service tonight, Morten Christensen. By the laws invested me by this enclave, you are now *shunned*. You'll miss services this evening and be questioned about your place in this community on the morrow." Smithson gestured to two large men. "You two. Apprehend him and take him to the old storehouse where he can sit and think about what he's done."

The two men approached, burly shoulders and wide chests, reaching for his arms. Morten backed away, curled his fist, and flexed his shoulders beneath his heavy coat. He drew Alma behind him and flashed Samuel a plea for help, but his next oldest son shook his head and remained by Lavinia's side. Uri huffed and shoved past them to stand beside Morten.

"I'm here, Father."

"This is not your fight, son," he said, gently pushing him away.

"It *is* my fight, Father. I'll not have them speak to you or handle you with such disrespect."

"No one will *handle* me." Morten glared at Smithson and turned a scowl on the two men. "Touch me, and you'll taste blood."

The pair exchanged a look, then one sneered and grabbed Morten's arm. Morten ripped free of the hold and snatched his wrist, twisting it upward and shoving him away so hard he staggered, slipped, and plunged into the wet grass. The next man tried to take Morten's other arm, but Morten checked him with his shoulder, sending him flying backward into the crowd, knocking people aside before they held him up. Women gasped. Men bristled and huffed.

Morten swept his finger across them and came to rest on Smithson. "No one will keep me from protecting my family."

"Your family is *here*," Smithson said and folded his arms. "*We* are your family."

"There are some lost sheep I must protect, and God help the man who tries to stop me."

Morten started to walk away when Alma came after him, catching his arm and half-turning him. "Father, I'll come with you!"

"Daughter, your heart is full of love, and I have no doubt you'd follow me through the belly of hell itself, but your place is here." Morten leaned closer and lowered his voice. "Stay vigilant. Keep an eye on Miriam and Uri. Don't allow them to be expelled."

With pain and worry etched on her face, she nodded. "Please be safe, Father."

"I will. Now let me go before a lot more of them try to hold me."

Alma let go, backing up and pulling Uri with her to join the rest of the gathered family.

"You'll be expelled..." Smithson said flatly. "And your family, too."

Morten started to walk away but paused, head down and voice low. "If that is my fate, so be it. But my family has nothing to do with this... and you heard from Samuel and Lavinia that they all tried to keep me from this. They are good and godly people, and I beg you to let them stay. If that's not enough..." He swallowed hard and almost choked. "Then I disavow them and say they are part of me no longer."

The crowd gasped. The kids—Esther and Lena, Mara and Noah —all cried out in horror to see their grandfather walking away. Morten pushed through the crowd, forcing aside a few men who tried to stand in his way, a hair's breadth from grabbing one man and throwing him into the mud, but the man stepped out of his way at the last moment. Whispers and murmurs followed him, accusations of his betrayal of God and their community while Smithson only stood there with his arms crossed.

Morten's stomach churned sickeningly as he broke from the crowd and started across the bridge. The water rushed beneath his feet, sometimes rising high enough to spray over the planks and hit his boots. Then he was on his own, marching down the lonely lane with no family or friends by his side. The tears came ruthless and cruel as the sight of his grandchildren's shocked faces were etched in his mind. It had been for their own good, the only way to keep Smithson from taking out his wrath on them. That would have to do until Morten could somehow bring them together again, and all he wanted to do was get Fitzpatrick saddled as quickly as he could before Smithson tried to stop him. Boots crunched behind him, and he turned to see Silas Toomer following him down the lane.

As he came up, Morten said, "If I offer you a ride, will you take me to the Nance's and make sure I can see my daughter?"

"Yes, sir," Silas replied. "Anything to get away from those creepy Amish. They're so weird... I almost didn't come..." He stuttered fearfully. "No offense, sir."

"No offense taken." Morten wiped tears off his cheeks and marched on.

CHAPTER TWENTY-THREE

Private Adelson, somewhere in Virginia

Adelson zipped up, splashed some water over his hands, and wiped them on his pants. The world smelled muddy, the mountainsides and hills were covered in a thick mist, and the road rolled to the north beneath the bridge they stood on. They'd pulled over somewhere on Highway 52 to relieve themselves and stretch their legs after the long and unproductive drive from Virginia.

The roads were just cracks and mudslides with wrecks and abandoned vehicles on the shoulders. Air fresheners dangled from rearview mirrors. Backseats were full of clothing, twelve-packs of soda pop, and other needless things. A little girl's doll in a backseat. A couple of cases of beer in a pickup truck bed. A Golden Retriever sitting in a puddle with his leash tied to the door handle.

The soldiers had stopped and called for the dog's owners all along the road before giving him some food and untying him from the door. Adelson had expected the dog to run away, but he'd hung around while they tossed him bits of jerky until it was time to go. He didn't need to ask the Sergeant if they could take the dog with them.

It would be a no-go because they had things to do and orders to carry out.

As they'd driven away, Adelson hid his tears watching the animal sitting in the wet road with his head tilted to the side as if waiting for them to come back. It was par for the course, another heartbreak, another punch to the gut that chipped away at his soul.

"Are you still upset about the dog?" Jamison asked and glanced over.

"Nah, he'll be okay," Adelson said, but his voice shook with emotion. "Why don't you quit asking me that? We left him ten miles back."

"Only ten miles?" Gress added, shaking himself and zipping up. "It feels like we've been driving for weeks since we left Stephanie and Laney. And don't worry about the dog, Adelson. He'll be fine. He'll find food and water like everyone else. Who knows, maybe the owners will come back."

"Maybe we shouldn't have let him go."

"It was the best thing for him."

"Yeah, who leaves a dog in the middle of all this tied to a door?" Jamison finished relieving himself and turned away from the long drop into the ravine.

"I'm going to go stretch my legs." Adelson walked back to the Humvee where they'd left it parked on the right-hand shoulder, west of where they were standing.

It was still bleak out but beautiful, too, with hills rising around them, so green and wet it almost hurt his eyes. The rain had stopped, but a mist clung to the mountaintops that made them glow ethereally. There weren't any blue skies, but something was breaking in the grayness, a light source cutting through the billowy fields. The Humvee windows beaded with droplets over spiderweb cracks, and dents riddled the sides along with several bullet holes. One radio antenna was torn off when those people with the school bus jumped them. Adelson moved past the Humvee and walked about ten more yards up the road, glancing back once before pulling a radio from his belt. Flipping it on, he searched the channels until he found the one he wanted. It crackled and hissed, the signal squelching and farting through the speaker.

"Laney, this is Josh. Are you there? Come back."

Adelson waited for her to answer with a gnawing anxiety. After several long seconds she finally did. "Hi, Josh. Yeah, I'm here."

"You sound tired."

"I've just been lying around and feeling useless. Stephanie is already doing stuff for the neighborhood, and we've only been here less than a day. Where are you?"

"Somewhere in West Virginia, I think. I was afraid we'd gotten out of range."

"What is the range on these?"

"Thirty-five miles or so. The roads are getting better, so we should make better progress. Anyway, I guess we'll be out of range soon enough, and I wanted to check on you and see how you were doing."

Laney paused, and he imagined she was smiling. "Thanks, Josh. I appreciate that. I think... I think things will be okay here. People seem to be pulling together and —"

"No, how are *you* doing."

"A lot better than before, but I'm still barely functioning."

"I can't imagine what you've been through."

"This has happened to a lot of people. Millions of us. You're still not sure about your family, are you?"

"No," he scoffed softly. "And I'm afraid to find out. It doesn't matter, anyway. I've got a job to do."

"You haven't thought about checking on them at all?"

"Every day, but Dad and Mom understand I've got bigger responsibilities right now. We used to talk about it a lot, actually. Pride, hard work, duty to country. My dad was in the Army, too. Spent some time in Afghanistan."

"Well, I hope you get to see them sometime." Another pause. "Just... don't worry about me, okay? I'll be fine here."

"Well, I'll worry about you, anyway. Maybe on our way back we can swing in and check on you guys. You know, check on the neighborhood."

"Right, the neighborhood," Laney laughed, and her voice sounded musical through the tinny walkie-talkie speaker.

Adelson's heart thumped, and he swallowed hard. "I mean... maybe we could go for a walk or something when I get there."

"A walk through this abysmal neighborhood? Sounds romantic."

"It doesn't have to be romantic," Adelson rushed. "That's not what I meant, unless... unless you wanted it to..." He winced, shook his head, tried to think of a way to start over but couldn't find one. His discomfort worsened as Gress and Jamison came up to the Humvee and watched the Private curiously.

"I know what you meant, Josh," Laney said. "I appreciate you looking out for me, and I'll be here if you can get back this way. Until then, be real careful, okay?"

The way she said it, the hopefulness in her tone, brought a grin to his face. "I will. I'll definitely be careful. You, too."

"Bye, Josh."

"Yeah, bye."

"Come on, Private," Gress called. "We're moving out."

"Yes, sir." Adelson jogged back to the Humvee where Jamison met him.

"Were you on the radio?"

"Yeah, just checking on Stephanie and them."

"More like checking up on *Laney*," Jamison said. "I saw the way you looked at her, man."

"She's been through a lot. Just making sure she was okay."

"Right." Jamison got in and slammed his door, and the Humvee's heavy diesel engine rumbled to life.

"I didn't authorize you to give them a radio, Private." Gress frowned as he leaned on the roof.

"Oh, yeah," Adelson stammered as he popped the back door and stood there. "I didn't even think about it, sir. I figured you'd be okay with it, and it was one of the older radios, anyway. We weren't using it, so..."

"Just get in the truck." Gress slid into the passenger seat and pulled his door shut.

Adelson rested one arm on the Humvee's roof, shaking his head in relief. He turned his eyes to the eastern sky, back the way they'd come, where a troubled but beautiful girl was waiting for him. He fought a sudden rise of guilt for not thinking of his parents first, but Laney's dark eyes and the spatter of freckles across her cheeks eased his mind like the remnants of a pleasant dream.

Warmth splashed across his face with a brightness that took his breath away. He looked around in confusion for the source of the blinding glow and found it in the sky. It was the sun, the actual *sun*, breaking through the clouds and bathing the sharp green hillsides in the brilliant color of an amber beer, or spilled honey, or... Laney's hazel eyes. It took Adelson a moment to catch his breath as a flock of sparrows sprang from the treetops and swooped across the valley, bursting with cheeps and chirps. He could've stood there all day, letting the light infuse him with vibrant energy, the sounds dancing in his ears like a beautiful song, but they had things to do, places to be... duties.

"Come on, Private!"

"Yes, sir!" Adelson laughed and got in.

READ THE NEXT BOOK IN THE SERIES

**Edge of Extinction Book 5
Available Here
books.to/aVDQO**

Printed in Great Britain
by Amazon